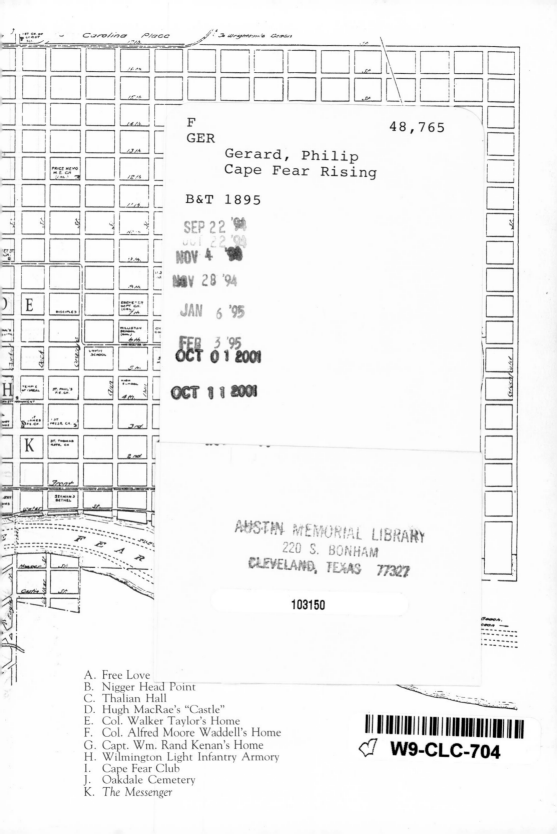

F
GER

48,765

Gerard, Philip
Cape Fear Rising

B&T 1895

A. Free Love
B. Nigger Head Point
C. Thalian Hall
D. Hugh MacRae's "Castle"
E. Col. Walker Taylor's Home
F. Col. Alfred Moore Waddell's Home
G. Capt. Wm. Rand Kenan's Home
H. Wilmington Light Infantry Armory
I. Cape Fear Club
J. Oakdale Cemetery
K. *The Messenger*

W9-CLC-704

CAPE FEAR RISING——————————————————

PHILIP GERARD————————

CAPE
FEAR
RISING

JOHN F. BLAIR, PUBLISHER WINSTON-SALEM, NORTH CAROLINA

DESIGN BY DEBRA LONG HAMPTON
PRINTED AND BOUND BY QUEBECOR AMERICA BOOK GROUP

*The paper in this book meets the guidelines
for permanence and durability of the
Committee on Production Guidelines for Book Longevity
of the Council on Library Resources.*

Library of Congress Cataloging-in-Publication Data

Gerard, Philip.
Cape Fear rising / Philip Gerard.
p.   cm.
ISBN 0-89587-108-4
1. Afro-Americans—North Carolina—Wilmington—History—19th century—Fiction.
2. Riots—North Carolina—Wilmington—History—19th century—Fiction.
3. Wilmington (N.C.)—Race relations—Fiction.   4. Wilmington (N.C.)—History—Fiction.
I. Title.
PS3557.E635C36   1994
813'.54—dc20   93–41369

For Kate,
à jamais _____

ACKNOWLEDGMENTS

The author is grateful to the following people for their valuable help in researching the historical figures and events portrayed in this novel:

The Cape Fear Museum staff, especially Harry Warren

Robert R. Crews, Wilmington Light Infantry Reserve Corps

Bob Ferguson, building manager, Public Services Division, city of Wilmington

Leland Smith and the staff of the Fort Fisher Museum and Historical Site

Michael Glancy

The Archives and Manuscripts staff of Joyner Library, East Carolina University

The Lower Cape Fear Historical Society archival staff, especially Diane C. Cashman and Merle Chamberlain

Aileen Leblanc of WHQR public radio

Dr. Melton McLaurin, UNC-Wilmington, Department of History

Dr. Daniel Noland, linguist, UNC-Wilmington, Department of English

The New Hanover County Courthouse Vital Records staff

The staff of the North Carolina Room at the New Hanover County Library

The staff of the William R. Perkins Library Special Collections, Duke University

The staff of William Madison Randall Library, UNC-Wilmington

The Thalian Hall staff

The staff of the United States Army Ordnance Museum, Aberdeen, Maryland

The staff of the Wilmington Railroad Museum

The staffs of the Southern Historical Collection, the North Carolina Collection, and the Photographic Services and Photographic Archives Sections at Wilson Library, UNC-Chapel Hill

Robert H. Wooley, historian

Thanks to Stephen D. Kirk for his good work in preparing this manuscript for publication.

The author is grateful for a research grant from UNC-Wilmington and a fellowship from the North Carolina Arts Council in support of this book.

This novel was inspired by events that actually happened. Some of the characters are based on historical persons. In taking dramatic liberties with the action, the author has tried to remain true to the spirit of the facts.

But this is fiction—only a storyteller's history.

An event has happened, upon which it is difficult to speak, and impossible to be silent.

Edmund Burke, 1789

PROLOGUE

1831

STRANGERS, THEY COME TO TOWN. Six men—black, furtive, traveling by night. They cross the Cape Fear River by rowboat from the
west bank and gather in the shadows of stacked cotton bales on the
wharf.

The August heat steams off the river in a clinging fog.

The six are frightened. There has been an uprising up north in
Virginia—black men murdering whites in their beds. The roads
are busy with armed riders—runaway patrols—galloping here
and there after rumors of fugitives.

But there is work here for free blacks, they've been told. This is a
free port. Full of West Indians, freedmen, mulattoes from white
mothers. A place that needs strong backs and clever hands. Worth
the risk. There's a man they have to see—owns a mill. Come
daylight, they'll find him and show him their papers. Meantime,
best lie low.

All but one are wearing homespun. Their faces are dusky and
lined, their hands horny and rough from work. The other, the one

they call Daniel Grant, is slender and lithe. His hands are smooth as a woman's, and yellow—like his face. His complexion is so fair that even in daylight he can pass for white. He wears a flannel suit and a linen shirt with a white man's name, the mill owner's, inked onto the inside of the left cuff. He is the only one of the six wearing shoes.

His voice is soft and resonant, a voice that comes up from his stomach and whispers things that sound so true five men have followed him a hundred miles from home to this river town.

They hunker on the wharf listening to the rush of the outgoing tide. The moon is invisible above the fog, silvering it with an otherworldly light.

One of the country men says, "The spirits is up and walking around, brothers." He carries a forked cypress switch to ward off evil spirits. Now, he rubs it between thumb and fingers until it is warm from friction.

"Hush, now," Grant says. "Don't go talking haints and voodoo. It's only the river fog."

"Feel that chill? The spirits is floating down the river to the ocean. Going back to Africa, brother." The country man rubs the forked stick some more. The love of Jesus is one thing, but a body needs every edge he can get in this wild river country.

"Just the night air cooling down," Grant says. The fishy stink of low tide fills the close air. " 'The Lord on high is mightier than the noise of many waters,' " he continues quietly, " 'yea, than the mighty waves of the sea.' "

"Amen," one of the men murmurs.

Another laughs. "For spirits, they's pretty ripe."

"Don't be taking it lightly, brother. Time of night to be indoors, bolt the shutters."

"Ain't that the word. Give me a soft place to lay my head."

They have been sleeping out-of-doors for weeks. For two whole days, they wandered lost in the swamps, eyes peeled for cottonmouths and gators. At last, they found the river. Providence had left a derelict rowboat stranded on the mud flats at the mouth of a feeder creek. "We'll just borrow this boat awhile," Grant had declared, and they oared across at turn of tide. The current was stalled, and the dark water piled up in foaming ridges—unnatural.

Now, the Cape Fear is once again rising.

Stiff and travel-weary, they settle in among the bales to sleep one last night in the open. But all at once, the river sounds change. There's murmuring out in the fog, the rasp of boots on rough boards—a boat?

Grant and the others peer into the fog. But it is a trick of the ear—the men come not from the water but from behind, down Market Street.

"Dust yourself off, brothers," Grant says when he sees them, "and mind your manners." In the sudden glow of a dozen lanterns, they all get to their feet, hands clasped at their stomachs, backs slightly stooped, heads nodded forward: don't look the man in the eye.

Except Grant. He stands erect, hands clasped behind his back. He balances on the balls of his feet, ready to move.

The crowd of whites, armed with tool handles and rifles, fills in around them, backing them against the river. They listen to the steady slap of ax handles against palms.

"What have we here?" A tall white man approaches. Unlike the others, he is unarmed. He wears a frock coat and a four-in-hand, even in this heat. The lanterns make it hotter. His hair and beard gleam with oil. As he speaks, his long, smooth fingers play with a silk handkerchief.

"Cap'n," Grant says, "pardon us for loitering at your wharf. We meant no harm. We have come seeking work."

"Hear that, Colonel?" one of the white men says. "Damned fugitives."

"You want to work?"

"Yes, cap'n. We only just arrived."

The white man lifts a lantern and thrusts it close to Grant's face. Grant doesn't look away. The man leans in, squinting. "Why, you're the creamiest nigger I ever did see!"

"A volunteer nigger," someone in the crowd says. "Could pass, if he was smart enough to try." Laughter.

"Bad night to be a volunteer nigger," someone else says. More laughter.

Grant says, "My daddy was a white—"

The Colonel slaps him—not hard, but so quickly that Grant is taken by surprise. The slap is almost ladylike—it hardly stings. "Don't ever let me hear you talking like that around here," the Colonel says quietly.

"Yes sir, cap'n."

"Don't look me in the eye, boy."

"Yes sir, cap'n."

"Why are you niggers skulking about at this hour? Plotting murder, are you?"

"We weren't skulking, cap'n. We're freedmen."

"Come into the light, all of you, where I can see you."

One by one, they shuffle closer to the lanterns. The Colonel scrutinizes their dark faces. "You one of Nat Turner's niggers?" he softly asks each in turn—speaking close to their faces. Grant can smell sweat, naphtha, perfume.

"No sir, cap'n."

"I think perhaps you are," he says to Grant. "Part of that murdering gang of wild apes up in Virginia. Going to slit our throats while we slept, were you?"

"We're freedmen, cap'n—I told you."

The Colonel yanks Grant's collar, tearing his shirt. "Where is your badge, boy?"

"Cap'n?" Something's wrong now, Grant thinks, getting more wrong every second.

"Every free nigger is required to wear a badge of cloth sewn onto his left shoulder—here." He cuffs Grant, hard. "The badge says 'Free.' Cost you a dollar at the town hall."

Someone murmurs, "Colonel, nobody goes by that old law."

"Cap'n, we don't mind buying a badge, once we working."

"Too late. Can't buy it now. You-all are unregistered niggers violating our curfew."

The country man fingers his stick and mutters, "Now they making up all kind of laws."

One of the white men snatches his stick and snaps it in half. "Don't be running that African voodoo on us."

"Colonel!" one of the men calls from the sea wall. "It's Parmele's skiff—got all his gear in it."

The Colonel folds his arms. "What have you done with the fisherman who owns this boat? What have you done with his body?"

"Wasn't no fisherman," the country man mutters.

"Please, cap'n, we're just poor field niggers looking for a job of work."

"Carter! Henry!" the Colonel says. "See if you can find Dal Parmele." The two men disappear into the darkness, and soon hooves are clopping fast on cobblestones. "What about you?" He grips Grant again by his linen shirt. "You a field nigger? You don't look like any field nigger I ever saw." He turns to his followers. "Gentlemen, what is your opinion of this fellow?"

"Damned rabble-rouser," one of them says. Others murmur assent.

"No sir, cap'n—"

"Yes, that's what I think. A rabble-rouser."

Grant remembers the name inked on his cuff. "Mr. MacIver can vouch for us, cap'n."

"MacIver? The Scots are all upriver. Make up another name." The men behind him laugh. "Are you the leader of these fugitives?"

"Cap'n, these are freedmen. They go where they please. We have papers—"

He tears the papers out of Grant's hand. "I don't see any papers."

"You didn't even look—"

"Don't back-sass me, boy," he warns softly. He riffles through the papers impatiently. "Well, what do we have here?" he announces, unfolding a yellowed newsprint pamphlet—David Walker's *Appeal to the Enslaved Negroes of the American South*. Walker, the son of a North Carolina slave, went to Boston to preach against the evils of slavery. Grant was given the tract by a liveried slave on a rice plantation across the river. He meant to throw it away in the swamp.

"Read us a lesson from your tract." He offers it to Grant.

"Cap'n, I swear, somebody just gave that—"

"Read us a lesson, boy."

Grant opens the pamphlet and, haltingly, reads aloud in the lantern light: " 'I tell you Americans—unless you speedily alter your course, you and your country are gone—' "

"You the ones is going to get gone!" somebody yells.

" 'God will not suffer us always to be oppressed—our sufferings will come to an end.' "

"That is quite enough. You six may be sure your sufferings will come to a speedy end."

"But cap'n—"

"You heard him, gentlemen." The Colonel holds up the pamphlet. "Preaching insurrection."

"Spell it out," says one of the men. "Read us the law."

The Colonel clasps his hands behind his back. "The Insurrection Law of 1741 requires that three or more slaves found guilty of conspiring to rebel must be put to death. These niggers claim to be free, but they have no proof. Therefore, under the law, they are held to be slaves. They are strangers—dangerous lurkers-about. They have on their persons evidence of conspiracy."

He turns to a man next to him, who is waving a horse pistol. "Take them to the marketplace. The time has come for Anglo-Saxon justice."

Sunrise, at the foot of Market Street. They have had their trial, in the slave marketplace. The white men line up in two ranks of twenty-odd each between the six black men and the river.

The river is running fast and high, the tide sweeping up from the sea in brown wavelets. There is no breeze. The sun is up behind the town, but the wharf still lies in shadow. Grant looks west across the river and, though he knows better, begins to calculate how far the other bank is, how long it will take to swim there—a quarter of a mile, more, the swift current choked with logs and debris. His hands are tied behind his back. Without his hands, any man in that fast water will surely drown.

"You came from the river," the Colonel says quietly. "Now go back where you came from."

On his signal, the first black man is shoved into the gauntlet. Hands behind him, he cannot quite maintain his balance. He lurches from side to side as the first blows strike him—ax handles, gun butts, fists, boots. Halfway down the line, he is snorting bloody mist.

Pistols are cocked.

He is four, then just three long steps from the sea wall, running—trying to run—on his knees.

They all fire at once. The bullets kick him headlong into the dirt. His body convulses, sprawling, legs spastic. Then he is still. They fire again into the corpse. Then there is a ringing silence into which the Colonel says softly, "Reload." It is almost military.

The crowd cheers them, even the women and children.

Grant watches. As each new man is fed to the gauntlet, he feels his tongue swell larger in his mouth. He has no words—his tongue is a dry lump. His eyes burn. He must quiet himself, he thinks. Regain control.

Names, he thinks. These country men have names. The Colonel never even asked their names. He concentrates, watches the third man reel into the gauntlet, racing toward the two sprawled bodies on the riverbank.

Tucker, he makes himself remember, that's his name. The first bullets knock the man down.

Big Gee. Willis. Terel. Coates.

Then they seize Grant by his elbows.

"You have no right!" He has found his voice. "We have papers!" His five companions lie in a single heap so close to the water they could reach out and wash their dead hands in it.

"Untie his hands," the Colonel orders, his tone full of regret.

Grant rubs circulation back into his wrists. But before he can grab or punch, strong hands are clamping his arms.

"As you seem to have a higher opinion of yourself than those blue-gum nigger cohorts of yours," the Colonel says, "we must take you down a peg."

Grant stares at the Colonel, stares at those soft gray eyes. But it is another man who has the knife. A fist closes on Grant's right index finger, yanking it taut at the knuckle. The knife flashes so fast, the finger is already gone before the pain blinds him in one quick burn. He wills himself to remain conscious.

The Colonel recites, as if he has said it before, " 'He shall bring upon them their own iniquity, and shall cut them off in their own wickedness. Yea, the Lord our God shall cut them off.' "

They take all the fingers, and the thumb. As each digit is severed, the Colonel's man tosses it to the crowd. Grant stares in horror at the mutilated stump of his hand, nausea washing over him. Then, running through his mind, over and over, is the old rhyme his daddy taught him in the fields, counting it out on his fingers: ought is an ought and a figure is a figure, all for the white man and nothin' for the nigger.

The back of his throat constricts. The crowd goes silent. His arm feels heavy and dead. He tucks it tightly into his left armpit, and, before they can shove him toward the gauntlet, he charges through it on his own, roaring. The Psalm of David is coming out of his mouth in tongues: " 'I will early destroy all the wicked of the land! I will cut off all wicked doers from the City of the Lord!' "

They are not quite ready for him. He is halfway down the lines before they lay a hand on him. He hears the snick of revolvers being cocked, like a chain of beads being counted, hears the bellowing of men on either side as a dull, surfy roar.

The sun is up over the town. The brown river glistens suddenly silver. Grant runs for it. He can make it—for one instant, he believes this. He is invisible, a wraith, a bloodless haint.

His feet are not touching the ground—he is flying, weightless, pure spirit. He can feel the wind rushing past his ears.

The world ends in a thunderclap, the river explodes behind his eyes.

———————

They untangle the heap of bodies and lay them in a row, heads toward the river. Somebody fetches a sharp, double-bladed ax. One man places a rock-maple block under each neck in turn. Another swings the ax—*thwack*. In this manner, they collect six Negro heads to be raised on poles along the roads leading into town—a warning to other strangers who might bring trouble.

Tucker's head is placed alongside the northbound road at Smith's Creek Bridge, facing north.

Big Gee's is raised beside the tollhouse on the Shell Road, leading to the ocean.

The heads of Willis and Terel are rowed across the river to the swampy peninsula where the channel forks into the Cape Fear and the Northeast Branch. The poles are twenty feet tall, so the heads can be seen from passing boats.

Coates's head is paraded up Market Street a mile and a half from the river, where the city peters out into longleaf pine forest, and is mounted beside the wrought-iron hitching post of a tavern.

They raise Grant's head right beside the ferry landing at the foot of Market Street, the place of execution. Boys wing stones at it with slingshots. Overhead, gulls wheel and rant, quarreling over the flesh. Men point it out to visitors. Women hurry by without looking up.

Black servants weep behind closed doors. Word carries to the cotton fields, to the mills, to the rice and turpentine plantations up and down the river. It is a bad time. Mothers keep their children close. Something is loose upon the land. Nat Turner is killing whitefolks in the Virginia tidewater, and no good will ever come of it. All the way up north in Boston, David Walker has been poisoned right outside his own tailor shop. Jesus is not coming again in this century.

Having slept off an evil drunk, Dal Parmele has retrieved his skiff and gone fishing.

Late in the afternoon, when the tide has turned, husky men working in pairs sling the decapitated bodies off the sea wall into the river. Headless, they all look alike. Each one floats briefly, tumbling in the current. A southwesterly breeze has risen, pushing whitecaps against the brown tide.

At last, the river has them all, surging toward the Atlantic, spiriting them away toward Africa.

Arms akimbo, the Colonel stands on the wharf watching them go. After a time, he sees only a greasy smear of blood on the receding tide. To the pairs of husky men, he remarks, "This has always been a peaceful town. A good town."

To himself, he says, " 'In those days there was no king in Israel, and every man did that which was right in his own eyes.' "

The men nod, grunt, then stoop to rinse their hands in the cool river.

PART I

THE WORD

1898

*The city of Wilmington has a population of
about 25,000. It is situated on the Cape Fear
river, twenty-five miles from its mouth, and at
the junction of the northwest and northeast
branches. The harbor is commodious, and is a
resort for vessels from all ports of the world.*

*There is a direct steamer line to New York, and
a good business is done by sailing vessels to all
domestic ports. Considerable trade is also done
with the West Indies by sailing vessels and
steamships. There are five railroad lines reaching the city, besides a short line to the coast,
which handles quantities of coast products. Fish
and game are abundant. There are two fine
pleasure and health resorts on the beach,
reached by rail and steamer. The beach is said to
be one of the finest on either side of the continent.
Malignant diseases are unknown. The death rate
is abnormally low. No city of the South offers
better natural and acquired advantages for men
of energy and enterprise.*

Wilmington, N.C.,
City Directory, 1897

CHAPTER ONE

Sunday, August 14

FROM THE OPEN WINDOW of the train, Sam Jenks watched the
river—wide and brown, here and there silvered by pools of glare.
The brown color came from tannin, his cousin Hugh MacRae had
explained in his letter. All that rotting pine and cypress leaching
into the current. The Cape Fear basin was practically tropical.
Hugh ought to know—he was native and had a cotton mill on the
river.

This was the regular train from Raleigh and Goldsboro that brought businessmen back to town after a weekend in the country. The car was full of men in summer-weight suits reading newspapers.

Sam leaned closer to the window, searching the brown water for something else—alligators. Hugh had sworn there were alligators down here, though Sam had not yet spied one. A wild country, Hugh had written: out in the swamp and lowland forest lurked water moccasins, copperheads, rattlers, whitetail deer, wild pigs, raccoons, and foxes.

Sam turned to his wife, Gray Ellen, and took her right hand in both of his. His hands were pink—he was blond, with a fair complexion. During the weeks at the sanatorium, he'd lost the sunburn he'd gotten in Cuba. Gray Ellen was black Irish, with brown eyes and tawny skin, even in winter. "This time, it's going to work out fine," he said. "I can feel it."

Gray Ellen didn't speak, didn't look his way.

"Chicago was a mistake," he said. "They don't give a man a chance." Sam was feeling stronger, confident again, now that he was no longer drinking.

"You've got a chance now." She was weary, had an edge. She hated traveling, hated moving. It took so much energy to start all over each time. The older she got, the harder it became. She was nearly thirty now, and it was very hard. This was the last move. The bargain was, they would settle here. If they moved again, it would be her choice. To a place she picked out. For her own reasons, not Sam's.

"All that's behind us now. I swear." He believed it, he could feel it. This was a new feeling he had, as if a great heaviness were evaporating from his body. The heaviness had been there so long that he had forgotten what it felt like to be without it.

It had been with him at Las Guasimas, in Cuba, as he wandered around the jungle in a feverish haze, unable to find out what was going on. It had been with him when he saw two men shot dead in front of him and a fellow correspondent named Edward Marshall take a Mauser ball in the back and later, leaning paralyzed against a tree, dictate his dispatch to Stephen Crane.

The copious rations of contraband whiskey hadn't kept away the fever. And the whiskey hadn't made him any braver. While the army moved on San Juan, Sam retreated. He made it by packet boat to Miami on July 1, the day the Rough Riders were charging up San Juan Hill and into the history books.

The biggest story of the war, and he missed it because he was too scared. And still he got home to Chicago too late.

Gray Ellen shifted in her seat. She could not get comfortable in this humid heat. "That's what you said when we left Philadelphia two years ago."

He dropped her hand. "Look, this isn't going to work if you keep carping. Forget Chicago. Forget Philly. We're here now. I'll be writing for a real newspaper."

He had written Cousin Hugh, asking for a job. They were only vaguely related, but Hugh put a lot of stock in family. "Come down here and help us promote the place," he'd written. "Forget Chicago—Wilmington is the city of the future."

Gray Ellen showed no reaction. Since losing the baby only six weeks earlier, she'd been like that a lot—distant. The day she miscarried, Sam was on a drunk in Miami. When he got home and found out, he went on another binge.

Next time, Sam was determined, it would go better. No reason why not. It was just bad luck before, and what could you do about luck? But luck could change. This was a new place. He'd been dry for a month. They said if you could beat it for a month, you could beat it for good. His head was clear of fever. He had his old ambition back.

Maybe he just wasn't cut out to be a war correspondent. But nobody would be shooting at him down here. Nothing was going to spoil this start.

Suddenly, the train lurched violently, and Sam was thrown against the window, Gray Ellen in his arms. A dapper gentleman across the aisle turned their way and smiled. He wore a silver goatee and held a brass-headed walking cane between his knees. "They are still working on the roadbed."

"Ah. Of course."

"During the War, you know, a train I was riding jumped the

tracks altogether. The carriages were stacked up like stove wood."
He smiled, as if he took great pride in having survived a railway
disaster. "I helped pull the injured out of the wreck. Several we
could not save."

During the war, Sam thought—at that very moment, the Rough
Riders were disembarking at Montauk Point to a ticker-tape parade down Broadway. At the front of the car, two returning soldiers shared a seat. "I hope they've fixed the track," he said.

The man with the goatee chuckled. "I should hope so—that was
more than thirty years ago. As I said, during the War. Headed
down to Charleston to witness the secession. I was a newspaperman then."

"You don't say." Sam reached across Gray Ellen and offered his
hand, then introduced himself.

The other man took Sam's hand in a surprisingly strong grip,
studied him with gray eyes, and kept holding onto his hand, as if
making up his mind about something. Finally, he said, "Alfred
Moore Waddell, at your service. And this must be your wife?"

He dropped Sam's hand and took Gray Ellen's, stroking it lightly.

"Gray Ellen," she said softly.

"Ah," Waddell said. "Scotch or Irish?"

"Scotch-Irish."

"Scotch-Irish! No finer stock on earth."

"Yes. Both of my grandfathers were rebels in a losing cause.
Pleased to meet you." She took back her hand, settled into her seat,
and closed her eyes. Sam wondered why she couldn't at least be
civil.

He kept his eye on Waddell. He'd had a lot of practice at observ-
ing people. That's what being a newspaperman was all about—
looking into people's eyes and finding trust or betrayal. Listening
to an earnest voice and deciding if it was lying or telling the truth.

Waddell had amazing eyes, he thought—the way they caught
and held you. There was a word for it—charisma. Was that too
strong? He wondered what line of work Waddell had been in before
retirement. Not newspapers—not for long. Preacher, maybe.

The train left the riverside and entered a thick lowland forest of longleaf and loblolly, red maple and sweet gum, lush as the Cuban rainforest. The right of way was overgrown with bright green wax myrtle and honeysuckle. Confederate jasmine entwined the telegraph poles, deep green leaves dotted by hundreds of withered, snowy blossoms. In the woods, between the bare, scaly trunks of the longleaf pines, dogwoods burgeoned. At one place, the roadbed was blanketed with fallen flower petals, white and pink. Oh, he thought, to have seen this country in bloom.

At a remote station, three rowdies wearing red shirts boarded at the back of the car. They jostled each other roughly and hooted at some vulgar joke. They took their seats and quieted down, and the train racketed through half an hour more of woods and swamp before stopping again.

This time, a single passenger boarded at the front. He was slender and fair and wore a pencil-thin moustache. He was dressed in a pearl-gray suit with a white shirt buttoned to the throat, without a tie. His gray fedora was banded in black silk. In one hand, he clutched a cloth bag, in the other, a small Bible.

As he passed their seats, the train started up, and he staggered a moment before recovering his balance. Gray Ellen looked up into his face and smiled. He nodded slightly and smiled back. Then he found an empty seat two rows behind them.

"Preacher," Sam said, "by the look of him."

"Handsome devil," Gray Ellen observed quietly, so the man across the aisle would not overhear. "Makes a person want to spend more time in church."

Waddell turned once to look at the preacher. Something about the man struck a queer note.

When the conductor came through, he stopped beside the preacher and collected his ticket. He loitered a moment longer than necessary.

At the rear of the car, the red-shirted rowdies were arguing. "Well, by God," one of them said loudly, rising, "I'll find out what color that boy is." Sam could tell by his tone that the man had been drinking—he surely knew the signs by now. The man lurched up the aisle, swaying with the movement of the train, and stopped when he got to the preacher's seat. Out the window, Sam could see the river again. But he turned to watch what was playing out two rows behind.

"You, preacher," the Red Shirt said. "I know you."

The preacher didn't even look up from his Bible. "I doubt it."

"Don't be back-sassing me, boy. I seen you in Tennessee, last year it was. Trouble in Johnson County, and you smack-dab in the middle of it."

"Sir, you are mistaken." Now, he looked up straight into the man's eyes, challenging him.

The other two Red Shirts moved up the aisle and stood behind the first man. "You trying to pass? Trying to make fools out of us, nigger?"

"I'm sure I don't know what you mean," the preacher said. Sam was transfixed by the man's calm demeanor—he himself would already have shoved a fist into the Red Shirt's eye. A sober man could always knock down a drunk.

Gray Ellen squeezed Sam's arm and whispered, "Do something."

"None of our business—local stuff."

"Help him, before it gets out of hand."

"Let it go by."

But instead, Gray Ellen turned and rose half out of her seat.

The Red Shirts grabbed the preacher by the coat and hauled him into the aisle. "You ought to be riding in the colored car, boy—didn't your mama ever learn you your place?" The preacher's hat fluttered to the floor and was lost under boots.

"Sam!" Gray Ellen whispered urgently.

The Red Shirts were manhandling the preacher up the aisle. Gray Ellen suddenly moved to block them. "What's going on here?" she demanded. "This gentleman, he was just minding his own business."

"That's right, ma'am—and you just mind yours."

Another of the Red Shirts said, "He'll just have to hoof it the rest of the way."

"You can't just throw a man off—"

One of the Red Shirts clutched her arm. "You best not—"

"Take your hands off my wife." Sam was standing now, and he edged out into the aisle, crowding Gray Ellen. The river flashed by through gaps in the trees, hung with gray Spanish moss. The Red Shirt released her arm, uncertain what to do. Sam was tall and lanky, but he had a reach. The Red Shirt looked him in the eye, then looked away.

Other people in the coach were craning their necks to see what was going on—they murmured and pointed. Sam couldn't tell whose side they were on.

"Gentlemen. Ma'am." It was one of the soldiers who had been sitting up front. Now, he loomed over their shoulders. Spreading his arms, he gathered Sam and Gray Ellen together like children. Gray Ellen smelled whiskey and horse sweat, mixed with cigar smoke, bay rum, and another odor she couldn't quite place.

"Just please take your seats, folks." He pressed a big hand onto Sam's shoulder and practically forced him into his seat. With Gray Ellen, he was gentler. "Please, ma'am," he said. He reminded her of pictures she'd seen of Colonel Roosevelt with the Rough Riders. She relaxed and sat—something about his touch made her defer to him.

"Now, boys," he addressed the Red Shirts, "this ain't the time or the place. The preacher here may not be aware of our customs."

The way he looked at the gray-suited preacher, hung between two Red Shirts like laundry, made it plain to Gray Ellen that the soldier didn't believe for a second what he was saying—he was just trying to keep the peace.

"Where's your manners?" he said. They bowed jerkily and murmured an apology to Gray Ellen. "That's fine. Now, boys, go on back to your seats." He slapped a hand onto the preacher's shoulder. The Red Shirts melted toward the back of the car, grumbling. The conductor squeezed by the soldier and disappeared into the forward vestibule.

The big soldier guided the preacher into his seat, handed him back his crushed hat, and winked at him without smiling. To Gray Ellen, he said, "Ma'am, I'm sorry as I can be. Some folks just get carried away." He grinned wryly, looking even more like Colonel

Roosevelt, moustache and all. He was older than she'd first thought—his hair was silver, brush-cut. His broad nose was a florid map of whiskey nights. But he looked fit—deep-chested and blocky in the shoulders. He held out a big red hand. "Captain Bill Kenan, ma'am. A pleasure."

"Likewise," she said, then introduced herself and Sam.

He glanced at the many bags in the overhead rack. "Coming to settle in our town, are you?"

Sam said, "We've heard there's lots of opportunity."

Kenan nodded. "So they tell me."

Gray Ellen said, "Would they really have thrown him off a moving train?"

"Don't let this give you the wrong impression. It's a good town."

"Are you just back from the Cuban war?" Sam asked to get off the subject. He might as well find out if the man knew about him.

Kenan laughed. "My war was over years ago. Now, I train the state militia."

Sam relaxed. "What's your specialty?"

Kenan beamed. "Guns," he said happily. "Ordnance."

That was the other smell, Gray Ellen realized: gun oil. Her father kept silver-plated shotguns in a glass case and cleaned them every Saturday.

Kenan went back to his seat, leaving the aisle clear. Gray Ellen was relieved. She squeezed Sam's arm—he had stood by her.

Across the aisle, old Waddell smiled enigmatically, narrowing his gray eyes but never losing his smile. A couple of miles down the track, he observed, "That Captain Kenan, he has quite a reputation in these parts. He was the sharpshooting champion of the entire Confederate army."

"Looks like a steady man," Sam said.

"The Duplin Rifles advanced closer to Washington than any other company in the Forty-third, and him out front." This was a story Waddell liked to tell, about a time of glory, of honor.

"They could see the unfinished Capitol dome shining above the battlefield." His eyes were dancing, and he used his hands in broad, fluttering gestures. "They could see workmen on the scaffolds." Waddell wished he'd been there himself, shoulder to shoulder with Bill Kenan, watching the president's black stovepipe hat sticking up above the parapet, shivering in a breeze of musket fire. "When the battle began, Lincoln was inspecting the troops at Fort Stevens. Captain Kenan—Lieutenant Kenan then—led the sharpshooters to within hollering distance of the fort. Took a shot at Abe Lincoln himself."

Gray Ellen said, "He missed, I take it."

"Yes, ma'am," Waddell said, missing the joke. "Killed the boy next to the president—a head shot."

"Oh, my."

"Kenan was wounded at Charleston, but he stayed with the regiment till Appomattox. Wasn't a single deserter in that outfit all during the War." He said it as if he himself were personally responsible.

The train rumbled over the trestle at Smith's Creek.

Sam said, "You were with the Forty-third?"

"Do I look like a foot soldier?"

No. He looked like a *Collier's* ink sketch of an antebellum cavalier, an aristocrat—hawk nose, receding hair, silver goatee.

"The Forty-first Regiment of the Third North Carolina—cavalry, sir."

Sam nodded. "Those fellows in the red shirts—that some kind of uniform?"

Waddell smiled and fingered the brass head of his cane. "An Irish fraternal group, I gather. Poor-bockers. Men who can't find work."

"Poor-bockers?"

"Local slang."

"What do they call themselves?" Sam asked.

"What else? The Red Shirts." He smiled, as if amused by the obvious lack of imagination. "Those boys are from out of town—lots of strangers coming in these days."

Like us, Sam thought. "I'm a newspaperman," he said. "A reporter."

"Bright young man might go far, he keeps his head." There was a twinkle in Waddell's eye. "Somebody who could tell the story of this place. Write it for the whole world."

"I'll remember that."

The train was out in the open now, running fast on good track. Across the river, another channel flowed into the Cape Fear under a high spit of land.

In the back of the carriage, the Red Shirts were stirring. They trundled up the aisle carrying cloth bags and string-tied bundles in brown paper. Two of them had Winchester rifles slung across their backs. They passed the preacher, but the last one stopped beside Gray Ellen. He leaned down and pointed across her body and out the window toward the river. "See that point of land yonder? They call that Nigger Head Point, sweetheart." He grinned. "Care to know how it got that name?"

"That's enough," Sam said. "Move along."

The Red Shirt joined his companions in the forward vestibule.

Outside the window, the river vanished and houses appeared—shotgun shacks and clapboard two-stories, some of them clean and tidy, others run-down, their paint peeling, pigs rooting among trash in the yards. Men loitered in the dirt streets—black men in a knot outside a drugstore, white men smoking on the stoop of a tavern. Sam had seen the ragged unemployed in other cities.

Waddell said, "Brooklyn. The darkies live here. And white laborers. Most of the Irish are in Dry Pond, over in that direction." He pointed out his own window. "Don't be alarmed—the train comes into the better part of town."

"Why do they call it Brooklyn?" Gray Ellen asked.

Waddell smiled. "Who knows? They do have a Manhattan Club there—sort of a *bal musette*. They go there to dance and carouse. The darkies do love their music."

"I see."

The conductor walked through the car announcing, "Wilmington, change for the Seaboard Airline, the Short Line, Charleston, and points west."

The train pulled under the long awnings of the Atlantic Coastline platform, thronged with women in sun hats and men in seersucker suits meeting the arrival. Redcaps scurried about retrieving bags.

"Come see me, hear?" Waddell said, handing Sam his card: A. M. Waddell, Lt. Col., C.S.A., Attorney-at-Law. "You lose it, I'm in the city directory," he said. "Mrs. Jenks." He bowed in the old, grand manner and left the train. On his seat, he left behind a copy of the latest *Raleigh News & Observer*, opened to an editorial cartoon of a giant black boot—labeled *The Negro*—crushing a tiny white man's back. The caption read, *A Serious Question—How Long Will This Last?*

The preacher quietly walked out the back of the car. Through the window, Gray Ellen watched him pause, hatless, on the platform, before he pushed through the crowd and past the swinging iron gate into the city.

One of the editors and owners of a paper was an associated press reporter and he let loose all that a credulous people would believe. They had most of the innocent people, women and children, with the feminine men believing everything that was printed, as well as the news that was circulated and peddled on the streets.

Benjamin F. Keith, wholesale merchant

CHAPTER TWO

Monday, August 15

WHEN SAM ARRIVED at the newsroom of the *Messenger* on Monday morning, the place was in an uproar. Men were gathered in a knot around a wooden desk piled high with books, papers, and a typewriter—talking loudly, disagreeing. Inside a glassed cubicle, a short man in rolled shirtsleeves marched back and forth in front of two other men, gesticulating wildly. He grabbed a newspaper from his desk, stabbed it with his finger, then flung it aside. The paper fluttered to the floor like a falling dove. None of the men bothered to pick it up.

Nobody noticed Sam standing in the doorway, sweating into his coat after climbing a flight of stairs. He moved across the room as if invisible, fingering his letter of introduction from Cousin Hugh, until he was close enough to hear the muffled voices behind the glass door, stenciled *Thos. Clawson, Editor.*

"That black son of a bitch has gone and done it this time!" the short man ranted. Clawson, Sam figured.

"Now, Tom, get hold of yourself."

"You get hold of yourself, Harry. I don't want to get hold of myself."

"You're the one sold him that Jonah Hoe printing press," Harry said. He was tall and bent, with a shock of white hair and a florid face—an aristocrat gone to seed.

"I want it back! I want him out of this town!"

"Rumor has it Alex Manly already left town," Harry said casually. "I hear he's in New Jersey." Sam had the distinct impression that Harry was enjoying all the hullabaloo. His bloodshot eyes were smiling.

"Well, somebody wrote that trash!"

"Mr. Clawson," the third man said, "don't you hear the clarion call?" He was a lean blade of a man in his mid-thirties. Sam sized him up: pale, a man who spent his days indoors, in offices, clubs, smoke-filled meeting rooms, hammering out the fine print of stock-for-cash deals, bond issues, third-party real-estate transfers.

Clawson wheeled to face the third man. "What are you talking about?"

"Reprint the damned thing." He spoke softly, with authority.

"Print the damned thing?" Clawson pounced on the discarded newspaper and waved it around, reading, " 'We suggest that the whites guard their women more closely'!"

Harry said, "No need to sell papers that way, Tom. We can't keep up with circulation now."

"In the meantime," the third man said, "buy up all the spare copies you can get your hands on and pass them out free on every street corner in the city."

Harry studied his own copy of Alex Manly's *Daily Record.* "A cut above his usual style, wouldn't you say? Pithy, active verbs, right to the point. A bit bold for Manly." Then he doubled over in a spasm of coughing. He fished out a soiled handkerchief from his immaculate white linen suit.

Clawson ignored him and kept reading, still marching back and forth: " 'Our experience among the poor white women of the country teaches us that women of that race are not any more particular in the matter of clandestine meetings with colored men, than are the white men with colored women'!"

Harry recovered. "Nobody reads that nigrah paper."

The third man trimmed a lean cigar and fired it from a wooden match. "Exactly my point—put it in the *Messenger*. They'll sure read it then."

Clawson wasn't listening. " 'Every Negro lynched is called a big, burly, black brute, when in fact many of those who have thus been dealt with had white men for their fathers—' "

"Such alliteration." Harry wiped his mouth once more with the handkerchief and stuffed it back into his pocket. "No one will take it seriously."

" '—and were not only *not* black and burly, but sufficiently attractive'—sufficiently attractive!—'for white girls of culture and refinement to fall in love with them'!"

The third man puffed his cigar. "Print it," he said again, putting a hand on Clawson's shoulder. It sounded like an order. "Run your own editorial right beside it. Tomorrow. Next week. Every day until the election."

Clawson noticed Sam standing outside the glassed cubicle. He jerked open the door. "You lost?"

Sam held out his letter of introduction. "I'm your new reporter."

"Like hell you are." Clawson slammed the door, and Sam stood perplexed, aware that the other voices in the newsroom had suddenly stopped, replaced by muffled laughter. He felt his face go hot. His armpits were soaked. The letter wilted in his hand. He brushed back his blond hair with a moist palm.

Before he could decide what to do next, the door swung open quietly and the white-haired gentleman called Harry held out his hand. "Harry Calabash," he said. "Honored."

Sam shook Harry's soft, damp hand.

"You must be Jenks—our war correspondent?"

Sam nodded. "Well, I was over there."

Calabash nodded slowly. "You arrive at an interesting juncture, Mr. Jenks. Come along." His voice was soft, lilting, almost effeminate. He spoke in theatrically unhurried phrases. Sam had heard a Southern drawl before, but Calabash affected an accent he could hardly comprehend. Despite a slight limp, Calabash moved nimbly among the desks, dodging through the narrow aisles toward an old hulk of a desk in the far alcove. He rummaged in the drawers. The clatter of typewriters filled the room now, writers at work. Copyboys dodged in and out. Sam kept his mouth shut.

"I understand you had some trouble on the train."

"Word gets around."

"It's a small town of a city, son. I'm an old reporter."

"There was an incident."

Without glancing up, Calabash said, "So I'm told."

"One of the soldiers settled it."

"Captain Kenan. Used to be collector of customs—best-paying job in the state, for the hours. Four thousand dollars per annum—that's a cool thousand more than Governor Russell himself makes. They kicked him out for a nigrah, fellow named Dancy."

"Hard news for him."

"Shoot, he'd a whole lot rather play soldier with the boys at the armory than ride a desk. Likes to get his arms around this life. Bill Kenan would have been Teddy Roosevelt, if Teddy Roosevelt hadn't already been invented."

"And Mr. Waddell?"

"*Colonel* Waddell," Calabash corrected. "He rode in with you, too? A local curiosity, like the statue in the square. Mostly harmless." He rummaged some more. "Eureka!" He held up penciled carbons clipped together. "Let us depart this sweatshop for a more agreeable locale."

Sam held out his letter, now stained with his fingerprints. "But I should—"

Calabash snapped the letter from his hand. "You should do what I tell you. I've been assigned to break you in. For heaven's sake, take off that coat before you keel over." Sam took off his coat, and Calabash slung it over the chair on top of his own. He took up a cane. From a peg above his desk, he grabbed a finger-creased Panama hat and set it lightly on his shaggy head. "And get you a hat."

They clattered down the wooden front stairs together and into the hazy heat of Market Street. "This humidity—makes a man fairly *ooze*," Calabash said. At that moment, from a stairwell doorway across the street, a lean figure emerged wearing a smart gray suit. A sign on the second floor read, *The Record Publishing Company*.

Calabash nodded toward him. "Alex Manly," he said.

"No," Sam said. "You're mistaken."

"Oh, I'm hardly ever that."

"Fellow's a preacher man. I met him on the train."

Calabash squinted toward the man as he crossed the street toward them. "You sure?"

The preacher walked briskly past them, so close that he brushed Sam's arm, though he did not acknowledge him.

After he had passed, Calabash said, "Thought you said you knew him."

"Not exactly."

"Well, by the living Jesus, he's the spitting image of Manly, right down to the fancy moustache."

"The fellow you were all talking about upstairs?"

Calabash nodded. "Let us retire to the waterfront."

Three blocks down the hill, they sat over a bare board table. Calabash sipped cold beer from a schooner. Sam drank iced tea. The far side of the Cape Fear was crowded with moored vessels— schooners, steam packets, several full-rigged ships. Tugboats worked up and down the river, hauling barges. The ferry plowed methodically back and forth across the river, hauling workers to the turpentine stills and shipyards on the far shore. Even indoors, he could whiff the bitter ammoniac odor of the Navasso Guano factory at the north end of the wharf. Big mule-drawn freight wagons rumbled over the cobblestones.

On the near wharf, an oceangoing steamship was taking on provisions from B. F. Keith's Warehouse & Dockage. Farther along, other vessels were being loaded with rice, timber, cotton, peanuts, tobacco, barrels of resin and case oil, naval stores. Gangs of black stevedores worked steam cranes and manhandled cargo nets. Not like the landing at Daiquiri in Cuba, Sam thought—soldiers falling out of boats, horses prodded over the side to drown.

He was impressed with all the activity—here was industry in high gear. Maybe Cousin Hugh was right, this was the future—how many tons of commodities were being transshipped before his very eyes while he sat idling?

Sam listened to hear the stevedores sing as they worked, but they only grunted, cursed, and joshed each other. "Quite a racket down here."

"Yes, but I like it—reminds me where I am." Calabash passed Sam his carbons. "Local politics. We have an election coming up in November."

Sam had covered the ward bosses in Chicago. He had hoped to get a more challenging beat than small-town party electioneering, and his disappointment was plain.

"Son, down here *life* is politics. And politics is life, period. The sooner you figure that out, the better off you're going to be. You ain't in Chicago now."

"Quite a list." Sam counted at least two dozen names. "Who's going to get elected?"

Calabash laughed dryly and shook his head. "It's a little more complex than that. Those are the rascals already in office." He savored his drink. "Won't be voting for a new mayor and aldermen for two more years yet."

"So, what? State and county offices?"

"Right. And Congress." Calabash leaned over the table close enough for Sam to get a blast of his breath. "Now, realize, son, that down here the state legislature controls the city charter."

Light was beginning to dawn. "So whoever goes to Raleigh has their hands on the local throttle."

"You're awfully bright for a Yankee."

Sam read the first page again. "Maybe I'm dense, but I don't get it—there are four slates of aldermen here. Which are the ones in office right now?"

Calabash drained his beer and waved for another. "Well, now, that depends on which of the five mayors you consider the legal man—Fishblate, Harriss, McLGreen, Silas Wright, or Colonel Walker Taylor."

"Another colonel? Is there anybody in town who isn't a colonel?"

Harry Calabash sighed like a nanny with a troublesome child. "Well, there's Silas Wright—he's only a doctor."

"Preacher kind?"

"Croaker kind."

"Why all the fuss about who runs city hall?"

"Come now—don't be so naive. Money. There's more money flowing into this town than any other place between Baltimore and Savannah."

"And it flows right through city hall." Just like Chicago.

Harry nodded. "Now, as I was saying. We have a Democrat judge who says Mr. Harriss is mayor, since Solly Fishblate was the last legal mayor and Fishblate handed the job over to Harriss."

"Why would he do that?"

Calabash rubbed his first two fingers against his thumb. "Lucre, son. Lucre. But somebody got crossed, and old Solly—who's now a Redeemer, which is nothing but a low subspecies of Democrat—wants his job back. Then we have a Republican judge—or maybe he's a Fusionist, I can't keep them straight—who's slapped an injunction on the Harriss crowd. McLGreen, he was a Reform Democrat last week. This week, he may be a Populist, which is really just a recycled Jeffersonian Democrat who hates the way the railroads have leveraged their capital with rate-fixing and bonds paid for by taxpayers. Then again, he may be a Free Silverite by now—like Mr. Keith down the wharf." He drained his schooner. "Got all that?"

Sam shook his head. So that's the way it was: worse than Chicago. "Not even a little bit."

"Good," Calabash said. "Now, forget everything I just said."

Sam just stared, not sure if he should laugh.

"You ever find yourself actually understanding all the political shenanigans in this town, you get back on that train before they lock you up with the imbecile children at City-County." He called for the waiter. "Can we get some whiskey here, please? It's almost ten o'clock in the morning—a man could die of dehydration around here."

"Yes, sir, Mr. Calabash," the Negro waiter said, and delivered two whiskeys in short order.

"There's lots of busy people running around getting into mischief," Harry said. "Mostly, their names don't matter."

"Mostly?"

"There's a few names that do. Trick is knowing which ones are which."

"How about a starting nine?" Sam said.

"Colonel Walker Taylor, George Rountree," Harry said. "Start with those names. Remember them. Watch out for them. When you meet them, pay attention to what they say."

"Right."

"And then there's John Allan Taylor—Colonel Walker Taylor's brother. They don't see eye to eye, those two. John Allan, he's pure business. Walk, he goes his own way. Military man, the strenuous life, Teddy Roosevelt. Thick with Bill Kenan. What he believes in ain't very complicated, and he believes in it all the way."

"And what does John Allan believe in?"

"You saw him in the office—cold fish. Knows red ink from black, the bottom line. Believes in the monthly balance sheet and the sanctity of railroad bonds."

Sam smiled—he had pegged him right. "Whatever you say. That the whole roster?"

"Not by a long shot. But I've told you too much in one lump already. You'll get all the pieces by and by—when you need them."

"Promise?"

"I don't make promises. Man who makes promises, he's already got his hand in your back pocket. But I do tend to repeat my wisdom from time to time—just in case you ain't listening the first time."

"I tend to listen good."

"Fine, fine. But everybody gets distracted."

Not if I can stay clear of the who-hit-john, I won't, Sam thought.

"One more thing," Harry said. "The mayor and aldermen don't have a free hand in this town."

"Oh?"

"Little club called the Board of Audit and Finance. Five men, all appointed by the governor."

There it is again, Sam thought, just like Chicago—that old fear of actual democracy. "So the aldermen can pass whatever laws they please, but the Finance Board holds the purse strings—contracts, hiring, bonds."

"You're catching on just fine. Used to be three Republicans and two Democrats. Now, the tables are turned."

"But the governor is a Republican."

"That fat old boy don't want no trouble." Governor Russell was a three-hundred-pound embarrassment. "Wants to keep the lid on down here. Keep things at a stalemate."

"So, whichever Board of Aldermen is ruled legal, they still have to pry loose their budget from the Democrats," Sam said.

"Sooner bleed a turnip."

"But the Democrats can't actually *do* anything without controlling the Board of Aldermen."

"That's a fact. Got to control both boards." Harry laughed. "Whereas, they've each got control of only one board."

Sam shook his head to clear it. "God bless democracy."

Calabash raised his glass and waited until Sam picked up his. "To the Bourbon Democrats."

"Bourbon Democrats?"

Calabash hacked into his bare hand. "Redeemers, son. Redeemers. Call themselves Bourbons. And they ain't named after the kings of France."

They clinked glasses, and Calabash drank. Sam shoved his glass across the table. He felt relieved he could do it so easily—no hesitation, not a second thought, no twinge of regret. "I took the cure, Harry. It's all yours."

Calabash hesitated. "What could it hurt to have just one?"

It was still easy to refuse—one drink and he'd have his old appetite back. He knew that as surely as he knew his own name. It was the one thing that could sink him, sink his marriage, for good. Calabash ought to know better. In Chicago, all the newspapermen Sam had known were like Calabash, sleepwalking between boozy good times and hangovers.

"It would kill me," Sam said.

"My word. You mean I'll have to work with you sober?"

"Harry, believe me—you wouldn't want it any other way."

Calabash sighed. "It's going to be a long campaign, son." Then he shot the whiskey to the back of his throat, smacked his lips, and set the glass down gently on the tablecloth.

"What's all this have to do with Mr. Manly?" Sam said.

"Mr. Alexander Manly is the editor of our rival newspaper, the *Record*. Negro paper. I fear he is about to be evicted."

Out the window, a band of five Red Shirts appeared on the wharf. Two had pistols shoved into their belts. They taunted the stevedores, oily with sweat. The stevedores ignored them. A white policeman stood by and did nothing.

Harry Calabash said quietly, "I do detest a bully." Sam said nothing—just watched the Red Shirts move down the wharf like a gang of schoolyard toughs out for mischief. "Well, let's go get you started."

Sam hesitated, then asked, "Do you think I might get away for lunch? I promised my cousin I'd meet him and get reacquainted. It's been years."

"Who's your cousin?"

"Hugh MacRae."

For the first time since Sam had met him, Calabash looked nonplussed. "Tom didn't tell me that."

"You know him?"

"He's only one of the three richest men in town. Put him on your list, too—right at the top. Where are you meeting him?"

"A place called the Cape Fear Club."

Calabash laughed, and then his laughter dissolved into a fit of coughing. "Joke's on me. Come on, let's check in at the office. You'll need your coat. Then I'll walk you over there." He got up from the table with difficulty, then stamped his left foot on the floor a couple of times, hard. "Leg stiffens up," he explained. "Got to get some fresh blood into it."

As they walked, the town was full of racket. Buildings were going up, shoehorned into alleys. Second and third stories were being added to old structures. Everywhere, workmen were hammering, sawing, slapping bricks onto mortar, stirring concrete in big, dented tubs. Sam took it all in. Something was strange about the scene, though, and all at once he realized what it was: from hod carrier to foreman, all the tradesmen were black.

On the way back up Market Street, thick with the traffic of drays, carriages, and freight wagons, Sam spotted Colonel Waddell strutting along the opposite sidewalk. He waved and called out, but the street was too noisy. The wagons crunched over the loose oyster-shell paving and stirred up a constant cloud of lime dust. Calabash held his handkerchief over his nose but hacked relentlessly anyway.

Another man, dressed in a black suit despite the heat, encountered Waddell from the other direction. The two stopped and conversed as pedestrians flowed around them.

Calabash pointed a crooked finger. "That man is a vector of ambition."

"The Colonel? But you said—"

"George Rountree—he already made the list. Vice president of the club that's serving you lunch today."

———

George Rountree had been avoiding Waddell for weeks. Waddell was a fossil, but canny and potentially troublesome. He had a way of getting into everybody's business and taking a piece of it.

"Morning, Colonel. Too hot to be walking."

Waddell took his arm. Rountree was a large man, powerfully built, his middle already running to fat though he was barely into his forties. Waddell steered him against a lamppost. "Mr. Rountree, I wonder if I might have a word with you."

"My office?"

"Too hot. The club?"

Rountree should have known—every time he had anything to do

with the old fox, it cost him money. But he was trapped. "Fine."

Three blocks away, in the dining room of the Cape Fear Club, which billed itself as the second-oldest men's club in the South, the air was cool and the dim light was easy on the eyes. Overhead, electric ceiling fans rotated lazily, gently humming. Heavy drapes and stout doors kept out the street noise. Plush Oriental carpets soaked up the occasional clatter of sterling forks on Dresden plates. A dozen early luncheon patrons sat in twos and threes over linen tablecloths and silver place settings, talking business—attorneys, importers, aldermen, wholesalers. Members and their guests. White men who owned things. Negro waiters in spotless white jackets and black bow ties glided noiselessly among the tables, the kitchen, and the bar, delivering entrées and iced drinks on silver platters.

Men came and went seriously, without socializing—no visiting table to table. This was a place of business, of public privacy, each table a confidential enclave.

In a corner alcove, behind a hand-rubbed mahogany bar, a white-haired Negro in a hunter-green waistcoat poured liquor. Behind him shimmered racks of crystal glasses, decanters in staggered rows, a bar-length mirror framed in brass.

Waddell sipped Chardonnay—he would allow himself one glass to go with the stuffed shrimp. Rountree wondered if Waddell expected him to pick up the tab again. It was common knowledge that Waddell's law practice was falling off. Lately, he'd been reduced to litigating petty squabbles over tradesmen's contracts, minor probate matters, police court. The Colonel had rich tastes and a new, young wife, but he hadn't gotten the dowry he'd expected from a deRosset, and his own resources were thin. Still, he'd always had a knack for getting other people to foot the bill—a born politician.

Holding it by the stem, Waddell carefully replaced his wineglass on the tablecloth and flicked his tongue across his lips. "Frankly, George, I'm a little put out. Apparently, the boys don't want me to help."

"Not at all," Rountree said. "It's early. It's a very early stage of things." He rubbed his bald head thoughtfully. He felt his baldness made him look distinguished. The silvering hair at his temples was razor-short.

"George." Waddell smiled with his lips. "We are both gentlemen. We both understand the need for discretion."

"I didn't mean—"

"Of course you didn't." The Colonel was still smiling.

"Nobody doubts your discretion." But the truth was, Rountree's associates didn't want their plans trumpeted all over town, not just yet. This was the quiet phase of the campaign—a time to plan, to marshal resources, to gather into a common purpose men who could be trusted.

"I fought for this country once, and by God, I'll do it again," Waddell said. "That's how strongly I feel about this matter."

"You're not the only one."

"There's nothing I wouldn't be willing to undertake."

Waddell had once gotten himself elected to a term in the United States House of Representatives. Ever since then, he'd been trying to get back into office. He had tried for the Senate, but Dan Russell, currently governor, had trounced him good. Rountree figured that, at this point, the Colonel would settle for any office—alderman, customs collector, health inspector—but he didn't say so. Waddell still had a following in town, in the capitol in Raleigh, on the State Democratic Committee. No sense starting a feud—just put him off awhile.

"It's time we took back this country," Waddell said, stabbing an index finger into the white tablecloth. His voice was a note too strident. The waiter glanced his way, then quickly went about his chores. "It's getting so it isn't safe to walk the streets. God-fearing women are being shoved into the gutter, gentlemen are being set upon by roving gangs—"

"You're preaching to the choir, Colonel."

More quietly, the Colonel said, "Some men can hold a crowd—maybe you need such a man."

Waddell could hold a crowd, Rountree had to admit. Waddell was one of the last of the old-time barnburners. He could throw his voice to a thousand people. He could work them up and gentle them down and then get them hot again, plying them with fiery slogans, sentimental clichés, and cheap showman's tricks. Mainly, he had that voice: sonorous, rhythmical, hypnotic. When he'd spoken at the old Opera House during his congressional canvass, it had sounded like the voice of God. It would get so soft the crowd would hush, leaning in to hear. Then in the next sentence, it would box their ears. Men came away with glassy eyes and balled fists; women came away in love.

But the others had been quite definite: keep Waddell out of it.

Maybe Rountree could distract him—the old fox was a fool for flattery. "Heard you at the Opera House, back when you were running for Congress."

"So long ago! And you still remember." Waddell beamed. "That was something. Did you know that I spoke off the cuff that day?"

"I had no idea."

"There wasn't time, you see. The nomination had only come vacant the day before. But you must have been a mere boy!"

Rountree had never thought of himself as a *mere* anything, but he nodded, remembering. It was the day he had decided to follow the law. "I was ten years old. You had five hundred people in the palm of your hand."

Waddell wagged a finger playfully. "Good people know the truth when they hear it. I was just the conduit." He sat back, smiling, and finished his shrimp with careful, precise bites.

To Rountree, Waddell was just a stage actor, too old to play the part he craved.

He wolfed down his well-done steak and gulped three straight cups of coffee after it. The coffee made him flush, but he needed the jolt to get through a long afternoon of business. "Look, Colonel, we've still got two and a half months. We've got things to settle with the people in Raleigh."

"Naturally."

"Perhaps when the time is right."

"A man could be persuaded."

"Maybe a speech." Rountree was slowly seeing the possibilities. They'd have to hold Waddell back for now, let things fall into place.

"Let me think about it," he said. When the time was exactly right, an old-fashioned barnburner might be just the thing.

Rountree consulted his railroad watch—not fancy, just accurate. "I have a client, if you'll excuse me."

At that moment, the waiter arrived with the check on a little silver tray. Rountree waited a beat for Waddell to reach for it. Waddell was a founding member of this club, and it was tradition for the senior man to host. But he patted his lips with his napkin and made no motion toward it. Rountree pasted the check to the table under his palm. With the other hand, he drew a fountain pen out of his pocket and unscrewed the cap one-handed—a trick he had picked up at Harvard—and scrawled his signature.

As the colored boy held the door for Rountree, Waddell was ordering another glass of wine. The day was turning out very well indeed.

The agent was waiting for Rountree at his office in the Allen Building. He never locked up during the lunch hour—that was the kind of city this was, the kind it would stay, if Rountree could help it. The agent got to his feet and smoothed his crumpled brown trousers. Rountree immediately went to his desk and unlocked it, not bothering to shake the man's hand. This was business—you didn't need to be friends for life.

"We've located the item you requested," the agent said. He fingered his straw hat nervously and wouldn't look Rountree in the eye. "Only thing is—"

"Yes?" Rountree was immediately alert. He'd half-expected this—these days, everybody tried to take advantage.

"—the price has gone up," the agent said quickly.

Rountree retrieved the papers he was after from his top drawer, slammed it, then came around the desk and stood facing the agent. He didn't have time for this foolishness. Rountree was taller and heavier, and the agent stepped back. "Your family business is in Kinston, am I right?"

"You know it is." Rountree had known the man's daddy for fifteen years.

"Kinston, that's my backyard." Rountree paused to let it sink in. "A contract is a contract. We will pay what we agreed."

"But there's another party who wants it."

"I have your signature on a purchase order." Rountree snapped the paper in his hand. "There's a figure next to it."

"Prices change, Mr. Rountree. If it were up to me . . ."

Rountree slipped a manila envelope from among the papers he had taken out of the drawer. He unwound the twine and opened it, then counted out fifteen hundred-dollar bills into the agent's hand. "Take the loss," he advised quietly.

The agent's eyes brightened. "Oh, I see. Well, we didn't expect cash."

Rountree shrugged. "No sense in extra paper. How about the other items?"

"All in stock—just a matter of sending them down from the factory in Connecticut."

"Thirteen dollars apiece."

The agent consulted his papers. "Right. Times two hundred and fifty."

"Exactly."

"Three thousand two hundred and fifty dollars."

"C.O.D."

"Of course." The agent fidgeted. "May I ask, why do you need so many?"

"No, you may not ask. When can we expect delivery on the main item?"

"Four to five weeks. It will have to be assembled. May I ask, is there someone here who is trained, that is, who knows how, who can handle . . . ?"

Rountree glared at him.

"Of course. The rest you can have anytime," the agent said.

"Fine. L. B. Sasser will take delivery at his drugstore."

"Yes, sir."

The agent was still fingering his hat, looking whipped, so Rountree clapped him on the shoulder and said, "I've got an edge on today—don't pay it any mind. Tell your daddy I was asking for him, hear?" Rountree shook his hand heartily.

"Yes, sir, thank you." The agent let out his breath, stuck his straw hat on crooked, and left quickly.

When the agent had gone, Rountree telephoned his wife, Meta, then telephoned Hugh MacRae to tell him the good news. But MacRae was at a luncheon appointment with his Yankee cousin. What the hell was he inviting down Yankee cousins for?

For what was coming up, the fewer damnyankees around, the better.

*Don't get mad at all the white people because of
the few who have forgotten. . . . In the first place,
we ask in all seriousness who is there among the
whole number that would make of himself a
murderer for the sake of carrying an election,
which, if it goes either way, must give white men
office?*

Daily Record

CHAPTER THREE

Monday, August 15

GRAY ELLEN JENKS WALKED from the Orton Hotel, where she and
Sam had temporary lodgings, to the brownstone Hemenway School
on Fifth near Chestnut. She had an appointment with superintendent Noble and a letter of introduction from Hugh MacRae. Sam
had asked for it.

She also had a manila folder full of references from principals
and senior teachers. She'd been the darling of Northside School in
Chicago—until Sam had fouled things up.

Once again, their life had been pulled up by its roots, but now
that she had been set down in this new, strange place, she might
as well make the best of it. She had no intention of sitting around
the house all day.

"We have two white schools, Mrs. Jenks," the superintendent told her. Noble spoke quietly, almost huskily. As he talked, he held his lapels like an amateur actor. He would have been uncommonly handsome but for his bad teeth. "This one and Union. May I get you a glass of tea?"

"No, thank you."

"Fine schools," he continued, looking out the open casement window at the giant elms that made a tunnel of the street. He turned back to his polished oak desk, its top clear except for a porcelain inkwell. He flipped through her letters. "Impressive," he said. "According to these, you must be a fine teacher. We'd be fortunate to engage you."

"That's very kind of you to say."

"Not at all." He lingered over the last reference, from Hugh MacRae. Then he handed the sheaf back to her. "Neither Hemenway nor Union, I'm afraid, has an opening."

"Oh. I was led to believe—"

"Now, Mrs. Jenks." He approached her, smiling. "The schools must remain above politics."

"Politics? I'm afraid I don't understand."

"I'm genuinely sorry I can't help you. Or Mr. MacRae. A man with such an *interest* in our schools."

"Mr. Noble, I really don't think—"

"Perhaps he can find a position for you at his mill. Or his bank."

She was beginning to understand. "Now, look—I'm not asking for any special favors."

"Mrs. Jenks," he cautioned her, still smiling. "You're new in this city. Don't say anything you might regret."

She glared at him—if only he were angry, direct. "Look, I'm sorry we got off on the wrong foot."

He flung his arms wide. "I'm a magnanimous man, Mrs. Jenks. I accept your apology."

Apology? She said, "I've taken up enough of your time."

"We have many local ladies who would be very good in the classroom, but we can't hire them, either. There's been a depression, you know."

"It's not a hobby, Mr. Noble. Not something I do to amuse myself in my spare time. I'm a trained teacher, I've got experience. It's my profession."

He smiled and held the door for her. "Yes, of course it is."

She turned to go but felt a soft hand on her arm. She faced him. He looked at her directly for the first time. He spoke more softly than ever. "A word of advice? Your high-handed attitude is going to put people off."

She was near tears, but she wasn't about to let this little cock see her cry. "I'll remember that." She bustled out of the office, skirts swishing. The secretary gave her a look and breezed into the superintendent's office behind her, and the door clicked shut. Gray Ellen dropped her letters. She stooped to pick them up and heard their voices behind the door.

"What is it that makes those people so pushy?" Noble was saying.

Us people? she wondered.

He went on, "They're always shoving their way to the front of the line." He was talking loudly now. "They come down here, throwing their weight around—well, they're just going to have to learn to pay their dues."

"She's new," the secretary said. "Give her time."

Noble said, "Well, I wouldn't hire the good Lord himself if Hugh MacRae recommended him." He banged something on the desk. "She probably got fired from her last job for moral turpitude."

Gray Ellen was flabbergasted. She took deep breaths to get control of herself. It was all she could do to restrain herself from marching back into that office.

The secretary reappeared, startled to see her. "You still here?" Her voice was uncertain—she wasn't sure how much Gray Ellen had overheard. She looked down at her desk, the neat stacks of papers.

"Don't worry, I'm on my way out. I guess I'll try the other schools."

"The colored? They're best left to their own people."

"I'm a teacher. My people are in the classroom."

———

Seven blocks away, at the Williston Colored School, the interview went better. "Do you have any local references?" John G. Norwood asked, after going through her letters of reference. He was polite but distracted. He kept checking his watch, as if he had another, more important meeting.

"No, I'm afraid not," she lied. She felt flushed and damp all over from the walk. She hoped it didn't stay this hot down here all the time—the heat sapped her energy.

"Never mind," he said. He started to say something else but stopped himself. "We've lost two teachers this year to illness." Then, after a moment's reflection, he said, "I can't promise anything. Folks frown on white ladies coming in here." He hastened to add, "But you wouldn't be the first." He paused, seemed genuinely regretful. "I'm afraid the pay . . ."

"I'm sure the salary will be satisfactory."

Norwood smiled. "Your attitude is commendable," he said, then shook her hand heartily. His hand, she noticed, was slippery from perspiration.

On her way out, she passed a delegation of black men, all young and well-dressed, heading for Norwood's office. She recognized the preacher from the train—fair-skinned, with wavy, neatly combed hair. He was as light-skinned as Norwood. When he didn't speak to her, she touched his arm. "Excuse me," she said. "Don't you remember? We met on the train."

He stared at her, a hard look, then his blue eyes softened. "You were the one," he said.

"Somebody had to do something," she explained. She was vaguely proud of herself.

"You should have let them throw me off," he said in a mellifluous voice.

"You *wanted* to provoke them? I don't under—"

"That's right," he said. "You don't. That's a good thing to remember."

"Come on, brother," said one of the young men. "The man's waiting."

The preacher never took his eyes off Gray Ellen.

"At least tell me your name," she said. "I'm—"

"I know who you are," he said in that same honey-dripping voice. "I have seen you before, in every city." He raised a finger and smiled graciously. "But you don't know who I am. You have no idea."

What in the world was this all about? The other men grinned at her. "That's right," they agreed. "Tell the woman the truth, preacher."

She was feeling bullied, the way the preacher must have felt on the train. Only, unlike him, she wasn't trying to provoke anybody to do anything. She was just getting mad. "You must have a name." She didn't care any longer who this arrogant man was, but she wasn't backing down. He smiled without showing any teeth, looking handsome and sly. "Never mind," she said. "Forget it. What do I care?" She turned from him.

"Mrs. Jenks," he said quietly.

She turned back, startled at the mention of her name.

"I am Ivanhoe Grant, a preacher of the Lord." He bowed ever so slightly from the waist.

"Fine," she said. "I'm very happy for you." How fitting, she thought—named after a silly medieval character in a book and a whiskey-sotted Yankee general.

"Perhaps I've misjudged you," he said sweetly.

She almost believed him. "Never mind. I'll just try to pick up the pieces of my shattered life and move on."

He laughed—a big, sonorous laugh. As soon as he laughed, against all better judgment, she found herself liking him. She had the uneasy sense that he had somehow been testing her, and now she had passed. He seemed to relax, but she was still agitated. This morning, everybody around her seemed to be talking in riddles, and she resented it—it was like hearing every second word of a question and being expected to come up with a good answer. She felt rattled and out of control, teased, but for what purpose? Everybody was saying something other than what they meant.

She had to get out of there, back to her rooms.

"Perhaps we'll meet again, Gray Ellen," he said. How did he know her first name, and what right had he to be so familiar?

"I doubt it," she said.

He kept smiling. "You got to be where you live," he said gently. "It's a small town."

Yes, she thought, heading for the air—and getting smaller every minute. Behind her, she could hear laughter and the shuffling of feet, then the careful shutting of a heavy door.

———

The Reverend Ivanhoe Grant and his ten companions crowded into John Norwood's office. Norwood was an alderman, a member of the school board, and one of the twenty most influential Negroes in town. He hobnobbed with Dr. Silas Wright, mayor, Benjamin Keith, the importer, and Sheriff George Z. French—all white men. They trusted his advice. He sat on the executive committee of the Republican party.

Norwood held up a copy of the *Daily Record*. His coat was off, his tie was undone, hanging in two limp ribbons from his unbuttoned celluloid collar. His shirtsleeves were rolled up on his thin forearms. "What in the hell does Manly think he's doing?" Norwood was angry. For years, he'd worked to bring the races together. Much of the time, that had meant compromising, giving up on little things to win bigger things.

"Telling the truth, brother," Preacher Grant said.

"You're not from around here."

"I was born here," Grant said. "I have only come back."

"Well, I never heard of your people. Heard all about you in Tennessee, though."

Grant smiled and bowed his head. "The Lord's will be done."

"The Lord's will shot down five black workingmen." It had been the familiar pattern: a rabble-rousing speech by a white man, an indignant meeting of blacks, more speeches and threats. All just talk until Grant showed up and goaded a few young men into action. Then in came the local thugs and the sheriff's deputies to quell the "Negro uprising."

Grant sat on the edge of Norwood's desk. He opened his hands like wings and softly flapped them in the air. "There is change in the air."

"That what brought you back—the smell of trouble?"

Grant's hands fluttered, his voice took on an incantatory tone. "Can you feel the change in the air, brothers? Can you feel it?"

They murmured assent. They didn't sound too sure.

"The time has come for the New Jerusalem."

"Amen," somebody said softly.

"Oh, don't get started," Norwood said.

"The time has come for the black man to walk in the sunlight with his head held high."

"Amen," said several in unison.

With an elegant, sweeping gesture of his right hand, Grant wiped the sweat off his forehead. The hand kept going and raised itself into the air, fist blinking into five outstretched fingers. His palm was white as a fish belly. "The hour has come for the black man to walk in the sunlight with his head held high and his eyes open wide." His inflection was rising, the voice taking on resonance and power.

"Praise Jesus."

His left hand aimed like an arrow at the cracked ceiling, toward heaven. "The hour has come for the black man to walk in the sunlight with his head held high and his eyes open wide and a *rifle* in his hands!"

"Tell the truth!"

"Walk in the sunlight with the Lord!"

"Head up high!"

"Mmm, mmm!"

Ivanhoe Grant was off the desk now, poised on the balls of his feet in the semicircle of listeners, his hands gripping an imaginary rifle. The hot little room rang with his words. "The hour has come for the black man to walk in the sunlight with his head held high and his eyes open wide and a rifle in his hands and his *finger* on the *trigger*!"

"Glory be to Jesus!"

"Amen, say it again!"

"Lord, Lord, Lord!"

Norwood wheeled on him, gripped his wrists, and pushed him out of the way. Grant's eyes flashed, but he did not resist. He had trained himself not to resist until it mattered. In the meantime, just absorb the violence. Let it pass through you. Let them waste their strength fighting what won't fight back. In time, even Norwood would come around.

"Now, listen to me," Norwood said. "This has gone far enough. This here's dangerous talk. A man could find himself strapped to the lynching tree for this kind of talk. Get ahold of yourselves."

Tom Miller, a real-estate investor and the most enterprising pawnbroker in town, said, "Maybe we've had ahold of ourselves too long, John. Maybe it's time we got ahold of something else." Miller made loans to lots of white clients, and lately, plenty of them were holding out on their payments, as if daring him to do something about it.

"Yeah."

"That's what I'm thinking."

Norwood persisted. "Look, we've made progress. We got Red Cross Street paved."

"Only 'cause it leads to the railroad station."

"We've got bicycle paths so our men can get to the mills without having to pay for a streetcar. We've got ten Negro policemen. We've got a closed sanitary sewer in Brooklyn now, instead of an open ditch. And the Negro ward down at City-County—"

"Editor Manly got us those things," Tom Miller said.

"You think he did it alone? He has been the voice of a united front. The ministers, the lawyers, the businessmen, the workers. And he got them by *leaning*. A firm, steady push. But no threats, no violence."

"We need more than bicycle paths, John. And we need it now."

"There's an election coming up."

"You think they're going to let you niggers vote?" It was Grant, laughing openly at them now. His words came slow and clear. "My, my, how you do carry on!" He paced in front of them, back and forth, hands clasped behind his bent back, shaking his head as if he could not comprehend such foolishness. Then he wheeled on them. "They're buying rifles and riot guns."

"We don't know that," Norwood snapped. He was getting tired of these histrionics. All Grant needed was a purple robe, maybe a choir swaying in rapture behind him. It was easy to get people riled up—they craved the drama. They'd wail and croon and clap their hands. With the right voice filling their ears with voodoo religion, they'd march straight into rifle barrels.

What was hard was getting them to do the unglamorous thing. Lean, he thought. Steady pressure, day after day, year after year, generation after generation. Use your head. Make the laws. Win the ballot. Bring your people up one at a time, each one helping the next.

"Open your eyes!" Grant hissed, balling his fists in front of his own eyes, then exploding them into star bursts of long fingers. "You stand here in your pretty white man's suits and talk like the white man and wear your hair like the white man and pay the white man's taxes. But roll up your sleeves. Look in a mirror. What color is the face under those white man's whiskers?" Ivanhoe Grant's face was running with sweat now, his beautifully combed hair glistening, his cheeks shining like yellow apples.

The men were murmuring and nodding. Some of them rubbed their faces, their wrists. Even Norwood, caught by the voice, reflexively glanced at the light olive skin beneath his rolled-up white sleeves, then felt tricked.

Norwood had lost control of the meeting, and he knew it. The whole point was to defuse the situation. Reassure these young hotheads so they wouldn't do anything rash and ruin all that he and the rest had worked so hard for—John Dancy, Armond Scott, Carter Peamon, Constable John Taylor, and all the other prominent black men who had lifted their community up to share in the prosperity of the largest, wealthiest city in the state. Its political center. The place where real and lasting reforms were happening every day.

They controlled the trades. The masons, the carpenters, the mechanics, the teamsters were all black men. They ran the waterfront—nothing moved into or out of the port without black men taking home honest wages. They had one all-Negro fire company— Phoenix Hose Reel Company No. 1, the best in the state. They had the trophy to prove it. They had lawyers at the bar and a black coroner. A Negro ran the customs house and another one ran the ferry. They had their own newspaper, their own schools run by their own principals.

But they could lose it all in a heartbeat. All the Redeemers wanted was the excuse, and Norwood refused to give it to them. The Republican party, the party of Lincoln, was his religion. It would be, he believed, the salvation of his race.

If any city in the South would lead the way to true equality for the Afro-American, Norwood believed, this one was it. He had the support of the Black Ministerial Union, the Society of Colored Ladies, the Negro Veterans Association, the Republican party, and—until today—Manly's *Daily Record*. He wasn't about to let a small band of hotheads set the clock back fifty years.

"Now, listen to me, all of you." Norwood spoke firmly. "They won't dare move against us. They'll fight us at the ballot box. Send Dockery to Congress. Return Marion Butler to the Senate. Lend your strength to Jeter Pritchard. Vote the Republican ticket—the black man's ticket. This is America—we have the vote. Your fathers and grandfathers died to win that vote. Don't waste it." Now, Norwood was sweating. He hadn't meant to give a speech— he was no good at speeches. What he had wanted was quiet talk in a private room among reasonable men. He hadn't counted on Ivanhoe Grant. Lord, it was hot.

Grant sat back on the desk, dabbing at his neck and cheeks with a squared white handkerchief, smiling at his own private joke. "And tell me this, Alderman Uncle Tom." He said it so smoothly it hardly sounded like an insult. "What color are the men who are going to count those votes?"

Norwood ignored him. "They won't move against us," he insisted evenly, for emphasis. "The fight is at the ballot box."

Pawnbroker Miller clenched his fists and held them up, then opened them into straining fingers, as Grant had done. "If they do move against us, I swear I will wash these hands in white men's blood."

Before anybody could reply, the door was flung open and sixteen-year-old David King burst in, out of breath and sweating, as if he'd run a long way. Doubled over, hands on knees, panting, he managed to deliver his message: "He's been evicted!"

Norwood said, "Who, boy?"

David straightened up, wiped the sweat out of his eyes, and massaged his left knee. He'd been born with a withered leg and was mildly retarded. "Editor Manly! They throwed him out! Closed down the *Record!*"

"Manly's in New Jersey," Tom Miller said, puzzled.

"That damned editorial," Norwood said. "We'll just see about this."

Ivanhoe Grant sat on Norwood's desk looking elegant and unsurprised. He rolled his eyes toward the ceiling and stage-whispered, "The New Jerusalem."

Halfway back to the Orton Hotel, at the corner of Market and Fourth, Gray Ellen Jenks was nearly knocked down by a colored boy running fast, pumping his fists hard and not stopping for anybody. Immediately, she wondered if he were a thief fleeing a policeman, then scolded herself for jumping to such a conclusion. That was mostly what was wrong with the world, she had decided a long time ago—everybody jumped to conclusions.

The boy ran gimpy, one leg cocked out straight. She watched him disappear up the street, a strange, scuttling figure.

An electric streetcar passed her, and she almost hailed it, to get a break from the muggy heat. It stopped at the corner, and the motorman stepped down to help two young white ladies aboard. When the black woman in line behind them boarded, the motorman stood aside, offering her no assistance. Gray Ellen decided to keep walking.

The lime dust from the oyster-shell paving parched her mouth and stung her eyes. Oyster-shell pavement—who'd ever heard of such a thing? Half the storefronts in town were dusted with it, their paint corroded by the lime, and the public parks were full of hacking children. The whiteness was blinding.

In the black neighborhood she had just come from, the streets were paved—those that were paved at all—with sawdust from the ice ships, spread to keep down the odor of fresh manure. But in neighborhoods like that, the manure didn't lie in the streets long enough to stop steaming: people rushed out to collect it for their rose gardens, their vegetable plots.

A sudden emptiness overcame her, a hollowness of the spirit: what was she doing here? All she wanted was a baby and a home, and a husband sober enough to give her both. And to work quietly at her profession. Was that so much for a woman to want?

A Negro man and his wife passed her, arm in arm, nodding good day. A black man and a white man strode by her going the other way, too engrossed in their conversation to notice her.

The sidewalks were jammed with well-dressed blacks—lawyers and commercial men. She'd never seen so many Negro professionals mingling with whites in Chicago or Philadelphia. No one here seemed to find it remarkable.

A black policeman on the opposite corner smiled and nodded. She felt ogled, felt the burn of a blush—silly, but she couldn't help it. She moved quickly up the street, not paying attention to where she was walking. Two white boys whipped past her chasing a colored boy. Black workmen and delivery boys crowded the alleys.

She smelled the river, the fish market, the sharp odor of the guano factory. Two mule-drawn freight wagons rumbled by, the hostlers whistling at her. She turned to see if they were white or Negro, then realized, all at once, that for the first time in her life, she was seeing the world in black and white.

She found herself back at Market Street. Up the block, across from the *Messenger* offices where Sam worked, there was a commotion in the street. She had no other pressing business, so she walked that way. A crowd of white men was gathered around the entrance to a saloon. Then she saw that the focus of attention wasn't the saloon but the rooms above it. Two black men were leaning out of the open windows on the second story dismantling a large, artfully lettered sign: *The Record Publishing Company.*

With a rope braced somewhere inside the building, they lowered the sign to street level, where other black men—not laborers, but men wearing clean shirts and snappy pinstriped vests, cravats undone—guided it into the bed of a two-mule dray.

The dray was already lying flat on its springs under the weight of a massive object behind the teamsters' seat—a shapeless hulk covered by an old green tarpaulin.

The white men were waving their fists and yelling so many things at once that Gray Ellen couldn't make out any of it. Some of them wore red shirts, like the rowdies on the train. A small knot of Negroes watched from the other corner.

A man in wire-rimmed glasses and leather printer's sleeves emerged from a stairwell door next to the saloon, and she realized what the tarpaulin must be hiding: a printing press.

The jeers grew louder, and for an instant, Gray Ellen expected violence.

But suddenly, a stocky, red-haired priest in a cassock and collar shoved himself between the crowd and the black man, and the Red Shirts at the front hesitated. The priest stood them off, crouching, fists balled.

Gray Ellen had drifted into the fringes of the crowd now. "Excuse me," she said to a pretty, petite woman. "What's going on here?"

"Don't you know, dearie?" the woman said. "They're clearing out that rat's nest."

"Excuse me?"

"The nigger paper, honey—that Manly devil. Throwing him out on his ear. About time, too, after what he wrote." The woman handed Gray Ellen a limp copy of the *Record* and snapped her index finger down on the editorial. "It's a slander to Southern womanhood, is what it is."

A fat woman in a faded print dress laid a damp hand on Gray Ellen's wrist. "Don't listen to that mess, honey. There's more to this than meets the eye." The petite woman walked away in a huff.

Gray Ellen cocked her head to listen amid the growing din of jeers and catcalls. "What do you mean?"

"Ain't from around here, are you? That nigrah paper wa'nt doing nobody no harm. Got carried away, is all."

"Who's the fellow in the sleeves?"

The fat woman squinted, then shook her head so her pink chins fluttered. "Can't say—but it's not Manly. Don't see Manly anywheres. You'll know Manly—pencil moustache, a real rooster. Smooth and cool—ice wouldn't melt in his mouth. Could be his new assistant."

"Who's the priest?" Gray Ellen had not yet visited her new church, St. Thomas's. This priest looked more like a prizefighter than a man of the cloth.

The fat woman chuckled in admiration. "That's Father Dennen, works with the coloreds over to St. Thomas's. A real hellion, that father."

"You're Catholic?"

The woman looked at her, horrified. "Honey, I'm a Christian woman, but I draw the line. I don't go in for all that wine guzzling first thing on a Sunday morning."

"Well, it's not exactly—"

"Just you take a look at what that Manly wrote—that's what's causing all the fuss, honey. Poor man wa'nt thinking clear, that's a fact."

Gray Ellen quickly read a few sentences of the editorial: "A Mrs. Felton from Georgia makes a speech before the Agricultural Society at Tybee, Ga., in which she advocates lynching as an extreme measure. This woman makes a strong plea for womanhood, and, if the alleged crimes of rape were half so frequent as is oftentimes reported, her plea would be worthy of consideration."

To Gray Ellen, the tone seemed reasonable. Maybe the controversial part came later. "Who is this Mrs. Felton?"

"Congressman's wife. Likes to sound off. It's politics, is what it is," the fat woman said. "MacRae and that crowd, they're the ones behind it. Wouldn't trust that man to give me change back for a dollar."

Lovely, Gray Ellen thought—twice in one day. Of all the people in this town to have for a sponsor. She'd never even met MacRae.

The *Record* staff all climbed onto the dray, perching on the sideboards. Gray Ellen noticed a girl among them, with a lovely, clear face. She wore a high-collared cotton blouse with balloon sleeves, her long muslin skirt wrapped by a blue denim apron. And eyeglasses. The girl clambered nimbly over the high sideboards.

At last, with a braying heave, the mules got the overburdened wagon moving, and it rumbled slowly through the heavy horse-drawn traffic up the long hill of Market Street, farther and farther from the river.

Hugh MacRae steered Sam through the shadowy breezeway and toward the dining room. MacRae was a lean-faced man with a high forehead and penetrating eyes. They'd both been born during the last year of the Civil War, but Sam thought of Hugh as older, since his business affairs were so important. Sam had met him for the first and only time almost ten years earlier, in Philadelphia, where Hugh was trying to buy hotels. Hugh had started and managed half a dozen corporations, most of them concerned with land development. He wanted to fill in the swamps east of Wilmington and build houses, factories, whole colonies. He had a vision.

"I believe in two things, Sam," he said, after they exchanged preliminaries. "Family and land. A man has to take care of his own people. And his people belong to the land."

Hugh MacRae looked as if he'd just leaped down from a horse after a fast, hard ride. His receding hair was mussed, his cheeks had high color. He impressed Sam as an energetic man always on the move, restless and easily bored. He had all sorts of deals working, all sorts of plans. He was an M.I.T. graduate, a self-made tycoon, a real-estate speculator. He was director of the National Bank of Wilmington. He was owner and president of Wilmington Cotton Mills, the second-largest cotton compress in town, after Sprunts' Champion Compress. He owned parcels of land all over the county and was busily buying up more.

"The only real standard of wealth is land," he explained. "They're not making any more land." His pet project was to build immigrant communities on the outskirts of town—Italian, German, Hungarian, Dutch. Separate enclaves of working men and women. Utopian labor communities. "White immigration," he said, "that will solve the race problem in the South once and for all."

Sam said, "I'm not sure I follow." They stood at the entrance to the dining room. The white maître d' hurried over from another table and bowed.

As they were led to their table, Hugh said, "A question of numbers. Right now, the numbers are way out of proportion. Part of it is our own fault—hell, we brought them here to work the rice plantations. But that's not the whole story."

Colonel Waddell passed by on his way out. "Good to see you again, sir." Sam held out his hand.

"If you'll excuse us," MacRae said. "Busy afternoon ahead."

They settled at their table. As the Negro waiter poured ice water into crystal stem glasses, MacRae observed, "That old boy Waddell was really something once. Politician. Orator. By God, he could really get your blood up. Now, well, events have sort of passed him by."

Before Sam could say anything, MacRae said, "I was surprised to get your letter. But it gave me an opportunity. You'll be an asset to this community."

Sam shrugged, but he was flattered. "I'm just a newspaperman."

"You didn't hesitate to go off to the war, do your duty. We can always use that kind of gumption."

"It wasn't so much."

"The proper way to measure a man is by his achievements. A man *is* what he *does*."

"I'm just a reporter. All I do is write the stories."

"You can tell our story to the world. You can look at us with a fresh eye, with a cosmopolitan perspective. What we're doing here will seem all the more remarkable to a newcomer."

Sam nodded. Waddell had said the same thing. Well, being a booster never hurt. "People always crave a good story."

MacRae smiled with his mouth closed. "This is the future down here. Nobody realizes it, but I know it. Land, that's where the money's going to be. Cotton's already on the way out. Same with turpentine."

The waiter delivered iced tea, and MacRae ordered lunch for them both in clipped tones. "Had two banks fail down here in two years—foolish investments," he said. "Too liberal with bad debts. I brought in New York money, fixed all that. Issued bonds guaranteed by the city. Guaranteed. Stability, that's what money likes. Order."

MacRae lectured on about politics, the stock market, the war in Cuba. "That spig army was no match for white men—you saw that for yourself."

Sam recalled the chaos of Las Guasimas. The Spanish regulars—the soldiers called them *spigs*—had shot from the tree line using smokeless powder. It was like fighting ghosts. The Americans were cut down in their ranks. "They got in their licks."

As the waiter delivered their appetizer of fruit compote, MacRae said, "Down here, the only fly in the ointment is the coloreds. Our city has become their mecca. In Raleigh, we believe it's deliberate."

"A plot?"

MacRae devoured his compote. "You're the reporter, you figure it out. Look at the census—three times as many coloreds as there were ten years ago."

"But that doesn't mean—"

"Doesn't mean what? It's getting to be a liability, if you know what I mean. Economically speaking. You should hear them in New York. At the Chevy Chase Club in Washington. Holding back development, they say. Who's going to put their money in a town run by coloreds? Which bank? Who's going to build a factory here? Who is going to patronize a beach resort surrounded by colored slums? Don't get me wrong. I have nothing against the colored man—in his proper place."

"I don't see the harm—"

"The harm is the filth, Sam. The filth. It is in our interest for them to be clean and decent. Our food is cooked by colored hands. Our children rest in the arms of colored nurses. Colored housekeepers make our beds and wash our underclothes. But when you get too many of them in one place, the result is squalor and crime."

"Well, poverty can—"

"They lack the instinct for civilization. Do you know that some white people are scared to emigrate to the South for fear of cannibalism? Cannibalism!"

"You don't believe that—"

"The signs are plain. Things don't change soon, we're in for another depression."

Sam was nonplussed. "Are you saying we shouldn't have come?"

MacRae smiled and said softly, "What I'm saying is—if you'll listen—what I'm saying is, we can't count on outsiders to bail us out again. We must take matters into our own hands." He squeezed the stem of his wineglass, and Sam waited for it to snap, but it didn't. "Seize control of our destiny."

Sam hadn't touched his compote. "Meaning?"

"Meaning there are eight thousand Christian whites in this town. Well, my God, you got seventeen thousand coloreds over there across the track. Just waiting to rise up on their hind legs, just biding their time. You got white Republicans putting ideas in their heads. Now, they want to vote."

"They're allowed to vote, the law says so." Sam was confused: he thought that business about voting had been settled years ago, during Reconstruction.

MacRae smiled but stopped eating, and Sam could tell he was annoyed. "Cousin, the law is not something written down in some book. The law is the way people live. How they do things. How they carry on their business and their families." The waiter leaned over the table to take their plates. "Hell, you can't have every ignorant cotton-field nigger voting for a two-dollar bribe. Where would this country be?"

Sam had no answer. He fidgeted in his chair, trying to concentrate on the opulent surroundings.

"Negro overpopulation, that's the virus killing this town, I've said it before and I'll say it again. And more coming in all the time. They've put the word out, see. Come to Wilmington, come to Darktown. Bring your mammy, bring your cousin. Bring your rifle."

Their entrées arrived. The steaming platter of braised pork loin hardly touched the tablecloth before MacRae attacked it with knife and fork. The waiter yanked his hand out of the way of the blade.

"I don't really believe—"

"You'll see a lot of things down here you'll find hard to believe."

Sam ate a few bites. The pork was succulent, tasting of light vinegar and parsley. "What did you mean, take matters into your own hands?"

MacRae sat back in his chair. "Just between you and me and the chandelier," he said confidentially, as the waiter poured their coffee, "the fuse has already been lit on this firecracker." He slurped his coffee. "Man, I love coffee on a hot day. Makes a man sweat out his poisons."

*I take pleasure in writing to you to let you
know that you are the sorriest scoundrel in
North Carolina. The article that you had in your
paper was a shame to the Old North State. . . .
And if I lived in Wilmington I would give you 24
hours to leave or I would blow your brains out.*

From an anonymous letter
to Alex Manly, signed only
"A. Man."

CHAPTER FOUR

Saturday, August 20

IN THE RIVER MIST of 3 A.M., the high side rails of Smith's Creek
Bridge loomed gray and ghostly. The road was deserted—just as
well. Instinctively, Frank Manly stopped the open carriage at the
foot of the bridge, listening for riders. The only sound was the
splash of fast, shallow water on rocks, rushing toward the Cape
Fear. The lone jet mare stood riveted in place, head up, sniffing the
damp air of the bottom.

Around them was thick swamp, impassable even in daylight.
Some night-hunting animal shrieked, and Frank shivered in the
heat. He didn't believe in spirits, but this was different. This was
live things that could hurt you, chew you right up. Fangs, claws,

stingers, and poison. Quicksand and gator wallows. Wouldn't be caught dead out there, he thought.

On the seat next to him sat his younger brother, thirty-two-year-old Alexander Lightfoot Manly, deep in thought. He'd been up for thirty hours, traveling. After the telegram, he'd taken the train south, getting off at Castle Hayne, twenty miles out. No use risking a lynch party at the Atlantic Coastline Station. But in the diffuse moonlight, he looked none the worse for all his hard travel. As usual, he wore a gray tailored suit and a high celluloid collar and cravat, along with a brushed gray derby over his wavy black hair. Though it was hot and muggy even at this hour, he wore kid gloves—a habit he'd picked up from his friend Dr. Wright, the mayor, who never appeared in public without white gloves. A black Prince Albert lay carefully folded behind the seat.

Satisfied there were no riders waiting on the road ahead, Frank urged the mare forward. She stepped delicately across the uneven planking of the bridge, the boards creaking quietly under the wheels.

"You stirred them up this time, brother, sure enough." Frank was the general manager of the paper. He had nothing to do with the editorial side, and had been in Greenville the day the editorial was published.

For a long moment, Alex Manly didn't reply. He was still brooding. It didn't make sense. He'd only been gone a few days, leaving young Jeffries, the new assistant editor, in charge. Jeffries was just an eager kid and not much of a writer. His prose tended toward dime-novel clichés and high-blown non sequiturs. Manly had hired him as a favor—an apprentice who would work for practically nothing. Surely, Jeffries hadn't written the editorial.

"Who was it, Frank?"

"Damned if I know. All I know is, I come back from Greenville and the office is closed, two Red Shirts standing guard with a bottle of save-the-baby. I kept right on going."

"As of now, Jeffries is fired."

"That boy's long gone. Norfolk, his girlie said."

Alex thought of his own fiancée, Carrie. Thank the Lord she was in London right now, singing on the stage, and not in the middle of this mess. Only last month, she'd been setting type for him. Now, the aristocrats of Europe were gathered at her feet.

"Is everyone safe? Mom and Pop?"

"For now," Frank said. He kept his eyes on the dark road. Alex was always the reckless one and Frank the tough, steady one. Like their other brothers, Henry and Lewin, they were descended from Charles Manly, an antebellum white governor of North Carolina who had freed all of his offspring by slave girls. Frank knew he himself could never pass for white in daylight—his skin was too dark, his hair too kinky, his nose too broad, and his lips too full. He preferred it that way—he suffered no ambivalence. He never went to sleep wondering who he was or where he belonged.

But Alex had always joked about "passing"—fooling the white man. He had a perfect ear—he could mimic an Irish teamster or a German baker. Frank never saw the humor, only endless confusion, an agony of choice. A man should not have to choose his race.

"How much black blood does it take to make a man black?" they used to argue. One grandparent made you a quadroon, one great-grandparent an octoroon. Named like exotic cigar wrappers, from light to dark.

Even if you had seven white great-grandparents out of eight, even if your skin was fairer than a swarthy Irishman's, you were not white. You were a mulatto, a high yellow, a colored, a darky, a black, a Negro.

Alex's fiancée, Carrie, was part Tuscarora Indian. Her people were trying to block their marriage—to them, Alex looked too white.

Among their own race, both brothers knew from long experience, shades of skin color seemed to matter almost more than to whites—light-skinned Negroes seemed to get hired faster by Negro bosses. They were trusted more quickly. Deferred to. Every preacher Frank had ever met was more white than black—like his own family, the progeny of white masters and black slaves.

But Frank Manly was not a man to stir things up. His main duty in life seemed to be to protect Alex from himself, and he was good at it. Strong and muscular, he had good physical instincts and an eye for trouble. He wondered why Alex had come back at all. What had ever possessed him to buy that damned printing press?

"Where is the press?" Alex asked quietly. Lights were coming into view up ahead—the houses of early-rising mill hands.

That goddamn printing press, Frank thought. Like it was some icon, the symbol of a divine mission. It was just a hunk of iron and a damned lot of trouble. They still owed Tom Clawson money on it. Well, at least Alex had asked about the people first. "They moved it, Lewin and the others. You missed all the hard work, brother."

"Someplace safe, I hope."

"Shoot. Ain't noplace safe. But we fixed it up with St. Luke's to rent us Free Love Hall. Two stories, good ventilation, more space than we had before."

Alex listened: the businessman talking. Practical, sensible. Next door to a colored church, not a bad location, he thought. Might keep off some of the rougher elements—*bocras* didn't like to mess with a church, superstitious that way. "So the ministers are with us."

"Wouldn't exactly say that," Frank said. The ministerial union had denounced the editorial as inflammatory but made a plea to support the *Record*. They'd printed subscription handbills and passed them out all over Brooklyn: *Pay up at once, if you please, so that we can combat the evil influences at work against our race*. It was the reminder Alex himself had written and run every day at the bottom of page one.

"Oh, well. They have to be cautious."

Frank continued, "Anyhow, the office is all set up. We're back in business."

Alex stiffened. "You haven't put out a new edition?"

"No, brother—waiting on you."

"Good. That's good." They didn't need another inflammatory editorial. "Brother Norwood must be tickled," Alex said.

Frank hooted. "Been kissing so much white ass, he's getting calluses on his lips."

They rode on, enjoying the breeze of movement.

"Alex?" He said it softly, so Alex knew it must be important.

"I'm listening."

"It's bad. You don't know how bad it is." After the eviction, Frank had been so worried that he tried to buy a pistol, but nobody was selling guns to blacks. A new unwritten ordinance. It was always the unwritten laws that got you.

Alex waited for more, but Frank said nothing. "You're suggesting we cease publication for a while."

"Only for a little while. Tempers are hot. Some mighty rough characters drifting into town. On the scout for that handsome face of yours."

"Something's in the wind, I know. I could smell it, too—all the way up in Asbury Park." It surely had a stink.

"Let it cool awhile, Alex. Hear what I'm saying? Give the man time to forget about us and get distracted by something else."

Alex thought, we are the only Negro daily newspaper in the country, but he's right. He wished Frank were wrong. It could've been worse—should've been worse. Next time, it would be. It stung his pride. It felt all wrong, against fairness, against everything he stood for as a journalist and reformer, but he said, "All right, Frank. We won't go to press for a while longer. But let's keep the staff together." Sometimes, you just had to hold onto your anger, let it burn in your belly. Sometimes, you said the most by saying nothing.

Frank relaxed. It was all right now, Alex was home. Everything was going to work out fine.

The buggy was among the outlying houses now, scattered kerosene lanterns flaring yellow lights across the dirt road. The electric lines didn't come out this far. Off to the left, in the darkness, lay Oakdale Cemetery, where the dead of seven generations of the best white families in the county rested in peace: Rose Greenhow, the Confederate spy who, weighted down by gold, drowned while swimming ashore from a foundering side-wheeler; Captain John Maffitt, the blockade runner; George Davis, attorney general of the Confederacy; generals, tycoons, planters, and their women. Alex had made a pilgrimage out there one rainy Monday just to read all the names.

Out of sight across the river, they could hear the rumble of a night freight laboring along the Seaboard Airline.

They passed through Brooklyn. There were no gas street lamps in this part of town. Through the thin clapboard walls, they could hear the clatter of pans and spoons, the husky murmur of sleepy voices. The sun wouldn't be up for another two hours. The dirt track under the buggy wheels turned to sand. The mare was tiring with the effort of pulling. She leaned forward and cut the sand with her hoofs, digging for traction. The tires made a soft *whoosh*.

Frank was dozing at the reins. No trouble would come to them here, among their own people. In a way, it was lucky they'd been chased away from downtown. Free Love Hall was across Market Street, half a dozen blocks up from the river, in a mixed working-class neighborhood. A Negro newspaper out there would be ignored. It was only six blocks, but in the right direction.

"Frank," Alex said. "One thing I don't understand."

Frank stirred and cleared his throat. "Only one thing? You a lucky man."

Alex drew a folded newspaper out of his inside coat pocket, and Frank realized he'd had it all along. It was still too dark to read the print, but they both knew what it said. "This Mrs. Felton, from Georgia. The congressman's wife."

Here we go, Frank thought. He can't leave it lie. Got to worry it till he lands us in more trouble. "What about her?"

"This whole editorial is on account of her speech, right?"

"That's the short of it. She some dumb *bocra*, saying nasty things about the colored man. Just like all the rest of them crackers. Should have let it go by."

"Frank, there's just one problem."

Of course there is, Frank thought: with Alex, there was always one more problem.

Alex said, "That speech is a year old. Why all the fuss now?"

Frank didn't say anything. A cold wind blew into his belly. He thought, somebody's messing with us. Somebody is surely messing with us.

Alex said, "Take me to the office. I want to see it."

"Now? I've been up half the night."

"Now's as good a time as any."

Frank sighed. "Whatever you say, brother. You're the man."

So instead of stopping at the neat yellow frame house at 514 McRae Street, where their parents and brothers were still asleep, Frank reluctantly clucked the horse on by. The windows were still dark. Alex didn't even look.

They rode down Red Cross for a block and a half to take advantage of the new paving, turned onto Seventh at Dr. Kirk's Central Baptist Church, and crossed Market after four blocks. The streetcars weren't running at that hour, but Frank, ever cautious, reined the mare to listen for the big eight-mule-team mill freighters that came barreling downhill to the wharf without lanterns.

In the glow of the gas street lamps, the street was empty. Up Market on the left, in one of the big houses that kept servants, electric lights were burning behind window shades in the downstairs parlor. Alex wondered who was entertaining at that hour.

Frank clucked the mare across Market. On the oyster shells, she moved at an easy pace. The brothers didn't talk. The only sounds were the *chick-chicking* of the mare's hoofs and the dull crunching of the wheels. Half a block past Williston School, they came to it— a white wood-frame building tucked between a private home and St. Luke's.

"You hung the sign?" Alex asked. His soft voice carried in the quiet.

Frank pointed. "Can't see it, but she's up there."

Alex nodded, approving. It was good to have a brother you could count on. "I'll stay here from now on. Sleep on the cot—you brought the cot?"

Frank nodded. Then he said, "What you going to do?"

"I don't know yet."

"You could always retract it."

Alex smiled in the dark. "Can't retract it—how would it look? Anyhow, they're going to do what they're going to do, regardless of what I print or don't print."

"You underestimate—"

"It'll blow over."

"You're always so sure about things. What if it don't?"

"Course it will. They've got an election to win. Congress, the statehouse, all those county offices. They can't have civil disorder."

"Ain't that the whole point? The election?"

"Let's boil up a pot of coffee. We can figure this thing out."

In Hugh MacRae's basement dining room on Market Street, nine men were gathered around a mahogany table. They had been talking since midnight. There was much to discuss, and this was a good place to discuss it. The dining room was accessible from an outside door beneath the front porch.

The house itself was a fortress, built of fieldstone and gray-stuccoed brick to resemble a castle, complete with rooftop battlements and an ivy-covered turret. The walls were a foot and a half thick. The lot was a full city block, fenced by high wrought-iron spikes set into granite footings. On granite standards at intervals along the fence burned electric security lights. The Princess Street side was closed off by a nine-foot-high brick wall.

"I was standing in the middle of Market Street—not fifty yards from my front door—conversing with a business associate." MacRae was telling the story of how he had finally decided enough was enough. "This gentleman was down from Raleigh. He had gone to the courthouse on a legal matter that morning and had to ask the nigger janitor for directions to the judge's chambers. Do you know that nigger spoke to him in the familiar?"

They nodded. They'd all heard this story before, enough to wonder if it were even true. But it confirmed them in their purpose.

"This gentleman was flabbergasted. Right there in the street, he was telling me, '*Our* niggers address us with some respect.' Just then, a dray came barreling down toward the wharf, a nigger driving. Now, he had plenty of room to go to one side of us or t'other. Point is, he aimed right down the middle of the road. We were forced to leap for safety."

They nodded, murmured their disgust.

"Leap to safety, gentlemen. Point is, that nigger driver forced us to take action." He smiled. "Maybe that boy did us a favor, after all. We are here tonight to contemplate just exactly what action we are going to take. And I can assure you, gentlemen," he said, looking around for effect, "the one action we will not take is to leap for safety."

"Hear, hear."

MacRae served the bourbon himself, out of the bottle, and set a crystal pitcher of well water on the sideboard for any man who needed a mixer. It was best to leave the servants out of this. His wife, Rena, and little Dorothy, going on seven, were asleep upstairs. He was doing this for them.

"So Rountree isn't coming at all? Doesn't George want to be in on this?" The question came from J. Allan Taylor. The others were owners of stores and livery stables, lumber companies and banks, wholesale firms and real-estate consortiums.

MacRae trimmed his second cigar of the evening. Vices were all right, among gentlemen. "Won't join us officially. Prefers to stay in the shadows. Feels he can be more useful that way."

L. B. Sasser, the druggist, said, "George will keep his mouth shut. That's his business. He's working the Raleigh end."

MacRae nodded. They'd spent the evening going over logistics. Using the thirty-two plat-maps completed by Sanborn-Perris in April for insurance bonding, they'd divided the city into sections, each with a captain to be named in the coming weeks. Each section was further broken down into blocks. On each block was designated a "stronghouse"—a physically invulnerable structure with a telephone.

The plats were color-coded according to structure: the stronghouses were all red—brick.

When the trouble started, the fire bells of the four white companies would ring simultaneously. Each block warden would set up headquarters in his stronghouse and wait by the telephone for orders from his section captain. Meanwhile, his men would gather all the women and children in the neighborhood and march them under protective guard to the stronghouse. Squads of militia would then evacuate them from each stronghouse and escort them to First Baptist Church at Fifth and Market, next door to the Wilmington Light Infantry Armory. Both buildings could hold out against any attack not supported by artillery.

J. Allan Taylor, MacRae's section-captain liaison, would transmit the orders of the Secret Nine to the captains. That way, if things went awry, they would not know the identities of the other eight men in this room. Taylor was pleased. Now, instead of just poring over endless balance sheets in a dreary office, he would be out in the open air maneuvering among other men of action. He couldn't wait for it to begin.

But they all knew it must wait until the election.

"Solly Fishblate wants in," L. B. Sasser said. "He's been asking around, knows something's up."

MacRae said, "He's part of the reason we're in this mess. If he'd shown more backbone as mayor . . . Anyhow, we don't need any Jews. This is Anglo-Saxon business."

"He's got some pull with the Dry Ponders. And the Red Shirts."

"We'll see. Maybe later. But not yet."

"What about Waddell?" J. Allan Taylor said. "Rountree mentioned him."

"Gentlemen, gentlemen," MacRae said. "We can't let everybody in. The whole project depends on discretion. A limited number of hand-picked men pursuing well-defined objectives."

Except for the Board of Audit and Finance, the city government was being run by Fusionists—Republicans united with Populists. The Redeemer Democrats had to carry the county and state elections, the first step in canceling out the power of the Fusionist Board of Aldermen. The Fusionist crowd was hostile to business. They blocked tax incentives and railroad bonds. They were strangling the financial arteries of capitalism.

Once the election was won, they could make their move on the city.

Taylor said, "We could write a lovely role for the old goat." The others laughed. It would be ironic to use that War of Secession relic to usher in the new century.

"Let me think it over," MacRae said. "Maybe when it gets closer to the election, if things aren't hot enough."

Sasser said, "They're going to be plenty hot, all right."

Taylor said, "Do we know where Manly is?"

MacRae laughed. "The joke was on us this time—he really is in New Jersey. Can't imagine he'll come back."

"Then who wrote—?"

"Does it matter? We've been baiting that boy for months, and somebody over there finally struck at our worm." MacRae hooked an index finger into his mouth and yanked, and the men laughed heartily. He finished his fourth bourbon of the evening, more than he usually allowed himself even on special occasions. But tonight he felt a pleasant glow, a lightness of mind and spirit. The camaraderie of men brought together in common cause. Men determined to fight for what they believed in. It stirred the soul just to think about it. He would have just one more. Hell, they were making history here. His ancestors had fought with Wolfe on the Plains of Abraham, battled Lord Cornwallis in the Revolution, stood off the Yankee fleet for four bloody years.

He wasn't going to be deterred by some crackpot social reformers who didn't understand business. He had a vision for this city.

"We'll have to get a good route map for the streetcars," Taylor said through the cigar smoke, "so we can move our people around fast."

"Right," MacRae said. "See to it, John."

"About that other business," L. B. Sasser said. He wasn't sure whether to bring it up, but he had to know what to do with it when it arrived.

"A few more weeks," MacRae said. "George assures me it's all set. You'll get instructions about where to put it and so forth."

Sasser nodded.

"The key," MacRae said, closing his fist slowly, feeling almost military, "is control. Control at every stage of the process. No mob stuff. Keep those damned Red Shirts on a leash."

Sasser said, "They're in sympathy with us."

"Look, I'll say this just once: the last thing we need is federal intervention. McKinley sends in troops because of civil disorder, we're finished. The Justice Department will void the election. Order. Control." He chopped the smoky air slowly with his hand. "Everything done according to plan." He looked around at their faces, looked each man in the eye. "I don't have to tell you, gentlemen, that even being here constitutes an act of criminal conspiracy."

He paused to watch the effect. These were men accustomed to dealing in commodities, not people. This was about people, about human nature, about will. Much less predictable. Hugh MacRae knew people.

Nobody spoke or drank. It was the moment of truth: if it was going to be called off, now was the time. MacRae enjoyed it—the quick shiver of danger, the rank smell of risk. You didn't get ahead in this man's world by playing it safe. He sipped his whiskey, the signal for the others to break their solemn tableau.

J. Allan Taylor said, "Before we go, Hugh. Rountree suggests we form a businessmen's committee. A legitimate body that can work in the open."

"Good idea. Make George the chairman—he knows the law."

The men set their glasses on the sideboard and filed toward the door, where MacRae stopped them. "Remember," he said quietly, "not a word of this to anyone, even your wives. Go out one at a time. Leave a few minutes between."

For almost half an hour, quick shadows slipped from under the porch and out the iron gate, walking fast down different streets. L. B. Sasser and J. Allan Taylor used the old smugglers' tunnel under Market Street and came up in front of the Wilmington Light Infantry Armory three blocks away—careful not to slam the passageway door and alert any members playing cards in the club rooms. Pierre Manning, an attorney for the banks, went into the tunnel a little behind them and stayed underground until St. James Church.

Across every back fence between the MacRae mansion and the river, barking dogs alerted the falling moon.

In the basement club rooms of the Wilmington Light Infantry

Armory, another meeting was getting under way. Colonel Walker Taylor presided. He had gathered five men he could trust on business so secret he would not confide it even to his own brother, J. Allan Taylor.

Walker Taylor was an immense, balding man with a nose like a beak. His thin hair was plastered across his scalp. He had enormous, dark bug-eyes and a handlebar moustache waxed into ridiculously long dagger points, like a Prussian general. After the War ruined his father, he'd gone to work at fourteen as an office boy for the deRosset & Northrop Insurance Agency. Three years later, he had started his own agency, and it was paying off for him.

Their grandfather had built this blockhouse as the family home long before the War. The floors and front facade were Italian marble, white as bone. There was a marble fireplace in every room. Upstairs was the only sunken marble bathtub in the state. The outside walls were English brick imported through Philadelphia, then hauled five hundred miles by ox train. He'd spent almost fifteen thousand dollars—a small fortune in 1824.

Their father, John D. Taylor, had enlisted as a private and risen to a colonel. Returning as the one-armed hero of the Battle of Bentonville, he had discovered that every stick of his property—including this house—had been confiscated by the Yankees. He never got it back. The family home had eventually been acquired by the Light Infantry.

This was the first and last time they would meet here. They would never meet in any location more than once.

The five were businessmen of long standing: Fennell, one of the incumbent alderman who had refused to give up his seat to the elected Fusionists; Meares, of the Seaboard Airline, engaged in a tariff war with the farmer Populists; Robertson, superintendent of the Clarendon Waterworks, which was fending off a bid to turn it into a publicly owned utility; Beery, another railroad man; and Smith, an insurance man whose firm had lately taken losses from arson.

They gathered around a kerosene lamp, preferring not to turn on the electric lights. It all seemed more dangerous in the flickering pale of a single lantern.

The light danced against the low brick walls hung with crossed sabers, regimental colors, racks of obsolete muskets from old, glorious wars. A dressmaker's mannequin in the corner by the fireplace wore the original green dress uniform of the Light Infantry, trimmed with orange and gold. On a nail above it hung the white-plumed hat.

On another wall hung a framed photograph of Captain Donald MacRae, Hugh's brother, who had commanded the Light Infantry in the Spanish War. They never saw action, just whiled away the war training in Brunswick, Georgia, as Company K, Second Regiment, North Carolina Volunteers.

"I hereby declare this meeting of Group Six open," Colonel Walker Taylor said crisply in a flat voice that died against the thick walls and low heart-pine ceiling. It was so hot that globules of pitch were bubbling out of the wood. "Come to order."

He should be presiding over this meeting in the boardroom at city hall, he was thinking. With the Fusionist board under a legal cloud, he had been elected mayor by the Democratic board—the same board Fennell belonged to. But for now, such distinctions were meaningless: he'd heard this morning that the state supreme court was about to validate the Fusionist board, beyond appeal. Wright's gang, half of them Negroes.

This meeting, however—Group Six—was the beginning of a new order. This was a potent tool for restoring justice, going back to the old values, the traditional ways. He was the leader by acclaim.

The men stopped chatting and listened. "You realize, gentlemen," Walker Taylor said dramatically, "the risk you take in even coming here. Your reputations, your livelihoods, your freedom." He paused, turned his bright eyes first on one solemn face, then another. "If we're caught, if word of what we're doing ever gets out . . . That's the first thing: no one must ever know our names. Not until the thing is finished." He smiled and leaned over the table. "Not until we've won. Then we can march down Market Street behind a brass band!"

"Hear, hear."

"But if something is to be done, we're the men who will have to do it."

"Absolutely."

"Nobody else."

Walker Taylor continued, "We cannot have the nigrah politicians running this town any longer. They're choking us. It's time to put the finish to Reconstruction."

"What's the plan?"

"Preparation, that's the key. In the event of an uprising, we have to be ready to act at a moment's notice."

"This is a big operation, then."

"We must put certain things in place. We'll have the element of surprise. The backing of a few good men, loyal men. Men we can count on."

Beery, of the Atlantic Coastline, said, "We'll need money. It's going to cost."

Walker Taylor clasped his hands. "I've already got a man working on that. Outside man—thought it best not to be formally involved. Doesn't care to know what we discuss at these meetings. Assures me he can operate with more latitude—legally speaking— from the periphery."

"We should suggest he form a merchants' committee. Chaired by a man who shares our views. Doesn't need to know about Group Six."

"Exactly," Walker Taylor said, smoothing a hand over his bald scalp. "A man we can trust completely. A man who knows how to keep secrets. George Rountree."

Sam Jenks reported to the *Messenger* office early. It was easy to get to work early these days. Without the cobwebs of a hangover in his eyes and a hammering headache between his ears, the world was clear and pleasant. There was a lucidity about things.

Sometimes, during a long day, there might be moments of panic, when he'd have to duck somewhere and force himself to breathe deeply once, twice, three times. But then he would be in control again. They'd warned him about the panic. Focus on one thing at a time, the doctor had said. Avoid conflicting responsibilities. Don't go looking for confusing choices. Steer clear of contradiction. It was not a question of whiskey but of character—so the doctor claimed.

Harry Calabash was nowhere around. Clawson stalked out of his glass cubicle and thrust a sheaf of loose papers into Sam's hand. "Night man brought these in a couple of hours ago. He was drunk. Give me something by noon." He was back behind glass before Sam had a chance to wish him good morning.

Sam sloughed off his wool coat. Today, he'd visit a tailor.

He put his feet up on his desk, the nearest one to Harry Calabash's alcove, and went through the papers. Police reports. Scrawled, half-legible. So now he was a police reporter. One report seemed to be about a break-in—a posse of white neighbors had tracked down a colored man for stealing chickens and silverware. Chickens and silverware? Make up your mind, Sam thought.

Another report said that a Negro deputy sheriff, Ed Bryant, had drawn his gun and threatened a streetcar motorman rather than pay the fare. To Sam, it seemed far-fetched—who would risk losing one of the best jobs in town over a nickel fare? But stranger things had happened. That's what journalism was, a record of outlandish things that really happened. The whole point was to dare the reader's credulity: you thought we told you some stupid, crazy, outrageous things yesterday? Well, what do you think of this?

While Sam was still reading, Clawson strode up behind him. "One more thing," he said. Sam turned his head but did not get up. "There's a rumor that Manly's back in town. That he plans to publish again."

"I'll check on it."

"Find out where he is. I want to talk to him."

"Yes, sir, Mr. Clawson."

Manly back in town? After they'd evicted his newspaper? After Mike Dowling, the Red Shirts' leader, had vowed to kill him if he ever showed his face again? Now, that was a story worth pursuing. And why did Clawson want to speak to Manly? He couldn't quite peg Clawson. He was an educated, reasonable man. Negro baiting wasn't his style. So why was he still running that Manly editorial every day on page one?

Sam rooted through Calabash's desk until he found a city directory. It listed Manly as residing on McRae Street, up in Brooklyn. But Manly wouldn't be careless enough to go home. He'd be hiding out in one of those shacks, among his own people, a screen of hard men around him.

———————

The sergeant behind the booking desk said, "Eddie Bryant may be colored, but that don't make him dumb enough to draw down on a streetcar driver." He had a laugh full of phlegm that came up from an impressive belly. Sam had seen cops in Chicago use their bellies as a muscle, bouncing little criminals into brick walls. This fellow looked as if he'd bounced a punk or two.

"I've got a report," Sam said quietly. No use pushing this copper—Clawson had said the night man was drunk.

"I got all kinds of reports," the desk sergeant said. "Don't mean they're true." He hawked an enormous wad of chaw into a brass cuspidor.

"Got a point." Sam leaned on the desk. He could be as laconic as anybody.

The sergeant scratched under his tunic. "Now, there's a boy I could show you. Made friends with a chicken that already had enough friends."

"I heard there was silverware," Sam said. "I heard some neighbors caught up with him."

"Spoons. Pair of silver spoons." The sergeant hollered to somebody in the back to watch the desk. Then he grabbed a ring of iron keys and led Sam down a corridor, through a steel door, and into the jail. The sergeant locked the steel door behind them. "But it was Red Shirts caught him."

The jail was quiet. Prisoners hunkered over their morning meal of grits and sausage. The sergeant opened a cell and Sam stared in at a skinny black boy sprawled unconscious on a cot against the far wall. His face was swathed in clean bandages, and his arm was tangled in a sling. There was blood on the pillow next to his mouth. "Sixteen years old," the sergeant said. "Name's David King. A good boy. Gammy leg. And a little slow." He tapped his skull. "His mama's a God-fearing woman, best cook in town. Domestic over on Fifth, near Princess. One of the better homes."

The boy was all beat up. No matter how many times Sam saw the victim of a beating, he couldn't get over it. All those fists and boots, pummeling. "Why in the world do you think he was stealing chickens?"

The sergeant looked him in the eye, as if to say, how stupid are you?

Sam didn't know what to make of this sergeant. He looked like every bully-copper he'd ever seen, but he was clearly upset about this boy, David King.

"Shoot, that boy didn't steal no chickens," the sergeant said. "Spoons belonged to his mama. He was on his way to Tom Miller's pawnshop."

"Why is he in jail, then?"

"Don't want nobody bothering the boy. Soon's he wakes up, he can go."

The sergeant led him out. Sam turned and held out his hand. The big sergeant eyed it for a second, then shook it slowly, squeezing, watching Sam's eyes for a hint of pain.

"Sam Jenks."

"Lockamy," the sergeant said, letting go the hand. "You get in trouble, and it looks like you will, you call for Alton Lockamy."

Sam was almost out the door before he remembered. He turned. "They say Alex Manly's back in town."

Sergeant Lockamy sighed. "I don't want to hear that," he said. "How do these rumors get started?"

Back at the office, Sam filed three takes on the David King story. The boy was not a thief, he reported. His mother was an upstanding woman in the community. The boy was a cripple. The Red Shirts got him and beat him.

He handed it off to the copyboy, who ran it to Clawson. It was five till ten. He stood up and reached for his hat. He'd look for a new suit. After that, he could spend the morning tracking down Manly.

Clawson was rapping on the window glass. He motioned Sam to come in, then slapped the pages of his story. "I sent you for a story about a housebreaker, outraged citizens defending their homes from riffraff—not a bleeding-heart editorial." He shoved the pages back at Sam. "Give me something I can use."

Sam stared at him. Surely, he wasn't saying to fabricate the story. Clawson stood with his back turned, hands jammed in his pockets.

Sam went out. He walked straight to Solly Fishblate's to pick out a new suit. Located next door to the Orton Hotel, Fishblate's Men's Furnishings was a long, narrow, low-ceilinged establishment with warped pinewood floors.

"Any friend of Harry," Solly Fishblate said. He was a short man with thinning black hair combed in a cloud of frizzy curls. Clean-shaven, fastidiously dressed in a full linen suit with a gardenia at the lapel—mid-fifties, Sam guessed. Hard to believe he had ever been mayor. Didn't have the force for it.

But then, before Sam even told him why he had come, Fishblate looped a measuring tape around his waist. "Thirty-four," he said. "Inseam, thirty-three. Very good. Very good."

He eased Sam's arms up, and Sam held them there while Fishblate measured his chest. "Thirty-eight," he pronounced, then stood rocking on his heels, eyeing Sam up and down, rubbing his smooth chin with his big, red hand. "You have a strong build." He patted Sam's back. "Your shoulders can carry a longer coat. This is your lucky day. You like silk? I got Chinese silk."

"I only need—"

Fishblate wagged a finger. "A man needs a change of clothes. A man must present himself in a certain fashion."

"Well, I—"

Fishblate waved off his objections. "Say no more. Look at the merchandise. Feel the quality." He steered Sam into a thicket of clothing racks. "For Harry, I give you a price. One must recognize the gentlemen of the press, am I right? Tell me I'm wrong. For Harry."

Sam walked out of Fishblate's having ordered two suits—one in cream and one in bone white—four shirts, two ties, and a pair of canvas shoes. He stepped onto the bright street wearing a snappy, new, yellow Panama, so light a man could forget he had anything

on his head at all. Gray Ellen wouldn't be pleased with his extrava-
gance, but he couldn't walk around in this heat in that heavy wool
sack he'd dragged down from Chicago. A man had to look like he
belonged in a place.

Sam had a plan for tracking down Manly: David King's mother.
Sergeant Lockamy had said she was employed on Fifth, in one of
the better homes. If he could get to her before she realized David
was in no real trouble with the law, she might be scared enough to
talk to him about Manly. If she knew where he was. If he was back.
If.

He strolled down Fifth under the canopy of elms, enjoying the
shade. At Fifth and Princess, he spotted two likely houses, both
frame Victorians with gleaming wraparound porches and lavish
gardens. He inquired at the nearer one. A colored maid with her
head wrapped in an orange scarf opened the door.

"Mrs. King?" he asked politely.

"Mrs. King?" she repeated suspiciously. "Bessie?"

Sam nodded.

"She just a housekeeper. She ain't done nothing wrong?"

"No, she's not in any trouble. I just need to talk to her."

"Across the street, that the house you want." She pointed with
the handle of her broom. "Colonel Waddell's place."

"Waddell?"

"Yes, suh. He live there, him and his missus."

"Thank you."

He crossed the empty street. As he was about to climb the stairs
onto the porch, a woman appeared from the side garden. "May I
help you?"

Sam introduced himself. She held out a hand covered by a soiled
gardening glove, then, realizing, quickly withdrew her hand and
peeled off the glove. She held out her hand again, and Sam took it
lightly. It was pale and small.

It would have been more proper for someone else to make the
introductions, but she was learning to be less formal about many
things. "Mrs. Gabrielle deRosset Waddell," she said, and curtsied
slightly. She pronounced it Dare-oh-zet, emphasizing the last syl-

lable. In her gardening apron, she was rather shapeless looking, but when she moved, Sam could see the slim lines of her figure.

"How do you do?" She can't be any older than Gray Ellen, Sam thought. It was common for wealthy older men to marry younger women, but somehow, he hadn't expected it in this case. He'd imagined the Colonel going home to a plump, matronly companion with a boxful of knitting and samplers. He had a new respect for the man. Gabrielle was striking—thick auburn hair, fine cheek-bones, lovely brown eyes.

"May I offer you some refreshment? It's such a hot day."

"Thank you, but no. Actually, I came to talk to your domestic."

"Bessie? She's out in the kitchen. Is something wrong?"

Odd, Sam reflected—why did any question at all immediately provoke the fear that something was wrong? "Oh, a minor matter. Her son, David. Had a little trouble, that's all."

Gabrielle cocked her hip. "She didn't mention it to me." Her eyes were lively and intelligent. Sam had the sudden insight that this woman was many different women, depending on the situation, on whom she was with. He could imagine her, late at night, sitting alone by a single candle writing sentimental poetry, then weeping over it. But only in private.

"If I could just speak to her—it won't take a minute."

Gabrielle gazed at him. He watched her brown eyes. He hadn't expected a white woman to be so protective of a servant, but then, he had never employed servants. Maybe they get that way, he thought. Maybe they feel responsible.

She took his arm. "Come with me," she said softly. She led him through the garden toward the back of the house, not looking at him.

To make conversation, Sam said, "It's so quiet back here. So peaceful."

Gabrielle glanced up, and he glimpsed sadness in her eyes. Only for an instant—then she looked away again. She said, "Not al-ways."

In the kitchen, he met Mrs. Bessie King, a wiry widow who couldn't stand still. "My David's a good boy," she said. "Wouldn't steal no chickens. I tear the skin right off his hide, he steal chickens."

"I'll be happy to put in a word for him."

"You a copper man?" She cocked her head and regarded Sam skeptically.

"Newspaper reporter."

"It's all right," Gabrielle said. "You can talk to him."

He wondered how she could be so sure. "I want to interview Alex Manly. I was told you might know where he is."

"Who told you a thing like that? What Mr. Manly got to do with my boy?"

"They're separate issues, of course—"

"My boy David got no truck with Manly."

"Bessie," Gabrielle said.

"What you going to do with Alex Manly when you catch him?"

Sam smiled. "I'm not trying to *catch* him, Mrs. King. All I want to do is interview him. For an article."

"Uh-huh. Talk. What about when you done talking?"

Gabrielle said, "It's all right, Bessie."

Bessie King pursed her lips, then said, "Well, I don't see what the big secret is. They even put up their sign."

"Sign?"

"The Manly brothers. The *Record.* Over on Seventh, next to St. Luke's."

"Is Alex Manly there?"

"Shoot, who knows where that dandy boy is?" She leaned toward a narrow backstairs door, nudged it open with her foot, and called, "Saffron, honey! Come down here." Then, when Sam looked puzzled, she explained, "My daughter, she help out over there."

A slim mulatto girl appeared in the doorway with a feather duster in her hand. She wore a plain cotton smock under an apron and had a white kerchief knotted around her temples. She came forward shyly. "Yes, Mama?"

"Baby, take this gentleman over to Free Love Hall. He looking for the Manlys."

Saffron lifted her eyes cautiously toward Sam. She laid the

duster aside and deftly slipped off the apron, which she hung on a nail behind the back door.

"We walking or riding?" she asked in a voice as quiet as paper.

"Walking," Sam said.

Saffron kicked up her legs one at a time and slipped off her sandals. "Summertime," she said. "Like to feel the sand between my toes."

As they left the kitchen, Sam thanked Bessie and then Gabrielle. He glanced back once, half out the door, and caught that same sad look in Gabrielle's brown eyes. She suddenly looked like a little girl who missed going barefoot—a young woman thrust into middle age.

Had they been alone, he might have kissed her on the cheek and whispered something tender and encouraging—the sort of thing a stranger could get shot for down here, he figured.

Instead, he walked out the door with an eighteen-year-old mulatto girl who moved as if she had no clothes on at all, gracefully unaware of her body. On the long, dusty walk to Free Love Hall, he watched her every chance he got.

Alex Manly is a white man—that was his first impression. They caught him at his toilet in a small back room of Free Love Hall, his starched shirt unbuttoned, his sleeves rolled. His face glistened. He held up his wet hands and forearms and stared at them, only mildly surprised.

"Alex Manly, I presume." Sam rubbed his neck and hoped somebody would offer him a glass of water. Saffron left and reappeared with a tin ladle of well water so cold and metallic it made his teeth ache. But he drank it all. She took the empty ladle and padded away, her bare feet *slap-slapping* on the scrubbed wood floor.

"You a Pinkerton agent?"

"Pinkerton? What?" Sam was caught off-guard.

A bigger man, more muscular and more recognizably Negro, had come in quietly. He said, "They been snooping around. Trying to find out are we plotting to overthrow the United States of America."

Sam studied his face—Frank Manly. Fit the description.

Alex laughed and toweled off his hands and face. "You're not from around here, are you?"

"Chicago, last," Sam said.

"Lot of Pinkerton men up that way. You a traveling man?" Frank Manly said.

"Some."

"Me, too—some. Let me see your badge."

"I told you, I don't have a badge. I work for Clawson, the *Messenger*. We've been looking for your brother."

"Well, I haven't been hiding out," Alex Manly said.

Sam pulled his notebook from his back pocket. "You're the biggest news in this town. Will you talk to me?"

Frank said, "This a bad idea, Alex."

"Come on upstairs with me," Alex said, buttoning his shirt.

As he led Sam up a bare pine staircase into the main office of the *Record*, Sam watched him—how he smiled at his own thoughts, how he moved, how he held his head—and thought of the words he would use to describe him in print: *lithe, articulate, cultured, handsome, charming, inscrutable*. He couldn't help smiling. Those were the same words he might have chosen to describe Gabrielle deRosset Waddell.

Alex Manly spread out back numbers of his newspaper on a broad table across from his printing press. "Go ahead, read," he urged. Sam admired the bold flag across the top of the front page: *The Daily Record—the latest news, price two cent, 25 cents per month*.

He glanced at the front page: "New York—Major Taylor, colored, today became the cycling wonder by beating Jimmie Michael and smashing all world's records."

The stories were set in narrow, lined columns, just like the *Messenger*'s, with modest headlines. There was news about the Cuban war—a story about a colored regiment coming home to medals and ticker tape for its part in the charge up San Juan Hill.

On page two, there were rhyming poems about friendship and nature, along with an advertisement for The Walker Taylor Insurance Agency: "Walker Taylor—He protects your interest in case of loss—Fire Insurance! Accident Insurance!"

There were also testimonials for Biddle University, "the leading institution in the South for the Higher Education of the Colored Race, exclusively for males."

"See?" Alex Manly said quietly. "We're just a hometown paper. A hometown within a hometown, you might say. I'm no Nat Turner."

Sam shifted from foot to foot. From across the room, where she stood sorting papers, Saffron watched him with amusement. She reached down and scratched an itch on her leg, raising the hem of her dress high. Sam admired her smooth brown leg, wondering if she'd showed it off deliberately. He said, "The editorial."

Alex swore. "That's all anybody knows about this paper. And what they know is taken out of context. Here." He handed Sam a copy of the complete editorial. "May as well get it right."

"I've seen it. Mike Dowling has sworn to kill you."

"Mike which?" Frank Manly said. He'd followed them upstairs. Sam hadn't heard him this time, either.

"That Red Shirt fellow."

"Bocra," Frank said.

"What?"

"White nigger," Alex said coolly.

Sam nodded—*poor-bocker*, Waddell's word on the train. Add *arrogant* to the description of Alex Manly, he thought. "What do you plan to do?"

Frank said, "What he got to be doing something for? Can't he just *be*?"

"It's all the same to me," Sam said. "I just came to hear your story."

"I'll tell my own story, when it's time," Alex said.

"Suit yourself. Meantime, I wouldn't open my door to strangers."

Frank interposed himself between Alex and Sam. "I believe this interview is over."

Sam stuffed his notebook into his back pocket. He hadn't written a line. "Tom Clawson would like a word with you, when you have time."

"I'm a busy man," Alex said ruefully. "Tell the man I'll pay him what I owe. Word of honor."

Sam was confused. "Pay him?"

"Never mind," Frank said. "Business."

Sam nodded. He turned to go. Apparently, Saffron was staying. She unfolded a pair of wire-rimmed spectacles and hooked them over her little ears. Behind the lenses, her dark eyes bloomed large and bright.

Sam said over his shoulder, "Tell Mrs. King that David will be home for supper."

Saffron didn't answer. He had hoped to hear her sweet, tremulous voice just once more.

Alex escorted him to the front door.

"What you're doing here," Sam said. "It takes gumption."

Alex Manly said, "We'll see."

By one o'clock, Sam handed Clawson a story about Alex Manly's return. The headline read, "Back in Business at Free Love Hall." Clawson read it quickly, then telephoned Walker Taylor at his office.

There is a black vampire hovering over our beloved North Carolina.

> Rebecca Stroud
> of Kinston, North Carolina,
> addressing a white
> supremacy rally

CHAPTER FIVE

Sunday, August 21

THE CHURCH BELLS WOKE HIM. The sunrise carillon at St. James Episcopal, scarcely three blocks away down Market. He'd married three different women in that church. Hands folded across his chest, Alfred Moore Waddell lay with his eyes closed against the early, dim light filtering through the lace curtains and limning the drawn shade of the Gibb door, lighting it in a sharp rectangle.

This was the best part of the morning. He opened his eyes a crack and listened, as if squinting would help him hear better. His hearing was not sharp, as in the old cavalry days. Then, he could hear a horse high-stepping across a gravel ford half a mile away and tell the regiment of the rider.

The mosquito netting draped on frames over his four-poster reminded him of sleeping under a tent during the War. He must remember to take his quinine capsule—it had been a wet summer, and malarial fever was breaking out all up and down the river. They hadn't had quinine in the army.

In the adjoining bedroom, nothing stirred. Gabrielle must still be sleeping. What if he were to wake up one morning and find her here, curled in bed beside him?—but the longing passed in an instant.

Gabrielle was an odd, quiet girl, he thought. She had that faraway look in her eye, as if, wherever they were together, everything that mattered in the world were happening someplace else.

He stared at the Gibb door, that ingenious device that slipped upward inside its frame and disappeared into the wall upstairs. Gabrielle had insisted on Gibb doors in all the second-story rooms. In the summer, they could be raised for cross-ventilation without the awkwardness of propped doors. One of them opened onto the oyster porch above the kitchen, from which Gabrielle could call out to the vendors in the alley, who would then leave their goods on the back stoop and chalk her account on their slates.

Let her have her whims. He'd already put two wives in their graves—sisters, Julia and Ellen Savage.

Julia was dead now these past twenty-two years. He had two children out in the world, a son named after him and a daughter, Elizabeth Savage Waddell—Miss Lizzie—both by Julia, who got him through the War.

Ellen, the younger sister, had passed away just three years ago come October. The sisters rested under a common headstone at Oakdale Cemetery. *Make them to be remembered with Thy saints*, read the inscription under the granite cross.

He'd never expected to marry again. But he had—just a little over a year after Ellen's death. The local wags had a good time over that one. Let them. It was good to have a woman to run the household and handle the servants. A man had other work. It was a fine piece of luck that she'd come with a new house, so he could move out of that firetrap on Third Street.

He shifted on his down mattress and untangled the nightshirt that had somehow gotten wrapped around his legs, constricting his circulation. The church bells rang a last note and then stopped, leaving the round, whole tone hanging in the air.

He would attend the late service.

Legs, that was his dream. And a horse, a strong, wild horse under him, rearing and plunging through water. He smiled, remembering the horse. Thrashing through sand, mud, swampy thicket. Then falling against a hill, pinning his legs. When he'd opened his eyes in the dream, the horse had become a locomotive, crushing his legs. Women screamed all around him, but he could see no one. He dragged himself out from under the locomotive, now become a horse again, and staggered to the top of a hill. His legs pained him so badly he could hardly stand. They swelled and throbbed. All around him, in the misty dark below, he could hear wailing voices. But he could see nothing. Some of the voices were calling his name. He stood on the hill, doused in moonlight, baffled, his legs going numb, threatening to buckle any second.

He poured himself a glass of water from the pitcher on his night table. Later, he would go down to the kitchen and drink a full quart of cold well water, fast, as he did every morning of his life. It cleared a man's bowels.

Waddell was a rational man. He understood that all dreams come from knowledge. In the night, his legs had gone stiff, he had tossed about and wrapped his nightshirt around them. His imagination had processed the information as a dream of crushed legs.

And the horse? Waddell sighed, enjoying his own company in the quiet of the cool room. Cavalry days. The time, on the Petersburg Pike, advancing on Richmond, when he had nearly been thrown during a sudden thunderstorm. Lightning had forked out of a purple anvil in the hot, turbulent sky. An oak tree split and burst into flame, scattering the column like an artillery barrage. Horses and riders reared and plunged, men hollered and cursed, raindrops big as pennies stung their necks and puffed dust in the road like ricocheting minie balls. It was as if they'd been ambushed, that was the feeling—the icy needle in the heart, lungs suddenly breathless, eyes instantly sharp as field glasses, ears blooming with sound.

Waddell's horse, Black Major, had careered off the road and up the high cutbank, out of control. He sawed back on the reins, and the horse wheeled, nearly toppling. Black Major flung his head backward, champing at his rider's knee, then rolled a wild brown eye. He was a big, spirited animal.

At the top of the hill, they had spun around in the rain, horse and rider. The world dissolved into a wet blur—the rain fell in a hard, gray screen, and he was blind. He just kept sawing the reins and Black Major kept spinning, head down, panic shivering along his spine, his flanks. He could feel the muscles tuning like wires even through the stiff cavalry saddle.

Then at last, the thunder had moved away, the rain had calmed to a slow patter, and the horse had stilled, bowing his head and snorting. Waddell had been so dizzy he could hardly keep his seat.

He sipped his water, put down the glass, then slid out of bed and used the chamber pot. This new house had an indoor privy complete with plumbing, but he preferred the pot first thing out of bed.

Black Major hadn't lasted the summer. Eighteen sixty-four, they lost the best of their horses that summer, rode them right into the ground. Lost them to artillery and Gatling guns. The Yankees fought like thugs, no respect for the forms. Horses stumbled and died and wound up in the bellies of marching men.

And now Black Major—one horse among all the mounts he had ridden during that campaign of quick advances and long retreats— had come back in a dream. Waddell hadn't sat a warhorse in years, except in parades.

Waddell did not dream often. Whenever he dreamed so exotically, he woke refreshed and certain that something important was about to happen.

He enjoyed watching his mind work. It was almost as if he could step outside of it and look in through a window at his own process of reasoning. The horse saddened him, old Black Major. He knew it was sentimental, but the death of horses had always affected him more profoundly than the death of men.

He was back in bed now, lying on top of the sheets. The day was already starting to warm up. In a little while, Aunt Bessie would arrive downstairs and begin closing up the house to keep in the cool night air.

The locomotive was an easy riddle: the train wreck on the way to Charleston. And the screaming? Two young ladies in the seat behind him, crushed to death—an awful thing. He had been pinned by luggage and the overturned seat but had managed to drag himself to safety. He'd always had a fool's luck. He had even pulled other injured passengers from the wreckage—only then did he seek first aid.

Arbitrary, how it all worked, he reflected. Things happened at random—where was the Almighty's plan? It was beyond him. Some died horribly, while others, even scoundrels, were spared. His legs ached this morning. He must get up, walk around, get some blood circulating in the cramped muscles.

Damned legs. In August of '64, his legs had gotten him out of the cavalry. A cavalry soldier wasn't supposed to need his legs the way a foot soldier did. But riding all day crooked the bones, splayed the joints, atrophied the muscles. How many cavalry soldiers had stunted, spindly legs? Even Bob Lee had short legs and walked with a permanent stiff limp.

Some days, Waddell had to have a boy rub his legs for an hour just to get the blood moving. And that was when he was a young man—God!

And then the strange fever had gotten into him. Swelled his legs until the flesh of his thighs burst apart like seams splitting, the tissue gone all buttery, oozing clear juice and smelling like sour milk. Nothing had ever terrified him so. It was as if his flesh were rotting before his eyes.

His dreams in those days were full of funeral biers and catafalques—he learned later that Abraham Lincoln had similar dreams before the actor from Baltimore put an end to him.

The surgeon wanted to amputate, but Waddell pulled rank. Only one in six was surviving the amputations anyway. Colonel Waddell kept his fine boots.

For weeks on end, Waddell lay delirious under the white shade of the hospital tent. Through tears in the rotten fabric, shards of blue shone through. He suffered nightmares of black, shapeless beasts feeding on his flesh—shadowy animals, rangy as wolves, gnawing the bones of his legs, sucking their marrow. In lucid moments between deliriums, he had come to think of them as the Dark Ones. Minions of the devil come to claim his soul by eating away his body.

Somewhere below his window, a horse and gig clattered along Fifth Street. He stroked his goatee and finger-combed his thinning hair.

It was hard to know who he was anymore. A man was defined by his place in the order of things. By his standing in the community. Alfred Moore Waddell was a minor lawyer in a city full of better ones. Like that Rountree—there was a man heading for a judge's seat. Waddell was a first-rate mind with a third-rate clientele. A voice men would follow, if he only had a podium. An ex-officer who had missed glory. A former congressman who could not pay the note on his own house without help from his wife.

He let his fingers knead the ridges of his skull.

He'd had his colonel's commission exactly a year to the day when he gave it up.

When it looked as if he might survive after all, he had been discharged from the makeshift hospital. The surgeon said, "I don't know what ails your legs—there's no medical name for it."

"But surely, in other cases of this kind—"

"There are no other cases of this kind—not in four years. You are a special piece of work."

"And yet you cured me."

The surgeon said, "Colonel, there are mysteries."

With his legs bound in bandages stripped from ladies' petticoats, Waddell took the train to Wilmington to wait out the rest of the war or die. The autumn of '64, he rode a carriage to a fishing shack on the ocean and bathed in salt water every day, taking the pain of the salt on raw flesh as a penance from the Almighty. If the legs killed him, at least he would die with the evil burned out of his soul.

The legs turned white and then red and then scabbed over nearly black. When the scabs shed, the flesh underneath was white as marble, with hairline scars and thin blue veins. It was beautiful. Then the legs had healed.

He groaned and stretched his left leg, then his right. He wiggled his toes. What would it feel like to have a good horse under him again, to be forging into battle? Just imagining it quickened his heart.

He wished he had been in a real cavalry charge—just once. Not one more indecisive skirmish in the woods, but an honest-to-God, full-bore, galloping, saber-clashing spectacle. In the crucible of frontal combat, a man might test himself. He might discover if other men would follow him. He might feel the rapture of the saber arcing in clenched fist, steel against steel, might shudder with the shock of meeting the enemy's line and turning it.

But a man might, instead, be found wanting.

Or a man might have his legs infected and lose heart. Something might go out of him that could never be put back.

That summer of healing, standing to his waist in the surf, leaning on a brace of canes, he had been visited by a premonition. It troubled him all the more because he didn't believe in premonitions—all that hillbilly voodoo was for the private soldiers, ignorant farm boys, sharecroppers and river rats and simple hired men. Waddell had studied law at the university in Chapel Hill under the best men of his age—Judge Battle and Samuel F. Phillips. He'd taken his first legal fee back in '55, on his twenty-first birthday—a four-dollar note issued by the Bank of Cape Fear. He was a man of reason and faculties.

But there was no denying the power of the vision. He balanced on wobbly, shivering legs, legs that felt like wooden stilts, and squinted toward the horizon, not believing his own eyes. There were ships out there—Yankee ships ranked in spiny silhouette against the rising sun, steaming south toward the river channel to take the fort that guarded the city.

If he watched long enough, they faded into the blear of the horizon. Illusion, he told himself. A trick of pain and medicine and shock. He was not a well man, He saw things that had not happened yet. Even the Yankees knew Fort Fisher was invincible.

Later, he walked the beach, feeling the flesh harden and tone in his legs. Even on cold, raw days, he waded into the frothing sea and remained there as long as he could stand it, gritting his teeth against the cold and the pain. A man's will could overcome anything. But when he looked out to sea, there was the line of ships, a vision stubborn as bad weather.

Finally, on Christmas 1864, real dreadnoughts darkened the sea. The Yankees swarmed ashore toward the Confederate lines. Every church bell in town tolled the news. Waddell buttoned on his dress grays and brushed them out.

Then a nor'easter blew the fleet back to Virginia, and he put away his uniform.

But three weeks later, the armada returned to finish the job, as he knew it would.

The bells always brought it back.

Fort Fisher, the Sevastopol of the Confederacy, Lee's last hope.

For a day and a night, the Yankees bombarded it. The vision was clear even now. Even now, the concussions rang in his ears.

He had been upriver from the fort with the other civilians, attending services that Sunday morning at St. James Church. Only a few men were in the congregation—too old, too young, or maimed. The rest were women and children. Widows and soon-to-be widows, sweethearts without hope, sisters and mothers of the Confederate dead and doomed.

At dawn, the naval guns went strangely silent. The fort was unbreached. No Yankees appeared on the beach. By eleven o'clock, the great church was full. The minister prayed, "From battle and murder and from sudden death . . ."

In a strangely female common voice, the congregation answered, "Good Lord, deliver us."

And at that moment, the cannons boomed again. There was no mistaking the relentless regularity. They had the range, firing broadside, firing fast and with discipline. Waddell couldn't help thinking that out there in the fleet was a fire-control officer who knew his business. They were battering down the fort. The litany went on.

He should go to the fort, he thought. It had vexed his mind all night. He had prayed about it to a God who answered with pure silence. He should commandeer a horse and ride to their aid—surely, they would need officers. It would not change the outcome. It was only a matter of honor.

In his heart, fear grappled with duty. Before the war, he'd been an ardent Unionist. Secession, he had written in the *Daily Herald*—which he owned and published—would invite invasion. In the carnival at Charleston, as the cannons fired across the harbor toward Sumter and the ladies applauded under parasols on the grass, they had laughed him off. Now, he was a prophet.

He no longer held a commission, he told himself. But his legs were healed. He was no invalid. He was a gentleman of quality, and he knew his duty. He could hardly bear the way the women looked at him, lolling in his pew, alive and well, holding a cane he scarcely needed anymore but always kept with him for appearances, while their own men stood in harm's way. He wore his uniform in church, as if he had a right to it.

He slumped in his pew at the end of the service, still praying. Then he walked stiffly home, loaded his dragoon revolver, buckled on his cavalry saber, and listened. He must go. He would go, he assured himself. Several times, he limped to the porch, the long saber rattling against his left knee, the pain in his legs growing sharper by the hour. He never left the house all day.

It would make no difference, he told himself.

He should have gone. But he only listened as the bombardment ceased, the signal that the killing had begun in earnest. Men swarming up the redoubts, fighting hand to hand in the traverses, swarming the firing pits, men so jammed together they had to hand their muskets forward to be fired by other men in the front line, so crowded that the dead were held upright by the ranks of the living—he could see it all in his mind's eye with the clarity of second sight. He no longer cared whether it was rational—the whole battle was erupting inside his head. He could smell gunpowder on the sea breeze, hear the death cry of men tearing like paper.

He could taste their fear. Their souls darkened the sky. In the afternoon, feverish, he went to bed.

The whole town was quiet. Colored boys were sent back and forth with news of the battle. Then for a while, there was no more news.

By nightfall, the fort had fallen.

The Yankees had the river and the last open port of the Confederacy. Even a fool could see it was all over now. No point in more dying. The Yankees took their time. Three weeks later, dressed in a clawhammer coat and sipping brandy, he watched them march into town. In the vanguard were colored troops.

So there was nothing mystical about the dream, after all. It was an emblem of all he had suffered—all his body had learned of pain and fear.

Only one part still troubled him: who were the ones wailing from down in the mist, and why were they calling his name?

Downstairs, Elizabeth Alma King, who called herself Bessie, let herself in the unlocked back kitchen door. A fat ginger cat, sprawled on the cold floor, got up and rubbed against her leg, bare under the gray skirts. It purred like a little engine and meowed.

"Hush, you cat," Bessie said and gently swept it across the smooth floor with her foot. The cat played with her shoe. "I swear, you just like a child." She poured some milk into a chipped dish and set it on the floor. The cat lapped it up.

"All God's creatures got to fill their belly," she said. She wrapped an apron around her middle and fumbled with the strings. A girlhood of chopping cotton had left her hands scarred and arthritic. She was still strong and slender—the other women at the Negro service at St. Thomas's envied her slim waist. Came from living close to the bone, she liked to say.

She kindled a fire in the stove. Lord, it was hot already. She left the door open to make a draft with the open window over the sink.

The Colonel liked his hot breakfast. But she wouldn't fool with lace waffles today.

The cat finished the milk and sprawled again on the floor, licking its front paws delicately. "My boy David," she told the cat, "he a good boy. He got a little devil in him, any boy got that. But they ain't no call to beat the boy. Ain't no call."

She thought she heard someone stirring upstairs. She paused in her work, cocked her head, turned an eye to the ceiling. She had a few minutes yet. This morning, she was working alone. Saffron was home with David. Saffron knew how to take care of a man. She'd put David right. She had all that loving in her and nobody to spend it on—her man had been taken in a mill accident. Yanked into the machinery, chewed right to the bone. They shut it down for two hours to pull him out, and when they did, he came out in pieces. An eighteen-year-old widow—it wasn't right. The Almighty just hadn't been paying attention.

The cat stretched and yawned, and Bessie shook her head, then wagged a crooked finger at the cat. "You got the blessed life. You got no trouble and toil. You got no chirren to squeeze your heart. You got no cares and woe, all you gets is the sweet milk." She reached down and stroked the cat, who leaned into her hand, craving more.

Now, she was sure someone was moving around upstairs. "That be the Colonel," she told the cat. "Man got worry on his mind. Man visit rooms at night."

She stirred up batter for flannel cakes and sliced off a rasher of pork to fry. She larded a frying pan and set it on the stove to sizzle. She moved across the kitchen into the pantry to fetch the preserves. A woman of gravity—some days, she felt like she was dragging the whole world around with her.

In the far corner of the pantry, near the ceiling, the brown spider quivered in her web, and Bessie smiled. "How do, Miz Spider," she said. A spider upright on the web was good luck. She looked for it every day. But if the spider hung upside down, death would visit the house before the next sunrise. She paused in the cool pantry, enjoying the stillness, the faint aroma of sealing wax and cured pine boards. The shelves were lined with neat rows of vacuum jars—green beans, strawberries, apple butter.

The presence of so much good food—stored carefully, each jar labeled with india ink—reassured her. Bessie knew that, as long as she worked in this house, she would never know want. It was insurance. Like a second family. She had a kind of right to this food. Her own hands had done most of the work of putting it up, though Miz Gabrielle had helped. "Whatever you need, come to me," Miz Gabrielle had told her in this very pantry almost two years ago, the day she had moved them all into the house as the Colonel's wife.

Whitefolks were always saying things such as that to show off, to remind you how much extra they had, but Bessie believed her: Miz Gabrielle had stood close to her and whispered it. She remembered her perfume, like gardenias. *Whatever you need.*

She went back to the kitchen and the early heat. The cat was perched on the window sill above the sink, tail curled around itself, looking out. Upstairs, she could hear the Colonel pissing away his night pizens. Miz Gabrielle must be still asleep.

She told the cat, "I be sleeping, too, that old peckerwood be my man." She ladled yellow batter into the sizzling skillet, where it hardened into brown coins. "I be sleeping morning, noon, and night. I be Sleeping Beauty, that man come sniffing around me for a taste." She laughed in the back of her throat. The cat ignored her.

She looked out the window past the cat. "My David never stole no chicken. Ain't no call, what they done to that boy. You got to give a boy a chance in this hard world." She wanted to reach out and stroke the cat, but her hands were full of work. The skillet hissed, and sweat dampened her forehead. It beaded on her upper lip and ran down. She tasted salt.

Breakfast frying was usually a good smell, sour and sweet at once. It filled up the soul and put a small ache in the belly. But not this morning. This morning, she had enough ache in her belly.

"Lord," she said softly to the cat as she shook the skillet, "feed my sheep. Feed my little lambs."

Sam woke to the peal of church bells. He opened his eyes and was pleased to see Gray Ellen lying next to him. They'd taken connecting rooms at the Orton and until last night had slept apart. They'd sat up late talking—soothing, quiet talk.

They'd cuddled on the bed, and soon she was fast asleep in his arms. He had not made love to her, but this was almost better. Little by little, she was trusting him again. Beside him now, lying under a single sheet, she stirred in her sleep. The early sunlight caught the sheet and made it shine. The mosquito netting filtered the light so that her face looked softer, younger than it had in years.

He slipped downstairs to the hotel kitchen and fetched a pot of coffee and a platter of breakfast rolls. Gray Ellen woke to breakfast in bed on a silver tray.

She sat up against the oak headboard and smiled. Sam looked handsome, his face and neck sun-browned against his white shirt, open at the collar. His eyes were clear these mornings. He was losing that haggard look of never having slept enough. Since he'd quit drinking, the years were falling away. She touched her own face to reassure herself of its smoothness.

"You and me," he said. "Let me court you."

She smiled. "You won my heart the first time." They'd met on a Sunday promenade along the Schuylkill in Philadelphia. All the other men wore hats, but his bright blond head had bobbed toward her, hatless, above the crowd. He was slim and strong, with an air of confidence lacking in all the other young men she knew. He had no bravado, and no false modesty either—just an accurate sense of his own abilities. "Someday, I'm going to be publisher of my own newspaper," he had told her matter-of-factly. Even in bad times, he always talked across to her, never down.

"After mass," she said, "let's go to the ocean."

It was a good moment. Gray Ellen thought, this is what it means to be married, a moment like this. A man and a woman together on a quiet morning for no special reason, saying nothing in particular, but saying it with love and tenderness. Tenderness, that's what the drinking took away. A drunken man could not be tender. But this—if this was the way it was to be from now on . . .

He took her hand and held it, saying nothing. She was aware that she was letting it start all over again. She had deliberately put distance between them—that was the only way she could heal. It was like cotton batting to insulate herself from his rough edges. He could no longer cut her, make her bleed inside. It had taken all her will and strength. If she let him win her again, let him back into her heart, she might never get loose again. It was a risk, but she longed to take it.

After a time, Sam said, "Do you think we'll be able to stay here?"

She sighed. It was exactly the wrong question for the moment, couldn't he see that? "I don't know," she said. "A lot of things can happen, I suppose."

"Meaning? I thought you liked it here, the job and all. You'll be teaching again real soon."

"Things are very different down here." She paused. He waited. "The people are different."

He nodded. "The way they talk." He thought of Harry making him work for every sentence. "I can hardly follow it sometimes."

She looked at him curiously. Maybe he was having a difficult adjustment, too—maybe that's why he'd brought it up. She hadn't considered that before—men just adapted so much more easily. The whole world was set up for men to adapt easily. "It's not just *how* they talk," she said. "It's what they *say*. What they *don't* say. Whenever I leave a room, I can feel them talking about me behind my back." She had told him all about her interview at Hemenway School. It was important he understand how small they had made her feel.

He poured more coffee, stirred in sugar. "Don't get paranoid, sweet. People are the same here as anywhere—some good, some bad."

"They wait on me last in the shops. They never include me in the conversation."

"You have to admit, the shops are full of bargains." There was nothing you couldn't find in the shops—the advantage of being in a deepwater port. And prices were a relief from Chicago. "Come on, we haven't been here very long. They'll get to know us."

"You hear all this talk about Southern hospitality. And they'll break their necks for you, all right, if you're family. Or if you've lived here for a hundred years. But if you're a stranger . . ."

Sam patted her hand. "You miss your family, I know. But isn't it beautiful here? The pinewoods, the ocean. The way the air smells off the river. I mean, you can *smell* this place."

She pushed away the tray and rested her head on his lap. "This place gets into your blood," she said. "I understand why they fought for it. Why they don't want to live anywhere else."

"Well, then."

"But they don't even want to *go* anywhere else. Even for a visit. Even as a tourist. Even in books. Down here, it's a flat earth."

"You've made your mind up too fast. You're not being fair."

"The Civil War's been over for thirty years, Sam. Nobody up north even talks about it. The world has moved on."

Sam nodded slowly and stroked her head. "All that is beside the point," he said. "You and me. I just want us to make a life here."

She fixed her eyes on his. "Oh, Sam," she said, and lightly touched his cheek.

———

Father Dennen preached an angry sermon during the late service at St. Thomas's—the white service. "We all have our place in God's eyes," he said. "The brother of whom you are the keeper may have red hair and freckles, like me. Or he may be swarthy, with a flat nose and thick lips. But every man's soul is the same color as the Lord God who made him."

At the door of St. Thomas's, an uninspired brick-and-frame building on Dock Street, Father Dennen greeted his congregants as they filed out after the late mass. Some shook his hand heartily and blessed him for a sensible sermon in dangerous times. But others pushed out roughly past him, deliberately snubbing the priest.

Sam shook Father Dennen's hand. He was much taller than the priest, but he could feel the raw strength in the man's handshake. Maybe that comes with having the courage of your convictions, Sam reflected. "Good sermon, Father," Sam said, eager to get on with the day he and Gray Ellen had planned. "We all needed to hear it."

Father Dennen held onto Sam's hand, then clapped his left hand behind Sam's elbow, pinching it. "You're Jenks."

"Yes, Father. Call me Sam."

"Well, Sam, I don't know what you're stirring up trouble for, but if I was you, I'd meditate on my immortal soul."

"Father?" Sam tried to pull his hand away, but the priest wasn't letting go. He was squeezing, pinching harder, as if this were some kind of contest. Other parishioners were backed up in the doorway, like cattle jammed in a chute. They wanted out.

"You're not from around here, are you?"

"Chicago, Father. But—"

"I been to cities. I see what you're up to. But let me tell you, it won't do here."

"What's wrong, Father?" Gray Ellen asked. Sam felt rescued.

"I understand you went to see Alex Manly," Father Dennen said quietly. "Leave him be. He's working for his people. Trying to keep his head down, do you see? There's no call to be trumpeting his good name all over your newspaper. Let Tom Clawson do his own dirty work."

Suddenly, Sam understood: the piece about Manly, back in business at Free Love Hall. He'd naturally expected it wouldn't run until Monday. "Have you got a copy?"

The priest unbuttoned his cassock above the waist, reached in, and produced a ragged copy of Saturday's *Messenger*. "Jenks, you complicate the work of the church militant."

He let go of Sam's hand and clapped him on the back hard enough to knock the wind out of him. Others filed out fast behind them. Sam stood under a locust tree, reading his article. People walked by and stared. Gray Ellen read it over his shoulder.

"The race-baiter Manly is back in business," read the lead. "The infamous author of the scandalous editorial defaming Southern Womanhood has set up shop in Free Love Hall, under the auspices of the Black Ministerial Union, and will continue inciting the Negroes to riot and mayhem. In the high-handed style to which his readers have become accustomed, the notorious advocate of rape and miscegenation was holding forth and granting interviews to the press and his disciples. 'The man who defames me shall be paid in full,' he vowed, waving his black fist, symbol of the movement to subvert constitutional Anglo-Saxon rule."

"Sam, how could you!" Gray Ellen said.

"Gray, you think I wrote this?"

"You said you wrote an article—"

"My God, the style is all puffed up, it's full of catch phrases."

"Manly didn't swear to get Clawson?"

"No, no. He owes the man some money or something. I didn't even write it in the piece—I just told Clawson that Manly'd make good on the debt, whatever it is. Manly asked me to."

She read the rest of it. "It gets worse," she said, her voice quiet and husky. "The article advises him to get out of town before—let me read it—'before the God-fearing white citizens of this town make an example out of him.' Good Lord, tell me they're not going to lynch him, Sam!"

He took her arm, and they started walking. "Nobody's going to lynch anybody. It's just hot air. These small-town newspapers, they get into rivalries to boost circulation. Haven't you ever read Mark Twain? He writes about this kind of stunt all the time."

"Well, you're all mixed up in it. I don't like that."

"I'll have a talk with Clawson first thing Monday. Nobody's going to butcher my copy like that. Not even the boss."

———

They put it out of their minds and passed a long, lazy day together. Borrowing the horse and buggy Cousin Hugh had made available at the livery stable downtown, they rode off down the Shell Road to see the beach. The breeze off the ocean cooled them, and they marveled at the different colors of the sky and sea away from the city—as if someone had taken a sepia photograph and painted in the colors brighter than real life.

At the wooden causeway, they looked out on low, marshy islands cut by finger channels. Beyond those lay the ocean. They crossed the causeway, overwhelmed by the soft breeze, the plovers and wheeling gulls. It was exactly what Gray Ellen needed today—to ride, to feel the air moving against her cheeks, to get away from the noise of other people. She didn't like living in a hotel, even a residential hotel. She wanted a little house on a quiet street, with a grocery on the corner and neighbors who sat on their porches in the evening trading stories about the day. She wanted a clean sky drifting over her backyard, and chips of starlight flickering on the leaves of her own spreading oak in the evening.

They left the buggy in the shade of the Oceanview Hotel and wandered along the wide, clean beach. The long green swells rolled ashore, dramatically serene. Holding his hand, she felt very much in love with her husband. The wind mussed his hair and burned color into his cheeks. He looked ruggedly handsome.

She stared into the wide-open sky, the long horizon in every direction, feeling a weight lifted from her spirit. She breathed in the air deeply.

Other couples roamed the beach, hand in hand. She felt a sense of release she had longed for ever since Chicago—the world seemed to open up, to promise everything.

She was slightly ashamed of herself for having already judged this place so harshly. "Lovely," she whispered, and Sam only nodded, threading his fingers into hers.

Then she unlaced her high shoes, kicked them off, gathered her skirts, and ran barefoot through the surf.

"What are you doing?" Sam laughed, then kicked off his own shoes and followed her into the ocean till the water foamed around his knees.

Afterward, they ate cold shrimp at a shack that catered to excursionists, then rode back to town in the dusk. The Shell Road had gone slate-colored in the evening shadows. The moon was up, and the horse had no trouble keeping to the level track at a slow but steady pace. On either side, the pinewoods seemed to press closer, filling their ears with a racket of bullfrogs and crickets, cicadas and owls. Once, a possum skittered across the road, her belly pouch fat with kits.

They came into the lights at Seventeenth Street and heard a commotion of shouting voices several blocks later. A gang of men and boys was running down Seventh, across their path. Sam reined up the horse, and they watched the mob stream by. Red-shirted men on horseback rode the fringes of the mob, shouting and brandishing rifles.

"Lord," Gray Ellen said, raising her hands to her mouth. If only they could have stayed at the shore a little while longer.

"The *Record*'s down that way, three blocks or so," Sam said.

"We must do something!"

Sam squirmed in his seat. The raucous crowd was spooking the horse, and he had to hold her reins firmly. For all the laughter and joshing, it seemed more like a college football game than a lynching. "You can't do anything against a mob."

"Do something. That's all I ask—do something!"

"Let me think, let me think." But he could not think. He was a reporter—his job was to find the action and get to the bottom of it. But he couldn't risk putting Gray Ellen in danger. He was torn. Part of him wanted to follow the crowd, but another part wanted to get as far away from the turmoil as this horse could take him.

"I'm going to turn around—go down Eighth and go in the back way. Hang on." The horse was easier to handle heading away from the clamor. He slowed for the corner and then clucked her along Eighth until they reached Nun Street. As they turned down Nun, they started seeing faces—Negro faces—staring up at them as they passed. A crowd of Negro men and boys surrounded Free Love Hall. One of them held their horse. "What y'all want to come down here for?"

"I need to see Manly. Warn him. There's a mob—"

"Manly's gone."

"Where? I need to—"

"Someplace safe from the Red Shirts—you think I'm going to tell you? You best ride on out of here before things get hot."

Suddenly, the buggy seemed surrounded by hostile black faces. Some of their hands held tool handles and brickbats. A couple of old double-barreled shotguns poked up among the crowd.

"You want me to tell him you were here?" It was a man dressed in a suit. A lawyer—Sam had seen him around town but didn't know his name.

Sam looked for Frank Manly but didn't spot him. He was distracted. He needed to get Gray Ellen out of here. "What?"

"Have you got a name? I'll tell him you tried to do him a good turn."

"Yes, yes. Tell him Sam—" Gray Ellen grabbed his arm. "Never mind," Sam said.

He turned the buggy and eased the horse through the crowd. Behind them, they could hear shouting, the clopping of horse's hoofs, the low, dangerous murmur of a mob of men getting set to do things that couldn't be taken back.

Gray Ellen craned her neck to watch as long as she could. Sam looked straight ahead. "Giddap!" he yelled at the horse, then whipped her across the rump.

The commotion was happening five long blocks from Hugh MacRae's mansion. As J. Allan Taylor and the Pinkertons they had hired apprised him of the situation, he paced the length of his library, furiously smoking a cigar. A lynching now would spoil everything. President McKinley would have federal troops here before morning.

The only solution he could think of was to go himself and try to reason with that fool Dowling. The white trash were sometimes worse than the nigrahs—unpredictable, didn't know their place.

"Get my buggy," he told his man. "Get it quick." To the Negro Pinkerton men, he advised, "Disappear." They went out through the smugglers' tunnel.

By the time he got to Free Love Hall, the situation was serious. After that foolish newspaper piece, word had gotten around that

Mike Dowling was going to hang Manly from a street lamp. A hundred or so Negroes now surrounded the *Record* to prevent him. Some of them were armed. There were no women or children—it was a fighting mob.

The Red Shirts were drunk and in disarray. Boys were mixed in with men. Some of the men had Winchesters, but plenty of them were just curious to see what was going to happen.

He spied Sergeant Lockamy facing down the white crowd. "Are you just going to let this happen?" he said.

"I've got six men. You tell me."

Walker Taylor rode up on a horse that looked too small to carry him. He had three men with him, also mounted. "Walk, can't we get that Mick under control?" MacRae said.

"Exactly," Walker Taylor said, wheeling his horse dramatically, "what I propose to do."

The Negroes weren't advancing. They remained in a defensive posture. Walker Taylor noted that and admired it. Inside Free Love Hall, three or four riflemen could shoot over the heads of their own people and decimate the white mob. Somebody was thinking. Because the white mob was disorganized, Walker Taylor knew that if he could turn the Red Shirts back, he could stop the whole thing. Mobs were stupid creatures. But after a certain stage, they could be dangerous. Some threshold would be crossed, and then nobody could claim control anymore—events would be propelled by sheer momentum. The thing would start to *want* to happen, and then it would. He had seen it happen in South Carolina once.

Luckily, this mob was still brewing. He could sense its half-heartedness. These men were out for mischief, not murder. Some were just starting on a drunk, while others were just sobering up.

Walker Taylor found Mike Dowling—disheveled, red shirt unbuttoned nearly to his waist—and two of his lieutenants on farm horses. They were passing a bottle.

"You're messing where you have no business, Mr. Dowling," Walker Taylor said.

"You country-club people really thrill me, and that's the truth."

Dowling swigged on the bottle and then tossed it away, toward the Negro crowd.

Walker Taylor watched it thump into the sand and hoped to God nobody would use it as an excuse to shoot in his direction—he was a pretty broad target.

"These swamp niggers is keeping good men out of work, and you're siding with them," Dowling said. "Well, Jesus, Mary, and Joseph!"

"This isn't the way," Walker Taylor said quietly. "I'm telling you to call it off."

"You're telling me!"

Walker Taylor leaned as close as he could. "There's riflemen on the second floor. You might as well paint a bull's-eye on your fat Irish kitchen."

Dowling looked uncertainly at the second story. "I ain't scared of no darky with a gun."

"There are five double-barreled shotguns in the front rank," Walker Taylor said coolly, making an automatic military appraisal. "Twelve-gauge, I think. They will blow you out of the saddle and take the saddle, too."

"Mike," one of the lieutenants said, "maybe this ain't a good idea."

"You going to let that nigger Manly get away with this?"

Walker Taylor said, "My Lord, you are thick! Manly's not even here. Don't you get any news at all in Dry Pond? Manly went back to New Jersey."

"Well, Jesus, Mike, that tears it."

"What do I have to do to persuade you?" Walker Taylor was running out of patience.

Dowling cocked his head, as though a beam of light had just lit up the inside of his skull. "Oh, I get it! You've got your own blessed plans! And you don't want us poor-bockers fucking it all up!" He grinned, showing broken front teeth.

Walker Taylor said, "Ride away. Now."

Dowling grinned. Then he noticed that Walker Taylor had his hand wrapped around the grip of a .45-caliber Colt, hidden under the flap of his jacket. He heard a wet click as Taylor let the hammer down and shoved the revolver back into his waistband. "Just so you know," Walker Taylor said, practically whispering. "There's nothing we're not prepared to do."

Dowling jerked upright in his saddle and whistled a clear, piercing note. "The nigger's gone to New Jersey!" he shouted. "We told him we'd drive him out, and we did! Leave these darkies to their supper!"

The mob began to bleed away by twos and threes. Dowling saluted Walker Taylor, still grinning, and then galloped up Seventh Street, scattering those on foot before him like barnyard chickens. He had some drinking to do. Things were turning out better than he could have hoped.

––––––––––

From the second floor of Free Love Hall, Alex Manly peered out cautiously onto the dispersing mob. Beside him, back against the wall, hunkered his brother Frank, a Winchester rifle cradled across his knees. Saffron King James was fetching them glasses of lemonade. She moved toward them from the stairs across the room, crouching, quiet as a breeze, careful to keep her silhouette out of the window.

"See what I mean about white reporters?" Frank said. "They out to nail your ass to the barn." He was angry—nobody ever took him seriously until it was too late. Especially Alex. Frank had rallied the other men just in time, or they might all be swinging from lampposts. "When things settle down, I be hunting a Sam Jenks for my trophy wall."

Saffron slid to the floor next to the men while they gulped lemonade. They'd been up here in the heat for two hours.

"Now you're talking Tom Miller's trash," Alex said. "We only need one like that."

"We best not be here next time they come."

"Next time?"

"Bank on it, brother."

"Why do you think they stopped at the last minute like that?"

Frank finished his drink and clunked the glass down on the floor next to his leg. "Didn't like the odds, I guess. Who knows what's on whitefolks' minds? Maybe nothing. Maybe just a hum like a 'lectric turbine."

The white mob had all but disappeared, the stragglers hurrying not to be left behind. The Negro men around the building relaxed and joshed. Some drifted home.

Alex Manly watched one figure emerge from the cover of a board fence and stand watching up Seventh Street after the retreating Red Shirts. He was a tall, lean man dressed in a gray suit. In the yellow lamplight, his face and hands fairly glowed. "Who is that fellow? Don't believe I've ever seen him around here before."

Frank bestirred himself for a look out the window. He thought, there he is down on the street, acting like he owns the neighborhood. "That's trouble," Frank said. "That's that goddamn preacher man, Ivanhoe Grant."

"Why trouble?"

"Man preach, but he don't preach in church. Skulk around behind the scenes, talking the talk, playing the tune."

Saffron said, "That's right. Preacher come around here while you were up north. Full of words, talking the talk."

Frank said, "Preacher be a shadow man. Inside man."

As Alex watched, Grant turned their way and stood gazing up at the window, his face caught full in the lamplight. "Amazing," Alex muttered, "truly remarkable."

"What?"

"Man looks just like me."

———

In the morning, Sam found Clawson in his office early, pencil in hand, poring over copy of the previous night's near-riot. He slashed away at sentences, cut whole paragraphs, inserted new details.

"You took a hatchet to my story," Sam said.

Clawson didn't look up. "All I did was punch it up. I'm an editor—haven't you read the masthead?"

"You have an obligation to the truth."

Clawson slapped the pencil onto his desk and stood up. "I have an obligation to sell newspapers."

"You're a professional."

"You want truth? Go to church." Clawson opened and slammed a file drawer, then hollered for a copyboy. "We all do things we don't like. That's how things get done."

"What are you talking about?"

"Ask your cousin. Meantime, write me a story I can use."

PART II

THE CAMPAIGN

*It was determined that this city and
county should be redeemed.*

George Rountree

CHAPTER SIX

Thursday, October 6

FOR A WHOLE MONTH, an uneasy surface calm prevailed. Whites
and blacks went about their business warily, avoiding open confrontation.

It was as if the town had rushed headlong to the brink, stared
into the chasm, and pulled back. Something irreparable had almost happened. Nobody had lynched a black man in Wilmington in
fifteen years, yet now, on the verge of the twentieth century, it had
almost come true. It scared them sober. For a short time, merchants were more civil, preachers less strident, agitators less
agitated. At Walker Taylor's urging, Mike Dowling left town to
visit relatives across the river.

For a while, Clawson backed off. He ran Sam's copy with only light editing—just a touch here and there to remind him who was boss. Sam tried hard to tell the truth about things nobody could argue with. The city was quiet, orderly, boring.

But then the incidents began. Small punctures in the social fabric, more and more frequent. Sam started to feel the seams of the town straining, pulling apart. He lay awake at night next to his unhappy wife and fancied he could hear the town stretched tight, tearing slowly, like sun-rotted tent poplin. It made him anxious. Would he be a reliable witness? Would he tell the story? Or would he run for cover, as he had in Cuba? He made up his mind to be braver.

A white laborer assaulted a black stevedore with a baseball bat, and a black policeman refused to arrest the attacker. "I'm not allowed to arrest whitefolks," he explained to the *Messenger*—a contention that Mayor Silas Wright hotly denied.

After the heaviest rainstorm in September, a gang of Negroes pushed a white woman into a muddy ditch. When Sergeant Lockamy happened by, they claimed she had slipped and they were only trying to pull her out.

Persons unknown desecrated the African Methodist Episcopal cemetery, smashing some tombstones with a sledgehammer and chalking obscenities on others. The caretaker spotted two Red Shirts fleeing into the woods.

Somebody fired a single pistol shot through the window of a streetcar as it passed through Brooklyn. Luckily, though the car was crowded with white shopgirls, nobody was injured.

A gang of white teenaged boys whipped a colored boy bloody with willow switches. They claimed he had stolen a wheel belonging to one of them. The colored boy said he didn't even know how to ride a wheel, so why would he steal one?

As Negro mill workers trooped through the streets to their jobs, bands of jobless white men loitering at tavern doors called, "Nigger!" and "Sambo!"

Every night the jail filled and every morning it emptied, as magistrates dismissed each other's cases. It wasn't exactly legal, but nothing seemed to be exactly legal these days. Justice was erratic and political. It was a good time to be a petty criminal, whatever color you were.

Fires broke out mysteriously in buildings all over town. It was rumored that the white firemen themselves were setting the fires to remind the Board of Aldermen just how vital they were. Like many other rumors, it didn't make much sense—the burned buildings were owned by both Republicans and Democrats, whites and blacks. But the town was mostly wooden. Three times in the last century, it had been razed by fire. Even the rumor of arson panicked sensible citizens. Night watchmen jumped at every shadow. In one week alone, they shot five prowling alley cats.

The weather remained hot and muggy, offering no relief for flaring tempers.

In the midst of the heat wave, organizers from the state Democratic party showed up and started Government Unions—white supremacy clubs. Within a week, they issued a Right-to-Work Resolution: from now on, employers were warned, they were to hire whites only.

Through September, the *Daily Record* published sporadically. It was no longer a true daily. The news featured church suppers, excursions by boat to Carolina Beach, recipes for summer squash, war news of black regiments fighting in the Philippines, inspirational poetry, pleas for moderation.

"We are one city, and we have got to get along together," read a typical piece. "The upcoming election makes for heated debates, but let us not forget the many advantages our white neighbors have shared with us."

Amazingly, most white merchants didn't pull their advertising. Subscriptions were up, and, for the first time in its six years of operation, the paper was making a reliable profit. Once a week, Alex Manly slipped a five-dollar bill into an envelope and posted it to Tom Clawson at the *Messenger*—installments on the Jonah Hoe printing press.

Manly, though, became a ghost. He visited his newspaper office at odd hours of the day and night so that no one could predict his movements. He stole through the back alleys of Brooklyn, convinced that if he were spotted in the open on the street, he would be shot down in cold blood. He believed that Pinkertons were following him. He no longer dared go downtown.

His brother Frank urged him to pack up the newspaper and go north. "Time is running out," Frank insisted, but, as usual, nobody listened.

"We'll wait it out," Alex said. "This will pass."

"It's the calm before the storm," Frank said. "They're getting ready." He had heard the rhythm of the town quicken, like a machine ratcheted up a gear. The pitch of ordinary talk grew more shrill. Vibrations shuddered along the downtown streets. The foundation of things was shifting—he could practically feel it under his feet. In random conversations, dangerous resonances made the air sing with threat. Loaded words ricocheted over their heads.

"When the election is over, we can get on with regular business," Alex said.

"That's a long time away," Frank said, tired of arguing. "Anything can happen." The cool days of November seemed like a country he would never visit again. He couldn't imagine the heat ever breaking.

"But it won't."

"Then why you skulking around like a fugitive from a chain gang?"

Alex was embarrassed by his fear. But he was not a man for guns. He was a thinker, a planner—not a street fighter. "Because just when you don't expect anything to happen, that's when it happens."

On September 27, the *Messenger* broke a story handed to it by the state purchasing agent for the Winchester Repeating Arms Company, which had taken an order from a cadre of local Negro businessmen for two hundred carbines. *The Wilmington Negroes Are Trying To Buy Guns!* announced the headline. Sam wrote the article. He had heard a persistent rumor that a Negro preacher was mixed up in the business, but he could never get a name or a confirmation, so he ran the names on the purchase order. The carbines were never delivered.

The *Messenger* continued to run an abridged version of the infamous "Manly editorial," and next to it each day was featured a new, lurid, sensationalized account of Negro rampage: *Black Beasts Attempt to Outrage the Young Daughter of a Respectable Farmer!* Often, the stories were wired out of Charlotte or Raleigh, and Sam began to suspect that the newswire was being used as a trick to make it impossible to verify such accounts. For all he knew, they were concocted in the back room of his own paper, then traded around the state with changing datelines.

Circulation tripled.

Except for the Winchester piece, his own stories were mild reports of street improvements, sermons, the comings and goings of socialites. He compiled the national news off the wire and retyped illegible letters from citizens so the compositors could make sense out of them. There was news happening all around him, but he could not pin down specifics. It made him cross and jumpy.

But he did not take a drink. Which was not easy.

Alcohol was ubiquitous, at least among the men. They drank from flasks on Sunday morning and from decanters at business luncheons on Tuesday. They sipped sherry before dinner and cognac after. Workmen swilled beer every night of the week in the taverns on every corner. The worst of them were along the wharf in Patty's Hollow, the red-light district. Prostitutes there could be had for three dollars, though the better class of customers frequented the brothels on Front Street, where a night of love cost twenty, including whiskey.

"It's not what I expected," Sam confided one evening to Gray Ellen. She was teaching now, and that seemed to absorb her, though he couldn't for the life of him imagine how she could spend all day with colored children.

"You knew when we came down here that you were going to have to start at the bottom," Gray Ellen said.

They were beginning to make a life here. It was difficult, there were many days when she was ready to give up and buy a ticket on the next train to Philadelphia, but she was determined to stick to their plan.

She made a point to visit the beach every Sunday—to drink in the open sky, the breezy quiet.

They had moved out of the Orton and into a house on Third near Ann Street, only blocks from Williston School. The rooms were sunny and included an indoor privy with a bathtub. Mature locust trees shaded the yard. Gray Ellen had found the place, arranged the move, decorated the bedroom and sitting room. Their landlady was the fat woman Gray Ellen had spoken to outside the old *Record* office the day of the eviction. She lived next door. She was not just fat but also pregnant, due in November.

"It's just, I feel I'm being cut out," Sam said. "Things are going on, and everybody's pretending nothing's happening. It's maddening." It was times like this when he could have used a drink. A bottle of beer, something to hold in his hands. A glass of whiskey and soda to dull the headaches he was getting more and more frequently in the oppressive heat.

"What's Harry say?" She was poring over her schoolbooks, devising lesson plans. She really wasn't in the mood for his grousing. She was back in her old form at school. The children were ill-prepared but eager, and she liked them. She had a feeling she could do some good here. Norwood was impressed by her and left her alone. She felt trusted. Shy parents brought her gifts of potato pie and plates of cold chicken and greens for lunch.

She spent as much time as possible with her schoolwork, to avoid facing the emptiness of the other times. Sam was moody lately, and she could have used a dose of his old humor.

"Harry's no help. They don't tell him anything."

"Who do they tell?"

"Good question." Maybe Cousin Hugh? He'd been spending a lot of time in Raleigh these past weeks. He and that lawyer Rountree. "People down here talk in some sort of code, and I'll be damned if I can catch onto it."

"We've been over this," she said. "You think I like it any better than you?" She was still waiting for a dinner invitation to the MacRaes'. She had met Hugh and his wife only accidentally, on the street. She suspected it was a deliberate slight.

"It's worse than that," he insisted. "The stakes are going up. Yesterday, I was looking for pencils. I started opening closets in the storeroom. Know what I found?"

"Not pencils."

"Winchesters—brand new. And pump shotguns, the kind they call riot guns. Forty, fifty guns. Cases of ammunition. A whole arsenal."

Gray Ellen stopped writing out lessons. "At a newspaper office?"

"Looks more like an armory now. I'm telling you, something is in the air. I mean, here I blow the whistle on one armed camp, and I wake up and find myself sitting smack in the middle of another one."

Gray Ellen stared out the window at the spreading branches of the locust trees and thought of the child she had lost. Sometimes, he came back to her like a little ghost, out of the blue, when she was feeling melancholy. She never knew what triggered the memory, but it always came sharp and all at once. She felt tears backing up behind her eyes. "I don't give a damn what they do to each other," she said, and went into the bedroom.

"Gray? What's wrong?" Before Chicago, he'd never seen her cry. She considered it a matter of pride to keep such emotional out-pourings to herself. But lately, she burst into tears for no reason at all. He never seemed to know what was wrong. One part of him wanted to help, but the other part just felt left out, exactly the way he felt at the office.

His instinct was to go after her, but that never worked, just made things worse. He would sit out here quietly, sipping tea and wishing it were scotch, staring out the window, listening to her cry, knowing that it was somehow about their lost baby and that somehow, as usual, he was to blame, wondering how her imagina-tion had made the jump from rifles in the storeroom to a baby she had miscarried months ago, wondering how a life that had started out so promising had ended up in a rented house in a strange place where everybody was getting ready to kill everybody else and acting like it was a family secret, while the woman he loved most in the world was miserable.

It was all supposed to have turned out different.

By now, they were supposed to have a family, their own house, a circle of smart and interesting friends, a full and useful life—success.

If only he knew what to say, how to make it right. It would have happened whether he was there or not, but he could have been a comfort. If only he hadn't blown it in Philadelphia and then Chicago. If only he didn't crave a slug of whiskey so bad he could actually feel the soothing buzz in his brain just from thinking about it. If only he were a better man in a better place. If only he had the words.

The right words made something true, or not. The right words couldn't be taken back later. "I love you," he had told her long ago, and those words were out in the world now, alive all by themselves. He couldn't call them back. She had said the same words out loud.

He listened to his wife weeping in the next room. The anger left him. He felt an ache under his ribs. He went in and put his arms around her—gently, gently—and rocked her. It didn't make her stop crying, but it was all he could do. He kept rocking her, staring out the bedroom window at the arms of the locust trees waving in a fitful breeze, light flickering off the leaves like sunlight shimmering on water.

Next morning, Hugh MacRae was sitting on Sam's desk when he arrived for work. "Burning daylight," he said. "Thought the army would have taught you better." He was wearing mud-speckled brown riding boots and a linen suit the color of sunflowers. When he slipped off the desk and tucked his thumbs into his waistband, the jacket flapped open, and Sam noticed he was wearing a shoulder rig with a horse pistol.

He clapped Sam on the back. "Leave your hat on. We're going on a little excursion, you and me."

"A story?"

"Right, a story."

"Whatever you say." Sam grabbed a fistful of pencils and stuck them into an inside pocket, then stuffed a notebook into his outside pocket. Hugh led him by the arm to the door before halting him at the top of the stairs. "Here," he said, handing Sam an object wrapped in a linen handkerchief.

"What's this?" Sam said, feeling the outline and the weight, knowing exactly what it was.

"You know how it works?"

Sam nodded and unwrapped the handkerchief. The navy pocket revolver smelled of gun oil. By the weight, he guessed it was fully loaded. He didn't know what else to do with it, so he stuck it into his jacket pocket.

"Relax," Hugh said. "Everybody's got to bring something to the party."

Sam followed Hugh's lead. He breathed deliberately to try to get his pulse under control.

Hugh led him at a brisk stride down to the wharf, where a steam tug was tied up, waiting. Clawson was already aboard, as were Walker Taylor—looking enormous in the uniform of the State Guard, complete with side arm—and George Rountree, the attorney. As Hugh and Sam stepped aboard, the three came forward, and everybody traded handshakes, then went into the pilothouse. At MacRae's signal, the whiskered captain snapped the brim of his greasy fedora and gave orders to cast off.

Sam steadied himself against the cabin wall as the stern dug in and the bow lifted, plowing a furrow in the outgoing tide as the boat steamed upriver. The river breeze rushed in at the open ports, cooling him so suddenly that he shivered.

Inside the pilothouse, the din of the engine made it impossible to talk without shouting. Hugh MacRae lit a cigar and paced like a man waiting for a telegram. Clawson lit a cigar of his own.

When they were well beyond the wharves, the railroad bridge, and the rafts of anchored ships, the boat lost way and the engine quieted to a low grumble. The captain nodded to MacRae, and they all followed him out onto the starboard deck, moving aft past the smokestack. Then they stood together at the rail, looking down onto the fantail.

Sam recognized big Bill Kenan at once, standing with two other soldiers next to a bulky object draped with a heavy tarpaulin. The tugboat was a mile or more upriver from the city, drifting down on the tide. Sam recognized the point of land coming up on his right. What was it the man on the train had called it? Nigger Head Point.

He heard murmuring and the shuffle of feet under the rear overhang of the cabin roof, but he could not see who was down there. Suddenly, Hugh MacRae took his cigar out of his mouth as if he were pulling a cork. "You men, come out from there. Let me see you."

Obediently, eight Negro men moved cautiously from under the overhang and stood blinking in the sun, looking up at MacRae.

"Take off your hats so I can see your faces," MacRae ordered, and the men complied. All were dressed in suits and ties—lawyers, merchants, undertakers. Sam recognized the man who had offered to take a message to Manly the night of the near-lynching, but he had never bothered to learn his name. And standing beside him, no mistake, was Frank Manly. He stared up at Sam, who wished he could suddenly vanish. He was acutely aware of the gun in his pocket—the bulge must be unmistakable to anybody staring as hard as Frank Manly.

The eight black men stood there on the swaying deck, hats in hands, not moving except as the boat moved.

"That's better. Now, if you will all move aft. That means to the very back."

The men looked at one another. Sam could read the bewilderment on their faces. Walker Taylor clasped his hands behind his back and rocked back on his legs, chest puffed out. Clawson stood out of the way.

Standing behind MacRae, George Rountree looked at his railroad watch and muttered gruffly, "Get on with it. This isn't a stage play at the Thalian."

MacRae turned on him with a shining intensity in his eyes. "But that's exactly what it is," he told Rountree, his voice a loud whisper.

"Just get on with it. I've got a full calendar this morning."

MacRae turned back and called to Kenan. "Captain. If you please."

In one hard pull, Kenan and his two men yanked off the tarpaulin. It was the first time Sam had seen a Gatling gun since Cuba. The sunlight glinted off the brass crank and receiver, gleamed dully off the ten blued revolving barrels. It was mounted on a steel tripod bolted to the deck. One of Kenan's assistants reached into a crate beneath the tripod and extracted a black-and-brass sleeve as long as his arm. He clicked it upright into the receiver, and Kenan swiveled the muzzle 180 degrees, sweeping it past the eight Negroes. They ducked and cowered, shielded their faces with their arms. Their mouths dropped open, but, if they said anything, their words were blown away on the breeze.

As Kenan steadied the muzzle over the starboard rail, they backed away from the gun, moving as far as they could toward the stern rail without going overboard. Sam stared off to starboard, where Nigger Head Point was coming abeam. What were those six posts near the water—a dock? As the boat drifted closer to the point, Sam realized what he was seeing: six large pumpkins impaled on poles.

Without further preliminaries, Captain Kenan cranked the gun. With the sudden burst of concussions, the black men fell against the rail, and one had to be grabbed before he toppled overboard. Kenan cranked off a hundred rounds, two hundred, five hundred, raking the shoreline while he found the range. The din was incredible, interrupted only for a split second as Kenan's crew changed magazines. They had practiced this.

On the shore, willows whipped as if caught by hurricane gusts. Mud spouted up in geysers. Deadfall logs were whittled into sawdust. Trees were splintered in half, foliage shredded. The pumpkins burst in quick, bright splashes. The poles disintegrated.

An old bull gator lifted his gray muzzle from the mud and disappeared in a spray of blood and hide.

Kenan had been shooting for a whole minute.

A thick fog of blue smoke drifted across the huddle of Negroes at the stern, floated up the river behind them on the breeze. Anybody watching from shore, Sam realized, would think the boat was on fire. He had forgotten that a Gatling gun made so much smoke. The Negroes were all doubled over, coughing.

Walker Taylor stood imperious as a schoolmaster. Rountree consulted his watch again. Clawson rocked on his heels. Hugh MacRae waited. The boat drifted south on the current, under the railroad bridge. The pall of smoke floated farther and farther astern, hanging over the brown water. Kenan's armed crew stood facing the black men, hands on pistol butts. Kenan slapped in a new magazine and looped his arm casually over the gun.

MacRae flipped the tails of his coat back offhandedly, so that his pistol in its black leather shoulder rig was visible. He started speaking, but, at first, Sam couldn't hear anything but the ringing in his ears.

"This little beauty here," Hugh MacRae said, pointing, "is an insurance policy." Walker Taylor, the insurance man, smiled. "It insures against a whole host of evil things." He waited, as if for someone to dare an interruption. "Nigrahs with Winchester rifles, for instance. Rabble-rousers and outside agitators. Civil disorder."

The Negroes stood silent, hats in hands, looking up. One of them had a growing dark stain at the crotch of his pants. He covered it with his hat.

MacRae said, "We mean to have order—do you understand?"

Slowly, reluctantly, the Negroes nodded. Sam wanted to protest, but he kept his mouth shut. Hugh had a look in his eyes that promised no mercy. He is a bully, Sam thought, but he is not bluffing. Then Sam was a bully, too, for doing nothing. For not objecting. For standing there with a loaded pistol in his pocket.

They already blamed him for nearly getting Alex Manly lynched. He was also the one who had written the Winchester piece. Now, he was a part of this, too. They would remember his face. They already knew his name.

But that was his job: watch, then write the story. What was the story? he thought. The man behind that gun is invincible. And the men behind the man behind that gun control this city. That was one story.

The seventeen thousand Negroes they were afraid of, that was another.

Kenan and his crew covered the gun with the tarpaulin. The city was coming up on the port bow. The captain ordered the engine put into gear. Rountree, Clawson, Walker Taylor, and Sam went back inside the pilothouse. Hugh MacRae remained where he was until the boat nudged the bumpers of the wharf and the crewmen looped lines over the bollards.

As the Negro men filed silently ashore, MacRae called out to them, "Tell your people what you witnessed today, hear?"

The eight black men vanished into the crowd of stevedores and sailors. MacRae flicked his cigar away into the river and dusted his hands against each other, as if they were soiled. He put an arm around Sam. "Write it up, Sam. No names. You understand."

"Military personnel," Sam said. "Or a company of militia officers."

MacRae smiled. "Exactly. I knew we could count on you. Being family and all."

"Of course you can count on me." Sam knew it was probably true, and he wished it weren't. He hated that Hugh was more sure of him than he was of himself.

When he stepped onto solid ground, his legs were uncertain. He could feel the wharf swaying under him, and he lurched for a few steps like a drunken man. He wasn't used to boats. If he'd thought about it at the time, he probably would have been sick. Now, he was thinking about it, and the adrenaline and the cordite stink and the bursting pumpkins backed up in his throat. He had tasted this at Las Guasimas.

I finally got to see an alligator, he thought.

He leaned into the gutter and heaved away his breakfast.

Then he went back to the office to write up the story.

*If something is not done to put down the
surly and rebellious attitude of the Negroes
towards the whites, we will have a repetition of
the Sepoy [India] Rebellion, which was ended
only after the British authorities had shot some
of the mutinous leaders out of the mouths of
cannon.*

Walter MacRae,
Hugh MacRae's uncle,
later mayor of
Wilmington

CHAPTER SEVEN

Friday, October 7

THE RIVER RAN FILMY under dirty-shirt clouds this afternoon. Sam
sat in Polson's Saloon with Harry Calabash and watched the
stevedores on the wharf work lethargically, like automatons. They
seemed to be hauling the same crates back and forth. There was no
joshing. The steamships on the river seemed painted in place. The
river itself was slowly congealing. The air smelled watery. Sam
breathed it into his lungs, and it tasted like rusty pipes. He could
not get his breath.

The government weather office predicted the heat would break
any day now. It was unseasonable, the kind of breathless, oppres-

sive calm that preceded a hurricane. But nobody down the coast was reporting any hurricanes. Everybody waited for a good nor'easter to blow away all the bad air.

Today's *Messenger* reported that certain New York businessmen were reneging on a major investment in Wilmington railroads and factories. The reason? Too many Negroes were flocking to the city, destabilizing the labor base. Whatever that meant. The situation, said the article—datelined New York—was volatile.

In another piece, datelined Raleigh, John Dancy was reported to advocate intermarriage between whites and blacks. Dancy was the Negro who had taken over Bill Kenan's old job as customs inspector. He denied ever making such remarks, but the denial didn't make the paper.

A story out of Charlotte—run beside yet another installment of Manly's infamous editorial—tallied up the Negroes who held offices in New Hanover County: four city aldermen, four deputy sheriffs out of a six-man department, the county coroner, the register of deeds and two clerks, a township constable, forty city and county magistrates, thirteen of twenty-four city police officers, the collector of customs, four health officers, and various assistants. Some eighty-six in all. An outrage, concluded the piece: "The Negroes of New Hanover County are 'too big for their britches'!"

"Why does he run that stuff?" Harry Calabash folded his copy of the newspaper and laid it on the table. "Wondered where you were off to so early yesterday, Samuel," he said laconically, sipping a neat whiskey. "I don't any longer get invited on such outings."

"Wasn't such a big honor."

The piece was out in today's *Messenger*: *Wilmington Light Infantry Unveils Instrument of Civil Order*. No mention of Clawson, Rountree, MacRae, or Walker Taylor. Kenan was referred to only as an officer in the army. The Negro men were named: John Norwood, Frank Manly, Carter Peamon, Tom Miller, David Jacobs, Jim Telfair, Norman Lindsay, and Armond Scott.

Clawson had given him the list of names—another list to keep track of. Sam had then pored over the city directory and asked Harry for whatever information wasn't listed there.

Armond Scott was the lawyer he had seen around town and then at the Manly near-lynching. Clean-cut, short-cropped hair; about thirty, innocent eyes. Graduate of Shaw University, admitted to the bar at twenty-one. Scott was the one who had pissed himself.

Norman Lindsay was a foreman at Wilmington Cotton Mills, MacRae's outfit. A working stiff.

Jim Telfair, a lay minister, was also manager of Sprunts' Champion Compress and a part-time copyeditor for Manly's *Daily Record*. Busy fellow, Sam reflected.

David Jacobs, a barber, was the county coroner.

Carter Peamon, another barber, was a ward boss in Brooklyn.

Tom Miller dabbled in real estate, but his bread and butter was his loan and pawn business.

John Norwood was Gray Ellen's boss over at Williston. She spoke highly of him.

And of course, he'd already met Frank Manly. The way Manly had glared at him still queered his stomach.

Harry wasn't paying much attention to Sam. He sat hunched over his drink, elbows propped on the table, brooding. Remembering, Sam was sure—a man like that must have plenty of things to remember, a lifetime all used up in one place.

"I'm no longer considered reliable," Harry said, with great regret. "Time was, nobody who was anybody would make a move without consulting Harry Calabash. Not in the whole damned county."

"Well, I felt like a fool." Sam played with the navy Colt in his pocket. He was already in the habit of carrying it. He picked up bad habits like his trousers picked up lint. "Makes me mad just to think about it."

" 'Ira furor brevis est.' "

"I know. I read my Horace at school, too: 'Anger is a brief madness.' "

"You're a man of principles, Samuel. I respect that."

If he only knew about Cuba, Sam thought. "One of the Negroes pissed his britches. Lawyer Scott."

"I've pissed myself over less."

Sam's ears still rang. "Made a din, all right." Blasted logs as thick as telegraph poles into toothpicks. What would such a gun do to human flesh? He could still see the pumpkins bursting.

"The gentlemen do love their toys." Harry ordered a second whiskey.

"A strange deal all the way around. I mean, who's in charge of what in this city?"

"That's a question, all right," Harry said. " 'I know nothing except the fact of my ignorance.' "

"Plato?"

"Socrates. Sorry, I can't give you the Greek. Too many years."

"Take Captain Kenan. He's with the State Guard, right?"

"After a fashion. Reserve status, or whatever they call it."

"But he's not part of the Wilmington Light Infantry."

"Oh, sure—he's one of the mucky-mucks."

"Is it a regiment, or what?" Sam said.

"Oh, I'd call it more of a club."

"A club?"

"You have to be a man of 'morally upright character.' Nominated and seconded. Then all the members vote. They each put either a white ball or a black ball in the box. Three black balls, you're out."

"Have they ever fought a battle?"

"Lord, the thought of those toy soldiers marching off to a real war. Where the other fellows have guns." Harry's laughter started him coughing.

"But the Civil War . . ."

"Oh, they mobilized. But the men just got absorbed by real regiments."

"And Cuba?"

"Never fired a shot. Volunteered, though—give 'em credit for that. Sweated out the war in Georgia."

"Then what are they doing with an armory?"

"Every club's got to have a clubhouse, Sam. Place to drink bad whiskey and smoke good cigars. Get away from their womenfolk."

"And a Gatling gun?"

"No," Calabash admitted, "that makes it a special club."

Sam drank his iced tea. He was getting awfully tired of tea. It was worst in the afternoon, when his mouth craved the bitter-sweet, frothy taste of lager beer. The heat made him so damned thirsty. "After that business yesterday, there's talk, Harry. Secret vigilante clubs. You ever heard of anything like that?"

Harry put down his glass and rocked back, leaning his chair against the wall, tucking his hands behind his neck. "Well, now, which clubs might you have in mind?"

"Secret clubs, Harry."

"You mean with spy codes? Secret handshakes? Mysterious symbols?"

"Don't make fun. This is serious. Maybe they do have secret codes or passwords—how do I know? I'm asking you."

"Well, let me see. There's the Masons—three or four lodges, pretty sinister boys. Then there's the Knights Templars, still searching for the Holy Grail. Hell, maybe they found it, tucked it away in their basement. We could walk over and check, it's only up on Front Street."

"Harry—"

"You got your Knights of the Golden Eagle, your Knights of Pythias, your Woodmen of the World—now, there's a cadre of revolutionary scoundrels."

"Harry, I didn't mean—"

"For pure deviltry, nobody beats the Fraternal Mystic Circle. They meet right across from city hall. Up to no good, I suspect."

"You know damn well what I mean."

"How about the Improved Order of Redmen?"

"Harry—"

"See, we Southern boys are joiners. About once a week, we need to sit ourselves down inside a room full of fellows just like our-selves who agree with everything we say."

"Sarcasm won't get it done, Harry."

"Course, we haven't even scratched the ladies' societies, the veterans' brigades, the church social clubs, the amateur theatrical troupes, or the Jews—the Jews are always up to something." He drank. "If it's juvenile delinquents you want, check out Walker

Taylor's Boys Brigade, marching around in Rough Rider clothes, carrying wooden rifles."

Sam let him rattle on until he was dry for whiskey and reached for his glass, then said evenly, "How about the Secret Nine?"

"What?" Harry said, coughing out the whiskey right into his bare hand. He dried the hand elaborately with his handkerchief and replaced it in his pocket.

"Group Six, Harry? Ever hear of them?"

Harry reached across the table, grabbed Sam's arms above the elbows, and pulled him in close. Harry could be strong when he wanted to be. "Lower your voice, if you please. Now, who you been talking to besides me?"

"I came to you first, Harry." No sense in dragging anyone else into this. He just needed to know if it was true.

"Three can keep a secret if two are dead." Harry let go. "You have to take care about who you're fooling with."

"I'm tired of fooling, Harry. I'm supposed to be a reporter."

"Tom Clawson doesn't want a reporter. He's got no use for bad news. He answers to MacRae. Haven't you figured that out?"

Sam glared at him. "What's the Secret Nine, Harry? Who are they?"

Harry Calabash shot the whiskey into the back of his throat and stood up. "Come on. Let's you and me take a walk."

They walked slowly in the oppressive heat, up the hill toward city hall and the courthouse, where they spotted Colonel Waddell hurrying inside. Harry said, pointing his cane at Waddell, "I'll tell you one gentleman who isn't in the club, and it's killing him."

Sam watched Waddell open the heavy door and disappear into the shadowy interior. Mentally, he added the Colonel to his list. He was starting to worry that Harry didn't know as much as he thought he knew. Or maybe he just wasn't telling Sam everything.

"You trust me, don't you, Harry?"

Harry looked the other way. "You have no idea what you are dealing with down here. The kind of money. How tight a circle you're trying to break."

"Do you trust me?"

"I don't trust myself. Or any man who drinks."

"I told you, I've taken the cure. Months ago. I'm dry."

"I don't trust any man who *can't* take a drink."

"That's not fair."

"First time you fall off the wagon, all sorts of things will come spewing out of your mouth." He spoke with the taste of experience bitter on his tongue. " 'Trust in God, and keep your powder dry.' Cromwell."

"They're going to use that Gatling gun, aren't they? Against the coloreds."

Harry turned and looked him square in the eye. In the gray sun, he looked old and used up, his face marked with deep lines scrawled haphazardly. The tousled white hair was lank. "Does that surprise you?"

"When, Harry? Election Day? Before?"

Harry turned away and shook his head slowly. He rubbed his eye briefly with the heel of his hand.

"When, Harry? Tell me."

Harry blew his nose and coughed. Sam was getting annoyed at the constant hacking—he wondered if Harry had the consumption. "No, I'm not tubercular," Harry said irritably, "though I soon will be if I keep sucking in this lime dust. The political fate of this city may well turn on which party declares for macadam."

"I want to get to the bottom of this."

"By God, you are arrogant. You believe you can come down here and get to the bottom of this thing in a few weeks. Well, I've been living here for sixty-three years, and I haven't gotten to the bottom of this city yet. It's a mystery. Anything that matters in this life is a mystery."

Harry got his breath. "Who knows when it will happen? I doubt if even the ones who are going to do it know when it's actually going to happen."

Sam touched Harry's sleeve. Under the thin fabric, the flesh was soft and loose. "Make a guess."

"My God, I'm tired of walking." Harry sat down on a bench across from the courthouse, and Sam joined him. Harry sighed long and thoughtfully, tapping his walking stick on the ground. "There are three possibilities. Or at least three that I count."

"Go on."

"All depends on how many cooks are stirring this particular stew. That's the trouble with planning a thing like this—everybody has his own recipe."

Sam recalled what Harry had called Rountree: *a vector of ambition*. How many other vectors of ambition were running around loose at night, or sitting behind closed doors, making clandestine appointments, circling dates on their private calendars?

"One," Harry said. "Next month, Governor Russell and his two pals, Oliver Dockery and Jeter Pritchard, are supposed to make speeches at Thalian Hall. Russell, he's the one we have to thank for the current crowd at city hall. If Dowling is back in town by then, if the Red Shirts are part of it, this city will lynch all three of them."

"White men?"

"Of course, white men. This isn't about race—it's about politics. I already told you that. Politics is just a kind of snobbery—who's in, who's out."

"A matter of class," Sam said. "Another club."

"You could say that. A man's class is the most important club of all. Got to be born into it, or buy your way in, if they'll let you. Like that place your cousin takes you for lunch."

"The Cape Fear Club."

"The second city hall. The real headquarters of the men that run this town. You notice how the regular city hall and the playhouse are in the same building? Where do you think the script is written?"

"I take it you don't belong."

"Course I belong. Where else am I going to do business?"

Every conversation with Harry seemed to go this way—it started out making sense, but, at some point, Sam was defeated by the logic. All he could do was listen and sort it all out later.

"You're some kind of cynic, all right," Sam said.

"I'm a newspaperman. You want the rosy view, go to church."

"Not my church. You must be thinking of the Protestants."

"Racism, that's just a special case of class snobbery. The people you don't want in your club," Harry said. "I thought you said you went to school."

"Once upon a time."

"Well, you're getting the graduate course now."

Sam wanted to get him back on track. "So that's one scenario for *when.*"

"Number two. On Election Day. If Governor Russell is foolish enough to come back here to vote, he will be taken by a mob. And he might—matter of honor and all."

"Of course." *Honor*, Sam thought. He was hearing that word a lot. "And the third scenario?"

"The most likely one. Just ask yourself two questions: who are they, and what do they want?"

"The men on the tugboat."

"Maybe others, too. We both know what they want. And a simple drunken mob won't get it for them."

"They want their city back."

Harry thumped his walking stick on the ground. "You have poetry in your soul, Samuel. Exactly. They can take back the state and national offices in the election, but they're stuck with the crowd in city hall for two more years. Business won't wait that long. There are bonds to issue, deals to make."

"MacRae? Or Walker Taylor?" Were the Secret Nine and Group Six working together? Or were they at odds?

"Whoever, they're going to need big Bill Kenan and his magical gun." Harry gazed off into the gray clouds and spoke as if he were quoting: "On a quiet day, after the election, when everybody has forgotten about secret clubs and nasty editorials, when everybody has let out their breath and is giving thanks to their Maker for peace and goodwill among men."

"Translation?"

"When the weather turns cold enough to clear the streets, and soldiers can maneuver in rank."

At that moment, Colonel Waddell emerged from the courthouse and took the steps in a fast, limping stride.

"Samuel, remember your Ovid: '*Medio tutissimus ibis.*' "

"I know, 'The middle path is safest.' " He'd been in the middle plenty lately.

He left Harry ruminating on the bench and followed Colonel Alfred Moore Waddell to his law office at Front and Princess streets.

"Mr. Jenks! A pleasure to see you. I was hoping you'd come calling one of these days." Waddell stood up behind his cluttered desk and reached across to shake Sam's hand. His jacket hung on a hook by the window. The armpits of his shirt were stained yellow with old sweat. The collar and cuffs were frayed.

"They have kept me busy."

Waddell waved the latest *Messenger*. "Crackerjack stuff. Terse, economical, precise. You should have been a lawyer."

"There's enough lawyers in the world already."

"Like they say, the only lawyer in town will starve to death—"

"And two lawyers will starve the town."

Waddell laughed dryly. "May I offer you a glass of spring water—or perhaps a splash of Tennessee sour mash? It's five o'clock somewhere."

"Water will be fine, thanks."

Waddell poured from a pewter pitcher into a dusty glass. He refilled his own chipped crystal wineglass with water and held it by the stem to drink. "Gabrielle tells me you came visiting."

Sam drank. The water tasted of tin and gave him a headache, it was so cold. Where did they get such cold water? "Looking for Manly. Talked to your servants."

"Of course, of course. They have an underground telephone, those darkies. Sometimes, I think we badly underestimate them."

"Wouldn't surprise me."

"Did you know that, after the War, I advocated giving educated Negroes the vote?"

"I didn't realize."

It had come back to haunt him. Fat Dan Russell had used Waddell's own speech to unseat him from Congress, calling him soft on Negroes. Now, Russell was the champion of the Negro cause. Given time, every noble aspiration got twisted. "I'm sure our ways must seem quaint to a Yankee," he said.

Odd, Sam reflected, draining the cold water: he'd never thought of himself as a Yankee till he'd come down here. Maybe that was the difference. These people thought of themselves as Southerners from the day they were born.

"Please, have a seat," Waddell said. Sam obliged. "And what brings you round today?"

Be as honest as you can, Sam's first editor had always advocated: lying gets too complicated too fast, use it only as a last resort. "I happened to see you at the courthouse. I realized I had not yet paid my respects."

Waddell nodded in approval: here was a young man who appreciated the forms. "Must have been quite an adventure out on the river."

"Oh, not really. Kid stuff, for an old soldier like you."

Waddell stood and paced the small office. "I do wish I could have been there. It must have been very *theatrical*, yes?"

Waddell spoke with a soft, mellifluous voice, like some of the professors Sam had admired at the University of Pennsylvania—those who always spoke partly to hear the sound of their own voices. That was all right, Sam decided: if I had a voice like that, I'd listen to it all day long.

"Oh, it was that," he said.

"We live in interesting times. Especially for an observer of the human scene, such as yourself. We have just won a glorious foreign war, a new century is about to dawn, the world is being redefined before our very eyes." His voice resonated in his nasal cavities so that it carried without sounding loud. Sam figured it must have to do with the bones of the skull.

"Sure looks that way," he said. Sam noticed for the first time the lined papers spread across Waddell's desk, each page filled with flowing cursive. A fountain pen lay uncapped. "Legal brief?" Sam indicated the papers.

Waddell beamed. "A speech. You haven't heard me speak, have

you? Of course not. Last week it was Kinston, week before that Goldsboro. Can't get out of bed in the morning without consulting the train schedule—reminds me of the days when I was canvassing for Congress."

"You running for office now?"

Waddell squinted one eye at Sam, as if he were not sure how to take that. "The Cause," he said quietly.

Sam looked blankly at Waddell, who picked up his pen, carefully capped it, and clipped it inside his shirt between the third and fourth buttons. His index finger and thumb were stained with black ink.

"White supremacy," Waddell explained, so matter-of-factly Sam wasn't sure he'd heard right. "Putting the affairs of the Old North State back into the hands of the race God intended to rule her, the Anglo Saxons."

What was he supposed to say to that?

Waddell smiled and touched his arm ingratiatingly. "Take yourself, for instance. Sturdy, blond, clear-eyed, intelligent. Nordic through and through. Born to take charge of things, not to go placidly along."

"You give me too much credit."

"Don't misunderstand me, we all know colored men who have risen in the world."

"Frederick Douglass, for instance?"

Waddell said, "Douglass once spoke at our own Thalian Hall—in the lecture room, of course, not the main stage."

"Of course."

"Powerful speaker." He sipped water and smiled, as if he'd just remembered something. "I used to play comic roles on that stage—can you feature that?"

Sam nodded. Thalian Hall and city hall were two parts of the same building. He could easily imagine Waddell gliding back and forth between politics and theater.

"Anyhow, it's a simple matter of King Numbers."

"Afraid I don't know that expression."

"Simple enough: education. Whites go to school—most of them

do, at any rate. Got some poor-bockers living back in the hills have
never seen a primer. A few watermen up the coast. But the nigrah,
he tends to be led around by the nose. Has no experience in self-
government. White man tells him how to vote, maybe pays him a
dollar, maybe not, and suddenly democracy don't mean much.
King Numbers, that's all it means. Who controls the nigrah vote.
It's a confounded racket."

"So the answer is to keep them from voting at all?"

"Until such time as the nigrah can make an intelligent choice,
yes. Get rid of the bosses, the coercion, the corruption. Stop taking
advantage of a gentle, timid people."

"I see."

"Democracy is a complicated business. You can't learn it overnight. Takes generations of practice."

Sam said, "So someday, when we live in a better world . . ."

Waddell could have been his favorite uncle, if he had any uncles.

"I notice the nigrahs aren't running Chicago."

Coming out of this man's mouth, it all sounded halfway reasonable. Maybe he had a point. Sam felt tricked, but he did not know
exactly why.

The door opened and Gabrielle deRosset Waddell appeared, her
face flushed from the heat and the walk. Across the room, Sam
could feel her heat. "Mr. Jenks," she said, curtsying slightly.
"What a pleasant surprise." She was clearly annoyed at finding
Sam here. She held a receipt in her hand.

"Mrs. Waddell."

Colonel Waddell stepped toward his wife. "Miz Gabby," he said,
and kissed her on the cheek. She flinched only slightly, but Sam
noticed.

"I had some business at Rivenbark's. We can talk about it later."
She tucked the receipt in her sleeve.

As she moved closer, Sam was overpowered by her scent—
gardenias and rose water mingled with perspiration. And her
heat—some women gave off heat, you could feel the air wavering
with it. He'd known only a few like that before. She had to know
the effect she was having on him. Women like her always knew.

Her brown eyes locked on his—he could not read her at all.

Gabrielle forced a smile.

The Colonel said, "Why don't we all retire from this sweltering office and refresh ourselves?"

Gabrielle took his arm, and Sam followed them out. Waddell didn't bother to lock the door.

They sat on café chairs at Johnson's Ice Cream Parlor and sipped iced soda water flavored with lemon.

"Apparently, you found Mr. Manly," Gabrielle said coolly.

"I'm afraid I did. But what happened later, well, it was frightening." Sam shook his head, eyes downcast. It had really shaken him up, and he wanted her to understand that. If she understood nothing else about him, he wanted her to know that. He was trying to do right. She watched him without giving anything away.

Colonel Waddell said, "A mob is never the answer to anything. Real solutions require planning."

"Let's not get into this," Gabrielle said.

"Of course," said the Colonel magnanimously. "I was forgetting the company."

"I didn't mean any harm, ma'am," Sam said.

"No, of course not. No one ever does." She said it flatly, tiredly. Not an accusation but an observation, of a thing that couldn't be helped.

Sam watched her across the table. She had a distant look in her eyes. She was somewhere else. He sensed that, if he reached out and touched her hand, he would feel nothing but the cold outline of a ghost.

"How is Bessie's boy David faring?" he said.

Gabrielle patted her loose chignon and said, "His arm has mended—I don't know about his spirit."

"Bessie's been with you a long time?"

"Is that the habit of all newspapermen?"

"Ma'am?"

"Can you only make conversation by asking questions? It's quite rude, you know."

Sam felt put in his place. He felt that way a lot lately.

"Miz Gabby," the Colonel said. "Fifteen years, Mr. Jenks, more or less."

"She was with the Colonel while he was still married to Miss Ellen," Gabrielle explained in a voice that made Sam wonder if she was looking forward to her widowhood. "Did you know Bessie was born into slavery?" She fiddled with her straw. He watched her white fingers play with it.

"She looks like a woman who's worked hard all her life."

"You can't begin to know, Mr. Jenks." Gabrielle cocked her head, parted her lips, but didn't speak further. Instead, she sucked on the paper straw, and he could see the lemon soda rising toward her mouth. She kept her eyes on him.

Sam tugged out his watch and glanced at it. He needed to get out of here, away from this woman, home to his own. "Time to go back," he said.

On the way out, they stopped at the counter to pay. Colonel Waddell said, "Blast it! Must have left my money in my other jacket. I fear I'm getting senile."

"Never mind," Sam said, handing a quarter to the girl behind the counter. "No change required." At five cents a soda, the tip was extravagant. He wanted Gabrielle to notice.

She put a hand on his sleeve. "You must join us for supper one evening soon."

"Thank you—of course."

"Bring your wife. Her name is—?"

"Gray Ellen."

She bit her lower lip. A curl of dark hair came loose from her chignon. "A lovely name," she said, "lovely."

Sam arrived home at six o'clock to an empty house. He'd stopped along the way to pick blue chrysanthemums from out front of St. Thomas's—a minor revenge on Father Dennen—but now had no wife to receive his bouquet.

He flung his wrinkled jacket on a chair and heard the revolver thunk against the wood. He'd have to remember to put it away later. Gray Ellen didn't even know he had it. He put the mums in a pitcher of water and left them on the kitchen counter, loosened his cravat, and settled into an Adirondack chair on the porch to wait.

Across town, in Brooklyn, Gray Ellen walked arm in arm with Ivanhoe Grant down Bladen Street. He'd practically kidnapped her from her classroom, and they'd ridden the streetcar into the heart of the Negro neighborhood. She was still wondering what she was doing here.

She had just been finishing up a spelling lesson, the last lesson of the day. The children were spelling in unison, "D-E-M-O-C-R-A-T, Democrat," and "R-E-P-U-B-L-I-C-A-N, Republican." She wanted them to be able to read the handbills come Election Day. She believed good spellers made better citizens.

The children giggled and vied with one another to see who could spell the loudest—they'd heard these words before. The little girls in the front row, sisters with tightly braided hair, recited in a single voice like a steam kettle. In the back, a huge, muscular boy recited in a clear tenor, almost a song. Somewhere in the middle, a skinny boy in filthy overalls croaked in a bullfrog bass, thumping out each letter. Gray Ellen loved the noise. It meant things were happening inside their heads. They were on their way to becoming people who could think for themselves.

This, she thought, her ears filled with children's voices, is where I live. More than ever, she longed for a child of her own. She could take her to the beach, raise her on the soothing rush of the surf. Teach her, love her, continue herself into another age.

When she dismissed the class, she realized he had been watching from the open doorway.

He stood in the hallway in his creased gray suit, Ivanhoe Grant, grinning his sweet grin, and she stood inside the sun-washed classroom, the children filing out rambunctiously between them, their little shoes clunking and scuffing across the scrubbed wooden floor.

Then the children were gone, and the classroom was empty. For her, there was always a sadness about an empty classroom at the end of the school day. The ghosts of voices lingered in the air, dusty with chalk. The desks sat in neat, useless rows.

Next month, next year, a dozen years into adulthood, maybe, some of them—one of them?—would remember her voice, the lesson it had carried that day, the pulse of her imagination and reason. If she were lucky, it would make a difference. Probably, she would never know. Every small lesson was an act of faith.

Into the quiet classroom strode Ivanhoe Grant. "Suffer the little children," he said, and smiled. His eyes were warm and glowing. She wondered how he could make them go warm and cold like that.

"Reverend Grant. Shouldn't you be out saving souls instead of haunting the schoolhouse?"

He stood right up close to her and laid his fine hands on her shoulders. She shuddered, feeling his electricity, but she could not pull out from under his hands. He stood so tall that she was looking straight into his black silk tie. He smelled musky and clean at the same time. She had never been touched like this by a Negro man before. Why didn't she balk?

"Salvation does not come to committees," he said. "Every man must go to the mountain alone."

"And every woman?"

"Especially every woman. Here beginneth the lesson." He let his hands fall from her shoulders but grabbed her elbow in a firm, gentle grip, coaxing her toward the door.

"Where are we going?"

"This lesson will cost you a nickel—have you got a nickel?"

She kept a purse in the bottom of the large cloth bag she carried her schoolbooks in. She broke away from him and went to the bottom drawer of her desk to get it. He waited. She was outside herself, looking in, marveling that she was about to go off with this man, this black stranger, without a word of warning, explanation, or persuasion. He hadn't even asked her permission to take her—where? She could—she should—say no. But something had gotten into her, a combination of the unseasonable heat, his audacity and sweet voice, her own stubbornness. She followed him out, and they boarded the crosstown streetcar at the corner of Seventh. He didn't touch her again until they stepped off the streetcar in Brooklyn.

"Where are we?"

"In another country," he said. "The Dark Continent. Bones in the noses and plates in the lips." He was making fun of her.

She looked down the row of unpainted shotgun shacks, the idle men loitering, smoking, pitching pennies. Negro men. On the sagging porches, black women rocked infants. Skinny dogs roamed in packs, chased by motley bands of Negro children.

"Time you saw where your children go when they go home."

"I've been in Negro neighborhoods before." She thought, we saw this from the window of the train, but it looks worse up close. She felt, irrationally, that her dark hair and brown skin weren't dark enough.

"You've been in places where the people go to work every day. For most of these men, work is seasonal. Seventy-five, maybe a hundred dollars a year."

"A year? How do they live?"

"You tell me."

"But so many of the women work—in private homes, taking in laundry, fancy sewing."

"The best ones can charge three dollars a week," he said. "Now that the Irish are trying to push them out, wages have dipped some."

The Irish? Sam had told her about Mike Dowling and his Red Shirts—was all that fuss about menial jobs? "Supply and demand," she said. "When the labor pool gets smaller, they'll have to pay more again."

"Half the men in this city are out of work right now—white and black. They're not interested in Adam Smith."

"Just how is it you know so much about it? You got here the same time I did."

"For me, it was a homecoming, teacher. The Lord brought me back."

Whenever anybody started talking about doing the will of God, she shuddered: somebody was going to suffer, soon.

She walked on, looking straight ahead. Heads turned as she approached, voices murmured as she passed. It was foolish to be here, a white woman walking with a black man she hardly knew. But then she scolded herself: why shouldn't she walk with a colored man? Why shouldn't she visit any part she pleased of the city where she lived? If she was really going to start a family in this place, she could not do it in fear.

"Poverty is awful," she said after a few steps. "What do you expect me to do about it?"

He bowed his legs, as if he were about to draw a sword. He whipped his right hand up suddenly and nearly jabbed her in the eye with his finger. He whispered, "It's not the poverty of their bodies that enrages me, teacher, but the poverty of their spirits."

"Blessed are the poor in spirit." She slapped down his finger. Ivanhoe Grant smiled, and she suddenly felt mean.

In a melodic tone, he said, "Teacher, there are more prosperous colored families in this city than you would ever believe. I'm talking about lawyers and moneylenders and businessmen. Oriental carpets and a grand piano in the parlor. Men and women who have been to school, some of them to college. Who hire out their laundry and eat fresh meat in the middle of the week, who read books and ponder the sacred. But they're poor, teacher—poor as the dumbest plantation nigger. And do you know why? Because they don't aspire. *Aspire*, teacher. Like in breath. Like in spirit. They live on the surface. They believe that what they have is enough."

"Maybe it is."

"What they have is everything there is, teacher," he said. He was right up in her face now. "Everything except freedom."

"Speak for yourself."

He drew back and made himself bigger. "I am a preacher of the Lord. My life must be large enough to encompass all the lives of my people."

"Just who are your people? Where is your church?"

"Look around you. This is my church." He stamped his foot in the sandy street. "Here is my pulpit."

Any minute now, Gray Ellen expected him to grab a passerby and start casting out devils. She wanted to get out of here, go home. Sam would be there by now. She should never have come out here with this wild man in a gray suit that never wrinkled.

"They cling to the surface," Grant said. He scuffed his shoe across the sand, raking out a large comma. "But the surface can be wiped away, just like that."

She waited for more, but apparently the sermon was finished. "As I said, what do you expect of me? I'm just a schoolteacher."

"I expect you to stop, look, and listen," he said. "Or the Glory Train gonna run you over. I expect you to open your eyes and ears and heart. I expect you to remember what you see here when your Mr. Jenks writes his little tales of Negro domination."

So that was it. A Chicago alderman had once tried to intimidate her to stop Sam from writing the truth. "Sam doesn't write that trash."

"You don't sound too sure, teacher. You do your homework?"

"My husband is a man of principles."

"They're all men of principles, teacher—that's what makes them dangerous." He had her walking again. The street was so deep in sand that she had trouble stepping.

He stopped her in front of a two-story frame house that rose out of the row of shotgun shacks like a rickety tower guarding the corner.

"Just what do you mean?" she said. "Who?"

He backed her against the house. The boards were sharp and warm against her spine. Across the street, a gang of idle men and boys watched. She could feel their eyes, hear their giggling laughter. For the first time, she feared for her physical safety—this man might do anything, and she was in the one place in the whole city where she could count on no help from anybody.

"Listen here, schoolteacher. This story has been a hundred years in the making. Two hundred. A millennium. Smoldering, burning from the inside out, gutting the foundations like a coal fire deep underground. About time it got some air. About time it burned in daylight."

"My God, you want to put a match to it."

He was a black shadow looming over her. "I want to burn the sin out of this wicked city."

She was astonished. "People will die."

"People will always die, praise the glory of Jesus!"

Gray Ellen felt a sudden sharp chill in her stomach. She held her breath. His eyes had gone cold as stars. Beads of perspiration jeweled his flawless yellow complexion. She could hear the quick beating of her own heart. She said, with all the control she could muster, "What do you want from me?"

"Come inside, teacher," he whispered, taking her hands. She felt his cool fingers playing with hers. "Give me succor in the hour of my trial."

She wrenched away and lurched along the clapboard wall, the boards cutting her back. The wall was the only thing keeping her up. "How dare you!" she wanted to shout, but what came out of her mouth was an inarticulate yelp. How had this happened? Had the whole point, from the schoolhouse until now, been only seduction? Were all the high-sounding words about social justice just a ruse to get her into bed?

As he stepped close again, she flailed at him with her balled fists.

He backed off, palms out, to show he meant no harm. "Teacher, teacher, calm yourself. I just want to be your friend."

"Get away! I don't need friends like you!"

The men across the street were still watching. One of them was pointing. Nobody was laughing.

He smiled and clasped his hands in front of him, bowed his head, watched her. "Teacher, don't tell me your heart is pure. Don't tell me you do not lust, as I do."

"Goddamn you," she said. Her hair was a mess, all unraveled on her shoulders and neck.

"His prerogative," Grant observed pleasantly. "But you were looking and talking like—"

"I was what?" Now, anger was overcoming fear. "Who do you think you are?"

"You heard me."

"How dare you! How dare you talk to me like this! How dare you touch a white woman—" It was out before she knew it. Now, she was all mixed up, angry at herself, furious at him, feeling dirty and low and victimized all at once. She felt had. He had pushed her into this.

Ivanhoe Grant smiled fiercely. "So it comes down to that. Then the lesson wasn't wasted, after all."

"Goddamn your lesson. Goddamn you."

"You're awfully dark, for a white woman. Maybe we've got more in common than you'd care to admit." He laughed.

"Don't you dare laugh about this!"

" 'Even in laughter the heart is sorrowful.' "

"Don't go spitting proverbs at me!"

His coolness infuriated her. His cool, plain arrogance, the arrogance only a man could have. She was angry that he had tried to seduce her, but just as angry that the seduction hadn't been genuine—which was crazy, and she knew it. She hated herself for being tricked so easily. For being so predictably what she was. She hated this man. She hated all men. She hated all black men, hated all the coloreds, everywhere.

"Go ahead and say it. It's on the tip of your tongue."

She glared at him.

"Nigger," he pronounced quietly. "Say it. Say it after me. You want to say it: *nigger*." He was talking louder.

She cast her eyes uncertainly from side to side, looking for a way out.

"It's easy, just repeat after me: N-I-G-G-E-R, nigger! See?"

"All right! Nigger! Nigger, nigger, nigger! Satisfied?"

"In the beginning was the Word, teacher."

Some of the men were coming across the street. Grant didn't seem to notice. Suddenly, they were all around her. Dear God, she prayed, don't let them damage me, let me be able to have another baby someday.

"You all right, miss?" one of them said timidly, straw hat in hand.

The man next to him let his half-smoked cigarette drop from his lip. "Laws, she a white woman!" he said in amazement.

"Look like she sick."

"Go on out of here, Charley Potatoes," one of them said to Grant. "You scaring the lady."

"We walk with you to the streetcar, ma'am."

Ivanhoe Grant lifted his hands toward heaven, fluttering his fingers. "In the beginning was the Word, teacher," he said coolly. "The Word." He dropped his arms, bowed his head, then disappeared into the house.

His rank smell lingered in the air. She could hardly stand the smell—the air stank of men.

On the streetcar home, she leaned out the window to blow it off her tangled dark hair, out of her dusty nose and throat.

Sam walked to the gate to meet her, cross from having waited for more than an hour. Something was wrong, he could tell. "Children acting up at school?" he said, taking her heavy cloth bag.

She smiled, but she was near tears. On the porch, he embraced her. He wanted her. He'd been waiting for her. She was his wife. He wanted to strip off her dress and kiss her shining black hair, her breasts, the insides of her thighs, feel her heat. He would do it gently. He would take hours.

She pulled away. "No," she said. "I'm not—I'm not ready."

Sam felt scolded. He stood on the porch as she went inside, expecting her to find the blue chrysanthemums he had brought her and rush back to him, linger in his arms, feel his love.

But instead, he heard her footsteps on the stairs, heavy and measured. Sweet Jesus, he wanted a drink. He went into the kitchen and ran a glass of water from the pump. The water was lukewarm and tasted of rust. He thought, the only place in town that doesn't have cold water.

The Old North State, the Home of Beauty,
Courage, Honor, Industry, Virtue, and
Independence.

Toast of the
Wilmington Light Infantry

CHAPTER EIGHT

Saturday, October 8

WILLIAM RAND KENAN stood in his shaded backyard on Nun Street a block and a half from the river and exercised with dumbbells. *Arms straight down by the sides, lift slowly till the arms are perpendicular to the trunk, hold them there, feel the muscles burn, expel the breath, and down.* Twenty repetitions, a thick towel scrubbed over the neck and face, then twenty overhead lifts. Next, Indian clubs. *Swing in a gentle arc, loose as swatting a baseball— down, over, around. Again.* Coordination. Grace. Control.

Then a quart of cold well water tasting of stone and iron.

The heat had broken at last. A cool breeze off the river rattled the high branches of the elms. The air smelled sweet, like the mountains. It carried the scent of storm and the first hint of burning leaves.

Kenan toweled off and threaded his thick arms through a white sweater. He patted his stomach—he hadn't carried that belly in the War, retreating to the Petersburg trenches with Ewell's tattered corps. He was a rail then, an eighteen-year-old recruit who'd left the University of North Carolina without a degree to follow his brothers, Thomas and James—colonel and captain—both wounded and captured at Gettysburg.

By nineteen, he had been promoted in the field to sergeant major. He wasn't shot until the summer of '64 at the Battle of Charleston. Then he made adjutant, and finished out the war an officer.

He'd survived. Couldn't even feel the wound anymore. He would sit in the big copper bathtub and try to find the scar where the minie ball had clipped off a chunk of flesh from his thigh, but it was gone. Like the War. A memory, a receding dream of blood, passion, and fear.

He grinned after the exertion—a prosperous man grown thick about the middle. But his middle was still hard. At fifty-four, he could still lift a grown man over his head, split half a cord of blackjack before breakfast, outshoot any man half his age.

He was alone today. His wife, Mary, was at Blowing Rock, in the mountains, with his three grown daughters. Usually, she went there only in summer, but this season, the heat had lasted so long. She'd be back within the week.

His boy, Bill Junior, was building a hydroelectric dam in Mexico. He'd passed through in June, back from a stint in Sault Sainte Marie. He was an alert boy, sharp as flint, good head for numbers. Engineer. Going to make his mark in this world. Hell, only twenty-six, and the boy had already been around the world—built a plant for Carbide Manufacturing in Sydney, Australia, then traveled home via Borneo, Sumatra, China, Japan, Ceylon, London, Berlin, Rome, Paris, and Niagara Falls.

Kenan used to sit up nights in his study, matching the postmarks of his son's letters to the globe—his thick finger carefully tracing out the boy's whereabouts, making it actual. It wasn't real until he could feel it under his hands. Once he had his hands on a thing, he had it for sure.

The boy got his talent for numbers from the old man. Kenan had been on the Board of Audit and Finance till this Fusionist crowd got in down at city hall. Damned meddling Governor Russell. No matter—he had plenty to keep him busy. He wasn't a wealthy man, but he had ample money in the bank. He had good credit and a good name, and, of the two, he valued the name more.

He walked between the kitchen—a separate outbuilding—and the main house, down the driveway to a woodshed crammed full of scrub oak sawed and split into stove-sized sticks. He'd left a little niche just inside the door. Dandy, the family Labrador retriever, had whelped nine pups night before last. Six had survived. He stepped into the shed and listened: they were chirruping like little birds. He grinned. God, he loved dogs. They were so uncomplicatedly loyal, so trusting. They craved affection so.

He hunkered over the wooden soapbox he had lined with castoff flannel shirts. Dandy lay on her side, fat with milk.

"How you doing today, little mother? Hey?" She licked his hand automatically. Her eyes were bright and her nose cold—she was doing just fine. The five black pups, fuzzy as bear cubs, jostled for places at the teats. They nestled in close, eyes closed, paws pressed on either side of a teat, suckling.

The sixth and smallest pup was brindled, black on gray, didn't even look like he belonged in the litter. But a litter could have two different sires, Kenan knew. That old gray mongrel down the street must have jumped the fence one day when nobody was watching. "You going to be a jumper, too, boy?" he whispered. It was comical and sad, the way the runt mewled like a cat. Kenan slipped his hand under him gently and scooped him out of the nest. "What's the matter, little barky?"

He sighed. Maybe this one wasn't going to make it. Dandy was an old girl to be having pups, and not all of her teats were giving milk. "Got a cold belly, do you?" Kenan carried the runt into the kitchen in the crook of his arm and fed it from a baby bottle he had borrowed from Hattie, the cook, figuring he might need it. He'd been around dogs all his life, and not every pup had what it took to make it in this world. In his younger days, when he'd run a dozen field dogs, he might have let the runt die. But he didn't keep sporting dogs anymore—Dandy was just the family pet. And the years had mellowed him. He shook his head—if the boys at the Light Infantry could see him now, perched on a kitchen stool in his athletic clothes, nipple-feeding a mongrel runt pup.

The hell with it, he figured, and laughed out loud. His voice filled the kitchen, and he laughed again just to hear it. What was the joy of being a strong man, if not reaching a hand out to the helpless?

He was an elder in the Presbyterian church now. He had learned such things. His life was settling into a deep goodness. He could see it in Mary's smile as she played the piano in the evenings when it was just the two of them, home alone. Feel it in the shy way she touched his cheek, and the way she went breathless, after all these years, when he suddenly hooked her around the waist and drew her into his big embrace.

The puppy fell asleep feeding. He put it back with the litter, tucked into Dandy's belly, and went into the house to change clothes.

The frame house—he'd built it almost thirty years ago—was bigger now, with the children grown. Time was, he'd felt crowded in that house, with Mary and the children—Mary Lily, Jessie, Sarah, and Bill Junior—and all their friends jostling and talking and playing underfoot. He used to retreat to the woods and fields, stay out for days, sometimes just watching, listening, walking, not shooting anything, until he was ready to come back into the city.

Summers, Mary would take the kids to the mountains, and he would go with the Guards. Back from training, he'd enjoy the peace and space for a few days. Then, missing the camaraderie of soldiers, he'd open the house to the young men of the Light Infantry.

For three years, he had been their commander. He had trained them properly, instilled in them discipline.

They'd start accumulating on his porch just before the dinner hour. Hattie would fix rabbit stew or stuffed quail, whatever game was on hand, and his table would buzz, lively with earnest conversation about tactics, maneuvers, politics, the future.

Now, the house seemed impossibly huge and empty. As he climbed the stairs to his bedroom, he was stung by a sudden melancholy. It was as if he were watching himself from outside the parlor window, a robust middle-aged man climbing stairs with a heavy tread, a man bereft of wife and family, rattling around in a chilly house all by himself.

He shook off the feeling. He was fine. Mary and the children were all fine. He had done well by them, better than he'd ever had any right to expect, starting out. He had always been certain he would die in battle. That he had lived through the War surprised him every morning of his life.

But he knew what had suddenly spooked him. It had come to him in a dream, and he almost never dreamed. Most nights, he slumbered like a child—he was quickly and restfully asleep, then, at first light, immediately and alertly awake. When he dreamed at all, they were heroic dreams—socking in the winning run, saving a child from a burning house, hitting the bull's-eye of an impossibly distant target.

But night before last, the same night Dandy was birthing her pups and losing three of them, Bill Kenan had dreamed about the gun.

He wriggled out of his sweater and flannel undershirt, stripped off his leggings, and sat on the bed, listening to the house creak in the breeze. Got to get some people in, he thought. A house was a live thing. It needed voices to keep it alive. Hattie would be back from her errands soon. He would tell her to plan for company tomorrow evening. Soon as he was dressed, he'd see what was left in the smokehouse. Maybe he could persuade Hattie to bake a Lady Baltimore cake—all those layers of sugar and almonds. The young men always craved the sweet stuff. He'd tell her to buy the fixings at Rivenbark's and make two—she could take the other one home to her family.

Kenan stood in the carriage barn behind the Wilmington Light

Infantry Armory, smoking a Havana cigar. The barn had three bays, but only the center one was occupied. It held a sturdy quartermaster's wagon: its chassis, box, and seat freshly painted French blue; its wheels, tongue, and doubletree painted cavalry yellow.

He unlaced the ropes holding the tarpaulin and yanked it down onto the sandy floor, then let down the tailgate and swung himself up into the box.

The Gatling gun's steel tripod mount was bolted to the bed of the wagon, as it had been bolted to the deck of the tugboat. The gun was mobile and high enough to fire over the heads of friendly ranks. The wagon box could carry a crew of three, with two more on the seat. Plenty of room for extra hoppers of ammunition.

The boxes of .30-.40 Krag rounds, each bullet longer than his index finger, were stored in the powder magazine under the armory's front stairs—behind marble walls two feet thick. Safe enough there till the time came to haul them out.

Cigar clamped in his teeth, he took up his place behind the gun and swiveled it back and forth, raking the walls with imaginary fire. Four hundred and eighty pounds, but it swung silently on greased bearings with just a nudge from his hand. The brass receiver felt cool. Absently, he studied the engraving scrolled across the brass housing: *Gatling Patented, Colt's Mfg. Co., Hartford, Ct.*

The brightwork gleamed—one of the boys must have been in to polish it this morning. He guessed they'd all be in here handling the gun every chance they got. He would, at that age. Hell, here he was now. But that was something else—or was it? Was it the dream scratching at his conscience, or was it just his old infatuation with the hard precision of firearms? He patted the brass. Already, Kenan could see his fingerprints coming up gray on the receiver. He scrubbed them off with his handkerchief.

"Lord, what a piece of ordnance," he said out loud. He listened to his voice settle in the empty space, which smelled of horses, paint, grease, gun oil, and tobacco. Fired six hundred rounds per minute— per minute! During the War, it had been a novelty weapon. Confederate commanders couldn't get it, and most Union commanders refused to use it. It violated their spirit of honor, of gentlemanly combat, their glorious frontal charges across fields glinting with bayonets, painted with staggered ranks of blue and gray troops, littered with the colorful dead.

Not U. S. Grant, though. Not the storekeeper. He had a head for numbers. He knew you could add up the numbers and the outcome would be plain as a baseball score. The numbers told a true story. And the War had become a war of numbers—how many dead and wounded, how many deserters, how many cases of yellow fever, how many muskets, cartridges, uniforms, horses. How many you had, how many the enemy had. How to reduce his numbers faster than he reduced yours. In the end, the only issue was efficiency.

Hand on the crank, Kenan swiveled the cool gun.

Efficiency.

The rotating drum, ten barrels strapped into a wheel and geared to the hand crank, was the key to its efficiency: as the barrels revolved, one was loaded, another fired, and another ejected its spent shell. Each barrel fired only once in ten shots, so it never got hot enough to melt.

Grant had used the old six-barreled Gatling guns against massed Confederate infantry at Petersburg and Richmond. Kenan had heard their stuttering fire above the yells and musket volleys, above even the artillery. Plain slaughter, men charging into that.

Only 250 rounds per minute, those obsolete Gatlings.

At San Juan Hill, Teddy Roosevelt's young lieutenants had turned the thing into an offensive weapon. They mounted the guns on light two-wheeled carriages and rushed them forward along with the general charge, stopping long enough to fire a magazine or two, then advancing again. He had talked to Rough Riders who had been there. The spigs had been blasted out of fortified trenches, killed behind wooden barricades thick as railroad ties. The Rough Riders said they'd never seen anything like it.

Kenan stood in the wagon feeling the sure, deadly weight of the gun, wondering if his dream would return tonight.

In the dream, he had been standing in this wagon exactly the way he was now. Two spirited horses were hitched in the doubletree, reins held tight by a groom in blue. Nobody else was in the wagon with him. It was parked in the middle of a street he didn't recognize—run-down shiplap houses, unpainted shotgun shacks, board fences with gaps like missing teeth.

Up the street surged a din of voices, but he could see no one. The light was very bad—a cloudy light that dimmed and flared, as if fires were being struck and damped. He squinted into the gloom. The voices grew louder, sounded closer—the low, menacing groundswell of a mob. Still, he could see no one.

He leaned over his Gatling gun, wondering—in the dream—where the troops were: Walker Taylor, the State Guards, the Naval Reserves, the Light Infantry.

All at once, the mob was upon him. It rushed toward him in a breaking wave, swelling the street, scraping against fences, overrunning front stoops. He looked down—the people were so jammed together they seemed to have no bodies, only faces. Their faces stared up at him, howling, mouths open, spittle flying from their red tongues.

At first, they were all Negroes—hideous, living caricatures, grotesque African masks, noses flared, eyes white with rage. His hand started the crank. The gun warmed. The fast muzzle flashes blinded him. He swept the sea of faces, hosed the crowd away like the firemen hosed the rats out of Sprunts' warehouse every spring. The faces burst, the bodies disintegrated, the crowd was washed away in a red and black smear.

But then, as he yanked out the empty hopper and slapped a full one into the receiver, the mob surged back. Again, he cranked the gun, spraying an arc of fire and lead into the faces.

And, in the dream, the faces were suddenly transformed into those of his children and Mary, blotted out before he could stop the crank. In the dream, his hand was riveted to the crank—there were literal rivets running through his knuckles into the brass handle. The crank was turning by itself now, as if driven by a strong motor, pulling his hand along with it, faster and faster, till he thought the bones would rip loose from his elbow, the sinew tear from his shoulder.

Into this killing field rushed the faces of his friends, his neighbors, men and women he had known for thirty years, boys he had grown up with, his comrades from the old regiment, his brothers, Tom and Jimmy. He could not stop. The crank turned so fast now it was just a bright blur. Ranks of faces thronged into view and then erupted, disappeared.

Last to storm the wagon was a rank of pumpkin heads—jack-o'-lantern faces. They burst apart, and their straw bodies fluttered to the street, weightless as feathers.

In the dream, he closed his eyes, willing it away. The gun at last stopped firing. When he opened his eyes, he was standing alone, naked except for boots, in a dogwood-shaded alley of Oakdale Cemetery. The wagon, the gun, the horses, the groom, the carnage of the mob—all were gone. In his ears rang a pulsing stillness of night birds and cicadas.

Before him under a full moon rose a low, grassy hill, fenced in black iron spikes. Stone steps led to the top. He recognized the place. He walked slowly up the hill, feeling an immense gravity settling in his chest. His boots might have been filled with cement. Among the low sepulchers stood an obelisk—bone marble, tall as a mounted man.

He stepped forward into the gloom and read the inscription, chiseled sharp as a saber cut: *William Rand Kenan 1845–1903.*
In the dream, he simply lay down at the foot of the obelisk, head to the warm stone, and stared at the moon while his body evaporated.

That was not even the end of the dream. As he lay there in the family plot, he could hear footsteps approaching, feel the shadows of people standing over him, hear their faint whispering.

But he was already gone, leaving behind on the hill only his name and the bare numbers of his lifetime.

He had awakened from the dream feeling curiously refreshed and calm, the muslin sheets cool against his naked body. He slept naked only when Mary was away. He could not call it a nightmare, not at the moment of waking. Sunlight was pouring through his window. For the first time in many years, he had overslept.

He had gotten up slowly, touching his legs, his arms, the muscles in his back, shoulders, chest. He had pulled on white athletic clothes and walked downstairs to lift dumbbells.

Now, Kenan climbed down from the wagon and secured the

tailgate. His cigar had gone out, and he didn't bother to relight it. Suddenly, he was afraid of being caught. He felt vaguely aware that it was wrong for him to be here. He couldn't say for sure what code he was violating, but he breathed the wrongness of where he was like atmosphere.

Quickly and neatly, he hauled the tarpaulin over the gun and tied it down. Before he went out, he listened. Through the barn wall, he heard horses nickering in the stables. Outside, he heard the cluck of boot heels on brick paving, men's voices, laughter. He held his breath until they passed.

It was clear to him: the gun had a soul. It wanted to be fired. It had a hunger for human targets.

A few minutes of brisk walking brought him home, where he spent the rest of the afternoon playing with the puppies, talking nonsense to his old dog, Dandy.

Early the next evening, Gray Ellen sat on the porch of their rented house with her landlady, Callie Register, a woman her own age who seemed more like a dowdy aunt. "My true name is Calliope," she'd confided to Gray Ellen when she rented the house—pronouncing it to rhyme with cantaloupe, in the manner of circus people. "Can you imagine—naming your only daughter after a steam organ?" She had a hearty, shrill laugh. "My parents met in the cheap seats of Dan Castello's Circus and Menagerie when it came to Kenansville. They sat through every show. When the circus left town, they left with it." She said there were Registers all over the county, white and black, cousins and strangers.

Sam had gone off to a so-called gentlemen's evening at Captain Kenan's. The sky was smeared yellow and pink through the trees. From time to time, a buggy passed along the street. The women were wrapped in knitted shawls against the chill. In a few minutes, it would be too cold to sit out any longer, and Gray Ellen would face the decision of whether to invite Callie inside the house. She didn't want to.

If Callie had been one of the girls she'd known in Philadelphia, somebody she could truly confide in, she might welcome the company. Callie was kind, obliging, generous. *Nice*. She encouraged Gray Ellen, cheered her up on bad days, brought her gossip and news. But she never knew when to leave.

Look how hard on people I've become, Gray Ellen reflected with a sudden small shame. It confused her to think she was no longer the kind of person she herself might seek out for company. These days, she had an edge. She was preoccupied, self-absorbed in a way that was strange to her nature. Even hateful at times. She couldn't help it. She didn't want to be, but she was. She was losing control.

Callie sat heavily in her chair, hands absently rubbing her swollen belly. "I wish Farley would get back," she said. With the baby getting closer, she was fretting.

She was afraid, Gray Ellen understood. Callie's last two babies had miscarried. In Callie's company, Gray Ellen's secret calamity always seemed diminished, and she resented it. She had a right to her special grief. Callie reminded her that the world just kept on spinning. Every woman had her own grief, and none was so very special. "Don't fret. He'll show up any day now."

Callie's husband, Farley, worked for the Atlantic Coastline as a track boss. His crew was down in South Carolina clearing a wreck—half a mile of freight train piled into a river. He'd been gone a month already. On-site, he lived out of a boxcar that he shared with a dozen other hands, sleeping on bunks and cooking over a sooty potbelly stove. Men, Gray Ellen thought, how they loved being part of a gang. Even a work gang. Even sleeping in an unheated boxcar and laboring sixteen hours a day for wages that would wind up in a bottle or the company store. What was the magnetism of gangs?

"I used to like it he was gone so much. I liked it that the house got so quiet and peaceful, I could walk from room to room and just listen to the peace. Then after the boys came along, it wasn't quiet anymore." She had twins, nasty little gangsters who chased cats and trampled flower beds and who everybody said took after Farley. But Farley was a gangly hillbilly from Boone, and the boys, at the age of eight, were already fat and white as milk. Their muscles had no tone—the bloat sagged off their arms and legs like soft cheese. Because there were two of them, they were bullies. Callie had left them next door alone.

"You want a boy or girl?" Gray Ellen asked.

"Don't matter. Whichever, this one's gonna be the quits."

"Pray for a girl. They've got more sense."

Callie laughed. "Ain't it the truth."

The light was fading and the chill seeped through her shawl, but Gray Ellen wanted to stay outside as long as possible. She felt sorry for Callie, but at least Callie belonged here. At least she was home. Two months in this place, and Gray Ellen still felt locked out, except at school. Still, whenever she tried to explain that to Callie, the only advice she got was, "Give it time, honey. You'll make your peace with this town."

But Gray Ellen didn't want to make her peace with any town. She wanted to be home, wherever that was. She wanted to love the place where she set down her roots. What was it Ivanhoe Grant had said that first time at Williston School, as she passed him on her way out after her interview?

You got to be where you live.

She lived here, but she wasn't here. It could be so lovely, especially along the river at dawn, or on the beach at sundown, bathing in the sea breeze. So why couldn't she love this place? She felt vaguely guilty about it. Whenever people asked her how she was settling in, she'd smile and say something pretty. But it didn't feel pretty. It felt hard. It felt lonely. She wondered if there was something wrong with her.

She'd given up trying to bare her soul to Callie. Callie would have her baby and, whatever she pretended, probably another three or four after that. She'd sit on her porch pining for a husband who, as the years wore on, would come home less and less. Like the tugboat crews, the river pilots, the drummers, the guardsmen, the sailors, the railroad engineers, all the other traveling men, ingenious with excuses to stay away from home.

Like Sam taking that assignment to cover the war in Cuba. And now, already, Sam was working two nights a week at the office. Now he had a new buddy, one of the men who had taken him out on the river the other day—the captain from the train. What was he getting mixed up with all these military types for? He was starting to do things she couldn't predict.

He was keeping company with Colonel Waddell, coming home with stories of the War. Whenever he spoke of Waddell, she could hear the adulation in his voice. And now he was toting a revolver.

He wasn't drinking, he'd remind her. As if that made up for everything.

"I best be getting back—round up the boys and scrub 'em down for bed," Callie said, and waddled across the lawn in the twilight, looking weary, moving slow.

She feels sorry for me, Gray Ellen thought. It made her want to weep.

At least that Negro preacher didn't feel sorry for her. Sure, he'd tricked her, but it was a kind of game. Somehow, he must figure that she counted, that her opinion could sway others. Of all the men in this town, Ivanhoe Grant had singled her out for attention. Not just as the wife of the cousin of Hugh MacRae, but for herself. Something in her nettled him, and he was out to convert her.

Maybe I should have let him kiss me, she thought. She felt illicit just thinking about it. Maybe she should have called his bluff, felt what it was like to fall into another man's arms right on a public street.

What would it have turned into later? A session of sweating sex in a run-down boardinghouse with a Negro man she half-despised, when she couldn't even face her own husband's tentative caresses? Was it wrong for her to want another man's hands on her? Was it just to get back at Sam? Or was there something else she longed for that Sam couldn't give her, some reckless passion she had never allowed herself?

She wasn't thinking in words, or even ideas, but in pictures, smells, the imagined touch of flesh. It scared her worse than a ghost story—and thrilled her the same way.

Was it just because he was a Negro, the object of every taboo she had ever learned? She shouldn't be thinking about this, she knew. Her heart beat faster just conjuring the fantasy. And what you envisioned for yourself—even as a remote fantasy—had a way of coming true. So her mother had warned.

Gray Ellen tucked her shawl tighter around her shoulders. She would sit out a little while longer, feel the night breeze blow silky on her cheek, imagine what people were doing at that moment in Chicago and Philadelphia and New York, out in the world.

At the door, Captain William Rand Kenan flung an arm around Sam and ushered him into the house. "Come on in, sport," Kenan said. Sam was pleased to be included. He liked the feel of Kenan's big arm draped across his back.

Colonel Walker Taylor stood, his back to the hall mirror, sipping red wine. Sam could see his bald spot reflected like a coin. He nodded in Sam's direction.

"You know Walk?" Kenan asked.

"Of course," Sam said.

Taylor quickstepped over and flung up his hand like a railroad semaphore. He made even Kenan look small. "You do nice work, Mr. Jenks."

"Very good of you to say so."

A clergyman holding a generous tumbler of bourbon got up from a chair. "Peyton Hoge," he said without smiling.

"Pastor Hoge is at First Presbyterian," Kenan said. "And here's Tom James. Captain James." A tall, well-built man of about forty shook Sam's hand. "Tom commands the Wilmington Light Infantry."

Captain James smiled ruefully at Sam, as if embarrassed. "Pretty tame stuff, compared to the action you saw in Cuba."

"Well, you know. It was a lot of noise and confusion, mostly." To change the subject, he said to Kenan, "Quite a show you put on, out there on the river." He figured Kenan would be eager to talk about it.

Kenan said dismissively, "A fine piece of ordnance. Let me get you a drink."

"Oh, just water will be fine."

Kenan paused, squinted, then understood completely. There were plenty of men who didn't have that kind of control. His estimation of Sam jumped a notch. Generally, newspapermen were physically timid, nuisances in the middle of action, men who'd never turn down somebody else's whiskey. Except the best ones—Steve Crane, Dick Davis. He'd heard Jenks had been with Roosevelt's army at San Juan Hill, and he wanted to hear about it. He had noted Sam's reaction on the river—how his jaw set, how alertly he watched everything, how his eyes never blinked. He didn't scurry to write it down. He wasn't scared. He just paid attention.

"How about root beer instead?"

"Even better."

Kenan thrust a sweating glass of root beer into Sam's hand. "Plenty of vittles on the sideboard," Kenan said. "We tend to be rather informal."

Other young men arrived. By the time they settled in to eat at the polished mahogany table in the dining room, there were a dozen guests. Though they had all arrived dressed in suits and ties, before long they took off their jackets, rolled up their sleeves, and opened their collars. They drank liberally and ate with gusto. Seated at one end of the table, Sam noticed how erectly the men—except for Pastor Hoge—sat to their meal, practicing a kind of barracks discipline. They were rowdy and colorful in their language, cursing freely even in front of the reverend, but they never lost the bearing of soldiers. Sam liked them. He liked being here among them. They seemed to think he belonged.

Among these men, he could almost believe he was as brave as they thought he was.

Kenan sat at the head of the table, beaming. A stout colored woman named Hattie tended the sideboard, carrying out newly cooked dishes of quail, venison, and rabbit. Kenan joshed with her and she scolded him right back and they both laughed. She adored him, that was clear. Sam hadn't felt this warm sense of exuberant well-being since the last time he'd drunk himself into jail.

"My boy writes me from Mexico," Kenan said. "Building a hydroelectric dam down there, you know. Has the damnedest time finding reliable men."

"Native labor," somebody said.

Walker Taylor said, "Well, we routed the spigs from Cuba," and winked at Sam. "We're sweeping through the Philippines. I suppose we'll be going into Guadalajara next."

"About time."

"Kipling had it right," the Reverend Hoge said. " 'Take up the White Man's Burden—and reap his old reward.' "

Kenan finished the verse: " 'The blame of those ye better, the hate of those ye guard.' "

"Hear, hear."

"The limeys didn't have Gatling guns, did they? Maybe they'd have done better," one of the young men said, and the others laughed.

Kenan glared at him. Sam was impressed by how suddenly, by his mere presence, he could take command.

"I just meant—"

"Never mind, son," Kenan said, back to his avuncular self. Turning that meat grinder on men, he thought. He said, "In the old days, it was different. Man to man. When you aimed your gun at a man, well, it was different."

Sam recalled the story he'd heard—Kenan taking a potshot at President Lincoln. Had any president ever died in battle? A lone man, the man sitting at the head of this table, had come within inches of ending the greatest American war in history. With a single shot. He might have been the most famous man in the world.

"Times are changing," Walker Taylor observed. "The twentieth century will be the golden age of American technology. I can remember when we didn't even have telephones in this town."

"Pretty soon, we'll have flying machines," said one of the young men. "There was an article in *Collier's.*"

"We already have balloons."

"Not balloons—actual machines," the young man persisted. "Winged aeroplanes. Can you imagine a machine that can soar over the heads of troops? Can you imagine if you mounted a Gatling gun on that? My God, one crew could command a whole battlefield." His eyes shone with the glimmer of a true believer who had never been under fire.

"You're dreaming," Captain James said. "We're years away from that. Decades away. Maybe another whole century. And machines are just machines. It still comes down to the man. His integrity. What he's able to do. What he's willing to do."

Kenan pondered that. In his dream, his will had not been able to command the machine. The machine had taken on a will of its own. This twentieth century was frightening. He wasn't sure it would have any use for a man like him. His son, he was the man of the future—a man who could control the machines.

For the next hour, they refought the great battles of the War of Secession: Lee should not have ordered Pickett to charge suicidally at Gettysburg, wiping out all those North Carolina boys; Grant could have been outflanked in the swamps of Vicksburg, if anybody had suspected he'd advance from that direction; Fort Fisher could have held out forever, even against ten thousand Yankees, if only General Braxton Bragg had acted decisively in the early, crucial hours of battle.

Sam listened intently, hoping to hear the secret of what made men courageous. And then he told them all about San Juan Hill, where he had never been.

After dinner, they went out into the backyard and arm-wrestled across a plank table. Kenan rolled up his sleeves and beat five of the young men in succession.

"Old Iron Bill," Sergeant Alton Lockamy said.

"Indestructible," agreed the young men, grinning.

Sam wondered what Kenan was trying to prove.

They took turns pissing into the oleanders along the board fence. Kenan woke the puppies and showed them off. The Reverend Hoge got very drunk and left quite suddenly. Walker Taylor drank very little and kept pulling out his gold watch.

Sam wondered what Gray Ellen was doing. He checked his own watch—almost ten o'clock. He wanted to stay, but he felt he should go. Just a few minutes longer. He wasn't drinking. This was good company. She would understand.

Inside again, they all smoked cigars. Sam took one from Kenan. A couple of the young men drifted away. At eleven, Walker Taylor went out as if he had somewhere else to go. At midnight, Captain James left. Realizing he was the only one still sitting in the parlor, Sam got up to leave also.

"Stay a minute," Kenan said, putting a firm hand on his arm.

"I should get home. It's already much later—"

"Yes, I know. But tell me, what was your reason for going out on the river?"

"Reason? I didn't have any reason." Hugh dragged me over there and gave me a pistol, he thought. "It was an assignment. I had no idea."

Kenan nodded, his face florid with liquor. His moustache bristled silver. "Yes, of course. I should have realized."

Sam recalled Frank Manly's livid face glaring up at him.

"It's a strange thing," Kenan went on. "People—civilians—think of military men as bloodthirsty killers. Craving battle, mayhem. Can't wait for it all to start, they think."

He stopped talking and focused his red eyes on Sam. Sam felt trapped: what was he expected to say? What did Kenan want to hear?

Kenan had drunk quite a lot, more than he had intended. It was Mary's being away, rattling around this empty house all day. The dream. "But we know better. We've been there, eh?"

"Right," Sam said.

Kenan smiled, realizing how drunk he must be to be badgering the poor fellow like this. Thing was, Jenks reminded him of his own boy. Not in his appearance—Bill Junior was far more handsome—but in his manner, how he paid attention to things. How he looked awhile, saw what was what and who was who, before he made up his mind. Most men nowadays didn't pay any damned attention. They were born with all the right answers. Never bothered to ask the questions. As the century came to a close, it seemed to Kenan, the world was spinning faster and faster. It was hard to keep up. Hard not to lose your head. Hard not to go along with the machine men.

When the century turned—what would happen then? Would it just spin out of control and unravel? The tombstone in his dream had read *1903*. Not possible.

He needed his own boy with him now. His time was running out. He didn't believe in dreams. Hysterical women with too-tight corsets were the ones who had morbid dreams, fretting over the melodrama. But he believed in this dream. The next century didn't belong to him. He wanted to do things right from now on, not make any more mistakes. He wanted to hand things over to his boy in good order, but he was afraid the order was coming apart. Gettysburg didn't matter anymore. Whether Pickett did or didn't charge. In the next war, it would just be machines anyway.

Why hadn't he made that shot at Fort Stevens? Of all the shots of his life—the turkeys he had won, the deer he had dropped, the pickets and artillery spotters he had picked off—why had he missed that single shot?

The most famous shot of his life—a miss.

But it wasn't a miss, not exactly. His heart hadn't been in the shot. President Lincoln was unarmed. He wore no uniform. His stovepipe hat stuck up above the parapet, an unmistakable target. He stood still as a post, staring straight toward the Confederate position. The man next to him squinted over the sights of a musket, and Kenan's shot killed him. He had felt the arc of his bullet flying into the soldier's face as if it were on a string. The president had never even ducked.

If only Lincoln had borrowed a rifle, taken a sporting potshot at the advancing skirmishers.

There was a lot to remember about those days, a lot to keep track of. Memories accumulated weight with the years. Things kept adding on. A man had to be careful to keep his center, remember what he stood for. He had missed, but he had not dishonored himself. Leave that to assassins like John Wilkes Booth. A man should face his enemy, take his chances.

Kenan didn't want to be alone tonight. What if the dream came back? If Jenks could stay awhile, they could have another cigar.

"Got to be going, Captain," Sam said. "It's been a pleasure."

Kenan nodded and shuffled toward the door. When he opened it to let Sam out, the night rushed in cool and full of sound. Things were happening out there, he knew. Men were meddling with the order. His boy was in Mexico building a dam. In the barn behind the armory, the gun was waiting, cool and silent, the ugliest open secret in town.

He poured himself another whiskey and sat up till the windows went light, listening to the clamor of the empty house, waiting for his wife to come home. At dawn, he slept and dreamed of Mexico, a chatter of voices in Spanish, an ocean breeze, horses cantering in the surf, the tropical sun warm on his weary face.

Walker Taylor took the block and a half to Third Street in long strides. He turned north another two blocks to First Presbyterian Church. With a key, he let himself in a back door, leaving it unlocked behind him. When he lectured Sunday school in the community hall of this church, as many as a hundred people would gather to listen. Boys and girls, but also full-grown men. Rough men. He could talk to them all.

Here was the place he had started his Boys Brigade—saving bad boys from falling into the gutter. Every July, he took them to Camp George, at the mouth of the river, near Southport. Only the boys who attended four weeks of lessons in a row were allowed to go. The boys adored him. They slept in tents and fished off the beach and told stories around driftwood campfires. They came home lean and brown, their little souls sturdier. He did it for them. They were his mission.

In the sacristy, Walker Taylor waited in the dark.

Within minutes, the other men drifted in: Fennell, Beery, Meares, Robertson, Smith. Walker Taylor lit a beeswax candle. It smelled sweet in the musty air.

"Rountree did a fine job procuring the thing," Beery said. "Quite a show on the river."

"It stays at the armory," Walker Taylor said. "The Wilmington Light Infantry have charge of it."

"But as commander of the State Guard—"

Walker Taylor nodded. "Right. In a crisis, they answer to me."

Fennell said, "I don't like Dan Russell coming down here to give a goddamn speech." Nobody said anything, but they all were embarrassed by cursing in the sacristy. "Nor Dockery, nor Pritchard."

"I don't see what we can do," Walker Taylor said. "It's a free country."

Fennell persisted. "But it will stir everybody up before it's time."

"Maybe we should just give our own speech," Smith said.

"Who could set the right tone?" Beery said. "It would have to be the right tone."

"Get 'em riled up, but keep the lid on."

"Right," Walker Taylor said. "Let me talk to George. He mentioned someone."

"Waddell," Beery said. "That old warhorse. That's who he wants."

Walker Taylor said, "We'll see. We'll just see."

"I like it," Smith said. "He can put fire in their bellies."

"He'll give us a stemwinder," Robertson said, "if anybody can do it."

"Man can hold a crowd," Beery said. "You better believe it."

Meares, who had not yet spoken, said, "You're playing with fire."

Beery said, "You want Colonel Taylor to be mayor, don't you? Isn't that what we want?"

The men all agreed that this was so.

"We've got to push," Beery said. "Not too hard, but not too soft, either."

Walker Taylor thought about being mayor. A man could accomplish a lot of good for people. In this town, a lot of things needed doing. He could do them—he and his army of good boys. "We've got to keep the Red Shirts in line," he said.

Fennell said, "They'll come in damned useful on Election Day."

Walker Taylor said, "Now, you listen to me. We're not vigilantes. We are defenders of the civil order."

"Men in this town want to work," Beery said. "White men. Mike Dowling is their hero."

"He's an out-of-work house painter."

"Nobody's hiring nigrahs anymore," Meares said.

Fennell said, "Nobody's firing 'em fast enough, either. This thing's going to go off."

Walker Taylor said, "Don't spoil the larger plan."

"Less than a month," somebody said.

"Can we rely on Kenan, when the time comes?" Beery said.

Walker Taylor gave him a look that made him sorry he'd asked.

"Will Colonel Davis interfere?" someone said. Charles Davis was acting adjutant general of the State Guard—Colonel Taylor's superior.

Walker Taylor said, "I have assurances that he will authorize a local solution."

The men nodded.

Walker Taylor said, "George will be around to collect money from each of you for the Businessmen's Committee. We have certain debts. He estimates we will need to raise about thirty thousand dollars. Encourage your colleagues to be generous."

They nodded and murmured. Things were getting accomplished. They'd already seen what they were getting for their money.

Beery said, "Solly Fishblate keeps sniffing around."

"Absolutely not," Walker Taylor said.

"What do I tell him?"

"Tell him he had his chance. He's permanently retired from politics."

"He'll keep his people from—"

"The people we need are sitting in this room. The people we need are on the Businessmen's Committee. We're trying to form a government, not a mob."

Fennell said, "What's the difference?"

"The difference is *law*," Walker Taylor said, his voice too big for the sacristy. "The difference is *order*. The difference is that we must be able to feel morally proud when it's over. We must be able to answer with a clear conscience those who will judge our actions a hundred years from now."

Fennell said, "Like I said, what's the difference?"

*The race question, which might be possibly
soluble without great trouble were all negroes all
negro, becomes a sociological problem of awful
possibility when we consider that miscegenation
has made and is making inroads into the Cauca-
sian race in this country to an extent little realized
by the masses of people.*

New York Times,
August 18, 1900

CHAPTER NINE

Saturday, October 15

THE WORD WAS OUT: no Negroes need apply.

The White Government Union had appointed a Labor Bureau to
find jobs for white men only. All employers had to hire through the
bureau or face the consequences. Hugh MacRae, the Businessmen's
Committee, and the Wilmington Light Infantry stood behind the
bureau with all their guns and law.

On the street corners of Brooklyn, boys passed out handbills.
"Mind your jobs, Negro workingmen," the handbills said in part.
"Stay out of politics. Don't vote, or else."

Or else what? Alex Manly wondered. How far would they go?
Frank Manly said they'd go as far as they had to: guns, shooting,

vigilantes in the streets. Alex wasn't convinced—he'd heard the rhetoric before. If they meant to act, they wouldn't be talking so much. They were clearly bluffing. This wasn't the era of the Ku Klux Klan, with midnight rides and lynchings at every country crossroads. This was a new day. Alex Manly had watched it come in. He'd written words that had coaxed it along. He was the daily voice of a whole people who had been silent far too long. It was a station worth guarding.

And the *Record* was finally beginning to turn a profit. That—not political rhetoric—was the true measure of the sea change, in this town and in cities all over the South. Negroes were at last becoming an economic force. The value of their skilled labor and the power of their pocketbooks would guarantee them greater and greater freedom. Bigotry didn't have a chance against the dollar.

Carrie had written him from London—all good news and gushing success. He reread the letter three times, not for the words but for the fair curve of her hand, the elegant, looping signature of an irresistible woman. He carried it in his pocket all day. If he closed his eyes, he could hear her full, throaty voice, see the broad Tuscarora Indian features that made her face so beautiful to him. Feeling confident again, he ventured out-of-doors alone to attend a meeting called by the Reverend Kirk to calm the jitters of the Negro community.

Six blocks straight uphill from the train station, five blocks north of Hugh MacRae's mansion, gaslights were burning at Central Baptist Church. The Reverend J. Allen Kirk, D.D., was vainly trying to bring his boisterous congregation under control. It wasn't his usual congregation. The church was packed with more men than he had ever seen—men whose wives and daughters and mothers were his usual flock, other men he had never seen before, rough men from the cotton mills, occasional laborers, brothers and cousins from the country, even a few troublemakers up from Charleston and Atlanta. The walls shuddered with the sheer press of human muscle. The heated air wavered over their heads, holding the mutter of troubled voices.

The floorboards flexed under the weight. The whole building

seemed to expand and contract with the great collective breathing of the congregation. The building was alive, moving, the flimsy container of a great frightened soul. In all his years of preaching the gospel of the Lord, he had never seen anything like it. Here was the active presence of grace in the world, the physical yearning for salvation, thundering hearts and sweating palms, tearful eyes and a hollow ache in the stomach.

They all felt it. He felt it. God was hovering over his congregation tonight. The Holy Ghost sheltered them under his brilliant wings. He smiled and took a deep breath, then another. The Holy Ghost would give him the words. He would trust to faith to tell them what they needed to hear.

The Reverend Kirk stood in the center of the chancel and listened, holding up one hand for silence. The noise went on.

The Reverend Kirk looped the stole over his high collar and marched to the pulpit with it fluttering as a crimson stripe against his brushed black suit. The pulpit was a little platform raised three steps above the level of the congregation. He solemnly climbed the steps and bowed his head, then lifted his arms in a stiff V, palms out to signify, once again, silence. The murmuring continued longer than he liked. "Brothers and sisters," he began. There was still some muttering in the back. A boot banged against a wooden pew. "Brothers and sisters, let us pray to Jesus."

But before he could say anything more, a tall figure in gray swooped into the chancel from a side door and began to speak. "We can talk to Jesus by and by!" the gray preacher, Ivanhoe Grant, shouted. His voice had a high melody to it. The shout soared over their heads and hung there, resonating against the pulse of the congregation.

The Reverend Kirk could feel their eyes turning toward the interloper. He opened his mouth, but the words he heard were Ivanhoe Grant's.

"Before we talk to *Jee*-sus, we got to talk to each other. *Jee*-sus doesn't want to hear us whine and wail and bawl like little babies in the crib. *Jee*-sus wants us to settle our business. *Jee*-sus wants us to help ourselves!"

The responses were tentative, muted.

"Amen."

"That's the word."

"Help ourselves, Lord Jesus."

The Reverend Kirk said, "What right have you to come in here—?"

Grant turned on him with fury. "I am a preacher of the Lord! I have been called to preach to my people in their hour of trial!"

"Tell the word."

"Preaching in the hour of trial."

The Reverend Kirk felt the soul of his congregation escaping him. He could not hold them. He stood in the pulpit, nonplussed. Ivanhoe Grant was glowing. He stalked the chancel, and his whole body shone with a nimbus of light. Even Kirk could not take his eyes off him. All he could think was that it must be some sort of evil trick.

"I'm talking about *earthly* business, friends. The work of this world."

"Tell about the work!"

"We all working for the Lord!"

Grant clasped his hands, bowed his head, and whispered so that they had to strain in absolute stillness to hear. "There is no more work."

Then he said it louder: "There is no more work."

Then he thundered it into their faces: "There is no more work!" They shrank back. "The *man* has taken away your work."

"The man!"

"Pity the workingman!"

The Reverend Kirk said, "Now hold on, don't go stirring up—"

"Ah, yes!" Grant turned on him again, hissing. "Lower your eyes, boy. Yassuh, boss. No suh, cap'n. I don't be needin' no work, boss!"

"They're not firing anybody," Kirk said. "Listen to me."

Ivanhoe Grant let loose a caterwauling laugh. "Of course they aren't firing anybody—not yet! You think the man can run his own mills? You think he can lay a straight course of bricks? You think he can stand up under twelve hours on the wharf that would kill a plow mule? They've got to keep some of us, or the city will fall apart. It's a simple matter of good *business*."

"Say the word, preacher."

"Keep this city keeping on."

Grant seemed to grow in stature as he talked. Kirk watched the man's back—it was as if he were inflating.

"Now, the *businessmen* of this community—the *white* businessmen of this city—made a proclamation today: no Negroes need apply. All new jobs will go to whites. The *strategy* is to replace us one by one. Man by man. Black man dies, white man take his place."

"Amen."

"Black man quits, white man take his place."

"Amen."

"Black man injured *on the job*, white man take his place."

"Black man fired—"

"White man take his place!"

"White man!"

"We losing that job!"

Ivanhoe Grant turned to stone and let them mutter, signify, testify, even shout, for a long minute. Then he held up one finger and the place quieted instantly. The gaslamps hissed.

The Reverend Kirk burned with envy and humiliation.

"Plenty of black men working," Grant whispered. "Plenty of black men got good jobs. Earn a pay envelope. Raise a family. Pay for the groceries. Pay for the streetcar. Pay for the gas company. Buy a dress for the wife, shoes for the little children. Plenty of black men working."

"Working, that's the truth."

"Plenty of good providers. Taxpayers. God-fearing men with quick minds and noble hearts and strong backs and nimble hands." His whisper had a soothing quality, like honey and whiskey on a sore throat.

He walked away from them, far back into the shadows until he all but disappeared. Some thought he had left. Kirk couldn't see him. Men in the back row stood up. The gaslamps whispered along the walls.

Suddenly, out of the shadows, the voice exploded at them: "But they dare not *vote!*" A woman in the front pew toppled into the arms of her neighbors. Grant strode forward, arriving in their midst with miraculous speed. His great voice filled the church like an organ. "Any black man who votes! Any black man who exercises his rights as a citizen and votes!" He flew out of the chancel, swung into a pew, and leaped up onto the seat, suddenly ten feet tall. An old, bent woman scrambled out of his way. "*That* man will be cast out! That man will be fired!"

"Word, preacher, word!"

"Can't vote in our own homeplace!"

While they shouted their anger, Ivanhoe Grant climbed down from the bench, threw off his coat, and approached the pulpit. The Reverend Kirk stared at him, trembling. I will not surrender my pulpit, Kirk thought, but he was already stepping down the three short steps, mesmerized.

He leaped into the pulpit—Ivanhoe Grant in his boiled white shirtsleeves, his arms raised in a stiff V, but his hands bent and loose at the ends of his cuffs, so that now he seemed to have wings. He appeared as an avenging angel poised over the congregation.

They quieted. Their eyes stared like birds' eyes, glassy and expectant. He said softly, "Let me tell you a story."

"Amen," they said. "Tell the story, brother."

"A stranger comes to town."

"Tell about the stranger."

"This was years ago. Before the War of Emancipation. Before Father Abraham. Before Reconstruction. Before this place was anyplace."

"In olden times," the bent crone in the front row said, "when prophets walked the land."

"Amen, sister."

He paused, watched their eyes, nodded. "A stranger comes to town. He is not alone. Six brothers, traveling together."

They knew this story. They whispered this story to their children when they misbehaved. They told it as a ghost story on windy nights camping by the river, as owls streaked through the swampy darkness and old, slimy bottom dwellers splashed out of the water to steal a hooded glance at the moon.

"They were no criminals," he said. "They were good men."

"Good men."

"Good men and godly."

"Godly men."

"Men who had cast off the yoke of slavery. Freedmen under the law."

"Free by law."

"Family men, looking for a job of work."

"Looking for a job."

"They were hauled to the marketplace like common criminals." His voice quavered. "The way Jesus was hauled before Pilate. And the Pharisees of this city judged them not by the laws of God but by the laws of hatred and fear."

"Pharisees, umh, umh!"

Ivanhoe Grant stood rigid, head bowed, eyes downcast, his voice silken, seamless. "And what was the sentence for being a black man in this town on that night?" He swept his eyes over them and breathed a single word: "Death."

Nobody spoke. He closed his eyes in a rapture of pain.

"The Pharisees put them to death. One by one. On the banks of the brown river that flows through this city and empties its sorrow into the sea. The river of fear."

He opened his eyes and fixed his gaze on all of them at once. Every man and woman was sure Ivanhoe Grant was staring into his or her private soul, the place where their sins stood clustered like canned goods on a shelf, labeled by weight and size and brand. They held their breath. Nobody said anything—they knew when to listen for the breath of the Holy Ghost. They wanted to hear it. If they held their breath long enough, straining their ears, there it was: in the fluttering of their own hearts.

Ivanhoe Grant said, "They cut off their heads." It was difficult to go on. He could feel the hot blade on his own neck. "They mounted the heads along the roads, as they mounted Jesus on the cross on the hill above Jerusalem."

"Amen," they said quietly.

He was clearly suffering. "On the hill of Calvary."

"Calvary, Lord, Lord."

"To warn against troublemakers. To keep the people down. But the people cannot be kept down. The people will rise!"

"Amen!"

"The people will rise on the wings of the Holy Ghost!"

"Amen!" they said more vigorously.

"Six strangers came to town. Their names are lost to history. The thieves crucified beside Jesus had names, but these black strangers had no names."

"No names."

That was part of the story they all knew, the part that made it folklore and not real truth.

"Except one." He held up a shining finger, straight as a blade. The silence was absolute. He waited for it to become intolerable. "Daniel John Grant," he whispered finally. "My father's father. My own blood kin."

The effect was electric. Alex Manly, standing in the back beside the door, could feel the energy crackle along the pews, leap the empty spaces, arcing distance. It crackled along his sleeves like static. It made the congregation buzz and murmur. So the story was true—not just a jack tale of haints and bogeymen and night spirits. If one of the men had a name, then the story was true. Now, all at once—now that it had really happened—it gained power. It loomed larger in their imaginations. It took on new meaning.

In one stroke, Ivanhoe Grant had altered entire childhoods, changed the story they lived by.

Alex Manly was amazed. The knowledge of what he had just heard struck his stomach like a bullet. His old fear returned. Something was possible that had not been possible a moment ago. He had been wrong about the threatening words—they were not empty. They were the voice of the bogeyman, and he was waiting for an answer.

Ivanhoe Grant lifted his long, beautiful arms and declared, "Every man and woman among you—*every* man and woman among you—must stand up and be counted. You cannot turn away from the earthly business of the Lord!"

The place erupted into a chaos of argument and shouting. In the melee, Ivanhoe Grant melted away. The Reverend Kirk mounted the pulpit with the trudging step of a hod carrier and pleaded, "Let us pray." But his voice was lost in the riot of other voices. He stood forlorn, staring out over his congregation, completely beyond him now, anger hard as a pill in his throat. He felt tricked. His sin was the sin of pride. He had deluded himself.

This, tonight, was not the trembling fervor of the Holy Ghost. This was the Other.

Alex Manly was so transfixed that the two Negro Pinkerton men had to shoulder him aside to get out the door. He didn't even notice them. And they were in such a hurry to report to J. Allan Taylor, they didn't recognize him.

———

Sam smelled like the tavern—Gray Ellen noticed it right away. It was in his clothes, in his hair—cigar smoke, stale beer, men. When he kissed her lightly on the cheek, though, there was no stink of whiskey. Thank God, she thought. But how many times could he say no? If he traveled with that Calabash creature very much longer, lingering in taverns and waterfront bars and gentlemen's clubs, sooner or later he was going to give in.

One moment of weakness, that was all it took. How could a woman live twenty-four hours of every day in fear of a single moment that would happen out of her sight, out of her control, a moment that could ruin her life in a swallow? How could she rely on character when, time after time, she had watched character bend so easily?

Sam changed out of his linen suit, which was already looking frayed and overworn, then washed up using a pitcher and bowl. She watched him from behind, how his back flexed each time he lifted his arms to his face. Maybe each time he said no, he grew stronger—was that possible? She didn't really believe it, but she had no choice. Maybe with men character was just habit.

She sat on the edge of the bed watching him. She was all mixed up. She wanted him to touch her without touching her. She wanted to hold him and stroke his hair and neck, bury her face in his strong shoulders and chest and feel his arms wrapping her in safe love.

She wanted him to understand what she was feeling, when she wasn't sure herself. She wanted him to know exactly what he ought to do, though she had no idea what that was.

He stripped his shirt off. She watched his back and thought, without meaning to, of Ivanhoe Grant. Where was he tonight? Whom was he with? A man like that—even a preacher man— surely he was with somebody. Especially a preacher man. *Give me succor in my hour of trial.* What a pitch. It had worked beautifully—made her just indignant enough to call him *nigger*. He'd worked all afternoon to make her say that one word, and she had. She couldn't believe she'd said it—it was a word she never used. Yet she had said it out loud. At the moment she said it, she believed it. It was the truth. It still amazed her. Made her want to knock his teeth out. The arrogance.

Sam stepped out of his trousers and folded them carelessly over a chair back. His white calves were too skinny, but his thighs and buttocks were muscled. The nightshirt fluttered down, covering them. If only he wouldn't turn, she could enjoy watching him. Without his wanting anything from her, without his desire.

But he did turn. All at once, she felt flustered, unsure what to do, as she felt every night now when he came to bed. In her nightdress, she felt naked, almost chilly. Gooseflesh rose on her bare arms. She felt herself coil reflexively, gathering herself inside herself, out of reach. She didn't want to, she just did. She thought of poor, fat Calliope, pining for her white-trash man—what she wouldn't give for a man like Sam. But that didn't help. Knowing didn't help. Feeling was all that mattered.

He stepped over to the bed and took her hand. She stood up as awkwardly as if this were their wedding night. Sam drew her in and hugged her. She told herself not to stiffen, but she did. If he would only wait until she could touch him.

"Look, it's all right," he said. "I'm tired, too."

"I'm not tired."

He sighed—so it was going to be like this. "Harry wanted to talk. I couldn't get away."

"Harry always wants to talk. Doesn't he have a wife?"

Sam loosened his arms around her and stepped back. "He's just an old drunk, he doesn't have anybody." He walked around to the other side of the bed and poured himself half a glass of water from the pitcher on the night table. She watched him drink it in one long gulp, wishing she could start this whole conversation over.

"It's this place," she said softly. "I thought the school would be enough."

"Nothing's ever enough, is it?"

She touched other people. She and Calliope patted each other's arms as they talked, without even noticing. She hugged the children at school, she told him so. She just could not bear to touch him.

"Sometimes," she said. She turned off the lamp and got into bed next to him, not touching.

He could still see her as a dim outline. "I don't know what you want."

The sadness in his tone disarmed her. "It's not what I want. It's figuring out how to get it. That's the hard part."

"I'm trying," he said. "I'm really trying my hardest."

"I know, I know." She shifted on the mattress, moving closer.

There was more to it—he wanted a child now. Suddenly, life seemed desperately short. It seemed vitally important that somebody carry on his name, his blood. Kenan talked about nothing but his son. All the other men had families to carry their lives into the future.

He lay there staring at the ceiling. He listened to her shallow breathing, felt her warm weight on the mattress, pulling him toward the center of the bed. He shifted a leg so he wouldn't accidentally brush her. In his mind's eye, he pictured Gabrielle, basket on her arm, tending her garden. He imagined her sad brown eyes, the fullness of her breasts, the bead of perspiration on her upper lip. How he had wanted to kiss her.

After a few minutes, Gray Ellen said, "Are you asleep?"

"Course not."

"Hold me," she said, and snuggled in under his arm, laying her head on his chest. Her hair smelled wonderful, like honeysuckle.

He stroked her black hair, falling loose on her shoulders. His whole body felt electrified.

"I do love you," she said.

He relaxed. Maybe this was going to be all right, whatever happened. Like the old days. If they could just make love once, then he wouldn't think about it so hard every time she got close. Maybe he should confide in her how much he, too, now wanted a child. Maybe that would make a difference.

"I just want everything to be perfect," he said.

She wriggled free of his arm and leaned over him, looking him in the eye. "It's not perfection that makes a woman fall in love. It's the flaws—that's what wins her heart."

"So a woman falls in love with what's wrong with a man."

"You twist it all up when you say it."

"There's nothing wrong with you."

She lay her head back on his chest and kissed it through his nightshirt. "Oh, there's plenty wrong with me, all right."

No, he thought, only one thing—you can't forget that I left you alone that night. "Nothing we can't fix," he said.

"Start fixing."

"You're sure?"

"Yes." She put her hands under his nightshirt, stroking his thighs and stomach. They kissed, at first brushing lips, tentatively, then holding the kiss. Gently, he touched her breast, kissed the nipple. She touched him, and he moaned in pleasure.

His sound stopped her. In the quiet dark, she could have gone through with it.

"What is it?" he asked.

"Shh," she said. "Don't talk."

"Tell me," he said. "It's all right."

The more he talked, the worse it was. "Don't talk."

He pushed her head back onto the pillow and moved over her. Suddenly, she felt claustrophobic, pinned. She couldn't move her arms. Too fast, she thought, too fast—slow down—but it was no use. Now, the darkness did not soothe her but made her feel even more closed in. She couldn't quite get her breath. What she needed was for something to come out of her, not for something more to go inside her.

"Wait," she said. "Please." She was losing herself—she had to stop before she was gone completely.

"What is it?" He was so worked up he could hardly speak.

"I can't," she whispered. "I'm sorry."

"It's all right," he said. Was she ever going to let him off the hook? Still, she had tried. She wanted to be a good wife.

She touched his cheek and pulled away at the same time. "Soon," she said. "I promise."

"Never mind," he said. He got up from the bed and pulled on his trousers.

"Where are you going?"

"For a walk. I don't think I can sleep just now."

Couldn't he see that what she needed was to be let alone, not left alone? "Suit yourself," she said. She waited till she heard his footsteps at the bottom of the stairs, the front door creak open then bump closed, before she cried.

———————

Out on the street, Sam shivered with the chill. He should have worn his jacket, but he couldn't very well go back for it now. If ever he needed a stiff drink, now was the time. He felt completely aroused, tingling. He walked fast up Ann Street, not noticing his direction, not going anywhere in particular. He felt lightheaded. If he walked fast enough, long enough, he would calm down, lose the thirst for a drink, go back to his bed and sleep without dreams.

The street was empty at this hour. He realized all at once that he had crossed into the Negro section. He'd heard there was some sort of meeting over in Brooklyn tonight. Clawson always seemed to know about everything that went on among the Negroes, almost as if he were getting daily reports. Sam still couldn't figure him out.

There was Gray Ellen's school on the right, Ebenezer Baptist

Church cater-corner across the intersection. He stopped and watched his breath cloud the still air in front of him. Out of the corner of his eye, he spotted movement—somebody walking. The figure crossed Ann Street and was illuminated briefly under the weak gas street lamp. The light glanced off her spectacles: Saffron King James.

He coughed loudly to announce himself, then crossed the street toward her.

"Mr. Jenks?" she said. "That you?" She watched warily as he approached.

"Good evening, Miss Saffron," he said pleasantly. "Yes, it's me. Sam."

She stood in the middle of the street under the light. All the windows around them were dark. She gathered her shawl tightly around her shoulders. "Chilly night to be out for a promenade," she said, and giggled.

She was headed in the direction of the *Record* office.

"Going to work at this hour?" he said.

She nodded. "Takes a long time to set the type. Do it right. I'm just a 'prentice—my fingers ain't learned yet. Got too many chores, most days."

He could see only one of her hands. The other was wrapped in her shawl, holding onto something.

"Mind if I walk with you awhile?"

"What will people think?" She giggled again, a high, sweet giggle.

"Who's going to see us? Let me walk you over there."

"Suit yourself. It's only a couple of blocks."

He fell into step beside her. She walked briskly.

"What do you have in your hand?"

She stopped and turned, slipped out her hand and opened it. She tossed a smooth rock into the air and caught it like a baseball. "Mama calls it my rock of virtue."

"Anybody tries to get fresh, you sock 'em?"

"Girl got to look after herself in this hard world."

The *Record* office was dark. Saffron reached down the neck of her dress, pulled out a string with a key tied to it, and opened the door. He hesitated.

"Come on in," she said. "I don't mind. Too cold out here."

"Just for a minute. Then I've got to get back." Gray Ellen would be lying awake, waiting for him. He looked around—were the Manlys here?

"Don't worry," she said. "Nobody else around tonight. Frank went home, and Alex is over at the church meeting. I got hours to work in peace."

She took his hand and led him upstairs in the dark. "Don't move," she said. She dropped her shawl on a chair, clunked down her rock, and lit a kerosene lamp but trimmed it low. He stood next to her, unsure what to do. Being so close to her in the confined space, he was overwhelmed by her physical presence. "Now, what is it you really want, Mr. Samuel Jenks?" She was close. Her breath smelled of peppermint candies.

"I told you, I was just out walking." Sam watched her body move, slender with young muscle.

"I saw you giving me the look. You best not be getting ideas."

"I just wanted company, that's all."

"That's what you cruising the street for, all right." She picked up her rock and tossed it up and down easily in her small hand.

Sam reached into his pocket and pulled out a thin fold of bills. "I've got some money," he said, before he even realized it.

She backed away. "I didn't think you were that kind." She sounded disappointed in him.

He put away his money, embarrassed. "Don't know what I was thinking. I'm sorry."

"Just 'cause I'm a poor colored girl, you think I don't have pride? You think I don't have aspirations?" She'd heard the word from the Reverend Grant, and this was the first time she'd had a chance to use it. "I'm going to nursing college someday."

He was confused. "Then why work for a newspaper?"

"That's my business," she said.

"Of course." He felt ashamed.

"So I can learn proper words. Ideas. I told you, I got aspirations. Now, get out of here."

Sam left without saying anything more. He walked home slowly. A cold drizzle had begun. It soaked his shirt, but he hardly noticed. Once home, he hesitated to go in. He walked twice around the block and then opened the front door and went upstairs to bed.

As he was undressing, Gray Ellen stirred in the dark and said, "Are you all right, Sam?"

"Don't worry," he said, unsure of his voice, "I didn't take a drink."

"I know," she said, "but are you all right?"

"Go to sleep."

We have been amazed, confounded, and a little ashamed of the acquiescence and quiescence of the men of North Carolina at the existing conditions; and more than once have asked ourselves wonderingly: Where *are the white men and the* shotguns?

Rebecca Cameron,
in a letter to Colonel
Alfred Moore Waddell

CHAPTER TEN

Monday, October 24

"A MAN CAN SIT IDLE and watch things fall apart only so long," Colonel Alfred Moore Waddell said, slapping the latest edition of the *Daily Record* on the linen tablecloth next to Sam's place. " 'Every Negro man with pride in his race must vote Republican in November, or else forfeit all claims to Manhood.' Indeed! Where do those darkies get off?"

Bessie King hovered at his elbow, trying to serve the soup.

Sam could read the headline: *30 Negroes Discharged From Employment Because of Their Determination to Enjoy Citizen Rights.*

Gabrielle, seated at the other end of the dinner table, nodded toward Bessie and admonished gently, "Colonel, please."

Waddell chuckled. "Aunt Bessie's not political. She doesn't hold with those rabble-rousing Negroes—do you, Aunt Bessie?"

"No, suh," she replied dully, eyes on the bowl of hot soup in her hand, poised over his lap. She thought, Lord, deliver me from temptation, hesitated, then set down the bowl.

"Still, we have guests. May we not leave politics for the brandy?"

"You're right, Miz Gabby. As usual. I was forgetting myself." He sipped wine and tossed the newspaper onto the sideboard.

Gray Ellen sat opposite Sam, and to her right was Father Christopher Dennen. Sam was alone on his side of the table. The soup was delicious—a white soup made with eggs and veal knuckle, one of Gabrielle's own recipes. Sam complimented her.

She said only, "I'm very lucky to have Bessie in the kitchen." Bessie, making the rounds with a water pitcher, beamed.

Gabrielle looked so lovely tonight that Sam had to make a conscious effort not to stare at her. Her black satin dress was cut low at the bodice and finished with sheer, gauzy lace that buttoned to her throat. The full rise of her breasts was apparent, even accented, under the bright chandelier. He thought it a daring dress to wear in such a close room. In a ballroom, among dancing, flirtatious women, it would have simply been part of the whirling elegance, drawing no more attention than a bathing dress on a beach. But here, it made her shine provocatively.

Her complexion glowed rose, her brown eyes caught the light, shimmering—even her hair shone. He admired the way she wore it swept up over her small ears, exposing the full curve of her neck. Her shapely hands were set off by small lace ruffles at the sleeves, and on her fingers glinted a polished yellow ivory cameo and a blue sapphire engagement ring, doubled onto the same finger as her wedding band.

Gray Ellen wore a plain black dress that revealed nothing.

Sam wore his old dark wool suit, newly brushed. The Colonel wore tails and a bow tie. His hair and goatee were oiled. Sam felt distinctly outclassed. He envied Father Dennen, with his careless red hair—he could wear the same cassock for all occasions.

"Father Dennen and I have an ongoing argument," Colonel

Waddell announced, after Bessie had served a main course of Spanish onions stuffed with ham, heavy cream, and breadcrumbs, along with a platter of St. Charles cornbread. "Regarding eternal punishment for the damned."

Great, Sam thought—small talk.

Father Dennen buttered a slab of bread. "The Scriptures are quite clear. I don't know why you persist."

"If I may play the Jesuit," Colonel Waddell said, and smiled foxily. "The Scriptures speak of eternal life, the resurrection of the body: 'Who shall change our vile body, that it may be fashioned like unto his glorious body.' St. Paul to the Philippians."

St. Paul, Gray Ellen thought—another true believer who had no use for women.

"Nicely quoted, as usual," Father Dennen said.

"And St. John tells us, 'Whosoever believeth in him should not perish, but have eternal life.' "

As he talked, Colonel Waddell sliced his entrée into strips with quick, sure strokes of his knife.

"Right so far," Father Dennen said, and bolted a slab of cornbread.

The women were talking low between themselves. "What a lovely dress," Gabrielle said.

"It's nothing," Gray Ellen said, "compared to yours. So elegant."

"I mean, the way you wear it."

Gray Ellen was taken off-guard by Gabrielle's directness, her sincere tone. She'd expected a haughty whiff of old money. "You're very gracious."

Gabrielle patted her arm and let her hand rest there a moment. "I'm glad you came tonight. You're not what I expected."

What had she expected?

"I mean, when Sam came by the house that day looking for Alex Manly, I guess I expected a blonde. Someone more Nordic." Gabrielle squeezed her arm. "I mean it as a compliment. You're so *warm*."

Gray Ellen felt herself blush. This woman was so much smoother, so much more adept at the social graces. For the first time in years, she felt like a bumpkin.

"Forgive me—I didn't mean to embarrass you."

Gray Ellen relaxed. "It's just that, well, down here, I haven't felt at my best. No one has seen me at my best. Have you ever felt that way?" What was it about this woman that drew her out so easily?

Gabrielle took her hand and squeezed it quickly. "I know perfectly. This town, it can be hard on a woman."

"But nowhere in Scripture are we told that the damned will live forever in hell," Colonel Waddell declaimed with gusto, brandishing his fork. "That's an invention of medieval folklore." He laughed. "The image of hideous, malformed *misérables* roasting forever in unquenchable flames."

Bessie, refilling wineglasses, thought, I know one miserable white billy goat I'd like to see roasting on a pitchfork, praise Jesus.

Father Dennen gulped a big swallow of wine and said, "What of St. Mark? 'But he that shall blaspheme against the Holy Ghost hath never forgiveness, but is in danger of eternal damnation.' "

"Ah!" said Waddell, flashing his knife. "But the language of Scripture is all thesis and antithesis! Do this, or else that will happen—eh, Father? Clear dichotomies of choice, time after time. Everything defined by what it is not. If damnation is the opposite of eternal life, then it must not only be punishment but an equally eternal death."

"You're stretching a point," Father Dennen said, taking another stuffed onion, big as an orange, from Bessie. "The Bible's more than rhetoric."

Sam was impressed that Father Dennen could be so civil—he'd never seen the priest be anything but fierce. But that's the mistake we always make, he thought. People are complicated, full of contradictions. It's what made it so hard to trust them, or to condemn them.

Still talking under the men, Gabrielle said, "I'll help you get along."

"When will I stop feeling like an outsider?"

Gabrielle smiled, her eyes crinkling. She whispered, "They say you're no longer a newcomer in this town when everybody who remembers that you moved here from someplace else is dead."

They laughed together. "That's a comfort," Gray Ellen said.

"Isn't it, though? After supper, we can walk in the garden."

Colonel Waddell said, "I still believe the terms of the Final Judgment will be realized by those who deliberately reject the plan of salvation."

"No clergyman would deny that. That's why it's called the Last Judgment," Father Dennen said impatiently. Under his clear tenor was now a gravelly edge.

"But I also believe that these terrors will end in eternal death." Waddell was all heated up. His gray eyes had the shine of a zealot's.

"But Colonel," Sam said mildly, "do you mean to claim that the human soul is not immortal?" He'd been trying, without success, to overhear the women's conversation. Whatever she was saying, Gabrielle was having an immediate effect on Gray Ellen—Gray looked animated, full of color.

Colonel Waddell smacked his hand on the tabletop, startling the women, who momentarily ceased talking. "Exactly!" He smiled at Father Dennen in triumph. "The human soul is not *necessarily* immortal."

The way he said it, with such logical bravado, made it sound to Sam like incontrovertible fact. Waddell's mind was so quick, his reasoning so clear.

Father Dennen wiped his lips with his napkin. "Well, if I can't make a promise to a man's immortal soul, then what have I got to offer? Where's my leverage?"

Standing by the sideboard, Bessie nodded. She would walk through fire for Father Dennen.

"The soul of a man who dies in grace can become immortal," Waddell said. "That's what redemption is!"

"Two sides of the same coin, if you ask me. Redemption, or damnation. Both will last a powerful long time."

Colonel Waddell said, "Immortality is earned, Father Dennen."

And you aim to earn yours, no matter what, Sam thought. Still, he was impressed with the breadth of the man's mind. Waddell had all sorts of theories about everything, and he read widely, even obscure works. He was always quoting some classical scholar nobody else had ever heard of. This room wasn't big enough for his voice. Lately, Sam couldn't hear enough of him.

Gabrielle said, "You've both been over this ground before." To Gray Ellen, she said, "They used to write letters back and forth in the newspaper. For a whole year, they weren't even on speaking terms."

"Still aren't," Father Dennen said, and Sam wasn't sure whether he was kidding. He couldn't fathom what had brought Father Dennen to this house for supper.

Gabrielle said, "None of us at this table plans to find out how long damnation takes—am I right, Father?"

He laughed. "Point well taken, Mrs. Waddell."

Bessie crossed herself and poured more wine.

Sam was glad to hear the subject change—with Bessie fussing over the table, he couldn't forget how he'd tried to betray his wife with Saffron.

Bessie cleared the plates and poured coffee, then served wedges of rum raisin cake glazed with warm sugar icing.

———————

After dessert, Gabrielle took Gray Ellen's hand and led her into the garden. The night air was cool, but not yet frosty. They strolled along the narrow brick path past hedges of azalea and Confederate jasmine that had long since lost their bloom, and now looked gray in the ambient light from the windows.

"You teach over at the colored school, don't you?"

Gray Ellen immediately became defensive. She'd understood too late that her job made her something of a social pariah. This was the first dinner invitation they'd had since arriving. Even Cousin Hugh had pointedly ignored them. She was still waiting to be invited to his home. Not that she wanted to go, but she felt she was entitled to be included. "Williston," she said. "It's a very progressive school."

"That kind of work, it must be very satisfying."

Gray Ellen studied her face for any sign of irony, but found none. "It does keep me sane."

Gabrielle laughed shortly. "I could use something like that."

For the first time all evening, Gray Ellen dropped her guard completely. She hadn't even considered that the wife of so prominent a lawyer, a former congressman at that, might be unhappy. "You haven't been married long."

"Two years next month. The Colonel was twice a widower."

"I see."

"Sisters. Dull as pumpkins, both of them, from what I've been told." She smiled. "But dutiful wives. Wonderful housekeepers."

"I know the sort."

"I'm lucky to have Bessie. Without her, the house would fall down around us. I can't bear to stay indoors all day."

"The children are like that for me. When I'm in front of the classroom, it feels like being outdoors."

"What I love is sewing. Making clothes, fancy stitching. I've made party dresses for all my friends."

"This one?" Gray Ellen touched Gabrielle's sleeve.

Gabrielle blushed. Even in the bad light, Gray Ellen could see she was embarrassed. "I didn't mean to brag. But I feel like I know you."

"It's lovely," Gray Ellen said. "I've admired it all evening."

"It's a bit too much, isn't it? I should save it for a ball."

"Have you been to any balls lately?"

"It'll be two years in November," she said, looking away.

They had made the circuit of the small, enclosed garden. The chill was settling on their shoulders, and their wraps were no longer enough for comfort. But neither wanted to go inside and join the men. The brisk air smelled clean. It carried the light scent of pine and wood smoke. Gray Ellen closed her eyes, tilted her head back, and breathed in the night.

"Your husband, he's a very handsome man," Gabrielle said.

Gray Ellen opened her eyes.

"He's very much in love with you," Gabrielle said.

"How can you tell?"

"At dinner, he wasn't paying any attention to the Colonel. He was looking at you the whole time."

"I thought he was looking at you," Gray Ellen said, then suddenly realized how mean the remark sounded. Tonight, she seemed to be saying the first thing that came to her mind.

Gabrielle hugged her briefly. "You mustn't think that," she said. "I'm afraid, wearing this dress, I was deliberately flirting." She laughed, but to Gray Ellen the laugh sounded forced and public. "I hardly ever get to flirt anymore. I enjoy distracting Father Dennen."

After a moment, Gray Ellen said, "Do you think he heard?"

Gabrielle said, "Don't be silly. Men never hear what we say."

"I wouldn't mind if he heard," Gray Ellen said. "I wouldn't mind if he paid that close attention."

Gabrielle took her hand again. "Let me make you a dress. It will give you an excuse to come over."

Gray Ellen nodded. Gabrielle led her toward the back door, then stopped her before going inside. Gray Ellen felt as if she were about to be kissed good night. Gabrielle took her other hand. "It can't be easy, working with the coloreds," she said.

"They're just people—"

"No, that's not what I meant." She put a hand to her mouth. "I always say it wrong. I meant, people don't understand. There's a meanness. Have you felt it?"

Gray Ellen's pulse was quickening. It felt lovely being with this woman. At last, someone who understood. "Yes, I've felt it. It's in the air."

"It didn't used to be that way. There used to be a kindness. There's so much money here now. It's growing so fast. People are forgetting themselves."

"Whatever it is, Sam's in the middle of it."

Gabrielle pulled her in gently and embraced her with surprising force. Gray Ellen was the taller, and their breasts nested together without the usual awkwardness of women embracing. Gabrielle kissed her on the neck, just under the ear, and Gray Ellen kissed her cheek.

Gabrielle let her go. "Promise me you'll take care."

"I promise," Gray Ellen said.

They went inside, where the air was already stuffy from cigar smoke. Gabrielle took her into the sewing room, off the kitchen. With a yellow tape, she measured Gray Ellen's waist, her neck, the length of her arm. Her touch was reassuring. They sat together in the window nook while Gabrielle passed bolts of fine cloth to her. Gray Ellen picked out a midnight-blue satin. The fabric was cool in her hands. Gabrielle draped it over the dressmaker's form, and Gray Ellen watched her fingers tucking and pinning it into a beautiful shape.

Gray Ellen said, "The fabric is so expensive. Let me pay—"

"Never mind. I bought more than I needed last time."

"But it's such an extravagant gift." Gray Ellen hated to take something for nothing.

"When you wear it, think of our friendship."

In the library after dinner, Sam took one of the four cracked leather chairs and lit a cigar, along with the other men. Waddell offered him brandy from a crystal decanter, but he declined. The library was cluttered with souvenirs and knickknacks—framed citations, a stuffed owl, a tarnished cavalry saber hanging on the wall over Waddell's head.

"A fine cigar," Father Dennen said, a snifter of brandy in his hand.

"Dash of cognac in the humidifier," the Colonel explained.

The room took on the heady aroma of cognac and Cuban tobacco.

"A man of taste," Sam said.

The Colonel laughed dryly. "God dwells in the details."

Father Dennen said, "So does the devil."

Colonel Waddell laughed and sat heavily in the chair behind his desk. Sam was fascinated by the eclectic library arrayed in leather bindings on floor-to-ceiling shelves—everything from Sophocles in Greek to Dante in Italian, with English classics and scientific books in between. And law books.

On Waddell's desk was a sheaf of white sheets with carbons. The top sheet was covered with penciled handwriting. Waddell saw the men looking. "My speech for tomorrow night."

"Do we get a preview?" Father Dennen asked, eyes alert.

"Afraid not, gentlemen." Waddell twirled the points of his moustache. "Public speaking is a dramatic art. One must create a certain *suspense*."

"I'm not sure I like the sound of that," Father Dennen said.

"*Honi soit qui mal y pense*, Father."

"This has all happened before," the priest said. "Last time, they killed only six—how many this time?"

Sam was confused.

Waddell said, "He means the uprising of 1831. They caught six rabble-rousers in league with Nat Turner."

"Wasn't any uprising. It was six innocent Negroes."

Sam said, "What happened?"

Father Dennen, looking at Waddell, said, "They cut their heads off and stuck them on poles. I've got parishioners who remember."

Waddell stiffened. "They had raped and murdered. My father told me the story. A lesson was required."

"The lesson is," Father Dennen said, "if you don't tell the story in its truth, you relive it over and over again. Can't you see that?"

"I know that's what you Catholics believe: your story, your mass, is a true story. But in my church, a story is just a story."

Sam said, "Your speech—can you give us a hint?"

"Come to Thalian Hall tomorrow evening."

"So Goldsboro wasn't enough. You're going to sing your bloody opera in your own hometown." Father Dennen puffed and exhaled smoke in a quick burst.

The Colonel was cool. "We had eight thousand people at Goldsboro. We'll have another thousand tomorrow night. They demand a hearing."

Father Dennen squinted at him. "I don't think you believe in this so-called Cause any more than I do."

"Father, you underestimate me."

"No, Colonel, that's one thing I don't do. Everyone else may underestimate you, but I know exactly what you're capable of." Father Dennen slugged down the rest of his brandy and set the glass on the desk rather hard. "If you'll excuse me, I have parish duties."

After the priest had gone, Colonel Waddell came around the desk. "A first-rate mind, but his sympathies are mistaken."

"You mean the Negroes."

" 'As a city upon a hill,' that's what we ought to be. A city with a grander vision, a place of enlightenment, a model for the Southern metropolis of the new century. Men should guide themselves by our light."

Before the Colonel could get carried away, Sam said, "What do you want?"

"You, too? You think I'm in this for personal ambition?" He sounded so hurt, Sam felt embarrassed for asking. He was constantly surprised by Waddell's eloquence, the utter sincerity of his tone. As always in his presence, Sam wanted more than anything for Waddell to take him into his confidence.

Colonel Waddell paced, limping jerkily, like a windup toy. "Do you know who discovered America?"

"Christopher Columbus, of course."

Waddell stood admiring his shelves of books, his back to Sam. "Five hundred years before Columbus, Norsemen from Finland had already colonized Newfoundland. They called it Vinland."

"I never realized."

Waddell fingered the spine of a fat brown book. "Most people don't. They accept whatever flimsy myth you put into their primer-book heads. But it's all here, in Dr. Shallowate's *History of the Hibernian Navigations*. The Nordic people came across the northern ocean in their celebrated longboats—*langships*." He turned on Sam and fixed him with his gray eyes. "Your people."

Sam was fascinated but also utterly confused—what had Viking raiders to do with Negro Republicans?

"They were a remarkable people, larger and stronger than any in southern Europe. Fearless and disciplined. Not like the swarthier races, who came later. And they brought no African slaves with them. Columbus started all that. The way he brought disease and ruin to the native peoples. The first thing he did was preside over the kidnapping and rape of a native woman. Later, he introduced the African slave to this hemisphere, on the sugar plantations. And the result has been misery on all sides, ever since."

This was not quite the Age of Discovery as Sam had learned it in grammar school. He was surprised to hear Waddell taking the side of the natives.

"It is always a dreadful mistake to mix the races," Colonel Waddell said quietly, sipping brandy. "The crew of the *Niña* carried syphilis home to Spain—the divine verdict on miscegenation! The Lord in his wisdom created the oceans to keep us apart."

"But we're not apart anymore," Sam said. "You can't change the past."

Waddell narrowed his eyes and stepped close to Sam. When he spoke, Sam inhaled the fumes of brandy on his breath. "No, but you can change the future. You can take the future into your two hands." He cupped his brandy snifter in both hands, like an offering. "You can make it whatever you want it to be."

Sam smoked his cigar and flicked the ash. The cigar made him lightheaded.

"I know you've been thrust into the middle of something you don't understand," the Colonel said. "You want to do the right thing. I pegged you for a man of character the moment I first laid eyes on you."

"What do you want from me?"

The Colonel gripped his arm, and Sam felt captured. "Help me. That's all. Be one of us, not against us."

"I'm not against you." But he wasn't sure. He wanted to remain passionately neutral.

Waddell stepped back and smiled, exhaling perfect wreaths of smoke. Sam had never been able to blow smoke rings. "You can do this thing, or you can do that thing, but you cannot do them both at once," the Colonel said. He drew on his cigar, and the end glowed. "Dichotomy. Choice. A man is either with us, or he is against us. There is no middle ground."

"I don't know what you want me to do." Sam felt an irrational desire to justify himself to this man, to please him. He sounded so reasonable.

Waddell's voice took on an avuncular tone. "You have been doing it all along—writing the truth."

Is that what I've been writing, Sam wondered?

"But now, I want something more. I want your loyalty. I want to know I can count on you." He clapped a hand on Sam's shoulder. Then, suddenly, he punched him lightly in the chest. "I want your heart."

Sam didn't speak. This was beyond politics now. It was a battle for souls. Maybe it had been that all along—the battle for the soul of this city. The particulars didn't matter. Paving contracts, dockage rights, railroad bonds, sewer rights of way—these were just the word made flesh.

It came to him, sitting in a leather chair in the presence of a Confederate colonel, inhaling cognac and Cuban leaf: he was at last being invited inside the club.

"What are you going to do?"

"No one will get hurt, I give you my word."

"Why do you need me?"

Waddell waved his cigar. "We don't. It will all happen whether you are part of it or not."

"What would I have to do?"

"Tell my story from the inside."

So he wanted a biographer to make him famous. "Let me think about it."

Waddell stubbed out his cigar. "Don't think too long. Afterward, it will matter who was with us. Names will be remembered. Loyalties will be counted."

Sam felt a chill. "I see."

"An enterprising young man like yourself could go far. The opportunities in this city will be nearly boundless."

Sam heard the back door open and close, heard the voices of the women.

Waddell gathered his speech in a neat sheaf and locked it in his top drawer. "I love the precision of rhetoric," he said happily. "Parallel structure. Either, or. Every word accounted for."

Mike Dowling was back in town.

In the wagon yard of Fire Station No. 2 at Sixth and Castle streets, barely three blocks from the *Daily Record* office, sixty Red

Shirts and their horses milled about. On the stern advice of Colonel Walker Taylor, Dowling was sober. It was seven-thirty, and a chilly dusk was already settling in.

"Form on me," he told his men. "Mount up."

With uncharacteristic discipline, the riders swung into line, two abreast, Winchesters and shotguns tucked into saddlebags. The column moved at a walk down Castle Street, wheeled onto Front Street, and broke into an easy trot as it passed through the business district, straddling the streetcar tracks. Pedestrians, many going in the same direction, stopped and stared. A few cheered. A policeman waved. Nobody challenged Dowling's little army. No Negroes dared these streets tonight.

Dowling kept his eyes straight ahead.

At Princess Street, the column turned right and cantered three blocks, then reined up at the front steps of Thalian Hall. There, Dowling's men formed a gauntlet to the door. Among the first to pass between their ranks was Colonel Alfred Moore Waddell, splendid in top hat and tails. "Cavalry," he observed happily, doffing his hat. From his horse, Dowling nodded. Behind Waddell came George Rountree, J. Allan Taylor and Colonel Walker Taylor, Captain William Rand Kenan, and every member of the Secret Nine and Group Six except Hugh MacRae, who slipped in by a side door to avoid the crowd. MacRaes had built this playhouse, and he knew all the back stairs.

Kenan glanced nervously at the mounted men. "Don't much like the look of that," he said to Walker Taylor.

"Don't fret, Bill. They'll behave. I read Dowling the riot act."

White men and women by the hundreds poured up the steps and packed the hall. Sam and Gray Ellen found seats in the front row of the mezzanine. She hadn't wanted to come, but Sam had insisted. Now, she marveled at the lavish appointments: pillars twined with a relief of painted grapevines; crimson velvet seats; crimson carpet on the main floor; an elaborate proscenium flanked by pillars and elevated private boxes, lavishly ornamented in gold leaf and carved rubies. The high, curving walls were a deep forest green, a warm contrast to all the crimson and gold. Electric lamps were strung under the curving rails of the mezzanine and balcony and bathed the stage in crisscrossing pools.

She was impressed. This could be the Philadelphia Academy of Music or Symphony Hall in Boston. On the stage, beyond the gleaming brass rail of the empty orchestra pit, sixty leading citizens took their seats in three semicircular tiers behind the podium.

After preliminary remarks by the Democratic chairman, the Reverend Peyton Hoge of First Presbyterian Church stood up. "During the War of Secession, our mills turned out iron for Confederate cannon," he announced before he'd even reached the podium. "Those cannon are long gone now, broken into scrap. But let us pray that the Confederate iron that went into their making—that determination—is as strong as ever."

The crowd applauded. A few whistled. Somebody behind Sam let loose a rebel yell.

"Among the finest citizens of this town are many who served the Cause."

Cheering and applause.

"In Oakdale Cemetery, a stone soldier in full dress uniform stands at parade rest, guarding the bodies of our fallen. In the so-called National Cemetery, only a short walk from this opera house, lie the two thousand Yankees who found out what a mob of nigrahs and Republicans are shortly going to learn: we will not be pushed around!"

Pastor Hoge waited for the applause to trail off, the house to settle down.

"Tonight, it is my great privilege to present a man who fought with equal bravery on the field of honor and in the halls of Congress. Ladies and gentlemen, I give you Colonel Alfred Moore Waddell!"

Waddell stood up slowly and remained standing at his chair as the applause and cheering went on. He smiled slightly, then walked casually toward the podium. The applause increased as Pastor Hoge—who, Sam thought, looked annoyed at Waddell for taking his time—shook his hand. Waddell braced his hands on the rails of the podium and swept the great hall with his eyes, nodding slightly toward the left balcony, the right balcony, the mezzanine. Then he clasped his hands behind him and stood rigid until the hall quieted. The silence was remarkable. Still, Waddell said nothing. He stood fixed in place, like the stone soldier at Oakdale. That was exactly the pose he struck—parade rest.

Sam was holding his breath, straining to hear. How many hundreds of others, he wondered, were doing the same?

"My fellow citizens," Waddell said at last, pronouncing each syllable as if it pained him. His voice was low and conversational, but by some trick he made it carry to the back rows. He looked around, and for an instant Sam wondered if he had forgotten his speech—Waddell had no paper in his hand. He stood looking up at the vaulted ceiling, as if his words were printed there.

"Last month." Again he waited, shook his head as if he himself could not quite believe what he was about to say. "Every month for the past *three* months, there have been in this city one hundred and forty burglaries. Person or persons unknown have violated the homes of law-abiding citizens and made off with their valuables an average of *once every five hours.*"

Angry murmuring, whispers.

"Four hundred and twenty times in the course of ninety days, criminals have destroyed the most basic right under the law—the right of an individual to be secure in his dwelling.

"And where are the miscreants, the vile perpetrators of such a crime spree?" He turned up his palms and continued speaking in a mild tone, as if he were baffled. "Are they in the county jail?" He looked around, as if waiting for an answer from the crowd.

"I have not heard of any arrests. Indeed," he said, his inflection now carrying a slight edge of anger, "I am in court five days in every week, and I don't recall that the courthouse has been choked with thieves. In fact, not one of those perpetrators has been arrested!"

Here we go, Sam thought—he's starting to get wound up.

But his voice backed down a notch. "The reason for this," he said, head down, staring up at the balcony as a preacher stares toward heaven with a bowed head. "The *reason* for this civic outrage is clear. As clear as black and white. What color are the magistrates? What color are far too many of our policemen? What color are these predators who plunder the common weal?

"They are," he said, as if controlling his rage with great difficulty, "the dregs of that other race. The *Negro* race. That gentle, childlike people dangerously mutating before our very eyes. And what, pray, is the cause of this mutation?"

Again he paused, and Sam expected another quiet answer. The crowd leaned forward in their seats.

"Power!" he shouted. "The corruption of power! The shameless manipulation of a whole race by greedy Republican scoundrels!"

He was warming up now.

He went on with the litany of abuses, now familiar through repetition in the pages of Clawson's newspaper: white women jostled off the sidewalks by Negro laborers, white professional men back-sassed by janitors, white children bullied by roving gangs of vicious Negro boys.

"They tell me the editor Manly is still in town. Still heaping abuse upon our womenfolk and our honor. Still printing slanderous lies upon the white race. Still daring us to do something about it!"

Sam scribbled impressions in his notebook: the arc of light along the proscenium; the pulsing nimbus outlining Waddell's hands, arms, and head; the malevolent undercurrent of outrage in the crowd. *Sizzling*, that was the character of the speech. The air was heating up.

He's got that light in his eye, Sam thought. That look of killing rapture. Then he gets that note in his voice, carries it along on a rising swell of pure words—not tumbling them out willy-nilly but firing them like rifle shots. Timing, Sam thought—that's his secret. He does it all with the pause. He does it all with the spaces between the words.

Waddell spoke for another forty-five minutes. He had them by their heartstrings, then he grabbed them by their throats. He had them soaring along on a wave of remembered glory, then answering his litanies in angry unison. He lifted them out of their seats and held them there—suspended in mid-sentence—with his voice.

"If there should be a race conflict here—God forbid!—the first men who should be held to strict accountability are their white leaders!"

"Hear, hear!"

"Damnyankee Republicans!"

"And the work should begin at the top of the list!" Waddell said.

"Damn right, Colonel!"

"Send them to hell!"

"I mean the governor of this state—the engineer of all the deviltry."

He paused again. Here it comes, Sam thought, the final windup. His heart was pounding. He loosened his tie. He could feel the swell of human energy filling the room. Gray Ellen watched, as she had all evening, with rigid indifference.

The Colonel spoke deliberately, summoning all the drama of a prosecutor demanding a capital verdict. "Will we of the Anglo-Saxon race stand for this any longer?"

"No!"

"A thousand times no! Let them understand that we will not live under these intolerable conditions. No society can stand it! We are resolved to change them, if we have to choke the current of the Cape Fear with carcasses!"

The house erupted. The crowd was on their feet, clapping wildly, screaming, shouting, singing old battle songs. Men pounded the seat backs, stamped their boots in unison. The balcony swayed. The whole building shook. Gray Ellen sat, unmoving, tears streaming down her face.

Sam timed the outburst—seven minutes. Waddell stood like the Confederate cemetery guard once more, drinking in the crowd's love. At that moment, standing between a thousand clamoring citizens and sixty of the most influential men in the city, he became the civic soul incarnate.

In the circle behind the podium, Hugh MacRae's face filled with blood. He hadn't counted on the old warhorse taking such complete control. Kenan looked to the exits, fearing a riot, wondering how they would get the women out before they were trampled. Rountree cursed himself out loud, though in the din no one could hear him. He should never have let this happen. They were going to tear down the hall and then march on Brooklyn, murdering and burning. Their careful plans had just been pulverized by an old-time barnburner. Walker Taylor was so stunned by the clamor he could not think straight. He wrung his big hands and hoped to God that Dowling and his men were not still lingering outside to lead the riot.

At length, Colonel Waddell held up his hand for silence, and got it.

"The time for smooth words has gone by. The extremest limit of forbearance has been reached. Negro domination," he said with a last, breathless pause, "shall henceforth be only a shameful memory!"

All at once, in the new clamor of applause and shouting, Sam realized that Gray Ellen was gone. He sprang up in time to see her disappearing into the crowd at the exit. He shouldered his way through the press of people and kept her in sight all the way down the stairs.

On the street, the cool air slapped him out of his daze. Gray Ellen had stopped under a street lamp at the foot of the steps.

"Gray!" he called, but his voice was lost in the noise of the crowd. He shoved his way toward her. She climbed the pediment of the street lamp and swung around it, holding on with one hand. She cupped the other hand in front of her mouth and began to shout. At first, Sam couldn't hear what she was shouting. Then, as he got closer, her words floated across the heads of the people beginning to mob the sidewalk.

She swung and shouted, tears streaming down her dirty face. "You lost the War!" she shouted, swinging around the pole.

People looked up. "She's drunk," somebody said.

"Can't you get it through your heads? You *lost* the goddamn *War!*" Her black hair was coming undone, falling around her face.

"Look at that black hair!" a man shouted. "You got painted with the tarbrush, did you, honey? Nigger in the family woodpile?" His companions laughed. Sam knocked the man down, and he disappeared under the tangle of feet.

She kept swinging and crying and shouting, "Don't you get it? You lost the War!"

Mike Dowling rode by, wheeled his horse in a tight circle, and shouted into her face, "Maybe we did, sweetheart—but we'll sure win this election!"

He galloped away. Sam snagged Gray Ellen around the waist and wrestled her, sobbing, to the street, where they rolled over and over on the oyster-shell paving until their clothes were coated white with lime dust.

PART III

THE BALLOT

There need be no surprise if a large number of colored voters are killed in North Carolina to-day or to-morrow. The preliminaries have all been arranged by the Democrats. The last thing to be done generally in the way of preparation for such an event is to send over the country a report of the riotous condition of the negroes and the fear of the whites, who expect an "outbreak" at any moment. That report was sent out by the Associated Press yesterday.

Philadelphia Press,
November 8, 1898

CHAPTER ELEVEN

Thursday, November 3

"BLESS ME FATHER, for I have sinned," Sam Jenks whispered into the confessional screen. The confessional box smelled of lacquer and mildew. "It has been many months since my last confession, and these are my sins." He'd been meaning to do this since Chicago. He told about his old drinking habits, his neglect of his wife. The awful fight they'd had after Thalian Hall.

Tomorrow was First Friday mass. He would start clean. The church always took you back. Always gave you a second chance.

He told about Saffron, keeping his voice low, embarrassed and ashamed at the sound of the words coming out of his mouth: "I tried to seduce a woman not my wife."

He waited for Father Cripps's bland, cheerful voice offering to absolve him. He was the priest scheduled to hear confessions. Instead, he heard a clear, fierce tenor, a voice not bothering to whisper, and full of righteous anger: "Black or white?"

"Father Dennen?" Christ, why couldn't that damned priest keep to his schedule? Sam wanted to bolt from the confessional box. But he was trapped—Father Dennen had surely recognized his voice already.

"Father Cripps is ill—never mind. Black or white?"

"Father?"

"The woman!"

"Black."

"Have you been back to her?"

Sam tried to swallow, but his throat suddenly felt constricted, dry. He could not clear it to speak.

"Have you been back to her?" Father Dennen repeated.

"Of course not. I didn't mean to go the first time."

"Of course not."

That was all he needed—irony from a priest. In the past months, his life had advanced beyond what any absolution could fix. Life was complicated, full of traps. A man trying hard to do the right thing would suddenly find himself doing exactly the wrong thing. "I always find myself exactly where I don't want to be," he explained weakly. Not just frequenting the saloons in Chicago or fleeing the battle in Cuba he'd been paid to witness, but seeing the mob at the *Record* office, witnessing the Gatling gun demonstration on the river, working at a newspaper office stacked with carbines, rolling around in the street with his hysterical wife.

"What?"

"I haven't got anything against . . . They're just trying to get along, I'm just trying . . . But on the river, and then my wife was angry, and there she was crossing the street under the lamp—it wasn't my idea to go looking for him anyway."

"Please, please," Father Dennen said, his voice less sure.

"I'm trying, Father. But I don't understand."

Father Dennen sighed. "At least you're honest." He sighed again, and Sam heard his callused hand rasping against the stubble of his chin. "But for the love of God, son—take charge of your life."

Sam said nothing. He waited for the lecture, the penance. But instead of assigning a penance, the priest said, "Why is your wife so angry at you? What have you done?"

It took him nearly half an hour to explain. "I left her alone when she needed me," he began. "Then I was a coward." He had never told the truth about Cuba to anybody but his wife. Now, he told Father Dennen.

When he had finished, he waited again for a penance. All he heard on the other side of the screen was the measured breathing of the priest. Now he knows everything, Sam thought. Now he can destroy me. Never again would he be able to face this man over a dinner table. He finally said tentatively, "A penance, Father?"

"If only the good Lord had supplied me a whipping post."

Sam was afraid of his anger. "I am trying to be a good man."

"No doubt. So are we all. It's hard to be a good man in these times. But that's no excuse. Marriage is a sacred institution. You are debasing it."

"Yes, Father."

"You want penance? Three things!" snapped the priest, the old ferocity back in his voice. Sam waited while Father Dennen milked the drama. "You will touch no strange woman."

"Yes, Father."

"You will do no harm to any man, black or white. Especially black."

"Yes, Father."

Father Dennen paused, breathing quick and shallow, like a prizefighter. "You will love your wife."

Sam barely whispered it: "Yes, Father."

"I know, I know—it's too hard," the priest said impatiently. "Do it anyway." And slammed shut the panel before Sam could even answer. Behind the lacquered wood, Sam could hear him murmuring in fast Latin. It must be the absolution and blessing, but the wood was too thick and he could not hear.

When he rose, his knees were stiff from kneeling so long. He cracked open the door. The church was empty—everybody had gone to watch the parade, he supposed. The priest had made him late. He hurried out the back way, furtive as a thief.

Gray Ellen spent the morning at the kitchen table poring over her students' copybooks. Some of her initial enthusiasm had begun to fade, and she was already looking forward to Christmas vacation. There were too many distractions for these children. Some of them were hopeless at spelling—there were so many letters they didn't pronounce, and they couldn't be persuaded to write down what they didn't say out loud. They looked on it as a kind of craziness. White teacher craziness.

Today had been proclaimed a holiday. She knew the reason, and it disgusted her, but she was grateful for a day to herself.

She sipped hot tea and watched out the open window as she worked. The breeze was riffling the boughs of the locust tree in the yard. The weather felt almost real today—brisk and refreshing.

When you're raised in a place, she reflected, the landscape enters your body. The silvery look of a rolling Pennsylvania meadow in the morning, the feel of a stormy breeze on your bare cheek, how a warm day smells sweet or musky. The colors of housetops darkened by hovering banks of clouds. No matter where you lived your life, what lovely, exotic lands you visited, your body craved the landscape of your youth. Your eyes and ears measured everything else against it.

This morning, the clear opal sky cast the world in a clean, mellow light, deepening the colors of things, limning their edges precisely. It was a light she could feel on her skin, full of hope and anticipation. The light made her feel at home—almost.

Calliope Register materialized at the back screen door. "Hey, Gray," she said, working hard to sound cheerful.

Gray Ellen sighed and closed the copybook. "Come on in. Have some tea?"

Callie came into the kitchen, so swollen with child she could hardly maneuver between the stove and the table. Her left eye was blackened, and proud flesh was rising on her cheek. Her right hand was wrapped in a dirty bandage.

"Let's go onto the porch, where we can be comfortable," Gray Ellen said.

She carried a tea tray onto the front porch, and Callie backed into the chair next to hers. "Thank you, dear. I swear to God, this baby is swishing back and forth inside me like a tub of laundry."

Babies again. "Is it all right? Did anything—?"

"Farley came back last night. Maybe you heard him."

"Yes, I'm afraid I did." It had been hard to ignore the crashing and banging, the shouted curses and the bawling of the twins. She hadn't heard Calliope make a sound. That meant she'd had practice.

"Oh, ain't nothing special with him," she said quickly. "That's how men are, I guess."

"Not all men," Gray Ellen said. "There's no excuse."

Callie looked embarrassed. She was having trouble getting her breath, talking in quick little spasms. "I ain't complaining. Far's a good man, mostly."

"Did he hurt you?"

She touched her eye and smiled faintly. "He done worse before."

Gray Ellen touched her arm. She couldn't help it. Part of her was outraged, but part of her understood perfectly. When you had so little, you couldn't afford to give up anything without something certain and better to take its place.

"I'm sorry," she said. Callie nodded but didn't look at her. "Has he calmed down?"

Callie laughed. Gray Ellen caught the bitter note. "He's gone, honey. First light. Off to a wreck in Goldsboro."

"At least he's working."

"I ain't talking no train, honey. He got laid off."

"Oh, I didn't realize."

"He comes in drunk. Boys are playing with their new jackknives, opening and closing the blades. He like to pitch a fit. 'What you throwing my hard-earned money away on toys for, woman?' he says to me. I say, 'Boy got to have a jackknife. How else he gonna play mumblety-peg with the other boys?' I bought them knives out of my laundry money. Then he whupped me. Whupped the boys. Start busting up the room."

"You don't have to stand for that. No woman—"

Callie's mouth went crooked as she talked. "Been slipping around. Whenever he goes slipping around, he's got to make like it's my fault." She shrugged. "Same with any man, I guess."

"I can't believe that."

"You better believe it, sweetie. You get off your high horse and look around. They get the itch, men do. Why, your own Sam—"

"What about Sam?"

Callie clasped her hands, looking straight ahead and rocking, though it was not a rocking chair. "Nothing," she said softly, pasting a white hand over her split lip. "Me and my big mouth."

Gray Ellen's cheeks stung. "Maybe you'd better go," she said, trying to control her voice.

"Maybe I'd better," Calliope said, laboring to heave herself out of the chair. "I wish I was pretty, but I'm not. I'm just a fat woman with a big mouth and too many babies." She was sobbing, making no attempt to wipe her eyes. The tears streamed down her face, leaving dirty tracks.

"Oh, for heaven's sake—sit down and finish your tea." It had been a clean, fine morning. Now, it was ruined. The beautiful light was wasted. She passed Callie a handkerchief. "Here, now, wipe your face."

"Thank you, dear. I don't mean to carry on like this." She mopped her face till the handkerchief was limp and filthy. She sipped from her cup and smacked her lips. "Nothing like a nice cup of tea when you're feeling low."

Across the fence, her two boys were yelping like wild dogs. "Come see the parade!" they shouted. "Come see the parade!"

The Red Shirts, Mike Dowling at their head, rode down Castle Street in a column of four, twenty deep. In the November light, their shirts looked crisp and military. The stocks of their

Winchesters gleamed with linseed oil—Dowling had ordered them to spruce up their rigs for today's gala. Most of them wore jaunty slouch hats, like Roosevelt's Rough Riders.

Dowling had borrowed a cavalry saber for the occasion, but he was unused to it, and it clanked against his boot as he rode, bruising his ankle.

As they passed knots of staring Negroes, they drew pistols and Winchesters and fired them into the air. The Negroes disappeared in a hurry. The mood in the ranks was jovial, lots of laughter. Men joshing, smelling the gun smoke in the autumn air.

They turned onto Third Street. "Coming into the finer neighborhoods," Dowling warned over his shoulder. "Holster them guns."

The two women seated on the porch at Third and Ann streets didn't wave. Dowling didn't care. Today, everybody would see who really ran this city. From a tall horse, a man could see a long way. He could listen to the good creak of leather, feel the muscled rhythm of the horse that carried him above the shit of the street, feel the power of mounted men eager to be commanded into action. He could see his own future as a golden glow at the end of a hard, fast ride.

Well behind the Red Shirts marched Colonel Walker Taylor and his Boys Brigade, uniformed in khaki, white wooden drill rifles on their shoulders. Taylor deliberately put as much distance as he could between his boys and Dowling's riders.

As the Red Shirts and the Boys Brigade proceeded through town, the crowd lining the streets fell in behind them and followed. At Chestnut Street, in back of the post office, the Red Shirts reined up in a park where tents had once been erected to house returning Confederate veterans. Today, those same old tents, flaps tied up, housed trestle tables and a brass band. At a brick barbecue pit, half a dozen men turned beef ribs and stirred pork barbecue in iron pots. Under the white canvas tents, ladies dished out coleslaw, cornbread, potatoes, okra, greens, and pecan pie.

From a solid silver tureen, two Daughters of the Confederacy ladled lemon punch.

The band was playing "The Battleship of Maine," a popular

marching song from the Cuban war. The Red Shirts picketed their mounts military fashion along a rope. The Boys Brigade milled around, admiring the horses, then stacked their toy rifles and formed up for barbecue.

By the time Sam arrived at the park, the party was well under way. White supremacy banners flew on ropes suspended between the ridgepoles. Boys waved American and Confederate flags. Colonel Waddell, Pastor Hoge, George Rountree, Walker and J. Allan Taylor, and Hugh MacRae were seated at a special reserved table at the head of the biggest tent, like a wedding party. Clawson was standing nearby, talking over Walker Taylor's shoulder.

"Well, at last—the press!" Colonel Waddell joked when Sam walked up.

"Big turnout," Sam said.

Over the music of the band and the clamor of shouted conversations, Rountree was talking seriously. He had been to see Governor Russell two weeks ago, along with Hoge.

Sam knew that, after a lot of leaning, Governor Russell had backed down, canceling last week's scheduled speech in Wilmington and promising to keep the Republicans from fielding a slate of candidates. He hedged, same as when he had let the Democrats take a majority on the Board of Audit and Finance. He was running scared. In 1870, when the Democrats swept the state ballot, they had impeached the Republican governor. Russell was too cagey to expose himself like that.

He laid down a condition: the two Democratic candidates most likely to impeach him must be taken off the ballot in favor of more moderate candidates. The delegation had agreed.

One of the new "moderate" nominees was George Rountree.

Meantime, the Republican slate had collapsed. Ben Keith, drafted to run for the state senate, had announced in a letter to the *Messenger* and other newspapers in town, "I cannot afford to sacrifice my business interests for political considerations." Twice, he'd been ambushed by thugs from the White Government Union, and the Red Shirts had enforced a boycott of his store. He was going broke and feared for his life. The daily mail brought anonymous threats to his family. Rountree visited him late one night and wrote the letter for him.

Dan Gore, candidate for the state house of representatives, and like Keith an alderman, had also gotten scared off. He was easier than Keith—a single brick through his front window, wrapped in a sheet of paper on which was scrawled a crude skull and crossbones. He vowed publicly to vote the white supremacy ticket. He gave Rountree fifty dollars for the campaign war chest.

Other champions of Fusionism and Negro suffrage—acting Sheriff George Z. French and Flavell Foster prominent among them—had quit the fight. Foster had been the Yankee commissar during the occupation of Wilmington at the end of the Civil War. Despite the fact that he'd doled out food and blankets generously to paroled Confederate prisoners, they'd never forgotten he was a Yankee.

The field was open. The ballot would include no Republican candidates for county commissioner, sheriff, coroner, clerk of superior court, or state house of representatives. The only black man slated to run in the first place, for register of deeds, had quietly withdrawn.

Oliver Dockery would still stand for the United States Congress against John D. Bellamy, and everybody already knew how that would turn out.

"Congratulations, George," Colonel Waddell said. "You're going to come out of this a state representative."

"We haven't won anything yet," Rountree said, put off by Waddell's tone. "Nobody votes till Tuesday."

"Still," Clawson, the editor, said, "it's all in place. We're ready to move anytime."

"That's enough," Rountree said, looking around at the crowd, who were mostly ignoring the men at the table. "The less said, the better."

Waddell smiled, made a sweeping gesture with his hand to include the gang of Brigade boys in khaki uniforms, the Red Shirts filtering past in twos and threes with full platters of barbecue, the other men and women making a noisy holiday. " *'Mene, Mene, Tekel, Upharsin.'* The handwriting is on the wall."

"Still, a little discretion, gentlemen. Things can change at any moment."

Pastor Hoge said, "I hear the nigrahs are going to put up their own slate of candidates."

Walker Taylor agreed. "I've heard that, too."

"They'll mob the polling places," Hugh MacRae said, fidgeting, twisting his hands together. He alone was neither eating nor drinking. "They've got the numbers."

Sam said, "Come on, you don't believe—"

The look in their eyes stopped him. Clawson squinted at him across the table. Everybody stopped eating. Walker Taylor held his glass to his lips but did not drink.

MacRae said mildly, "We've got more experience than you in these matters. You just pay attention and write it up." Sam heard the threat in his voice. It was a voice that could say anything and make it come true.

Mike Dowling entered the tent and shuffled toward them between the rows of tables, a Red Shirt flanking him left and right— bodyguards. Dismounted, he was a short man with a heavy torso, apish arms, and bandy legs. The rusty cavalry saber bounced against his leg.

"Well, if it ain't Himself," Clawson said.

"Delusions of grandeur," Walker Taylor said.

Waddell added, "Somebody ought to show the gentleman the proper way to wear a sword."

Walker Taylor said, "He's got almost a hundred rifles behind him now."

Dowling and his men nodded as they passed. Sam saw the bulge of a flask in his back pocket. Dowling commandeered an empty table, stood at the head, and waited until his Red Shirts were lined up along both sides. Then, when he nodded, they all sat down together.

"Thinks he's in the officers' mess," Waddell observed.

"Never mind him," Rountree said. "I know how to handle that kind."

Sam said, "How's that?"

Rountree struck a match to a cigar. "Give him a job. Something with a uniform and gold braid that doesn't carry a gun." He tossed away the match.

MacRae laughed and said, "George, you've got a way of cutting right to the heart of things."

From the other direction appeared Solly Fishblate. "Look what's coming," MacRae observed.

Waddell said, "It's getting so a gentleman can't enjoy his dinner in peace."

The Reverend Hoge said, "Did the old Jew ever ante up for the campaign war chest?"

Rountree nodded. "Took me three visits. Finally squeezed fifty dollars out of him."

"Blood from a stone," MacRae observed.

Fishblate wasn't carrying any food. He stood before them, arms crossed, mouth and cheek jumping in a nervous tic. "Gentlemen," he said, face flushed, out of breath, as if he'd run all the way from his shop on Front Street. "I had no idea you were planning such a show." He stood rocking on his heels, holding his left arm as if it were broken, waiting for somebody to invite him to sit down. No one did.

"Rumors," Fishblate blurted out. "To my ears come these rumors." His arms uncrossed and boxed his own ears, then flailed the air. "Secret plans, secret committees, things to happen after the election."

"Let's control ourselves," Walker Taylor said.

"Town's full of rumors," Rountree observed, drawing on his cigar. "What else is new?"

"I have met with my people. It was not easy, on such short notice, but they listen to Sol Fishblate. They are willing to go along." He collected himself and caught his breath. "I want you to know," he continued in a lower voice, and paused, studying their faces, "that I am willing to serve again."

Rountree looked puzzled. "How's that?" He held his cigar casually, his index finger hooked over it.

Fishblate grabbed the handkerchief out of his front pocket and mopped his brow and neck. "To serve again. As your mayor."

MacRae said quietly, "You're jumping the gun."

"But the secret committee, the plan."

Walker Taylor said, "There's no secret committee—get that out of your head."

Rountree said, "There's no secret plan. We're going to win back the county and the legislature. That's as far as it goes."

"But I contributed money. I was given to understand—"

"We all kicked in," Walker Taylor said. "Put this town back on a stable footing."

"Make it safe again for decent white women to walk the streets," Waddell said. This was the first he'd heard anybody mention this mayoral business. Suddenly, he was very sure he'd been left out of some important conversations. He'd have to ask a few discreet questions in the right quarters. But there was no need to include Solly Fishblate, not yet—if Fishblate's administration hadn't been so incompetent, they wouldn't be in this mess. He might talk to him later, though, in private.

"But as long as Dr. Wright and his crowd—"

"Let it be, Solly," MacRae advised. "Now, run along out of here—we've got business."

Fishblate, too, found an empty table, across the aisle from Dowling's, and it soon filled with his old Dry Pond cronies. They bent their heads over the table and talked with their bodies.

When Fishblate had gone, Sam asked his cousin directly, "What about it? Is there a secret committee?" He expected wild anger, maybe even a fist.

MacRae only sighed and said, "You've been reading too many romances," and patted him on the back.

"Secret plan, that's rich," Walker Taylor said.

George Rountree said, "Sam, there's not a thing going on here that we're not proud to do in the light of day, out in the open, with the whole town watching. That's why it's called democracy."

Outside the tent, the breeze had freshened into a wind, snapping the flags. The white supremacy banner bellied like a sail, and under it Walker Taylor's Boys Brigade performed close-order drill with their wooden toy rifles. Their mothers and fathers shouted "Bravo!" and clapped till their hands warmed with blood. Other boys looked on, envy shining in their eyes.

Walker Taylor looked on proudly. These were the boys everybody else had given up on, the bad boys, the truants and shoplifters and little gangsters, and he'd drilled them into a corps of proud soldiers for progress. It was only the beginning of what he could do for this town.

Bring it to order, then all things were possible.

Behind the drilling boys, the Red Shirts mounted their horses, sleeved their Winchesters, and quietly headed for Brooklyn.

In his first-floor library half a block from Market Street and just around the corner from Hugh MacRae's mansion, J. Allan Taylor sipped brandy, waiting for the Pinkertons. He wondered how much Walker knew. They'd need Walker when the trouble came—a first-rate military man like him was hard to find. But Walker was naive about politics. He actually believed he was going to be mayor when this was all over.

The Pinkertons were half an hour late. It was going on one. The grandfather clock ticked away the minutes. He'd left the kitchen door open for them, but he'd left no outside lights burning—couldn't risk their being seen. After the demonstration today, the speeches and the marching music, then the Red Shirts' rampage through Brooklyn all evening—smashing up shops, shooting rifles—he wasn't sure they'd dare venture into this part of town at all after dark.

He was just pouring another short brandy when they darkened the door of his library. He was startled. He had expected to hear them at the back door—door thunking shut, feet shuffling across the kitchen floorboards, voices muttering. But they had simply materialized without warning.

"Don't just stand around," he said softly, so as not to wake his family. "Come in."

The two Negro men entered warily and sat on the edge of the

chairs he had arranged in front of his desk. He got up heavily—realizing all at once how very tired he was, how late it was, how curiously old he was feeling tonight—and drew closed the French doors.

Both men wore rumpled city suits without ties—one blue, one brown. They held their slouch hats on their knees and fidgeted nervously. The one in the brown suit was smaller-framed, wore a moustache, and did all the talking. His name was Albert Tully.

"We've been up and down this town," he said. "We've peeked into windows, listened at bedroom doors, praised the Lord in seven churches, got our hair cut eleven times, treated every brother in Brooklyn to free beer." He cleared his throat. "We got the story, boss."

Taylor briefly wondered whether to offer the Pinkertons brandy, but thought better of the idea. Still, he felt awkward sipping his own, so he let the snifter sit untouched on the desk. "Keep your voice down, please," he said.

"Beg pardon, boss."

"So tell me a story."

Albert looked at the quiet one, who nodded and fingered his hat, turning it endlessly across his knee.

"It's a bad story, boss. Raining sticks and stones out there tonight."

"Go on."

"There's a high-yellow rabble-rouser behind it all," he said.

Taylor nodded. "Manly."

He shook his head. "Not Manly, boss. Another man. Stranger in town. Preacher fellow, goes by the name of Grant. Ivanhoe Grant."

"Never heard of him."

"You will."

"What about him?"

"Stirring 'em up plenty."

"They got guns?"

"More than you'd care to know."

Taylor wondered what could persuade a man to inform on his own people. Surely, there was more to it than money. "Hasn't your friend got anything to say for himself?"

The Negro in the blue suit stopped twirling his hat and smiled. "I be the quiet type, boss," he said with a certain pride. He narrowed his eyes. "I walk through walls. I slide down chimbleys. Invisible man, that's me." He touched his vest with a delicate finger. "Slip into bed between man and wife and listen to sweet nothings all night long." He didn't smile.

"Lester here is a ghost," Albert Tully explained.

Taylor looked unnerved.

Albert Tully chuckled. "That's a word we use in the trade for a pure spy. Man can find out things without getting found out. Get inside all the right places—and get out again."

"Get inside your head," Lester said.

"Do they have a plan?"

"Wouldn't call it no plan, perzactly," Lester said.

"Going to be a surprise," Albert Tully said. "On Election Day, they're going to mob the precincts, vote their own men in by hook or crook."

"We've got that covered," Taylor said, thinking of all the armies at their disposal—the Red Shirts, the Light Infantry, the Naval Reserves, the State Guards. All the good men he could count on to lead them—Donald MacRae, Bill Kenan, Roger Moore, Tom James. "What else?"

"Servants," Albert Tully went on. "On election night, they will rise up against their masters. Burn their houses to the ground."

"What? Burn their houses?"

Albert Tully leaned so far forward he was practically sitting on thin air. "They've been bragging, boss—every child in Brooklyn has a can of kerosene and knows how to strike a match."

"My God, I hadn't realized—"

"It's the truth, boss," Albert Tully said, and Lester nodded. "That's how they're talking. Burn the sin out of this town. Like some Bible story. Tom Miller, the loan man, he says he's going to wash his hands in white man's blood."

"Tom Miller?" Taylor dipped his pen in the inkwell and started taking notes. "Tell me everything," he said. "Give me names and places. Especially names." MacRae would want chapter and verse. Now, there could be no doubt—they must act. With this new intelligence, they would have to strike even harder. Shoot to kill. The lesson would have to be even more thorough.

The two Pinkertons sat in his library telling their story until after three. "One last thing," Albert Tully said, looking sly. "I got some news about your war hero at the newspaper."

"Do tell."

Taylor paid them in cash, but made a notation in his ledger so the committee could reimburse him later. When they had gone, he downed his brandy in one quick gulp, then poured another for sipping. So they meant to tear this town apart. They meant to tear down the old order. Well, there would be order. He and Hugh would see to that. It began with the list of names copied in a neat hand, running down the page in two precise rows.

———————

Rountree met the Pinkertons at his office in the Allen Building rather than at his home. He disliked letting business intrude on his family life. A gentleman kept things where they belonged—to maintain perspective.

He checked his railroad watch—nearly one. They were late. He couldn't abide lateness. Passion and time were all a man had in life. With a careful calendar, he could do his life's work three times over.

And why in the world did they insist on these midnight rendez-vous? My God, he'd bought a Gatling gun in broad daylight. Surely, their secrets weren't so dangerous. Must be their training, he reflected. Their instinctive distrust of daylight. Their love of shadows, secrecy, masquerade.

He heard them talking loudly in the hall, then watched their shadows bloom through the frosted glass of his door. "It's open," he said.

Two white men entered, both in soft clothes, wearing caps. With their rough faces and square hands, their clodhopper brogans and soiled corduroys, they had been passing for laborers in Brooklyn all week. Smith and Brown.

"You're late."

Brown said, "Fellow can get lost in these streets."

"Never mind." It wasn't worth the trouble to upbraid police agents. They ran on their own clock. In any case, they'd come with reliable references from a judge he knew in Chicago. They'd give him the straight story.

Smith opened a notebook. Rountree wondered how he kept it so crisp and clean under the circumstances. The agent pulled out a miraculously sharp pencil, licked the point, then licked his thumb and flipped through the pages, occasionally checking off some item.

"Well?"

Smith smiled sardonically. The agents were still standing, as if to announce that this wouldn't take long. Smith said, "We've been high and low, Mr. Rountree. We've been in the mills, under porches, inside the churches."

How had they managed that? Blackface, like in the minstrel shows?

Brown said, "We've bought a round of drinks in every tavern between here and Virginia."

Rountree said, "Get to the point."

Smith shrugged and closed his notebook, as if disappointed not to be able to recite dates and times and places and names. "Point is, you've wasted a little money. And we've wasted a good deal of time."

"Meaning?"

"Meaning there's no uprising. There's not fifteen guns in all of Brooklyn."

Brown said, "A few old squirrel rifles, a Civil War pistol or two, a couple of one-bang shotguns. Like that."

Rountree leaned forward, squinting, as if to bring their words into focus. "No organization? No leaders? No plan to take the polling places?"

Smith scratched his head with the sharp end of the pencil. "Somebody's been filling your head full of tall tales, Mr. Rountree. Sure, there's a half-dozen hotheads, big talkers. Winged some stones at streetcars after Mr. Dowling's tour, then ran like hell.

Maybe one of 'em will get up the nerve to throw a rock through your window some dark night. Maybe."

"But we understood there were hundreds—"

"They had a church meeting. You know how they do—jump up and razzle-dazzle around. Ain't no harm."

"Didn't come to nothing," Brown agreed. "Lot of hot air. One fellow with a big mouth, preacher man, but I've seen his kind before. When things get hot, they turn tail and skedaddle. Couple of Sunday-school teachers with birches could keep that whole Darktown buttoned up."

"So you're not expecting a riot?" Rountree asked. He had to be sure they were all talking about the same thing. Colonel Walker Taylor would want to know. So would Hugh MacRae.

Smith chuckled. "Not unless you start it." He flipped open his notebook. "You don't believe me, look it up. Times, dates, places. All the places where nothing was happening, all the times when nobody was up to anything. It's yours, anyhow—you paid for it." He tossed the notebook onto Rountree's polished desk.

"Names?"

"All the names of all the coloreds who weren't up to no good," Brown interjected, grinning.

"You're looking for the bogeyman, Mr. Rountree," Smith said. "Well, he don't live in Brooklyn. All you got in Brooklyn is a whole lot of factory niggers who just want to be left alone."

"You agree with this report?" Rountree said to Brown.

Brown shrugged. "Don't know how you-all did it, but you've raised the tamest collection of niggers this side of the grave. They'll sit still for anything, long as you let 'em work. My advice is leave 'em be."

Rountree showed the Pinkerton men out. Was this good news or bad news? One thing was sure: it surprised him. He had been preparing to defend his home and city against hordes of black vandals with guns. According to the Pinkertons, they could take this thing easy. Turn down the flame a bit. All those guns and speeches—maybe they'd overreacted.

This would take some hard thinking. The whites were lathered up, and the blacks were lying down. Keep Waddell in check, Rountree thought. Let it roll on nice and easy. Think about Raleigh, the statehouse, a bigger world than this.

He had to win on Tuesday. Had to keep the lid on somehow. No violence—there must absolutely be no violence. It was no longer necessary. It wouldn't be legal.

He locked his office door and went outside. The narrow streets looked broad, so empty. He walked home right down the center of the street. Business could wait until morning.

From the pulpits of North Carolina the doctrine
of white supremacy was preached in the same
breath with the story of Christ's love.

Henry L. West,
journalist

CHAPTER TWELVE

Monday, November 7

WHY SHE WENT SEEKING him out, she couldn't explain. Not to
herself, certainly not to her husband. Ivanhoe Grant had humili-
ated her, but what Gray Ellen wanted was not revenge. She
wanted to understand. In Waddell's speech, she had glimpsed
something profoundly ugly, something completely outside her experience. Until she understood it, she would have no idea what to
do next.

She went looking for Grant at the boardinghouse where he'd
cornered her that day as he toured her through the slums. The
neighborhood was alive with the sounds of people, their smells,
their chatter, the noise and clutter of their lives. Shirts snapped on
laundry lines. Somebody was hammering a nail. Water was run-

ning out of a pump. Children shrieked. Two women laughed and slapped their fat thighs. A skinny dog yipped after a creaky peddler's cart. A spoon clanged against a pot. A door slammed.

Rain was predicted. As she walked, she felt somehow safer with her umbrella in her hand.

She let herself in the front door, which wobbled on rusty hinges. Inside were a dim hallway and a rickety staircase. The place smelled of rotten wood and mildew. She sneezed in the dust-hazy air. On the second floor, she listened at a closed door: shoes scraping the floor, fingers tapping, a man clearing his throat. She knocked. The door wasn't closed properly, and it sprang open and banged against the wall like a gunshot. A man in the chair by the window, working at a small desk, jerked his head around, terrified.

"Reverend Grant," she said, startled breathless herself, "I didn't mean to frighten you."

He remained alert as prey, blue eyes focused on her. Something was different about him—the spectacles. She had never seen him wearing spectacles. They made him look bookish and shy. His right hand held a pencil. Before him on the desk lay a tablet of lined pages. He didn't get up. The room was tiny—a narrow, unmade bed, a night table and basin, a dirty brown carpet, and the little desk by the window. A breeze fluttered the papers.

"Close the door, schoolteacher, before I lose all my work."

She did as she was told. "What are you doing?" she said.

He stood up. He was jacketless. The sleeves of his white shirt were limp from perspiration, as if he'd been working for a long time. His tie was undone at the collar. He picked up the tablet and smacked it against his palm. "I have watched and I have listened and I have bided my time." He tossed the tablet onto the desk, then set the pencil on it.

"You're making a record."

He smiled and nodded. "Exactly. If anything should happen, people must know what was said and done here."

"What's going to happen?"

"I am not a prophet. Something may happen. Who can say?"

"Who do you work for?"

He shook his head, clapped his hands, and paced the little room. "You are a piece of work, schoolteacher. Who do I work for?" He turned on her and put his face right into hers so she could feel his heat. "The Lord Jesus Christ, our God and Savior!" he said.

"I'm not impressed." She sat in the only chair in the room, by the desk, and stood the umbrella against it.

He kept pacing. "Now, you going to tell me what you're doing here?"

She didn't have an answer. Or the answer she had was not the kind that lent itself to words. He was the only man in town who took her seriously. Maybe it was just that. A few months ago, she could never have imagined herself coming to a place like this in search of a man like Ivanhoe Grant.

"You know, you could get me hanged just by being here."

It had occurred to her. "You didn't seem too worried about that last time." Right out on the street, she recalled. No pretending about it—pure bullying. If she'd given in, he'd have surely taken advantage.

"There's a lot more to worry a man these days." He glanced out the window, as if making sure she hadn't been followed. "Now, what are you doing here?"

"You tell me."

He sat on the desk and leaned over her. "I think you don't know what to make of me. I believe I baffle you."

"Go on." She couldn't look away from him.

"You've never met a man like me before. I'm not *nice*. And that excites you."

"Don't go too far."

He shrugged elaborately. "I don't mean only sexually, although if you're honest—"

"I said, don't go too far." She started to get up, but it was a halfhearted attempt. She'd come here looking for a solution. This man did have a certain power about him. He stuck in her imagination. Her memory kept coming back to him, fascinated. He had that smooth, bedtime voice that took her off-guard, then poked her in the eye with truth.

"There is an excitement of the heart, teacher, as well as of the body. A tingling of the mind in the active presence of new ideas. A trembling of the soul."

Yes, she had felt all those. But that wasn't it. "How about fear?"

"Fear? Ah, then you have come to me as a confessor."

"I already have a confessor."

He nodded. "The priest."

"Yes." She had told Father Dennen everything. She only wished Sam would confess to him, too.

"You tell him *everything*?"

She pondered that. "Not everything."

"Not everything," he whispered. "Then I am the one who hears the things you cannot even confess to your priest." He kissed her. She held her breath, wondering what to expect. His mouth had a slightly metallic taste, like the taste of well water from a tin cup. It was not unpleasant.

He drew back. "I am forcing nothing," he warned her. "You came to me."

She could not bring herself to speak. He was right and he was also wrong—at this instant, she was powerless to do anything but let the world happen to her. She was under his spell.

He pulled her over backward in the chair. She felt herself falling and cried out, weakly.

"I will not let you fall," he said gently. "You shall not even stub your toe." The odd remark sounded vaguely scriptural to her. He eased her back and then rolled her off the fallen chair and onto the brown rug. He was surprisingly heavy on top of her.

She waited for the passion to flood into her, but nothing happened. She was not even really afraid, did not even feel guilty. She watched herself as if she were a detached observer peeking in the window: half-undressed now, she lay on her back, arms flung limply over her head, on a dirty brown carpet in a cell-like room in a tawdry boardinghouse in the Negro section of a city she had come to loathe.

The image astonished her. Then her vision filled with his blue eyes, the sweat gleaming along his razor-sharp moustache. She was disappointed—she had expected a mad loss of control, a sudden violent surge of guilty emotions, a heart-pounding tumult of caresses. Meanwhile, he was peeling off her blouse.

"Wait," she said.

He must have heard the sadness in her voice. She wasn't struggling, just politely asking.

He got off her. "So, you can't make up your mind." He wasn't even breathing hard. "I am forcing nothing. Just go home and forget about this."

As he stood over her, shirtless, she saw that something was wrong with the skin of his stomach and chest. Slowly, she got to her feet, feeling the breeze fretting through the open window. "Your stomach, those marks."

"What?" He stood confused, one hand holding his shirt, the other touching a pink scar on his stomach. There were more scars, livid pink slashes.

"Your scars." She moved toward him, fascinated, and traced her fingers over the long scar on his belly.

He laughed. She felt his laugh under her fingers. "You're tickling me," he said. He wasn't laughing anymore. He pushed her back, gently but insistently. "Last man tickled me, he used a cat."

"A cat?"

"You know, teacher—the kind with nine tails? The kind where each leather tail is knotted wet around a steel rivet and then dried in the sun till it's nice and tight?"

"They whipped you?"

"Jesus, Mary, and Joseph, woman! You have no idea what goes on in this world. Lynching—it's an old custom in these parts."

"Turn around. Let me see."

"You don't want—"

"Turn around." She turned him and saw the bare flesh of his back. She swallowed the bile that rose in her throat. His flesh was pink, white, and black, crosshatched in overlapping scars. The texture was *corrugated*—that was the only word that described it. She said the word to herself, to remember the effect later.

"Have you ever seen a lynching?" he asked quietly, his back to her, staring out the curtainless window. "Do you know what happens when a man is whipped?"

She said nothing. She had never seen such a thing in her life.

"They tie your arms up over your head, like this." He raised his arms and crossed his wrists, then let them down and picked up her umbrella. He whacked it against the desk. She jumped. "At first, it stings. You close your eyes and you can see the stripes on your back—each one as it is laid on, as if your eyes were watching through your own skin."

Whack! "How it makes a long, red welt."

Whack! The rubber tips at the ends of the umbrella ribs ricocheted against the wall. "You feel the knot biting, then flicking off. Each time it flicks off, a little piece of flesh goes with it." *Whack!* "By the third lash, the welts start to bleed. They don't sting anymore—now, they burn. Now, it's like fire is being poured onto your back." He flailed at the desk with the umbrella till it was beaten shapeless, the fabric shredded. He flung it away.

She wanted him to shut up, she didn't want to hear any more about it, but she didn't dare speak.

"Like liquid fire. You keep your weight on your feet no matter how bad it hurts, so your arms don't pull out of their sockets. You say to yourself, Lord, help me keep standing on my feet. You promise him anything."

"Please," she managed to say.

"No, I don't guess you want to hear all this. But I believe this is what you came here for. I do believe that."

"I don't think—"

"Let me tell you this," he said, still not looking at her. "I have never told this before to anyone." He paused, but she said nothing. "Whipping a man is hard work. In the old days, on the plantations, they used to make a black man give the whippings. Black on black. Insult to injury."

He waited for her to say something, but she didn't. "Sometimes, the man doing the whipping, he has to take a break. Let another fellow take over. Man can hurt his back, whipping another man. So for a few seconds each time, you think it's over. They're done. They've lost the stomach for it. There are women in the crowd, young children. Surely, they'll put a stop to it."

He forced a laugh, shook his head. "But you know what? They

never lose the stomach for it—not in my experience. They want you to scream. They want you bawling like a baby. Especially the women.

"You've already pissed yourself," he said. "And your pants are soaked with blood—feels like greasy water. Your shoes are full of blood, but it don't do you no good in your shoes. You start to feel dizzy, your eyes go all swimmy, you wonder if you're going to pass out and break your own arms."

"Please, that's enough." Her insides were churning and her throat was dry. The room seemed suddenly too hot, yet she had gooseflesh on her arms and breasts. She realized all at once that her breasts were uncovered, her nipples erect against his ruined flesh, that she was standing at his back nearly naked. She grabbed her blouse and held it over herself.

"And if you're mule-stubborn, you don't cry out. You're a stone man. Swallow the pain. Take the pain." He punched the flat of his fist against his stomach. "Pack it into your stomach, close it like a fist. The pain makes you strong.

"But you're getting weaker—can't help it. Your spirit leaking out onto the ground. They can smell it. Start shouting louder. They can smell the kill. They're all yelling now, everybody wants a piece of you. Man with the whip, he swings it harder. You feel the sting of the knot on your shoulder bones—all the flesh is peeled off. The bones make a different noise, hollow, like whacking a water pipe when it's froze."

He was talking so fast she could hardly keep up. "The crowd is moving now. Men and women both, fending off with their hands. See, you're getting all over them. Little chunks of you—your flesh and blood, chips of your bones—flying into their eyes. Ruining their nice clothes. They jump back. The women squeal. Makes them crazy, they love it so. The men hoot. Strings of your flesh are hanging off the bushes. Coon dogs are fighting over the scraps."

Ivanhoe Grant was out of breath. He braced himself against the desk, palms flat, arms rigid. She stood watching an arm's length away. His breathing was ragged.

He said quietly, sadly, "When your back is all used up, they start on the legs. Sooner or later, you got to fall down. Then they put a rope around your neck and lift you up." Around his neck was a ring of rough flesh—his high collar always covered it.

"They hanged you? Then how did . . . ?"

He sighed and then spoke quietly. "If the good Lord sends a fearful storm of lightning. If everybody runs for cover and leaves the nigger tied to the tree. That's how."

She waited. His breathing calmed, deepened, took on power, control. When his voice came again, it was the voice of the pulpit, mystical, chanting: "He is baptized in a cold rain while the fire of the Holy Ghost blazes across the sky, cracking trees, burning the air into smoke. With fire and water is he baptized. They drift out of the woods like smoke, dark faces and dark hands, and they carry him away from that place. And in his delirium, he speaks in the tongues of the Holy Ghost. He gets the call, teacher. He is blessed by the Almighty, chosen of God. Forever after, untouchable."

He undid the buttons of his fly, then tugged down his trousers. The scars continued down his buttocks, thighs, and calves. Only his face and hands were unscathed. Naked, he was revolting to look at, worse to touch. Grotesque. Yet her fingers wanted to feel the rough flesh.

"Don't touch me," he said quietly. "That's not why you came here. Sit. Talk to me. Tell me what's in your heart."

"Who are you?"

He laughed without enthusiasm. "I am the devil on your shoulder. I am whatever you make me."

All morning long, activity was frantic at the *Messenger*. The newswire telegraphed nonstop, copyboys came and went, and Clawson stormed around importantly—dictating assignments, yanking copy out of typewriter platens, yelling at reporters, pausing only to shout into the telephone.

J. Allan Taylor was in half a dozen times. Clawson's office was crowded with rough men Sam had never seen before. They came in long enough to pick up a rifle or shotgun, stuff their pockets with ammunition, then shuffle out in twos and threes, hats pulled down hard over their eyes in the manner of country men.

Sam sat at his desk working on a piece about the election. Police Chief Melton was so rattled with premonitions of violence that he'd asked the Board of Audit and Finance to authorize the hiring of two hundred special officers to guard the polls. The board had hemmed and hawed and refused to spend the money. Meanwhile, armed Red Shirts and Rough Riders patrolled the streets in squadrons. The coppers avoided them.

The Board of Aldermen had met in emergency session and declared it illegal to sell alcoholic beverages within a mile of the city limits—but everywhere saloons were doing a brisk business and men were drinking openly on street corners. From what Sam could tell, every white man in the city had bought a gun.

The local Democratic party had assigned twenty-five men to each of the precinct polling places tomorrow.

The Wilmington Light Infantry and the Naval Reserves were on alert.

Schools were closed. Vigilantes acting for the Businessmen's Committee rode the streetcars.

Housewives were buying canned goods and kerosene for lamps.

Many domestic servants had not reported for work this morning.

The town was full of strangers.

Where was Harry Calabash? Sam could guess: sprawled on his bed, obliviously drunk. He could use Harry today. He'd already lost track of half the names that mattered, and more were coming up all the time. There were so many factions, so many different parties, so many levels of the same parties.

The Fusionists had broken with the Populists, and both had disowned the Republicans, who, they declared, had shown no backbone against the white supremacy campaign.

The state Democratic party was feuding with the New Hanover County Democratic party over George Rountree's place on the ticket. "Go to hell," Rountree had reportedly told Furnifold Simmons, the state chairman and himself a candidate for the United States Senate. "We're going to run our campaign to suit ourselves." Wilmington was the real capital. The party was here. The will.

Mayor Silas Wright was nowhere to be found, nor Sheriff French. Most of the aldermen had disappeared after their emergency meeting.

All sorts of military men were taking their uniforms out of storage: Colonel Roger Moore, somebody named Morton with the Naval Reserves, another fellow named McIlhenny. Sam just couldn't keep the players straight anymore.

All those vectors of ambition were converging on the polls. If there was a single, secret plan, it couldn't possibly be carried out amid this chaos of factionalism. Everybody was at odds. Nobody was going to get what he wanted. Everybody was going to step all over everybody else's neat designs. Liquor, guns, politics, money, and white supremacy—quite a recipe.

Sam was aware of someone standing over him. "Colonel Waddell. Surprised to see you here."

"The air smells of ozone," Waddell declared, sniffing dramatically.

"Pardon me?"

Waddell slapped him on the back. "Storm coming," he said happily. "Clear the air, make it so a man can breathe deeply again."

A storm was coming, all right.

"Can you get away?" Waddell said. "We can talk over lunch."

Sam glanced toward Clawson, who was looking his way through the glass and motioning him to go along. He didn't look happy about it.

Sam grabbed his coat and followed Waddell to the door.

At the top of the stairs, Harry Calabash passed them going into the office. "Samuel," he said. "Off to conquer new worlds, I see."

Waddell looked on, annoyed.

"You all right?" Sam said. "I missed you."

"Never better." Harry looked tired, but his suit was immaculately cleaned and pressed, and he'd obviously been to the barber. He looked like a man with a purpose. Sam couldn't smell liquor on his breath. Two men shouldered past them carrying Winchesters. "Democracy in action, eh?"

"Harry, we have to talk."

Harry patted the pocket of Sam's jacket, the one with the revolver. "Ruins the drape of your suit."

"Mind your own business, Harry."

———

Gabrielle emerged from her sewing room—the old servants'
quarters behind the kitchen—to take lunch with them. Before
they sat down in the dining room, however, she and Colonel
Waddell excused themselves to the library to discuss some household matter. He could just make out the rising inflection of her
voice through the closed doors. He didn't mean to listen, but it was
a habit he had long cultivated for his profession.

Saffron King James wiped her hands on her apron and rested
them on her hips.

"Look, I'm sorry," Sam said. "What I did that night was wrong. I
beg your pardon."

"Don't fret. I ain't going to get you in trouble with your boss."

"The Colonel's not my boss."

"Sure act like it."

Sam glanced at the French doors of the study, still closed.
Gabrielle's voice was high and angry. He could make out a few
words—they were quarreling over money, household expenses.
"Look," he said to Saffron, "things are getting plenty hot around
here. You better watch yourself."

"What you talking?"

"Tomorrow, stay off the streets. Find a hole and crawl in it."

"That what you going to do, find yourself a hole?" She laughed.

"Forget it," he said. "No use talking to you."

She said, "Too bad you got to go home to that ice queen."

"Don't you dare talk about my wife." He raised his hand, but he
wasn't sure what he meant to do. He couldn't strike her—he'd
never struck a woman in his life. But he had to do something, so he
walked into the dining room.

She followed. "She thaw out sometimes, with the right man."

"What?" He turned.

She went around the table and played with her apron strings.
"Some girls fancy a preacher man. Not me, but some girls."

"What are you talking about? Tell me plain."

"Shoot, ain't no use talking to you." She grinned, then disappeared through the swinging door into the kitchen, where he heard her laughing.

Then another door slammed, and Sam heard Waddell's crooning murmur from behind the closed doors of the library. Presently, he and Gabrielle appeared in the dining room. Her face was flushed, and she would not meet his eye. She said, "Bessie's down at the market. I'll serve the lunch."

While she busied herself in the kitchen, Waddell poured them both glasses of iced tea from a pitcher on the sideboard. "I hope you've thought about what I said."

"Of course. But I still don't understand why you need me."

"Things are starting to happen. When they're done happening, this will be a different city. The old virtues will matter again—loyalty, honor."

Sam sipped his tea. God, he was beginning to hate the stuff.

"I'll be frank," Waddell said. "My own son—"

"You don't have to explain."

"Let me finish. A man wants to be remembered. To pass on his legacy. I have a son, but he is no good to me. No good at all. I need someone I can count on."

"To tell your story."

"Somebody who has mettle, who is not easily swayed. You were in Cuba—you won't flinch."

Sam shrugged. It was easy to watch other men being brave, even in Cuba. "A lot of men fit that description."

Waddell waved a hand. "Not as many as you'd think. Not like the old days." He wagged a finger. "But you—I saw it in your eyes that first day on the train. You would not meddle in other men's business, until it was a matter of personal honor."

When the Red Shirt had grabbed Gray Ellen. Given another chance, Sam knew now, he might take sides sooner.

"Mainly, I need someone who has no debts." Waddell waited for it to sink in. "Someone who is not connected to the regimes of the past."

"Hugh MacRae—my cousin, remember?"

"I can work with Hugh. But I need a sort of protégé, if you take my meaning."

"I already have a job. I don't have any training in the law."

Waddell smiled. "What you need to learn, I can teach you."

"If I go along?"

"Keep on writing for Tom Clawson. When the time is right, I'll call for you." He moved very close to Sam. "I'll only call once. After that, events will pass you by."

Sam nodded. He was tempted to make a declaration of allegiance here and now. All his career, he had been dogged by bad luck, bad timing, bad habits. Chicago had been his first big chance. Then going to Cuba with the army. He'd fouled up both.

Now, he had cleaned up his life. He was ready. It was about time he hooked up with a winner. Waddell looked like the right horse. He had that aura of success, a man in exactly the right place at exactly the right moment. Never mind his household troubles—he had lost two wives, and look who he'd ended up with. He always came out ahead.

Still, it felt wrong.

Gabrielle took too long preparing lunch. When she finally came into the dining room, her eyes were red. She wouldn't look at Sam all during the meal. Waddell stuffed himself happily, talking non-stop—between mouthfuls of cold ham and pickles—about the Hibernian navigators, Columbus, and Manifest Destiny. To Sam, he seemed an old man to be entertaining such grand ambitions, but then he remembered Joshua Slocum, another old man, who had just sailed alone around the world on a salvaged oyster dredge and now dined with the Roosevelts. The world was changing. Anything was possible. The trick was to reach out and grab the main chance. Sam intended to grab as hard as he could.

As he and Colonel Waddell left by the front door to go back downtown, Bessie King was hurrying up the driveway on her way around back, carrying a parcel wrapped in white butcher's paper.

"Hello, Aunt Bessie," Waddell called.

Bessie stopped and glared at them both. She nodded slightly, then continued around back.

Colonel Waddell rapped the ground with his walking stick. "Damned insolent coloreds. Under my own roof! I simply will not have it!"

Sam expected the Colonel to turn around and go back inside to discipline Bessie, but instead he kept walking toward Market Street.

In the kitchen, Bessie unwrapped the porkchops for supper and commenced to butterfly and season them. That boy David was going to get himself into trouble, running with that preacher and those Manly boys. No good was going to come of it. And now that newspaperman was back, plotting with the Colonel.

She checked on the spider in the pantry and felt reassured that she was still upright in her web. Calm down, she told herself. Other folks crazy, no reason you got to be crazy, too.

Gabrielle came up beside her. "Bessie, why don't you stay here with us for a few days?"

"Miz Gabby?" She wasn't sure she'd heard right.

"Saffron and David, too, if you want."

"But the Colonel—"

"You leave him to me. This is your home, too. Use the sewing room—I'll clear out my things."

"I don't know."

She laid a hand on Bessie's wrist. "I just feel safer with you in the house."

"If you put it that way."

"There's one bed in there. And a couple of old army cots."

"I know, I know. Down in the basement. My David can haul 'em up."

When Gabrielle had gone, Bessie went back to preparing the porkchops. "Living with the whitefolks," she said to the empty kitchen, shaking her head. It was a long way from the cotton fields. "The world sure turning topsy-turvy."

———————

Except that this time Gray Ellen was not with him, and that he was sitting on the stage behind Waddell, Sam had a strong sense of

déjà vu. Thalian Hall was once again packed with white faces—
mostly men. There were fewer women than previously. Several
orators spoke as the crowd filtered in, boisterous, joshing, making
the most of the fun. From this new vantage point, the hall seemed
intimate, a fancy parlor. He was astonished that he could recognize so many faces so clearly so far into the back rows.

Waddell again waited for the house to quiet completely before
speaking. He knew he was the man they had all come to hear.
Once again, he played their emotions perfectly. His speech was the
same as before, the same one he had been delivering all over the
state at rallies and barbecues, changing it only slightly, honing the
metaphors, injecting local anecdotes.

"Men, the crisis is upon us!" he declared, then waited a whole
minute for the uproar of applause and cheers to die down. "This
city, the county, and the Old North State shall be rid of Negro
domination—once and forever!" Again, a din of cheers, men banging their fists on the arms of their seats.

His voice took on a measured tone. "You have the courage. You
are brave. You are the sons of noble ancestry." They murmured
assent.

"You are Anglo-Saxons. You are armed and prepared, and you
will do your duty."

"Hear, hear!"

"Be ready at a moment's notice. Go to the polls tomorrow, and if
you find the Negro out voting, tell him to leave the polls! And if he
refuses—"

Murmuring, angry muttering, a rebel yell.

"—kill him! Shoot him down in his tracks!" He banged his fist on
the podium.

The hall exploded in whoops and cheers. Was this just hyperbole? Sam wondered. Or did the Colonel honestly expect them all
to come out shooting tomorrow? Hyperbole, he decided—an orator's
trick. Otherwise, the notion was just too far-fetched. They were,
after all, on the verge of the twentieth century. Sam checked his
watch: five minutes passed this time before the Colonel could
continue. Tonight, he was going to burn the place down.

"We shall win tomorrow, if we have to do it with guns." He pivoted and pointed his finger like a pistol. "Let every man go to the polls ready and willing to *rule* or *die*."

Another uproar of assent. Then it got very quiet. Sam could see only Waddell's back, his erect posture, the black clawhammer coat draped perfectly, without a single wrinkle. The silver head shimmering in the limelight.

So quietly Sam could barely hear, he continued, "If you fail at this time, you deserve to be spit upon."

He leaned and spat, right onto the stage.

Something was happening at the back of the hall. In the midst of the shouting and applause, Sam couldn't hear the fight, but he could see black heads bobbing in the crowd at the top of the aisle. He left by the back way and ran around to the front steps, where the police were dispersing a gang of Negroes—a dozen or so, Sam calculated. They scattered, except for one lying face down on the steps with two policemen pinning him. They drove their knees into the small of his back until he stopped struggling, then handcuffed him and led him across the street to jail. Sam recognized one of the cops as Sergeant Lockamy.

"Frank Thompson, that's the name of the fellow they just hauled away," Harry Calabash said.

"Where have you been hiding?"

"Thalian Hall, like everybody else. Your stage debut."

The crowd was streaming out of Thalian Hall, more boisterous than ever. Men were passing flasks, shouting and arguing, laughing.

"You want to talk, Harry? You're all spruced up—what's the occasion?"

"I felt a need this morning to be *professional*."

Sam nodded. "Come with me."

"We're just rushing to and fro tonight, aren't we? Where are we off to now?"

"The jail. Talk to this Thompson."

By the time they covered the two hundred yards to the jail, a new mob was forming. The Negroes chased away from Thalian had returned with plenty of friends. The swarmed around the jail and made threatening noises, but none of them went in.

"They'll never get anywhere like this," Harry observed sadly. "Haven't got anybody to lead them."

For the moment, the white crowd milling around the corner at Thalian Hall seemed oblivious to the scene at the jail. But it wouldn't take them long to get wise. Just then, Sergeant Lockamy appeared on the steps of the jail. Next to him stood John G. Norwood. Norwood stepped forward and raised his hands for silence. He kept waiting, but the crowd wouldn't quiet down. He spoke anyway, his voice high and trembling. He's scared to death, Sam thought.

"Brothers, brothers!" Norwood said. "This is no way to do!"

"They got Frank!"

"He is not going to be harmed, believe me."

"Uncle Tom!"

"Why should we believe you?"

Lockamy stepped forward and said, "We'll let him out in the morning, after he sleeps it off."

"Go to your homes," Norwood said. "Don't start any trouble." Over the heads of the black crowd, he could see whites in twos and threes beginning to straggle toward the jail, curious about what was going on, what new speech they were missing. "Go home—now!" Norwood's voice took on more authority.

Now, two more black men came out of the crowd and took their places beside Norwood—Carter Peamon and the Reverend J. Allen Kirk. Father Christopher Dennen, red hair fiery in the gas carriage lamps mounted on either side of the jail doorway, stood by like a statue of conscience.

They took turns entreating the crowd to break up. A sudden cloudburst that had been threatening all evening began to drench them. The rain was cold and fierce, while it lasted. The Negroes milled around uncertainly, then began to drift away.

"That's it," Harry observed. "Don't give them any excuse."

The rain passed quickly, leaving the air sharp with lime and earth.

Tom Clawson pulled a buggy up to the curb. "Sam, can I borrow you for an errand?"

Harry said, "You're a popular fellow tonight. How about a drink later at Polson's?"

"Right." Sam climbed aboard the buggy.

Clawson slapped a Winchester across Sam's knees, then drove fast up Princess to Seventh without speaking. As they crossed Seventh, Sam noticed lights blazing in Hugh MacRae's mansion. Across the street, Walker Taylor's house was also lit up so brightly that Sam worried at first it was on fire. Clawson appeared not to notice. He urged the horse down South Seventh toward Free Love Hall. When Sam saw where they were headed, he said, "I hope you don't expect me to shoot anybody, Mr. Clawson."

"With any luck, you won't have to. But you never can tell—it's a spooky night. I want you to watch my back."

Sam said, "I don't get your angle in all this."

"Makes you think I have an angle?"

"You're playing fast and loose." Sam was taking a chance. "But you're not Hearst—you know better. Yet here you are, drumming up a war."

Clawson kept his eyes on the road. "Don't push it. I didn't like you when I hired you. I'm not sure I like you any better now."

"That's your problem. But you can't fool me. You're no vigilante."

"Well, you got one thing right."

At Free Love Hall, Frank Manly came out of the shadows and approached the buggy from behind. "Mr. Clawson, that you?"

"Look, there isn't a lot of time. Get Alex, will you?"

"What you got to say to Alex?"

"Oh, for Pete's sake." Too fast for Sam to stop him, Clawson was out of the buggy and rapping on the locked front door. "Alex! Come out, I have to talk to you."

Frank said, "It's okay, Alex—open up."

Sam laid aside his Winchester, but he stayed in the buggy. He didn't want anybody paying attention to him in this neighborhood at this hour of the night. Frank Manly stared at him, arms crossed, blood in his eye.

The door opened. Alex Manly appeared, looking drawn and groggy. "Mr. Clawson? Why didn't you say so? Come on in."

"No need. I just came to warn you—this time, they mean business."

"What exactly was it they meant last time?"

"You're smart enough to know the difference. I'm telling you, get out while you can. Get gone and stay gone."

Alex Manly was buttoning his shirt. He hadn't put out the newspaper in days and had been sleeping at the office for some time now, trying to make up his mind about the future. "But the printing press, we can't just—"

"Leave it behind. I'll come collect it, by and by. When all this blows over."

Alex Manly laughed. "You must have me mixed up with another gentleman. Gentleman who doesn't know business. I own more than half of that press now."

"And I still own the other half. And the half you do own won't be much good to you when you're hanging from a lamppost."

"That what your whitefolks committee going to do to me?"

"It's a thought. Look, this has gone far enough. I don't want to see you hurt."

"You just don't want to lose your investment."

"I'm telling you for your own good. I must be crazy even to try and talk sense to you." He turned and stalked back to the buggy.

"Wait a minute, Mr. Clawson." Manly came outside, and the two stood next to the buggy. "All I'm saying is, I've got an investment to protect."

Clawson pushed him away. "You just don't get it, do you? This town's all worked up. There's a mob down at city hall getting the ropes ready, and they've got your lamppost all picked out. Don't hold me responsible—I wash my hands."

"You wash your hands?" Alex Manly shouted furiously. Sam tensed, expecting him to strike Clawson. Then Sam would have to intervene. But Manly didn't—he wasn't that kind of fighter. Sam relaxed. "That trash you've been printing? Driving a wedge between white and black? Just what do you call that?"

"Don't forget who sold you your printing press. Who got you started in this business so you could tell your side of the story. Don't forget that."

"Lot of good that's doing me now."

"Just out of curiosity," Clawson said, "who wrote that editorial?"

"What makes you so sure I didn't?"

Clawson shook his head. "Not your style. Come on, for the record. Who wrote it?"

Alex was still angry. "A black man."

Sam wanted to get out of there. He said, "Mr. Clawson, he has a point about the money."

Clawson dug in his pocket. "Here. Twenty-five dollars—it's all I've got."

"Ought is an ought, and a figure is a figure," Alex Manly said, sighing in disgust.

Frank said, "All for the white man, and nothin' for the nigger."

"Now, there's no call—"

"It's not enough," Alex said. "You're short by a hundred."

"It'll have to be enough," Clawson said, and climbed aboard the buggy. "Leave a receipt with the press, so there won't be any trouble about it later." It had always been a handshake deal. At the time, Clawson had been happy to unload the old press. Who could have figured it would cause so much mischief?

Manly looked up at them. "I can't decide if you're trying to cheat me or save my life."

"Good," Clawson said. "Giddap!"

Clawson drove home down Market Street to take advantage of the street lamps and the lights from houses. From Seventh down to the Cape Fear, armed men were deployed in pairs on every street corner.

As they passed the Wilmington Light Infantry Armory, Sam heard the sound of men's voices singing a marching chorus. "They'll be bunking up the whole lot of them, on alert," Clawson said. "Hundred and fifty men, or nearly. Makes a body feel safe just to think about it."

Sam wanted to go home and see Gray Ellen. He hadn't talked to her all day, he'd been so busy running around. But he needed to see Harry, too. Clawson let him off at Polson's Saloon.

"Just one thing, Sam," Clawson said before Sam climbed out. "Where we went tonight? What you heard?"

"I know. None of it happened."

Clawson clapped him on the back. "Maybe you're not as dumb as I thought."

Sam hopped out of the buggy and turned. "So which was it, Mr. Clawson? Were you saving his life, or just trying to cheat him?"

Clawson smiled and leaned toward him. "Sometimes in life, son, there transpires what is known as a coincidence of interests. Tell Harry I want him sober tomorrow."

Sam didn't go into the tavern right away. He lingered in the open air trying to take in all that had happened today. What had Saffron meant?—*some girls fancy a preacher man.* Just talking, he figured. A girl like that, she was liable to say anything.

Sam inhaled the river, ripe and tangy. The rain had roiled the waters. Low tide, he reminded himself. He checked the piling at the ferry landing: six feet under the high-water mark. The current was stalled. The tide was about to turn. From now on, he could watch the Cape Fear rising.

Voting was not a right but a privilege, and
should be exercised only by qualified people.

George Rountree

CHAPTER THIRTEEN

Tuesday, November 8

ELECTION DAY DAWNED chilly and clear. The first Negroes to venture outside found handbills tacked to their doors, plastered on shop windows, hammered onto telephone poles. *Remember the 6*, the handbills declared over a crude skull and crossbones. Which six? The answer was far from clear.

Alex Manly yanked the handbill from the back door of the *Record*. Three possibilities occurred to him: the six leading Republicans who had been ousted from the ticket; the six white businessmen who made up Group Six, a white supremacy organization he had learned about only yesterday; and the six Negroes who, according to the legend, were lynched in 1831, their severed heads mounted on poles on all the roads leading out of town. Lately, folks had been retelling that story a lot.

He stood reading, shirtless, in the chilly backyard of Free Love Hall. The rest of the text left no room for ambiguity: *These degenerate sons of the white race whose positions made them influential in putting Negro rule on the whites, will suffer the penalty of their responsibility for any disturbance consequent on the determination of the white men of this county to carry the election at any cost.*

So it hasn't even happened yet and they've already picked out their scapegoats, he reflected—Benny Keith, Flavell Foster, Father Dennen, all the Yankees who had come here to seek their fortunes. And Mayor Wright and any others, black or white, who were trying to see past color. Inarticulate anger welled in him. He was not used to being inarticulate. He was used to speaking his mind. He had spent years mastering the craft of persuasion, the art of eloquence. But he had no say anymore.

He crushed the handbill in his fist. In this city, despite everything, he was still a stranger.

Frank stood suddenly at his shoulder. "White man don't come around on ordinary business," he said softly.

"Don't I know, brother. Don't I know." Clawson's visit last night. His final warning.

"They'll be coming around on extraordinary business, directly."

"No need to spell it out. I can read."

"So you can, brother. Horse and buggy waiting. Just say the word."

Castle Hayne again, under cover of darkness, slinking away like a common criminal, leaving behind everything—his people, his voice.

"Going to be a moon tonight," Frank said. "Can't be helped."

"What will be," Alex said.

"I have sent a wire to New Jersey. They will cable Carrie in London. Another two months, she'll be home. You'll forget all this."

Home, Alex thought. Where would that be from now on? New Jersey, Asbury Park? Maybe Philadelphia? How would he face Carrie? How would he explain that he had run away?

"I will shame her," he said.

"Shame ain't got nothing to do with it." Frank was getting angry. "Common sense. It ain't worth getting killed."

"No, brother, you're right. You're always right."

"Tonight. Soon as it gets full dark."

"What about the others?"

"They don't want the others."

Alex stood dumbly, looking down the alley at the new day. The world seemed suddenly narrow, constricted, seemed to lead inevitably to a place he didn't want to go. Had he been so foolish to think he could change things? How had all his choices, all the grand possibilities he had dreamed, disappeared so quickly?

"Don't go out today, brother," Frank said.

"I have to vote."

Frank spat. "They're going to stuff the ballot boxes anyhow—and they'll be laying for you, you show your face."

Alex knew he was right. His vote wouldn't count—none of their votes would. The whole thing was already cooked. He was surprised to learn that he wasn't up to a symbolic act of courage—a grand gesture. He had always assumed he would be. Now, he had nothing, not even his good opinion of himself.

"Get inside. There's riders all over town. I don't want no brother of mine to wind up with his head stuck on a pole. They might remember he has kin." Frank steered Alex through the back door of Free Love Hall and locked it behind them.

Before it was fully light, Mike Dowling assembled his Red Shirts behind the post office and led them at a walk past the Orton Hotel on Front Street, then around the corner onto Market, heading away from the river. The horses walked with their heads up, nostrils steaming, nickering nervously.

Off to the right, they passed the Gothic tower of St. James Church, crowned with cypress pinnacles, built to stand the weather. They paraded past the Temple of Israel, a Moorish-style oddity dedicated for its Jewish congregation in 1876 with a speech by Colonel Alfred Moore Waddell.

Half a block farther on, to the left, members of the Wilmington

Light Infantry and the Wilmington Naval Reserves were already forming up on the lawn facing the street. The milling soldiers watched Dowling's men with curiosity. A few of them waved. The Red Shirts did not wave back. Their faces were set. They were on a mission. They were past fooling around. Some of the horses balked at the sight of so many uniforms and tossed their heads. Their riders slapped the horses' necks reassuringly and half-stood in the stirrups to gentle them. The column was quiet except for the murmuring of rider to horse, the creak of stiff saddles, the jingle of harnesses.

Now, Dowling urged his little sorrel horse into a trot, and the column followed suit. He barely noticed the fortresslike First Baptist Church at the corner of Fifth Street.

At Seventh Street, a lone rider waited for them in the middle of the intersection—Hugh MacRae.

"Whoa, boys," Dowling called, reining up.

MacRae sat on his big bay hunter, one leg crossed over the pommel of the English saddle, looking bored and irritated. His high, soft boots were spattered with mud, and his hair was wind-blown and disheveled, as if he'd just galloped miles cross-country. In fact, he had ridden less than a block, in no particular hurry.

"Want to come along to the party?" Dowling said. He could not get his horse to stand still—she was prancing all over the road.

MacRae waited patiently for him to get his mount under control. His own hunter, seventeen hands tall, dwarfed the skittish sorrel. "Just what do you think you are up to?"

Dowling sawed at the reins, cursed, and half-stood in the stirrups. "You heard Colonel Waddell last night—we've waited long enough. We're going to take back this town." Dowling looked over his shoulder for support and saw the sullen faces of his men. They all knew Hugh MacRae.

"Just how do you propose to do that?" MacRae's hunter remained so still the two of them could have been a monument. Waddell was getting out of hand—these poor-bockers were starting to take him literally. His first instinct had been right: keep Waddell out of it. Rountree had agreed. It had been the others, dazzled by the myth of the Confederacy, who had insisted. Well, whenever you went against your best instincts, sooner or later you paid.

"Burn down that nigger paper," Dowling said. "It ain't very complicated. Lynch that dandy little monkey that runs it."

"Quite a plan," MacRae said. Turn him on his side, MacRae thought, and the sawdust would run out his ear.

"We'd be glad to have you along."

"But you're overlooking other considerations."

"Such as?"

Off his right flank came a sound that stopped Dowling's heart: the metallic slap of eighty rifle bolts. The Wilmington Light Infantry, armed with high-powered Krag-Jorgensen carbines, had double-timed up Market underground, in the tunnel, and come out ahead of the Red Shirts. Now, they were formed up in ranks, three deep, blocking Seventh Street. The front two ranks, kneeling and standing, aimed their rifles for volley fire. The third rank stood in reserve.

Behind the milling Red Shirts, Captain Kenan and his crew had quietly drawn up the Gatling gun, taken the tarp off, and leveled the gun at the mounted Red Shirts. Between the Gatling gun and the ranks of riflemen, they'd have the Red Shirts in a deadly crossfire.

Don't do anything stupid, Kenan thought. Don't make me crank this fine brass handle. Go slow. Listen to Mr. MacRae. If we fire on you, we'll kill a lot of good horses.

Behind the wagon, sixty Naval Reserves, bayonets fixed, stood ready to deploy as skirmishers.

Dowling twisted his neck, taking it all in. "How did you know—?"

MacRae said, "The telephone, Mike. New invention. Why don't you have your men dismount and water their horses?"

Dowling glared at him. All along the block, people were leaning out open windows to see what was happening. Dowling gave a signal. His men dismounted and shielded themselves behind their horses. It was unthinkable that the infantry would fire on them. But they were dealing with MacRae.

"Let's just talk awhile, you and me," MacRae said.

Dowling followed him into L. B. Sasser's drugstore, where Sasser, a member of MacRae's Secret Nine, joined them at a table in the back room.

"I don't have to tell you," MacRae began, "that we face a delicate situation here."

"Don't pussyfoot around," Dowling said too loudly. With enough bravado, he could reassure himself. "Delicate, hell. Me and my boys, we try to set things right. Well, we sure know who our friends are."

"We're all on the same side," MacRae said coolly. Sasser's clerk brought them all coffee.

"Funny way to show it, then—drawing down on my boys."

Sasser said, "Shut up, you goddamn mackerel-snapper. Listen to your betters."

Dowling shoved back from the table and jumped up, spilling his coffee. "That's it! I've taken about all I'm going to take! You goddamn high-hats have it all worked out! Well, Mike Dowling wants in on the action, see? I want of piece of this thing. Me and my boys—"

"What do you want, Mike?" MacRae said gently. "Sit down." He said to the clerk, "Bring the boy more coffee." MacRae was younger than Dowling, but nobody remarked the irony.

The clerk obliged, then mopped up the spill with a towel.

Dowling tried to get his rage under control. He was all jacked up this morning. His hands were shaking so hard he couldn't bring the cup to his lips. His mouth was full of the sour taste of adrenaline. He couldn't get his spit. He had worked himself up to what they must do today, and this was no time to lose his nerve. He steadied the cup. Finally, he managed a sip. "We want to work. We want jobs. Them niggers got all the good jobs locked up."

"We can do that," MacRae said amiably. "Honest white men ought to work."

"Right," Sasser said. "Bring a little dignity back to the working classes."

Dowling scowled, but before he could say anything else, MacRae said, "Would you like to be a fireman, Mike?"

It had never crossed his mind. "A fireman, huh?" He rolled his eyes toward the pressed-tin ceiling, as if imagining himself driving the big hook-and-ladder wagon. "Sure, that would be a fine thing. One of them city jobs. They can't fire you over every pizzlin' thing."

"You can lead men, Mike. You've got the makings of an officer."

"I got a hundred rifles waiting out front," Dowling agreed. He was slurping freely now from his coffee cup, his hands no longer trembling.

Seventy-five at most, MacRae thought. Get the numbers right—don't fool yourself. A man fools himself with numbers, he loses track of the world.

"My boys. They listen to me," Dowling said. He looked warily at Sasser, then MacRae. "Them fireman's coats, they got fine brass buttons."

"They do that," MacRae said. "Coat like that, it would look good on—"

"And the chief—"

"There can be only one chief," MacRae said quietly.

Dowling looked uncertain. He said, tentatively, "Assistant chief?"

MacRae stared at his coffee.

Dowling cleared his throat. "Mighty proud thing to be a captain."

MacRae smiled and nodded. "You'd make a fine captain, Mike. Truly."

Dowling relaxed and smacked his lips, as if waiting to be offered something stronger than coffee. When nobody offered any whiskey, he pulled out his own flask and dumped a slug into his coffee.

"You can appreciate our position, can't you?" MacRae said.

Dowling frowned. With the whiskey hot on his tongue, he was feeling a bit cocky now. They understood he was a man to be reckoned with. They were taking him into their confidence—they had no choice—so he might as well speak his mind. "Mr. MacRae, I got to say I just don't get it. Me and my boys, we could have this whole business settled within the hour."

Sasser was losing patience. "You dumb Mick."

"L. B., please! Look, Mike, here's the thing. We move now, there's a chance the federal court will declare the election invalid.

Troops come in, it's the Yankee occupation all over again. Reconstruction, and the niggers in charge. We lose everything. The election's got to happen first, see?"

Dowling slurped the rest of his whiskey-laced coffee. He was one of the mucky-mucks now. He had opinions. "Hang the election, I say. We'll run things the way we want to run 'em."

Suddenly, MacRae banged his fist on the table so forcefully that Dowling fell backward in his chair and had to grab the edge of the table to keep from sprawling on the floor. MacRae stood and planted one fist on the table. He poked an index finger into Dowling's face. "Now, you listen to me. You're going to take your men and ride home. You're going to do nothing else until you hear from me. Got it?"

Dowling nodded. "Yes, sir." He should have known better than to trust the damned high-hats.

"Good. This thing is way too big for you, Mike. Way too big. You're pissing with the big dogs now—be careful you don't get pissed *on*."

Dowling recovered himself enough to be angry again. "Just what makes you think you can tell me what to do? My men and me ride out of here, who's going to follow us? The Light Infantry can't stand around all day."

"You are a piece of goddamn work," MacRae said, almost amused. What would it take to get through to this blockhead? "L. B., have your clerk call my house. Tell them to bring it over."

They waited in silence for several minutes for MacRae's man to arrive from up the street. Donald MacRae, Hugh's brother, smartly turned out in the gray-and-red tunic of the Wilmington Light Infantry, clomped in carrying a portfolio. MacRae drew out a document and tossed it offhandedly onto the table.

L. B. Sasser said, "Thought we were keeping that under wraps."

Dowling picked it up and read the first paragraph with great difficulty. He scrutinized it for a few minutes, then gave up. "What is it?"

Sasser grabbed the document with a sigh of disgust and read, " 'Believing that the Constitution of the United States contemplated a government to be carried on by an enlightened people—' "

"There's going to be a mass meeting tomorrow," Hugh MacRae explained.

" '—believing that its framers did not anticipate the enfranchisement of an ignorant population of African origin—' "

MacRae said, "We'll read the whole proclamation then."

" '—and did not contemplate for their descendants subjection to an inferior race, we the undersigned—' "

"They're all going to sign it, every businessman in town."

" '—citizens of the City of Wilmington and County of New Hanover, do hereby declare that we will no longer be ruled, and will never again be ruled, by men of African origin.' "

"There are seven articles, altogether," MacRae explained. "I wrote it myself."

Dowling was still puzzled. "What is it?"

MacRae said, "We call it the White Man's Declaration of Independence."

"What good will it do?"

MacRae rose from his chair. The interview was over. "Go home, Mike. You're twenty-four hours early."

Sam Jenks had spent a restless night.

He'd stayed out late at Polson's Saloon watching Harry get drunk and listening to stories from the old days, when the Klan rode in gangs along country lanes and pregnant slaves were whipped lying belly-down in depressions scooped into the earth, to protect their unborn babies—the masters' property. Harry was full of grisly plantation tales.

Sam experienced an attack of clarity at Polson's, and he craved a long whiskey to sluice away his guilt and blur the outlines of the life he could see forming itself out of his present actions. But he didn't drink. He watched other men drink themselves stuporous and patiently waited for Harry to run out of stories.

Sometime after midnight, in between thundershowers, Sam had

managed to get him home. "Thought you'd dried yourself out," he said, knowing Harry couldn't hear him. Harry looked ridiculously old in the dim lamplight, face creased and drawn around the eyes, yet slack around the mouth and jowly from whiskey fat. He was just an old ghost now, fading away. And nobody was even watching, except Sam, who didn't want to look.

When Sam had arrived home, Gray Ellen was already asleep. He climbed into bed next to her. Her scent was overpowering—perspiration and perfume.

He had needed to talk to her, to caress her and feel her settle the world back into balance. He wanted to tell her everything he'd seen, explain to her all his conflicting instincts. She was his one fixed point.

Instead, he stared at the ceiling shadows. During the night, the thunder came and went, brooding over the town. Before dawn, it rained hard. He listened to it drumming on the roof. From time to time, the wind flung the rain against the window like handfuls of bird shot. His dreams were like broken glass—jumbled shards of images with edges that cut.

He woke up exhausted.

Gray Ellen was already downstairs sipping hot tea. He stole up behind her as she stared out the window, seeming as distant as if they had never met. He stood for almost a minute, unable to make himself speak to her.

"Don't stand there all morning," she said quietly, still looking out the window. "Come sit down. There's biscuits on the stove. I can fry up some eggs."

"I'm not very hungry." His stomach was full of acid.

"Suit yourself."

"No school today?"

"Of course there isn't." She, too, had slept badly, and she didn't have the strength to talk about the things that, sooner or later, they must talk about. Sam was sober—that was a good thing. She refused to be the one to give him the excuse to take a drink.

"There was another rally last night," Sam said.

"Your friend the Colonel? How I detest that strutting cock."

"He's a man of principle. He has a duty—"

" 'When a stupid man is doing something he is ashamed of, he always declares it is his duty'—Bernard Shaw."

What right had she to run down a man of such stature? " 'Nothing is ever done in this world until men are prepared to kill one another if it is not done.' " She wasn't the only one who could quote literary truth. Anybody could find an eloquent epigram for any kind of shrill philosophy. It was the first thing you learned on newspapers.

"At least you haven't forgotten everything you studied."

Sam backed off. His head was splitting. "Look, I don't want to fight today."

"Neither do I." Gray Ellen sighed. She knew she was making it hard for him. She couldn't help herself. Until yesterday, she'd had no idea how much he owed her. Ivanhoe Grant had opened her eyes. In his room, she had wept for hours, grieving for her lost life. She knew it was only a matter of his being there at the right time, but still there was something mystical about the man. He existed outside right and wrong—blessed and evil all at once.

She would have her life back, with or without Sam. She knew that now. A single, strange encounter had clarified things. She wished she could talk about it with him, make him understand what she needed. But how could she tell him that selfless devotion to a husband wasn't enough, had never been enough? As for Ivanhoe Grant, Gray Ellen never wanted to see him again. A man like that belonged in memory, not in real life.

Sam slumped into a chair at the table and rested his chin on steepled hands. His cheeks were sallow. His eyes had no clarity.

"After breakfast," she said matter-of-factly, ignoring the fact that he was eating no breakfast, "why don't you come out with me to vote?"

"What's the point? It's all fixed. That much I've figured out." He wasn't even sure he objected to the fix. The men who were going in were competent, serious, and experienced. Maybe, in a city like this, democracy was overrated. What had the Negroes ever contributed to the place besides a lot of Holy Roller churches and gang labor?

"The point is to vote. That's the point."

There she was again, stuck on principle. "What do you want to go out for?" Sam said. "You can't vote."

Right, she thought: a woman isn't even trusted that far. "You vote for me."

"How do you know who I'll vote for?"

"I'll know."

"Maybe it won't be anybody you like."

"I just want to see you do it."

He didn't say anything. She wasn't fooling.

She said quietly, "It starts with this. Today."

He nodded, slowly. His stomach was settling down. He had a long day ahead. What time was he supposed to meet Harry? No matter—Harry would be late. Harry was always late. Sam might as well be late for a change. "Ready when you are."

She sipped her tea, taking her time.

Sam attempted to vote in the community hall of First Presbyterian Church, the place where Colonel Walker Taylor drilled his Boys Brigade. Half a dozen armed men in rough clothes milled around the entrance. He waited in line behind other men in coats and ties.

Inside, the elections officer—a grocer Sam saw at least twice a week—asked his name, then checked it against the rolls in a ledger-sized book. "You're not in here, Jenks."

"I live at Third and Ann."

"Property owner?"

"No."

"Got a birth certificate?"

"Of course not. You know who I am."

"How about a deed to your house?"

"I just told you, I'm not a property owner."

"Been here long?"

"Since August. You ought to know."

"That's not long enough."

"Listen, I can be vouched for. My cousin, Hugh MacRae—"

"You're holding up the line, Jenks. Next time."

"What is this?" Sam said.

"Special registration. Too many transients and undesirables trying to influence things."

"By whose order?"

The clerk shrugged. "By order of the people who order such things. How the hell should I know?"

"So you're not going to let me vote."

"Ain't up to me."

"But all the same, I can't vote."

"Move along, or I'll call the sheriff."

"I don't believe this." Sam cast about for somebody he knew, some face he could count on. He recognized nobody.

"You don't have to believe it. You just have to vamoose."

Outside, Gray Ellen was waiting, hands tucked into her shawl against the wind. Sam said nothing, just took her arm and started walking toward home.

She said, "So, are you going to tell me who you voted for?"

He laughed tiredly. "I can sure tell you who I didn't vote for."

———————

Sam spent the day with Harry Calabash riding the streetcars from precinct to precinct, gauging the mood of the city. Few Negroes were out. The ones they saw in Brooklyn moved furtively in nervous clusters, heads down, mouths shut.

Downtown, white women promenaded alone or in pairs, accompanied by armed husbands and brothers. The Red Shirts patrolled in squadrons, sullen men who had been ordered not to shoot, not today. Their Winchesters rode in saddle boots. From time to time, they slapped the oiled stocks to reassure themselves that they were still there.

Eventually, bored and hungry, Sam and Harry wound up at the Cape Fear Club, which was holding an open house for reporters from all over the East. At the door, two uniformed privates from the Wilmington Light Infantry—hardly out of their teens—looked them over closely and then, recognizing Harry, let them pass.

Inside the foyer, four more soldiers sat cross-legged on the floor, dealing poker. Their rifles were stacked carefully against a maroon leather reading chair. A Negro waiter set down a tray of sandwiches and beer on the floor beside them.

"Sentries," Harry explained, shaking his head.

Sam entertained a sudden ridiculous vision of a Negro mob storming the old club. Or maybe not so ridiculous. It was known to be the de facto headquarters of the Democratic party and the white supremacy campaign. And the club building, like most of the older structures in the city, was built of clapboards over heart-pine frames, loaded with flammable pitch. A little kerosene, the flicker of a match . . .

He sat at the bar with Harry and sipped his coffee. Next to every window in the place sat an armed soldier. No doubt, there were more upstairs, laying out their fields of fire.

Maybe they had a right to protect themselves, Sam figured. MacRae, Rountree, the Taylors. After all, men like them had built this town. They were the engine of its progress from a sleepy little colonial port to a major export center that shipped out a quarter of a million bales of cotton a year onto the world's markets. Ships from all over the world called here. Every railroad in the South converged here. Men like MacRae, Rountree, and the Taylors created employment for thousands, white and black. They were family men, decent men, men who pulled together for the common good. They founded charities, looked after orphans, supported the feeble-minded and the poor with their taxes.

These men—not a few colored ministers, lawyers, and barbers— had done that. They had made Wilmington the political and economic center of the state. They had a stake here. They weren't drifters or seasonal laborers, but men who had put down roots, men whose families had fought the Indians and the British and, yes, even the Yankees to stay here. Their ancestors were in Oakdale Cemetery, their children attended the schools, their taxes had built City-County Hospital. They were on for the long haul.

If things went wrong, Sam knew, they had a lot to lose. They had families, a community, a way of life. They cherished those things. Why wouldn't they fight to keep them?

But the nagging question kept coming back: who exactly was trying to take them away?

Sam pushed away his coffee cup and asked the colored bartender for an iced drink. "Didn't expect it to be so quiet today," he observed, sipping root beer.

Harry slugged down a shot of whiskey, then sipped another over ice. "It's early yet. Stick around."

"I'm not going anywhere."

"You might could be going someplace, you ride the right coat-tails."

Sam ignored the remark. What did Harry know about Colonel Waddell or his plans? Why shouldn't a man take advantage of the luckiest break he'd had in years? He hadn't been asked to compromise anything yet.

"So," Harry said, staring at the bright rows of bottles behind the bar, "you're cutting me out."

"What?"

"Whatever deal you've got working, you're going to keep it to yourself. Figure you can't trust old Harry anymore. Old Harry's unreliable."

"You're way out of line, Harry."

"I suppose I was a fool to expect you to be different."

"Look, Harry—"

"I never held back with you, Sam. I gave it to you straight. I'm the memory of this town, the only honest one it has. And you got the benefit."

"Don't go too far, Harry. I've been hauling your carcass home too many nights. Don't tell me what I owe you."

Harry smiled. "You're right, of course. Make whatever deal you can. Somebody ought to come out of this with something worthwhile."

"It's not like that."

"Whatever you say. Bartender?"

So now even Harry thought he was up to no good, Sam thought. First the Negroes, then Gray Ellen, now his only friend. Well, he might as well be up to no good—he was already paying the price. They sat together, brooding separately.

"Look at them," Sam said after a while, meaning the other reporters, from papers in New York, Baltimore, Philadelphia, and Washington. "They're going to file their eyewitness accounts from the bar."

Harry coughed into his handkerchief. Sam saw the smear of bloody phlegm before he refolded it. "Why the hell not?" Harry said. "They're getting the same story we got, with a lot less wear and tear."

Colored waiters moved among the reporters delivering drinks, smiling, carrying messages between tables. Men in dark suits passed out cigars and shook hands, working the room.

Sam sipped his awful root beer. The heavy sweetness made his teeth ache. "Still, doesn't seem very professional."

Harry ordered another drink. "That's what happens when you take the suspense out of politics. Makes it like watching a horse race you know is fixed."

Just then, a military courier—Sam couldn't keep the uniforms straight, but he wore plenty of buttons and epaulets and a big horse pistol in a buttoned holster—rushed into the room and made for the back. He rushed out just as suddenly, a dozen men in suits trailing behind him.

"What's happening?" Sam asked one of the men as he rushed by.

"Trouble up in Brooklyn. Nothing to be alarmed about. Stay put and enjoy your drink."

Sam grabbed Harry's arm. "Like hell."

They rode a streetcar packed with the vigilantes Sam had seen coming and going from the *Messenger* for weeks. When they arrived at the polling place in Brooklyn a quarter of an hour later, they scarcely recognized it. That morning when they had visited, it had been quiet as a church hall, guarded by a handful of rifle-toting white "specials" from one or another vigilance group. Now, it was under siege by a crowd of Negroes.

At the edge of the mob, they met a woman reporter from New York wearing a crimson Eaton jacket. She scribbled furious notes in the most illegible scrawl Sam had ever seen. "What do you know?" he asked, dispensing with formal introductions.

"Quite a row brewing," she said happily, still scribbling. The streetcar vigilantes had meanwhile shouldered their way through the mob to join their comrades inside the polling place, where some two dozen white men were handling the vote of a largely Negro precinct. "They've been turning away Negroes who want to vote. They say they're not eligible. Some kind of special registration."

Harry said, "Never heard of such a thing."

Sam said, "So they went home and got their pals."

"It's all sort of spontaneous," she said. "Nobody seems to be in charge. Of the Negroes, I mean."

Sam said, "Seen any preachers?"

She nodded. "Just one. Handsome devil. He was around when it all got started, then he vanished. Guess he got scared off."

"Right," Sam said. "That must be it."

She said, "They're not even armed."

"I see a few ax handles," Harry commented.

"But all the guns are on the other side," she said. "And more coming all the time. Do you think they'll open fire?"

By now, scores of white men were facing off more than a hundred Negroes. The standoff had an inertia to it—it wasn't going anywhere without a good, strong push. Sam could feel everybody's reluctance to push. It was in the air. He could see it on the faces of the Negroes, the uncertainty in their eyes.

Captain James arrived with a handful of men. Sam admired the fact that he hadn't trotted out his whole force. All those pretty uniforms on this side of the tracks would surely have provoked a riot, and a riot would quickly have turned into slaughter.

"Aren't you frightened?" Sam asked the woman reporter.

"Frightened?"

"Gadding about in that pretty jacket, asking questions, in the middle of all this?"

She smiled a yearbook smile. "I'm just a woman. Everybody tells me everything."

Sam mounted a wagon bed to see over the crowd.

"What's happening?" Harry asked.

On the front porch of the hall, a familiar group was speaking to the crowd—John Norwood, Carter Peamon, Armond Scott, and Father Dennen. Sam couldn't hear everything they said, but it was clear they were exhorting the Negroes to disperse. "Leadership," he told Harry. "That's what's happening."

Again, just as at the jailhouse last night, the crowd evaporated. Miraculous, Sam mused—the right man says the right words, and real things happen in the world. Or don't happen.

And all this today was about words—speeches and pamphlets, handbills and editorials. Little black marks on paper inserted into the slot of a locked wooden box. The marks became numbers, the numbers were placed beside names, and the names determined the law. Then real people had to live under the law. It held them from the moment they left for work in the morning until the last lamp in the house was extinguished at bedtime. It held them even while they slept.

In fifteen minutes, the confrontation was over and the boredom was back. Sam climbed down from the wagon. The woman in the crimson jacket was still scribbling. He watched her fingers, thin and sharp as pencils. Her green eyes were focused on the notebook. Her face was lean, her little nose pointy as a beak. Tough girl, he thought. The kind that loves to watch. He hoped she was paying close attention. She wouldn't blink. She would write the exact truth.

Sam said, "Something's holding everybody back."

"I told you," Harry said. "It won't happen today."

The woman reporter asked, "What are you talking about?"

Harry said, "Let's get back to the club. I want to go over my notes."

"I'm coming, too," she said, grabbing Sam's arm.

He broke away. "Sorry," he said. "Club rules. Gentlemen only."

They hitched a ride on one of the streetcars that were making regular circuits of the city carrying crews of white vigilantes. The woman reporter followed, but they left her at the door of the Cape Fear Club, where she snagged Colonel Waddell on his way out. He happily consented to an interview.

To nobody's surprise, the Democrats swept the election. In the Fifth Precinct of First Ward, whose rolls registered 324 black and 31 white voters, nearly 500 votes were tallied for the Democratic slate.

In Fourth Ward, with 546 registered voters, Democrat John D. Bellamy won nearly twice that number of votes for a seat in the United States House of Representatives, easily beating Oliver Dockery.

Furnifold Simmons, the state Democratic chairman, won a United States Senate seat from incumbent Republican Marion L. Butler.

All across the ticket, the few Republicans who ran were routed. They lost the courts, the county commission, and representation in the United States Congress. The state legislature was now packed with an overwhelming majority of white supremacist Democrats, who held it in their power to change the charter of Wilmington— and would certainly do so. The days of the Fusionist city government were numbered.

Half the dead in Oakdale Cemetery voted the Democratic ticket. The other half didn't vote.

By eleven that night, the city was quiet. The reporters had filed their stories. The election officers had gone home. Brooklyn was deserted. Only a few saloons downtown remained open for business—illegally. No policemen appeared to cite them. Sergeant Alton Lockamy passed Polson's on his way home and stopped in for a quick beer himself. He couldn't quite believe Election Day had come and gone without a single attack. The worst was over.

At the Wilmington Light Infantry Armory, the soldiers had long since stacked their weapons upstairs and retired to their homes. They were still on alert, but that was only a precaution. The Gatling gun was safely stored behind locked doors, neatly covered and under constant guard, its ammunition secured in the marble bunker under the front steps. The club rooms were dark.

Colonel Walker Taylor was finishing off a brandy nightcap before going up to bed.

Captain William Rand Kenan lay awake next to his wife, listening to her soft breathing with a quiet joy. He had done nothing to be ashamed of. There had been no bloodshed. The real power of any weapon—even a Gatling gun—was the choice of whether to use it. In a sense, as soon as you fired your weapon, it had failed to do what it was designed for: it had failed to change the enemy's behavior to your advantage.

Today, he reflected, had been a perfect example of that. They had deployed their weapon, and its very presence, the threat of use, had caused seventy-five horsemen to dismount and then disband peacefully. There had been no wounded horses to shoot, no bodies to carry from the field, no prayers to say for the dying. It had been the most efficient kind of military exercise.

There had been no chaos of battle to disrupt the orderly plans for taking back the city. The right men would go to the state capitol and to Washington and start the process.

The old house on Nun Street creaked familiarly in the late breeze. He'd left the window open—he would sleep well tonight. He touched his wife, gently, so as not to wake her. He loved her warmth. Next to her, he was protected from the force of his dreams. She turned on her side, and he tucked his body against hers, feeling their two heartbeats together. Somewhere out in the world, his son was making him proud.

———

In a meeting parlor of the Cape Fear Club, George Rountree sat tabulating results from all over the state as they came in on the wire. Messenger boys jogged back and forth from the Western Union office at the train depot. A colored boy brought him fresh black coffee in a bone china cup. Rountree lit another cigar. He was still wearing his jacket and vest. His tie was still knotted perfectly at his throat.

Rountree was going to the statehouse, he knew that. A warm satisfaction settled in his chest. The whole deal had worked out with such little friction and such precise timing that he was still slightly amazed.

But that was the least of it. He and his fellow Democrats had been delivered a ringing mandate to take charge of the Old North State, to put the Negro in his place and send the carpetbaggers packing. When the magnitude of the Democratic victory became apparent, he relaxed a bit, loosened his tie, took a long draw on his cigar. It wasn't over yet. He would stay until he had all the numbers, all the names. Tomorrow, he could sleep in. Nothing was happening tomorrow. They'd been ready to put down an uprising today, but the only mob that had almost gotten out of hand was Dowling and his damned rednecks.

The section captains had kept the Businessmen's Committee informed of events all over the city. The telephones had worked fine. There had been few surprises.

Still, it never hurt to be prepared. Preparation was the key to everything. The first principle of the lawyer was to know in advance the answers to the hard questions.

Hugh MacRae stuck his head in the door. He'd been in another parlor conferring with some businessmen, probably that so-called secret group of his. "You're going to do great things for us in Raleigh, George—congratulations."

Rountree shook MacRae's hand without standing up. "You expecting any trouble tomorrow?"

MacRae winked. "Not a bit. It's all over."

"Looks like all our precautions were for nothing." After Rountree had shared the Pinkertons' report, even MacRae had agreed force would no longer be necessary.

"Never hurts to have your structure in place," MacRae said. "Let them try and take the city from us now."

"Right. By spring, we can have the charter amended and a special election for a mayor and board."

"Don't worry about all that now. You've got time. We're organized, that's the main thing."

MacRae went out. Rountree had never entirely trusted MacRae, and he didn't trust him now. He'd always had the impression that the secret groups—MacRae's and Walker Taylor's both—intended much more immediate action. But maybe that wasn't necessary now. All the cloak-and-dagger stuff made fine melodrama, but he and other level-headed men like him would do the real work for the Cause in the light of day, by law. The Republicans or Fusionists or whatever they called themselves were finished in this county.

King Numbers was dead. Rountree already had notes for a draft of a bill to limit the franchise to voters who had the education to use it wisely.

No more illiterate hordes of Negroes voting according to the orders of a white party boss. Rountree believed deeply in democracy—the democracy of educated, competent men of free will. With a little more work, it would come to pass here.

In a few hours, he would go home to sleep the sleep of the just. For now, he sat awhile longer, waiting for one more wire, enjoying the finest cigar he had smoked in years.

Solomon Fishblate hurried up Fifth Street. He had never liked the chill. He found Waddell's house without trouble and rapped lightly at the front door. He expected the servant to open it, but instead the Colonel himself appeared. Of course, it was late—the servant must have already gone home.

"Come in, Your Honor," Waddell said, deliberately addressing Fishblate as if he were still mayor.

Fishblate entered and took off his hat and coat. He smiled. It felt good to be treated with some respect for a change. A short time ago, he had been a man to be reckoned with in this city. But this new crowd had left him out of everything. How had it all changed so suddenly?

"Come into the study," Waddell said. "The maid has gone home, of course, but Miz Gabby is asleep upstairs, so we must talk gently." Bessie King and her daughter Saffron were, in fact, asleep in his own back room, but he had no idea.

Waddell settled into a leather chair, and Fishblate sat down in its mate, waiting for Colonel Waddell to explain why he had summoned him.

Waddell waited a suspenseful interval, then said, "Solly—may I call you Solly, sir?" Fishblate nodded, hat in his hands. "Solly, you and I have been relegated to the margins of things. Left out in the cold, so to speak."

"Yes, we have."

"They—I mean the men who are running this particular show—

call on us when they need us, then conveniently shunt us aside. Am I right?"

"Indeed you are, Colonel."

"There prevails a certain, shall we say, *ingratitude*?"

Fishblate nodded vigorously. "They forget the sacrifices certain parties have made in their interest."

"Exactly." Waddell clapped his hands together lightly. "And I'm forgetting my manners—may I offer you some refreshment? Wine or brandy?"

"Brandy, if you please."

The Colonel poured him a full snifter. Now, this was more like it—being waited on by the blue bloods. Here was a man who appreciated his standing in the world.

They settled back with their brandies. "You are aware of the meeting tomorrow," Waddell said.

"Of course. Would I forget a meeting at which I am to preside?" They had asked him to preside as a sop, he knew. As he understood it, the meeting would be largely ceremonial. They got the meat, he got the scraps.

Waddell chuckled. "I mean no disrespect. It was only a way of broaching the subject. They've asked you to chair the meeting because you enjoy, shall we say, a certain influence over the Red Shirts."

"Lot of those Micks, they come from my district. MacRae figures I can keep them in line."

"Can you?"

"Of course not. Mike Dowling, that hothead. Brains of a turnip. Nobody can keep that crowd in line. Any day now, boom. They're going to blow off."

"But MacRae's people don't know that."

Fishblate shrugged. "Why tell a person what he doesn't want to hear?"

Waddell rose and paced the room with difficulty—his legs were stiffening up something fierce in this chill. "No doubt they also want to show that they have the backing of the former administration."

"No doubt."

"Then, sir, I have a proposition."

"I'm listening." Here it comes, Fishblate thought—he was about to be invited inside again. Good. The outside was no place to be, not after today.

"Tomorrow, invite me up to the platform. First thing."

"Now, why would I do that?"

"You know," Waddell said, still pacing, the legs unstiffening a little with the circulation, "I've often thought what a good mayor you made. In those days, business was good. Things proceeded with a certain order. You could count on the police, the magistrates. Now, it has all unraveled into chaos."

"King Numbers," Fishblate agreed ruefully. "You are suggesting what?"

"MacRae has his own ideas about who ought to be mayor. So does Walker Taylor. So does George Rountree. So do a lot of people."

"And you don't have ideas?"

Waddell finished his brandy and put the glass on his desk. "Certainly, I've got ideas." He looked Fishblate square in the eye.

"Me?" He didn't quite believe it could be so easy.

"Why not? I sure as blazes don't want the job—got my hands full. But I need a man I can count on."

"And you can count on me? Why?" Fishblate was still skeptical. He'd been in politics too long to take anything at face value. Nothing came free. If he could only determine what Waddell stood to gain, then he could rest easy. The first rule of politics: find out the stakes.

"Because you're a known quantity," Waddell said. "Because you don't trust Hugh MacRae. Because you've already got people you can call on to make a government. Because you can keep the streetcars running and the electricity on and the fire companies sober."

"Keep going."

"That's all there is."

Fishblate shook his head and stood up, as if to go. He wasn't buying. "I mean, what's in it for you? What's your end?"

Waddell sat on the edge of his desk and struck a pose. "Simple. Next year, support me for governor."

Fishblate nodded. Of course—why hadn't he seen it? Waddell still had influential friends all over the state from his congressional days. But he would need Wilmington. And the mayor would control the party here. Whoever wound up mayor could make or break a campaign. "I could double-cross you."

"You won't."

Fishblate smiled, nodding. "No, you're right. A deal's a deal." Everybody knew that when Solly Fishblate made a bargain, he stuck to it.

"Then you agree?"

"How do I know you can do it? Just because I let you address the meeting? You've made plenty of speeches already."

Waddell laughed from his belly. When he finished, he leaned over Fishblate, circled an arm around his neck, and whispered, "Timing."

"Timing," Fishblate repeated, now himself on the verge of laughter, recognizing the truth when he heard it.

For in the hearts of all true Southerners
there exists an affection that is almost akin to
love or devotion for the "old fashioned darkies,"
many of whom possessed "white hearts" in
black bodies.

Gunner Jesse Blake,
quoted by Harry Hayden

CHAPTER FOURTEEN

Wednesday, November 9

THEY WERE HEADED OUT Seventh Street toward Castle Hayne Road,
Alex and Frank Manly. They wore their Sunday suits for traveling. Alex huddled into the turned-up collar of his Prince Albert, his
brushed gray derby pulled low on his forehead. Frank wore a
charcoal greatcoat and scarf against the damp chill. His slouch hat
was pulled down over the tops of his ears. Both men wore gloves.

Out of sight under the buggy seat, each had stowed his single
portmanteau, packed with all he would take from the city. Frank
kept insisting they could come back in a few weeks or months,
when things had calmed down, but Alex didn't believe it. The

buggy was open to the air, but the top was raised, giving the illusion of protection from the cold.

Far off, the carillon at St. James Church sounded one o'clock. There was no hurry—they had four hours to make the train at Castle Hayne. They must not seem to be running away, or else they would excite the suspicion of one of the vigilante groups that systematically patrolled the streets.

Alex was brooding. He understood that he was at the end of something, but he could not imagine a future. The night lay ahead, black and formless. Exile. He mused out loud, "Lately, we always seem to be doing one thing and pretending we're doing another."

Frank said, "Well, ain't that all the fashion?"

"All the same, I don't care for sneaking around in the dead of night, just to be able to do what I've got a perfect right to do already. That's nigger stuff. That's the kind of life we've been trying to outgrow for a hundred and fifty years. I want a life out in the daylight. I want to look people in the eye, say what's on my mind."

"You've done plenty of that, little brother. Why do you think we're out here in the open on a bone-cold night dodging white men with guns that want to lynch us?"

"Proves my point exactly. You can go so far, then they pull back on the leash."

"If I ever catch up with that boy Jeffries," Frank said, "I'm gonna yank his leash but good."

"He was just speaking his mind." If it was Jeffries who wrote it, Alex thought. It had been such a guaranteed provocation.

"Somebody put him up to it," Frank said. "I'd like to know who."

"Doesn't matter now." That was the sort of thing nobody ever found out. The *why* of a thing was always just smoke. The facts were all you had. "By the time the white men get done writing the history of this election, you won't even know there ever was an Afro-American newspaper in this town."

"The office is all locked up, pastor has the only key," Frank said. "You've made your record. Nobody can pretend different."

"Oh, you might be surprised what people can pretend."

They were crossing Market now. Here, the patrols were frequent.

Alex said, "The Hoe press will be gone. Tom Clawson will collect it first thing."

"Ain't the only printing press on the planet. We'll find another one."

Alex didn't think so. He didn't think he had the zeal to start it all again. For six years now, he'd been pushing, and he felt suddenly weary. For six years, he'd pushed his rock uphill, and now it was rolling pell-mell right back down the hill. If he didn't get out of the way, it would roll right over him. Some community leader—slinking out of town in the dead of night.

A party of five riders appeared from the direction of the river. They spurred their horses to a trot when they spotted the buggy.

"Uh-oh," Frank said. "Trouble coming in a crowd."

"Pull up your scarf," Alex said. "Relax. And whatever happens, don't open your mouth."

Frank cursed and pulled back on the reins, stopping the buggy in the middle of the intersection. The horsemen slowed to a walk. When they got near enough, the lead rider called out, "Where you boys traveling so late?"

Alex waited till he was closer. He didn't feel like shouting. He wanted this thing to be as calm as possible. "Heard there might be some excitement down in Brooklyn tonight," he said, looking the rider in the eye. The rider had no lantern, and the buggy top shielded the brothers from the gaslight on the corner.

The lead rider, joined now by the other four, laughed. "Niggers don't much like the cold. I don't reckon they'll make trouble tonight."

"We're on the lookout for the Manlys," Alex said. "We only have one horse between us, or we'd go mounted, like you. That's the proper way to hunt blackbirds."

The riders laughed and blew out clouds of breath. The horses snorted, impatient to be moving.

"We heard they might try to slip out tonight or tomorrow," the leader said. "We're on the lookout ourselves." He peered into the buggy. In the shadows, Frank sat very still. "Hey, you boys don't have no rifles."

Alex said, "We heard they wasn't armed."

"Just the same, you'll need more than a buggy whip," the leader said. "Piner—let me have that Winchester."

One of the riders drew a carbine out of his saddle sheath and passed it to the leader. "Piner'd rather use his pistol anyway. He's a gentleman." They all laughed. The leader passed the Winchester, stock first, to Alex Manly. "Y'all know how to shoot a rifle?"

Alex took the Winchester and, pointing it toward the stars, jacked a round into the chamber, then carefully let down the hammer.

The leader nodded in approval. "That goes back to Tom Clawson down at the *Messenger* when you're through with it. Property of the Businessmen's Committee."

"We'll take good care of it." Alex laid the rifle across his knees.

"Good hunting, boys."

The horsemen trotted off, and Frank clucked the mare forward. He didn't speak for a long block as the carriage wheels hissed through the oyster-shell paving. Then he said, "Passing for white. Tonight, of all nights. Goddamnit, Alex—I've got to climb down and piss." The tension broke, and the brothers hooted and giggled for six more blocks.

They struck Castle Hayne Road and in twenty minutes were crossing Smith's Creek Bridge. "Hold up, Frank," Alex said. He peered down into the darkness below the bridge and cocked his ear to the sound of running water. Then he flung the rifle from the carriage and listened until he heard the splash. "Drive on, brother. We've got a train to catch."

Nobody had told George Rountree about the meeting. He found out about it when his wife, Meta, woke him at nine, waving a copy of the *Messenger* in his face. He'd been at the club till after three, and he was groggy and disoriented. "What?" he said automatically. "Mrs. Rountree?"

"I hated to wake you, George, but the meeting's in an hour."

"Meeting?" he said. "There's no meeting today." He sat up and rubbed his fatigue-burned eyes.

She handed him the newspaper. "See? All white citizens are requested to assemble at ten o'clock." She bit her lip. "You told me that part was over."

"I thought it was. Lay out a suit and a fresh collar." He sat in bed for a moment longer, rubbing his temples and the bald dome of his head. Hugh MacRae, you son of a bitch, he thought. Or was it Waddell? There were just too goddamn many chiefs and too goddamn few good Indians.

He splashed cold water on his face, shaved quickly, dressed, and hurried out to find somebody who knew something. On Front Street, he fell in with a knot of white men headed for the meeting. They knew only what they'd read in the paper. He quickened his stride and broke away from them, cutting across a vacant lot on Mulberry behind Colonel Roger Moore's house. Moore had already gone to the meeting. It was ten minutes till ten. Rountree practically ran the remaining two blocks and arrived at the courthouse in a sweat, breathing hard. He took a minute to collect himself, carefully mopped his brow, neck, and pate with his handkerchief, then strode up the stairs to the main courtroom.

There was not an empty seat. A thousand white men and women jammed the seats, the aisles, the hallway, the stairs.

In the jury box sat a dozen leading citizens, including Senator-elect John D. Bellamy, Solomon Fishblate, and Tom Clawson, along with Hugh MacRae and every other member of the Secret Nine. Conspicuously absent was Alfred Moore Waddell.

Rountree took in the scene at a glance. MacRae. He was operating outside the party now, outside the legitimate Businessmen's Committee. And what in the world was Solly Fishblate doing in the foreman's seat? A machine boss from the old days. Didn't have any principles, didn't believe in the Cause. He had no standing at all. Yet there he was, seated next to Senator Bellamy, and here he, George Rountree, was—in the back of the courtroom, practically out the door.

Without hesitation, Rountree shouldered his way down the aisle, stepped over the wooden railing, grabbed a chair from behind the court reporter's desk, and sat down at the far end of the jury box, next to Hugh MacRae. The courtroom resounded with the murmur of the crowd. Babel, Rountree thought—an utter nonsense of voices, five hundred different conversations, words overlapping words, the chirping laughter of women and the raucous braying of men, the creak of wooden seats and the scrape of feet, whispers and shouts, men calling out to their cohorts across the aisle and women giggling and arguing fiercely among themselves, pimply Red Shirt hooligans chanting "White is Right!" and old soldiers singing off-key the marching songs of bygone days best forgotten.

MacRae leaned over, smiling without showing any teeth. "Glad you could join us, George."

"Like hell," Rountree said. "Why wasn't I consulted about this?"

MacRae turned up his pink palms. "There was no need."

"I'm on the Executive Committee of the Democratic—"

"It's gone beyond that now, George. This is phase two."

"You can't just—"

"It's done, George." MacRae stared at him, practically nose to nose. Rountree was the larger man, but he backed off. "Now, you can either go along, or you can just plain go," MacRae said. "Your choice."

Rountree was confused. They had won—what more was there to gain? "We got what we wanted already."

"You got what *you* wanted. There's still some unfinished business."

"Don't give me that shit!" Rountree was talking too loud, trying to be heard above the rising din of the unruly crowd. While he was talking to MacRae, Solly Fishblate had left his seat and mounted the judge's bench. He raised his hands for silence. All at once, the crowd hushed, and in the sudden instant of silence, the tail end of Rountree's last remark rang out over the house: *shit*!

The audience erupted in laughter. Even Fishblate broke up—it was always a treat to see a blue blood make an ass of himself in public. Rountree was puzzled at first, then, realizing his voice had carried to every corner of the courtroom, he ducked his head and massaged his temples with his fingers. Now, he had a headache to go with his burning eyes.

Solly Fishblate stood behind the bench, gripping it hard, as if to keep himself from falling. He slouched, apparently overwhelmed by the weight of the crowd, and in a reedy voice made a few opening remarks. Fishblate yielded the floor to Senator-elect Bellamy, who opened with a standard acceptance speech full of purple sentiment and hyperbole. Striding back and forth in front of the bench like a prosecuting attorney, he expressed his gratitude in as many words as possible. He reminded them that he would not soon forget who had sent him to Washington: the Anglo-Saxon race.

The crowd gave him a thunderous standing ovation. They were in a jubilant mood this morning. Bellamy bowed and soaked up the applause till it began to peter out into sporadic clapping. Then he sat down.

Hugh MacRae was on the edge of his chair, holding a sheaf of white pages in his hand, when Fishblate, still on the bench, blurted out, "And now, a special treat. I direct your attention to that champion of our Cause—"

Hugh MacRae smiled and winked sideways at Rountree.

"—that sterling citizen of the world and the Old North State—"

MacRae straightened his cuffs and adjusted his tie.

"—that paragon of Southern chivalry, who has sacrificed so much to bring about the victory we now enjoy—"

MacRae leaned forward in his chair, ready to stand.

"Colonel Alfred Moore Waddell!"

MacRae stood up, startled. Waddell, who had been waiting in the judge's chambers, marched out of thin air and crossed in front of Rountree and MacRae. Seeing the papers still held out in MacRae's right hand, he bowed slightly from the waist, snatched them with the precise gesture of a fencing master, and carried them to the center of the courtroom.

MacRae climbed out of the jury box, two steps behind him. Before he could take back his papers, Waddell was already addressing the crowd, waving the papers over his head. "I have just been handed some urgent resolutions," he said in his ringing baritone, "of which I heartily approve!" He riffled through them quickly, nodding, his quick eyes taking in the gist of the document.

"Ladies and gentlemen," he began again in a serious tone. "I have been called upon to deliver a declaration that will gladden your civic hearts." He nodded toward MacRae, and the crowd responded with cheers and applause. MacRae bowed and stepped back.

"It is a declaration every bit as momentous as that sacred declaration which inspired a revolution of free men to wrest their destiny from a foreign colonial power.

"Ladies and gentlemen, I give you the White Man's Declaration of Independence!"

Theatrically, he held up the crisp, shining white pages and slowly waved them from right to left, like a magician proving the reality of an illusion.

When the crowd quieted, he began to read: " 'Believing that the Constitution of the United States contemplated a government to be carried on by enlightened people . . .' "

As Waddell read the preamble, Rountree turned to MacRae, whose face was crimson. "Those are exactly my words, Hugh."

"So what?" MacRae said, so angry he could hardly speak. "They belong to everybody now."

"So be it."

Rountree, like the rest of those present, was entranced by the reading of principles he had long believed. Unlike the others, though, he was already calculating what part he would play in the rest of this meeting. He'd been ambushed in this court before. He was no amateur.

MacRae sat rigid, arms folded tight across his chest.

Waddell was in his glory. Fishblate had not known about this declaration—Waddell had counted on that. Waddell had heard about it by accident, a stray remark from a lady newspaper reporter in a crimson jacket. He hadn't laid eyes on it until a few minutes ago, when he'd stolen it right out of MacRae's hand in front of a full house. No matter. His eyes always read ahead of his voice—an orator's trick—and he would win their loyalty forever by telling them what they had waited all these months to hear. This declaration was not just another rousing call to action, but an official, codified pronouncement, blessed by every man they had just elected, about the new state of the world.

The prose was delicious. From Hugh MacRae's mouth, Waddell thought, it would have been just a litany of familiar phrases, no more emotionally riveting than a grocery list. But Waddell listened to the words, their rhythms and sounds, the resonances of ideas, and delivered the declaration with all the passion in his actor's heart. He wound up the preamble: " 'While we recognize the authority of the United States, and will yield to it if exerted, we would not for a moment believe that it is the purpose of more than sixty millions of our own race to subject us permanently to a fate to which no Anglo-Saxon has ever been forced to submit.' "

The crowd roared. Waddell waited till the applause reached its crescendo, then held up a single finger to begin counting off the seven resolutions. The crowd stilled.

The resolutions were predictable. The genius lay in codifying them as articles of popular government backed by the full weight of the law. The genius was in doing it right here in court.

The first resolution called for respectable taxpayers to once again control the city's fate. The second warned that whites stirring up Negro unrest would be summarily dealt with. The third stated that the Negro was a renegade element in the city.

Once more, Waddell had to wait for the surfy roar of the assembly to die down.

" 'Fourth—That the progressive element in any community is the white population and that the giving of nearly all the employment to Negro laborers has been against the best interests of this city and county.' "

The Red Shirts, led by Dowling, erupted in a chorus of hip-hip-hoorays.

" 'Fifth—That we propose in future to give to white men a large part of the employment heretofore given to Negroes.' "

The Red Shirts whistled and cheered.

" 'Sixth—' " Waddell continued, the first phrases lost in the din, " '—we are prepared to treat the Negroes with justice and consideration—' "

All over the courtroom, men and women were on their feet, cheering him on. He had them. He was their hero.

" '—but we are equally prepared now and immediately to enforce what we know to be our rights.' " He caught his breath and looked around. His heart was wild with exhilaration. He was a one-man oratorical cavalry charge. He could read the joy on their faces. Their noisy approval vibrated in his chest. This city now belonged to him.

He paused for a minute, three minutes, five whole minutes before the courtroom was quiet enough for him to continue with the last resolution. " 'Seven—That a climax was reached when the Negro paper of this city published an article so vile and slanderous that it would—in most communities—have resulted in the lynching of the editor.' "

He finished slowly, calling for the *Record* to be shut down for good: " 'We demand that Alex Manly leave this city forever—within twenty-four hours.' "

Hurrahs, cheers, applause. The walls and ceiling vibrated with human noise.

" 'If the demand is agreed to within twelve hours, we counsel forbearance on the part of all white men.' " Pause. " 'If, however, the demand is refused, or if no answer is given within the time mentioned, then the editor, Manly, will be expelled by force.' So say we all!"

Even Waddell was not prepared for the ovation that now cascaded over him. The sheer force of it bowed his head and pushed him back physically into the bench. The men from the jury box crowded around him, pummeling his back and wringing his hand.

Before he knew what was happening, a contingent of Red Shirts mobbed the bench and lifted him onto their shoulders. They paraded him back and forth before the bench, then carried him up and down the aisles, where men and women reached out to shake his hand, pat him on the back, kiss him, thump his shoulders, touch him. He was breathless, filled with a rapture of adoration, scared to death of being torn limb from limb.

Solomon Fishblate was momentarily dismayed. Had Waddell known about the declaration all along? No, he couldn't have. He just had that dumb actor's luck. He could walk through hellfire and come out with a lit cigar. Fishblate used the confusion to collect his wits, then once again seized the moment. "I propose an eighth resolution!" he called from the bench, over and over, until at last the crowd realized he was speaking and gradually quieted.

The Red Shirts gently lowered Waddell back onto his feet. He was as startled as anybody, for the first time in his life at a loss for words. He had gotten what he'd come for. Dumbly, he stretched out his hand, indicating that Fishblate should continue.

"I move that Mayor Wright, Chief of Police J. R. Melton, and the entire Board of Aldermen be notified to vacate immediately!"

"Hear, hear!"

"Throw the rascals out!"

"No more nigger lovers in city hall!"

A minor din ensued. George Rountree saw the opening he had been waiting for. He jumped up and asked to be recognized. Waddell, still in a mild euphoric stupor, obliged. "I move we appoint a committee of five to take Mr. Fishblate's resolution under consideration."

MacRae's men, eager to brake the frenzied momentum of the Waddell-Fishblate faction, approved. Rountree was appointed chairman, and four others were quickly called to join him.

While they retired to the judge's chambers to deliberate, Waddell spoke again to the courtroom. The euphoria was wearing off now, and he was a little frightened of what he had set in motion. "Let us not be hasty in resorting to violent measures," he said without his previous fire. "The editor of the *Record* will be dealt with."

Others took turns delivering brief orations endorsing the declaration. Within a half-hour, the committee of five returned. Rountree had reworded Fishblate's amendment to keep it within the law. Now, the mayor, police chief, and Board of Aldermen were charged with "being a constant menace to the peace and welfare of this community." Therefore, they would be notified that they *ought* to resign.

The best men of the community lined up at the bench to affix their signatures to the completed declaration. In addition to the party in the jury box, almost half those present in the courthouse—445 white men—signed, including Walker and J. Allan Taylor, Mike Dowling, Tom Clawson, the Reverend Peyton Hoge, Captain Thomas James, and William Rand Kenan. Virtually every prominent name in town was represented: Bellamy, Bryan, Cameron, Collier, Corbett, Davis, deRosset, Duke, French, Mayo, Moore, Nutt, Rivenbark, Savage, Worth, Yopp.

Conspicuous by their absence were other names: Keith, Foster, Sprunt, Chadbourn, Calabash, Jenks.

When the courtroom at last began to empty, Hugh MacRae's Secret Nine, Waddell, Fishblate, and Rountree remained behind.

Rountree said, "We had better present this to a delegation from the Negro community right away, or it will lose force."

"Exactly right," Waddell said. "Round up some niggers that can read."

Rountree said, "Summon them to meet a duly appointed committee."

"I've got a committee in mind, George," Waddell said. He had a lot to say about things now. He put an arm around Hugh MacRae. "Hugh, will you serve?"

MacRae recognized Waddell's invitation as a peace offering for the stunt he had pulled earlier. It was not enough, but it was a start—Waddell wasn't forgetting who was in charge of this show. "Certainly I'll serve."

They haggled for another fifteen minutes. In the end, Waddell's committee included all of MacRae's Secret Nine. But not George Rountree.

Sam Jenks and Harry Calabash had watched the whole thing from front-row seats. On his way out of the courthouse, Waddell waved Sam over. "We'll need a neutral observer. Get your pencil ready." Harry started to say something, but Waddell cut him off.

"One observer will be sufficient." He looped an arm around Sam's neck and escorted him up the aisle toward the door.

It was unprecedented that a delegation of Negroes be ushered into the Cape Fear Club through the front door. It was Waddell's idea: bring them into the big house, let them see firsthand the world they were up against. MacRae made sure to decorate the foyer and front parlor with two squads from the Wilmington Light Infantry in full kit—just in case.

Among the thirty-two black leaders rounded up by Dowling's Red Shirts and escorted to the meeting were barber Carter Peamon, pawnbroker Tom Miller, lawyers Armond Scott and W. E. Henderson, and Jim Telfair of the *Record*. The others included a postal clerk, a butcher, a coal dealer, two undertakers, several laborers, and an alderman, Elijah Green. Only one minister, Sam noticed. There were key faces missing: the Manlys, most obviously, but also John Norwood, the Reverend J. Allen Kirk, the other ministers. Probably they were unavailable on such short notice. The Red Shirts had cast their net and dragged in whomever they caught.

The black men, nearly all wearing suits, were directed into the largest meeting room and told to sit against the wall in two rows behind a long board table. Waddell sat at the head of the table, hands folded on a sheaf of papers.

Across the table from the Negro delegation sat the newly formed Committee of Twenty-five—bank directors, railroad presidents, mill owners, insurance men, attorneys, brokers, two ministers, and a doctor.

Sam stood near the door. When everyone had crowded into the room, Waddell addressed the Negroes without preliminaries: "There will be no talking. No discussion. No argument. We are presenting an ultimatum."

Then, without heat or fire, he read the White Man's Declaration of Independence. The black men listened, first puzzled, then angry, then full of fear. Lawyer Henderson stood. "Colonel, you'll be pleased to know that the Manlys have already left town."

"Who's that sitting next to you?" Hugh MacRae demanded.

"Carter Peamon, sir," Peamon said.

"If you're not the spitting image . . ."

Henderson continued trying to make his point. "The *Daily Record* is now defunct."

"Sit down!" Waddell said. "I don't want to hear a damned word out of you. Give us your answer in writing."

"But Colonel—"

"Sit down! I'm not finished."

Henderson slumped into his seat. Carter Peamon shifted nervously in his chair—MacRae kept staring at him. Sam had to admit Peamon looked a lot like Manly—same light complexion, same stylish moustache, same slight build.

Waddell read the amendment encouraging the present mayor and aldermen to resign. Alderman Elijah Green opened his mouth to protest, but nothing came out. He turned his hat in his hands. To Sam, he looked like a defendant who had just read the guilty verdict in the faces of the jury.

"You will have until tomorrow morning at seven-thirty to reply in writing. Deliver it to my house on Fifth Street." Waddell looked into their faces. Nobody said anything. "If you comply with all our demands, we may avoid violence. Otherwise," he said, glancing back at Hugh MacRae, "we will take strong measures."

Sam waited for the discussion, the argument, the heated debate. For a change, nearly everybody who mattered was assembled in one room together across a table. Surely, now was the time to talk things out, negotiate, come to some kind of understanding everybody could live with.

He understood Waddell's tactic: start with an unequivocal, impossible demand. He had seen union negotiations, political haggling, railroad commission budget hearings, congressional debates. Always, they started from a fixed point. Always, they declared irreconcilable differences, then proceeded—over the course of hours of tedious, wearing talk—to reconcile them.

But nobody on either side of the table said anything. The

Negroes sat, polite as kids in Sunday school, waiting to be dismissed. Come on, Sam thought—say something! Now's your chance! Prove you can't be pushed around.

But nobody objected or protested or even cursed. Then get what you deserve, Sam thought.

The whites sat tense and upright.

At that precise moment, in the unbearable silence of a room full of fifty-eight grown men who all tacitly agreed they had nothing to say to one another, Sam understood the South.

Waddell sat rigid, enforcing the silence. When even he couldn't stand it any longer, he abruptly presented a typewritten copy of the declaration to lawyer Henderson and stood up, a signal to the others. The white men exited first, collecting down the corridor at the bar. Sam stood at the doorway next to an armed guard. The Negroes filed past him with their heads down, except for Tom Miller, who paused, looked him in the eye, and shot him with his index finger. Sam remembered him from the tugboat. Now, he was part of this, too.

Sam joined the other white men at the bar. Hand trembling, he drank a tall glass of mineral water to soothe his dry throat. George Rountree appeared across the room, talking heatedly with Hugh MacRae and J. Allan Taylor. As Sam watched them wag their fists and shake their heads in the filtered, golden light of late afternoon, as he tried to comprehend the shifting alliances of this affair, Harry Calabash stole up on him.

"I take it events have escalated to a new level."

"Jesus, Harry—I've never seen anything like this before."

"Seen what? Bartender!"

"Somebody who really won't give in. I mean, everybody always *says* they won't give in, but sooner or later everybody gives in on something."

"Maybe there's still some hope for your soul."

"They won the election," Sam said. "What more do they want?"

Harry sighed. "You haven't been listening, Samuel. They've never been subtle about it. What do you think all that white supremacy talk was about?"

"Talk, that's what. I thought it was just talk. People don't actually believe that crap, do they?"

"Don't ask me to tell you what people believe. I can't even say for sure what I believe. How about you? You've been having it both ways for some time now."

"Harry, philosophy doesn't help. Leave me out of it."

"I believe a man can convince himself he believes in something—"

"Goddamnit, Harry—make sense." He shoved Harry's glass out of reach. "Lay off the sauce."

"—if what he convinces himself he believes will get him ahead in the world." Harry stood and stretched to retrieve the glass.

Sam raised his glass of mineral water. "The hell with you."

"To vectors of ambition."

Sam drank the rest of his water and still felt parched. "Now what, Harry?"

"You tell me. I wasn't at the secret meeting."

"You heard the whole thing at the courthouse. They've got till tomorrow morning to give in to the demands. In writing."

"Yes, we must have it in writing. Make it all neat and legal."

"That's the plan, all right."

"Well, you should be glad. Colonel Waddell apparently likes the cut of your jib. You'll be sailing right along with the new wind that's blowing."

"You don't think much of me, do you?"

"You don't care what I think," Harry said. "You look at me and you pray, 'Lord, don't let me end up like that.' You're young. You want the good life."

"I want something to show for it."

"For what?"

"*It.* You know. Work, labor, toil, strain, worry. Love."

"Ah, love. Now we're down to the nut."

"Cut it out, Harry. What do you know about it?"

"More than you realize, my boy."

"Spare me more stories about the old plantation. Some goddamn tale of lost love—jilted under the magnolias by a buxom Southern belle."

Harry held his glass in both hands and bent over the bar, not drinking, staring into the sparkling crystal. "There's another kind of love, Sam. Maybe you've never run across it."

"I've seen all kinds."

Harry sighed. "I'm talking about love of a *place*."

"Patriotism," Sam said. "You're very big on that down here."

Harry shook his head. "No, not patriotism. You're not listening. Not love of country. Love of a *place*."

"This place."

Harry rubbed the glass between his palms as though he were trying to ignite it from friction. "Yes, this place. Does that surprise you?"

Sam shrugged. "I've moved around quite a lot. One place is pretty much like another." But the soft ocean breeze had stuck in his nostrils, as the deep green of the pine tops against the opal sky had stuck in his eyes.

The colored bartender freshened Harry's whiskey without being summoned and stood with his back to them, a few paces away. Sam could feel him listening. The man's green jacket was flat and smooth as a billiard felt.

"You're wrong," Harry said quietly. "I feel sorry for you—to be as old as you are, and not to know that."

Sam laughed. "You just said how young I was."

Harry was staring into the crystal again, frowning, as if this were very important to him and he must get it right. "A man can live his whole life in a place and not belong to it. Nor it to him." He squinted at Sam to see if he was paying attention. "Or he can step off the train in a place he's never laid eyes on before and belong to it body and soul, world without end."

"Amen." Sam smiled.

"You don't believe me."

"Sure—the first part. Seems to me that's where Alex Manly comes in."

"Not just him."

"Oh, stop being so serious, Harry."

"It doesn't get any more serious than this. It's time you understood that."

"You love this place."

Harry nodded slowly, looking him in the eye. "So do you."

"Not me," Sam lied.

He gestured for more mineral water. The bartender leaned over slowly to pour it from a quart bottle, and Sam half expected him to put in his two cents. He had intelligent eyes and the soft hands of an intellectual. Probably studying at night to be a lawyer, Sam figured. He had no idea what these people did at night—not just the blacks, but the whites, too. They drank and talked, he knew that. And the ones like his neighbor, Farley, beat up their women. But what else? What made them stay here? What made them love it here so bad they'd suffer almost anything to live out their lives between the river and the sea?

Harry said, "It's the sound of your childhood, gets in your blood. The smell of mint under the kitchen window. The rotten stink of the river at low tide. The chatter of cicadas and pine borers on a humid night. In your imagination, you always live in the place where you were brought up."

"Wait a minute—how about the man stepping off the train?"

"He's lived there all his life, only he doesn't know it yet. In temperament. In books, maybe. Or the music he's listened to, the paintings he's seen. In dreams and desires. The women he's loved."

Sam waited for him to drink his whiskey, craving to join him.

"There is a landscape of the soul, Samuel. We walk around on this rocky planet, swatting skeeters and slipping in the mud. But we also walk around on the little postage stamp of ground inside our heads." He tapped an index finger against his temple. "That's our real compass. That's the place we know every inch of by heart."

"Too early in the day for speeches, Harry."

Harry shook his head. "No, no. It's late. Later than you know."

"You're drunk again."

Harry smiled and raised his glass. "Samuel, you've got to find your place."

"I'm here, aren't I?"

"That's not what I mean. You have to make this place your own. Or you have to go. There's no third choice."

"Harry, if I knew how to do that . . ."

"Where were you brought up?"

"Philadelphia."

"That doesn't tell me anything."

"A gritty little tenement on the Schuylkill River. My father was a riveter, fell off a scaffold and broke his back. He hung on for a couple of years. I sold newspapers on the corner, that's how I got started. Then a printer took me on as his apprentice. From there to the compositing room of a newspaper. Quit before I went deaf."

"So you've worked your way up."

"You could say that. I was a scholarship boy at Penn—only lasted two years. Otherwise, I pay as I go."

"And you couldn't wait to leave your life behind."

"Right. And sometimes it couldn't wait to leave me behind."

Harry sipped his drink and nodded. "But don't you ever miss it? Don't you ever want to go back where you come from?"

Sam thought about that. He tried to recall a single image from childhood, a single smell or taste. The touch of his mother's hand at bedtime, tucking the covers around his shoulders while he pretended to be asleep. But he didn't really remember that. He was cheating—making up a memory. She might have done exactly that, and the room might have been sweet with her rose water and the scent of baking rolls still in her apron and in her hair. Her voice might have been soft and husky, her lips dry and cool as they brushed across his cheek.

But really, he couldn't remember. The room was just a room. His mother, dead now for years, was just a pretty, shy face in a frame, too young ever to have been the dour woman he knew. Philadelphia was a name on the map, an indistinct geometry of dark, square buildings against a gray sky. The details were blurred. The drinking must have wiped it all out, he figured. He had never understood, before today, the extent of what he had lost. He had drunk to forget—that old joke.

"No," Sam said. "I'm here now. I don't ever want to go back."

"Are you, Sam?" Harry asked sadly. "Are you really here with us now?"

*In Peru or Nicaragua or Paris we should call
this revolution. It is no less revolution in North
Carolina.*

> The New York Independent,
> quoted in the
> Philadelphia Press

CHAPTER FIFTEEN

Wednesday, November 9

JOHN G. NORWOOD went to his office at Williston School early and
worked all day behind closed doors. His regular work routine had
been interrupted enough already by this white supremacy nonsense. The politics were settled for now. They'd lost ground, but
they could make it up next time. This election was an aberration.
History favored the Republicans.

At three o'clock, he stood in the corridor to watch the children
burst out of their classrooms. He was feeling low today, weary of
talk and politics and weighty matters, and seeing the children
lifted his spirits. Their squealing banter delighted him, made him
feel younger, free of all the responsibilities he had taken on. Over

the heads of passing children, he could see Gray Ellen Jenks standing beyond her desk, watching out the window.

Against all odds, Mrs. Jenks had proven herself a fine teacher. She clearly had the gift. Partly, the gift was just plain, old-fashioned love. Partly, it was a questioning intelligence. Real teachers had a kind of longing, a searching excitement of soul. They wanted to find out things. They didn't settle for the old, easy answers. They lived in their minds more than in the world. Real teachers were often disappointed in life.

They had to guard against this disappointment or give in to a deep sadness about the nature of the world. The difficulty of learning anything. The impossibility of knowing anything for sure. That was the risk, and it got them all sooner or later. The thing was to carry on as long as possible, and to seek strength from the Lord.

When you don't know for sure, you have to go on what you believe.

Or was he only idealizing? So what if he idealized the calling?—it was the key to the future of his race. He knew this as surely as he knew Christ had died on the cross. Ignorance was the enemy. White supremacy was just ignorance made flesh.

In a few years, or a few decades, there would be another kind of white man in the South—a white man as color-blind as Mrs. Jenks. They might still be named MacRae and Taylor and Rountree and even Dowling, but they would have moved beyond the old antagonism. They would understand that The Negro was as mythical as The White Man. There were as many kinds of Negroes as there were Negro people. Color was the least useful way to categorize anybody.

The evil genius of the white supremacy campaign was that it had managed to erase all other distinctions among men. It had created the Black Monolith. Only fear of difference mattered. Like any irrational proposition, it was impervious to logical argument.

The irony was clear as water to Norwood: the Negro community's greatest liability was that it did not act as a unified community. It was a fractured, fragmented coalition of bickering interests. Like any other community, really—but as far as the MacRae crowd was concerned, it was a single-minded threat stamped only by its color.

The children were all gone now. Mrs. Jenks came toward the door of her classroom. She looked wan and dispirited—he wondered how her own people treated her. He should have paid more attention, but there were so many good people to look out for. Her arms were heavily laden with books and themes.

"Mr. Norwood—I didn't realize you were in today."

"Oh? I'm always in at this time of day."

She felt uncomfortable to be caught in the middle of this business again. Bad enough that Sam was in it up to his neck. "I just meant, with all that's going on downtown—"

"What's going on downtown?" Suddenly, his pulse quickened.

"Look, I steer clear of politics."

"It's a man's business. But tell me, please."

"Another meeting," she said. "One of those white supremacy carnivals."

"Not much we can do about that. Anyhow, the election's over."

She pursed her lips, wondering how much of what Sam had told her was supposed to be confidential. It couldn't possibly matter now. She wasn't obliged to keep his secrets. "They're presenting some list of demands or something."

"Who's presenting?"

"The usual crowd, I guess." Sam hadn't been specific.

"To whom?"

Maybe they'd deliberately left him out. "To your people."

My people, he thought. *Your people*. How easily we use those terms. "Oh? And when is all this supposed to happen?"

She shrugged, shifting the weight of the books in her arms. "The meeting was this morning. I don't know about the rest."

He stood in front of her unintentionally blocking her exit, nodding dumbly. How could he have been so naive? He should get to a telephone and call—whom? Maybe he ought to just get downtown as fast as possible and start asking questions. But what might he be walking into? He'd seen how that Colonel could get them worked up. No need to be the first black face they saw after a session like that.

Bare feet slapped on the pinewood floor at the end of the corridor. David King ran toward them with his crippled gait. "Mr. Norwood! Mr. Norwood! You got to come quick!"

"Calm down, boy. What is it?"

"There's been an old tomatum."

"Ultimatum?"

"That's right, that's right." His arms were windmilling, and he couldn't keep his head still. "They meeting at Jacobs' Barbershop right now. Mr. Jacobs say to fetch you."

David Jacobs was also the county coroner. "Thank you, David. Run along and get a drink of water."

When Norwood turned back toward Mrs. Jenks, she said, "Isn't it ever going to end? What else can they possibly want from you people?"

"Hush," he said, patting her arm. "You go on home."

When Norwood joined the thirty-two men who had been rounded up for the meeting with Waddell, others who had not been at that meeting were also present. He immediately spotted Ivanhoe Grant.

Jacobs' Barbershop was on Dock Street, a stone's throw from the river. It had three barber chairs in a long, narrow space heated by potbelly stoves at either end and lit with electricity. Jacobs was a prominent man, and his clients were all white. Both side walls were hung with mirrors, creating the illusion of a larger space. If a man stared into the mirror, he could see himself multiplied to infinity.

Seated in the middle barber chair, lawyer Henderson was presiding, or trying to, amid the clamor of argument and denunciation. Jacobs sat to his left and Carter Peamon to his right.

"What's going on?" Norwood asked Armond Scott.

Scott passed him a two-page typewritten carbon with a list of signatures appended. "Read this," he said.

Tom Miller, the pawnbroker and real-estate man, said, "I warned you! I told you they wouldn't be satisfied with no damned election."

"Gentlemen," Henderson said. "Let's not bicker among ourselves."

"Where's Manly?" Norwood demanded.

Armond Scott snorted. "Long gone. Him and his brother both."

"About time."

Tom Miller had the floor. "You want to make peace, that's your business. But not me. I'm nobody's *boy*."

"Nobody said you were, Tom."

"I still say we stand up and fight! Get our guns and give the sons of bitches what for!"

Some of the men cheered and hooted.

"We've got them outnumbered three to one! Three black guns against every white gun."

"Just where you planning to get guns, Tom?" Norwood spoke in a loud voice full of a confidence he was not feeling. Things were unraveling fast.

"Out of our closets, our attics."

"They got all the guns, Tom. You know that." For months now, it had been impossible for a black man anywhere in the county—anywhere in the state—to buy a gun. They'd scraped up only a handful, enough to show off at Free Love Hall that first time. "You want to turn this city into a shooting gallery? That what you want?" Norwood turned on the crowd now, grabbing men by the lapels, asking them personally.

"Time we did something," one man said.

"Time the black man stood up for himself 'round here."

"Time we shoot up this town."

Norwood cursed. He was not a man to curse—he knew it would get their attention. "Shoot up this town?" He walked among the crowd and it parted to let him pass nearly the length of the shop. "Shoot up this town? Just what part of this town you figure on shooting up? Market Street? You think they're going to let a bunch of marauding *niggers* shoot up Market Street? All those fine homes?"

"We've got to do something, John," Carter Peamon said.

Norwood paid no attention to him. "Let me tell you this, and get it right: if the shooting starts, the shooting gallery is going to be Brooklyn. And guess who gets to be the clay ducks?"

Men murmured sullenly. He was right, and they knew it. The Wilmington Light Infantry and Naval Reserves had been parading all over the place lately, showing off their fine rifles. And some of the men in the room had watched the Gatling gun firsthand, out on the river.

Lawyer Henderson didn't say anything. Jacobs spun his chair slowly back and forth, shaking his head. Peamon stared into the mirror.

Ivanhoe Grant said from somewhere, sweet and low, "If you ain't the sorriest bunch of plantation niggers I ever saw."

Norwood said, "That's not fair, Reverend. It's all right for you to raise hell, but we have to live here after you're long gone. We've got families, property. We're on for the long haul."

"Everybody got to live somewhere." Grant emerged from the back, shaking his head, smiling big. He paused to light a cigar and smoke it awhile, waiting for them to want to hear what he had to say.

Henderson said, "I don't recall inviting you in here anyway."

"The Lord invited me," Grant said quietly. "The Lord invites me anywhere the black man won't say boo to the white man."

"Man has a point," Tom Miller said. He, too, lit a cigar, as if to show that he wouldn't take any guff from anybody, white or black. The atmosphere quickly became smoky and close. Somebody accidentally kicked over a brass spittoon, and it clanged under the men's feet till somebody else righted it.

The men were all talking at once. Grant stood nonchalantly smoking. After a while, he started laughing—soft at first, then so loud that, gradually, the other talk quieted. Once again, all eyes were turned on him.

Norwood, annoyed, said, "Just what is it that amuses you so, Reverend?"

"You are one precious gaggle of niggers," Grant said, hardly able to speak through his laughter. "Man might mistake you for the United States Congress."

"This is an important matter," Norwood insisted. "We're the duly appointed Committee of Colored Citizens."

"You're a bunch of scared niggers in a barbershop."

Everybody objected at once. Grant stood casually puffing on his corona, oblivious. Armond Scott, a young lawyer, stared at him, captured by his clear blue eyes and the sureness of his manner.

Sitting above the pandemonium of angry voices, Henderson raised his arms for order. When that didn't work, he took off his shoe and banged it on the arm of the barber chair. "Gentlemen, gentlemen, gentlemen," he kept repeating uselessly.

"Go ahead—shout me down!" Ivanhoe Grant said suddenly, with such force that the room quieted. Henderson put his shoe back on. Aware that some of the younger men, including Scott, were listening hard, Grant said more softly, "Do whatever you think is right. In the end, it won't matter. It will happen."

"Just like that?"

"Just like that." He snapped his fingers crisply. "Don't any of you get it?" He held up his cigar. "You're not in charge of this. Never were. They're going to do what they've been planning to do all along."

Norwood smiled and seized upon Grant's own logic. "So if it doesn't matter what we do, why not be reasonable? Why not take the moral high ground?"

"Call it that, if you want," Grant said. "I call it giving in." He sidled over and stood nose to nose with Norwood. "What I'm telling you is, your only chance is to stand up to them."

"Why? What kind of chance is that?"

Grant shook his head, as if incredulous that any grown man could be so thick. "Because," he said with forced patience, "that's the one thing they won't expect."

The meeting lasted another hour and a half. Norwood and Henderson prevailed, as Grant knew they would. He had made his speech for today. He knew why they wouldn't take the risk. But they were taking the same risk anyway, without any pride. For the last half of the meeting, he looked on with detachment. What will be, will be, he thought. You can't stop it.

"So we're agreed," Henderson said at last. The men murmured assent without enthusiasm. "Mr. Jacobs, if you please," he said, trying to invest the proceedings with a formality appropriate to the gravity of the moment.

Jacobs, who as coroner was accustomed to filling out meticulous death certificates in a fine cursive hand, acted as secretary. He read the final draft of their reply: " 'We the colored citizens to whom was referred the matter of expulsion from this community of the persons and press of Alex Manly, beg most respectfully—' "

"Beg," Tom Miller said, and spat on the floor. "Beg."

" '—to say that we are in no wise responsible for, nor in any way endorse, the obnoxious article that called forth your activities.' "

"That's right," Carter Peamon said. "We're not taking the blame, so we're not really giving in. All this fuss about a man that's already gone."

Tom Miller said, "We're giving in. At least admit it."

Jacobs continued, " 'Neither are we authorized to act for him in this matter, but, in the interest of peace, we will most willingly use our influence to have your wishes carried out. Very respectfully,' etcetera."

"Fine," Henderson said. "That ought to smooth their feathers." He handed Jacobs an envelope, and Jacobs addressed it to the Honorable Alfred M. Waddell, 16 North Fifth Street, City. At Norwood's insistence, he added, "Please deliver at House."

He sealed the envelope and handed it back to Henderson, who held it up like a prize. "Now, who's going to deliver it?"

"Give it to me," Tom Miller said. "I'll deliver it on the end of a brick!"

Some of the men laughed.

Norwood said, "I suggest a delegation of three—Jacobs, Henderson, and myself. Let them see we have a united leadership."

Carter Peamon, who had been a precinct boss and had held various minor county posts, said, "That's exactly the wrong thing to do. We don't want to go making this thing out to be too important."

"He's right," Henderson agreed. "We've got to salvage some pride out of this."

"Right," Jacobs said. "You see President McKinley delivering his own mail?"

"Who wants to be our envoy?" Henderson said.

Ivanhoe Grant stepped forward.

"Not you," Norwood started to protest.

"I'm exactly the wrong mailman," Grant said, smiling to show all his teeth. Norwood could see he was mocking them, playing the sambo. "But I wish to nominate young Armond Scott here." He had never met Scott before today, but the boy clearly thought Grant had hung the moon. Grant had been watching his face.

"Good idea," someone said. "Send a lawyer. That's how they do this kind of thing."

Others murmured assent.

"What about it, Armond?" Henderson said.

They were all looking at him—he couldn't very well say no. "Well, sure," he said, without any certainty in his voice. "Sure, I'd be honored."

Several men slapped him on the back and nudged him toward Henderson, who leaned down from his chair and handed Scott the letter. Scott carefully slipped it into the inside pocket of his coat.

"Gentlemen, we are adjourned," Henderson said. "Leave here in twos and threes. Stay close to home, and don't do anything stupid." His last remark seemed to be addressed personally to Tom Miller, who spat and banged out the door ahead of the others, all by himself.

Within a few minutes, most of the men had scattered, hurrying in little knots up Dock Street, away from the river, their hats jammed low over their ears in the twilight chill, their eyes nervously glancing over their shoulders in case they were being followed.

Henderson asked Norwood, "Why hasn't the Board of Aldermen acted? What's Mayor Wright doing?"

Norwood could tell he was scared. He understood for the first time that Henderson had been working very hard to appear composed. Now, he just looked like a man worried sick about his family and his livelihood.

Norwood shook his head. "I've been trying to get them to meet for a month now. Everybody's too scared, I guess. Dr. Wright has disappeared. Some say he's hiding out, some say he's long gone and not coming back."

"That's unheard of—he's the mayor."

"You read the last part of their so-called declaration. They want us all out of there. We dodged that part in our answer."

"Can they do that?" Henderson said.

"I didn't think they could do what they've already done. But the board, we're a duly elected government. I don't see how they can get around that."

"Who becomes mayor if the mayor's left town?"

"The board would appoint one," Norwood said.

"What about the board? What if they're scared off?"

"It's never happened. They could nominate their own successors, I guess, but the full board would have to vote it."

Norwood heard his own words as if somebody else were speaking them. He was talking out loud about the overthrow of the government—*his* government—as if it might actually happen. But it was a crazy idea. This was modern times, not the old plantation days. They couldn't chase off the whole board, and none of them, including himself, would ever nominate successors that would please the white supremacists.

"I think we're safe," he said, after mulling it over. "Too many people would have to go along. You could never get that many people to go along with anything that dirty."

"Let's hope so," Henderson said. "Meanwhile, get that damned board together. We're breaking our backs trying to abide by the law, but the law is wearing thin."

"I hear you, brother. I hear you."

———

Ivanhoe Grant caught up with Armond Scott at the corner of Front Street, just as Scott was stepping into the street in the direction of downtown. He came up behind Scott and startled him.

"Oh, it's you, Reverend. Guess I'm a bit jumpy." He patted the letter in his breast pocket.

"I'd be jumpy as a cat with that mail in my pocket," Grant said amiably. They walked together for half a block. Clearly, Scott was in no hurry to get where he had to go. "You're a brave man," Grant said.

"What do you mean?" Scott stopped and glanced left, then right, his hand over his heart.

"Didn't hear no army of volunteers fighting you for the job."

"You nominated me."

"I know, I know. Thought I was doing you a favor, giving you some standing among those men. They need some fresh thinking."

"New blood."

"That's right, new blood. But maybe I put you on the spot."

Scott shrugged and started walking again, this time with more purpose. "I'll leave it off with Colonel Waddell and be on my way."

Grant stopped at the corner of Market, and Scott stopped, too. "Go on your way?" Grant said. "Son, you're making some powerful assumptions."

"I don't see it."

"You know why I didn't volunteer?"

A pair of white men crossed the street up ahead. Grant waited to see if they would come his way, but the men seemed preoccupied with other business and disappeared up Market in a hurry. "I figured, I show my black face in that pretty neighborhood, I'll wind up like my granddaddy."

"I heard you at the church meeting. Doesn't change what I have to do."

Grant ignored him. "Figure I might as well paint a bull's-eye on my back. They're apt to have rifles in every window by now. I mean, do you realize where Colonel Waddell lives?"

"I've never gone visiting, if that's what you mean."

Grant pulled Scott into the doorway of a hardware store closed for the night. "Just off of Market, on Fifth," he said. He pointed up Market Street, away from the river. "Half a block east of him, right up this street, you got John D. Bellamy's mansion. Just past that, you've got Hugh MacRae's castle. Across the street from that, you've got Colonel Walker Taylor's house."

"So?"

"On the west corner of Market and Fifth, there's First Baptist Church, which at this very minute is full of vigilantes. Practically next door to that is the Light Infantry Armory." Grant lowered his voice to a whisper. "All connected by secret underground passages."

"Go on—secret passages."

"Tunnels right under the street. Go in here, come out there, like magic." He snapped his fingers. "White man can be wherever he wants to be, just like that. Might as well be invisible."

"Never heard of such a thing." Scott chuckled nervously. Actually, he had heard tales of the old smugglers' tunnels, but he had always assumed they were just stories.

"We're talking about the heart of the heart of White Town, brother. Three blocks that way. You think they're going to let you wander around loose in that neighborhood?"

"I'm just the delivery boy."

"You'll be running the gauntlet. You think they're going to wait long enough to find out what you're delivering?"

The streets were weirdly deserted. Scott turned the corner and started walking resolutely east on Market in the direction of Waddell's house. He hurried across Second Street, then Third. Approaching Fourth, with the Wilmington Light Infantry Armory coming up on his left, he slowed.

Grant clapped him on the shoulder and stopped him, held up his finger for silence. Scott strained his ears. Far off, like distant surf, he could hear a vague murmur. "Hear that?" Grant said. He prodded Scott on, keeping to the right side of the street. A hundred yards away, in the yard of the armory, uniformed troops were drilling with bayonets. An officer with a sword gave the commands. Each rank of skirmishers advanced toward a line of straw dummies hanged from a gallows. The gallows was newly framed of clean, blond wood.

With each thrust of the bayonets, the rank of soldiers shouted in unison. Their sound was a kind of roar. The bayonets ripped into the burlap dummies.

"Know why they yell?"

Scott shook his head. He was afraid to ask.

"So they can't hear the cartilage tearing," Grant explained in a whisper. Scott was rattled.

Up ahead, men jammed the street. Scott and Grant were only a block and a half from Waddell's house. Between them and it lay First Baptist Church, on the left corner. The roar of the drilling infantrymen was nothing compared to the roar that suddenly rose from the mob in the street.

"Mass meeting," Grant said, head cocked to listen. "Somebody's giving another speech. Whatever he said, they liked hearing it."

Scott stared at him dumbly.

"See their torches?" Grant said. Market Street was bathed in light—from the gaslights on the corners, as well as from a hundred kerosene torches flaring orange and smoking into the clear night. Once they emerged from under the shadows of the trees, they would surely be spotted.

"Church rally," Grant whispered. "Can you beat it? Calling on our humble Lord to bless their mischief!" They both stared toward First Baptist Church, which rose above the crowd like a medieval fortress. "They're voting on who to lynch."

Armond Scott was afraid. There must be five hundred white men here, he thought, and their mood is ugly. "We could circle round, come up from the other side."

"You don't think they'll be waiting on that side, too? Use your melon."

Scott was stymied. A few minutes ago, carrying the message to Waddell's house had seemed like a minor chore. Now, it seemed suicidal. Scott wrung his hands. He looked up Market, daring himself to walk farther.

Grant put an arm around his shoulder. The boy was trembling. Grant spoke slowly, gently. "Take it to the post office. Let some white man wearing the proper uniform deliver it for you."

He could backtrack down Market Street, walk north on Front for two blocks, and be rid of it. "But that's not the plan! I promised—"

"You promised you'd get it there. Right?"

"Well, yes, Reverend, but—"

"If they shoot you down in the middle of Market Street, is the note going to get there?"

Scott was confused. Grant's voice was so sure, so confident, and he was a righteous man. "No, I guess not."

"You guess not? Well, I don't have to guess. I can say for sure."

Another roar went up from the crowd. Scott could see their backs and the torches, pumping up and down in clenched hands. He looked at his shoes, as if he couldn't get over how mud-spattered they were. He said, tentatively, "The post office? But it won't arrive on time."

"We post it now, it'll make the early mail."

Scott pondered that. "The man said seven-thirty."

Grant laughed and clapped him on the back. "You lawyers. It was a figure of speech, that's all."

Scott looked skeptical.

"Look. Didn't the declaration itself say they demanded an answer within twelve hours? Right in the text?"

Scott was on firm ground now—he understood documents. "Right. Within twelve hours."

"And what time did you meet with Waddell and his bunch?"

"Three-thirty sharp. The meeting lasted half an hour."

"So twelve hours from four o'clock makes four in the morning. Yet he said seven-thirty." He knew Scott was too scared to think straight. "Does that sound to you like they care whether it gets there at four in the morning, or seven-thirty, or eight-thirty, just so long as we give in?"

Scott thought about it awhile, then smiled. "When you put it that way . . ."

"Anyway, they already have their answer. Didn't lawyer Henderson say he told them Manly was already gone? Didn't he tell them we meant no trouble?"

"He did that. He's a man to speak his mind."

"So the written reply is really just a formality. Something for the record. They're not in any suspense."

Scott relaxed. "No use me getting all shot up over this thing." He laughed with nervous relief.

Grant shook his hand. "I admire a man with common sense."

They doubled back down Market Street together, keeping to the shadows, and hurried along Front Street two blocks to the post office. On the steps of the massive marble building, Scott stopped short. "Damn!"

"What is it?"

"They're closed—and I haven't got a stamp."

Grant smiled, reached into his coat pocket, and extracted a glassine envelope full of stamps. "Here," he said, offering it to Scott. "Better paste two on it, just to be sure. No sense taking any chances."

John Norwood left Jacobs' Barbershop alone. He wasn't sure where he was going. See if Mayor Wright was in his rooms at the Orton Hotel, maybe. Find Flavell Foster or Ben Keith, buy a little insurance from the vigilantes. He had to walk awhile and think this thing through. He had a hunch there was precious little time left for quiet reflection.

Scott had taken the letter—good, that was done. Scott was young but reliable. As a lawyer, he was only fair, but he had a bright future as a politician. People took to him immediately. He had charm, good looks, and a winning smile, and he was a team player. He ought to be putting the letter into Colonel Waddell's hands any minute now.

Up ahead, Norwood spied two men walking together. One was lean and blond. Even from behind, he recognized the other's halting gait, the sloped shoulders and walking cane. "Hold up there, Mr. Calabash," he said.

Harry Calabash turned, startled. Sam Jenks turned with him, alert for attack. "Oh, it's you, John," Harry said. "How are you this evening?"

"You know better than to ask me that."

"Have you met Mr. Jenks?"

Norwood bobbed his head and held out his hand. "His wife is one of our finest teachers. Can't say I admire his own work as much."

"Ah. Of course."

"We've sent the reply," Norwood said, almost defiantly.

"What do you want me to say, John—that everything's going to be fine?"

"I don't expect anything but fairness, Harry."

Calabash shook his head. "Listen to him, Sam. Fairness, that's all he wants. What city has he been living in?"

"Shouldn't you be getting on home?" Sam said to Harry. Harry was drunk, and he didn't want Norwood talking him into anything.

Norwood said, "You never come around anymore, Harry. You never talk to us anymore."

"Can't be helped," Harry said. "I'm not a free agent, you know— I work for a man."

"And your friend?"

Sam Jenks looked insolent and wary.

Harry said, "Look—"

"Forget it. Forget you ever saw me. I'll go back to my people and you go back to yours."

"Aw, don't be that way."

"What way should I be? I'm part of this government. I'm an elected official. White people voted for me, too."

"I know. I was one of them."

"Then write the truth for a change, Harry. You know how it is. Write it that way."

"John, John. You've been in politics long enough to know. Somewhere between my typewriter and the front page, the truth changes."

"And you take no responsibility?"

"I work for a man."

"So it's not your fault? Is that what you mean?"

"These days, John, most things are my fault. Good night."

Harry turned and went on his way, Sam beside him. The sky was clear and full of stars. Sam looked up and picked out the Big Dipper. He had never seen a sky so big. He could almost feel the earth rolling under his feet.

Norwood stood and watched them until they were just shadows, no longer in the shapes of men. He felt the starlight on his skin. The sky was a map of old journeys running deep in his blood. The Big Dipper, pointing toward the North Star—in the old days, the slaves had followed it north to freedom. "The drinking gourd," he whispered to himself. "Follow the drinking gourd."

PART IV

THE COUP

No trade at Wilmington. Spirits of turpentine—
nothing doing. Rosin—nothing doing. Crude
turpentine—nothing doing.

Associated Press
Market Report,
November 11, 1898

CHAPTER SIXTEEN

Thursday, November 10

SAFFRON WAS STILL ASLEEP in Miz Gabrielle's sewing room. The headless dressmaker's dummy stood in the corner, draped with folds of fine satin for Gray Ellen Jenks's evening gown.

Bessie King busied herself in the kitchen.

David hadn't come back last night. Bessie didn't know exactly where he was. If there was trouble, that boy would find it, though he was a good boy at heart. Everybody said so. But he didn't think too clear. He was the kind of boy things happened to, never the right things.

Bessie served Colonel Waddell in the dining room, where he ate alone. He seemed all stirred up this morning, high color in his cheeks. Kept rubbing his legs and cursing softly, "Damned cavalry legs." Let him suffer, she thought. Pain was a boon to character.

She ducked into the pantry to fetch another jar of marmalade, and there she saw it: her spider, hanging on her web upside down. "Lordy," she said out loud, and crossed herself. She grabbed the marmalade and went out quickly.

"Something spook you?" the Colonel asked as she clattered down a plate of eggs, bacon, and cheese grits in front of him.

She looked at him and saw a ghost. She saw him melting away like a haint, a bad dream of a bad man. "No, suh," she said, ducking her head.

"Do you know what today is, Aunt Bessie? What anniversary?"

"Suh?"

"Ninety-nine years ago, Napoleon seized the throne of France."

"Yes, suh."

He sipped coffee. "Go see if Miz Gabby is up yet. When you've served her breakfast, take the rest of the day off."

"Yes, Colonel."

"And Aunt Bessie? Stay off the streets today."

"Colonel?"

He smiled. "Nothing you'd understand," he said, and forked into his eggs. "Just politics."

She left in a swish of skirts.

Waddell ate with gusto. He'd need a hearty meal today. Lately, his appetite was enormous. His muscles were stretching, unbending, craving exercise, like the muscles of a young man. His brain was humming like an electric coil. His voice was tuned and strong. Only his legs gave him pain—cramps, poor circulation, knees that grated. Nothing a good, brisk walk wouldn't cure.

In his mind, he counted off the men he would have to contend with. Hugh MacRae was the most formidable, but, for the time being, their interests coincided. And Hugh's brother Donald did as Hugh told him.

Next in order of prominence came the Taylor brothers.

Colonel Walker Taylor, officially in charge of the State Guard, could be a problem. He seemed to want to run things. But he favored posture—intimidation and threat—over outright violence: stand up straight, shoulder to shoulder, and you won't have to fire a shot. That was good. Walker Taylor had high-minded ideas about duty and honor. He would act with restraint. Still, if things got out of control, he was a brave man who would give orders to shoot to kill. Waddell must be careful when and how to use him.

J. Allan Taylor, who held no official claim to anything, was the brother to watch. He had close ties to Hugh MacRae and lacked Walker's patience and restraint. He would charge in and do the job, quick and dirty and mean. He wanted results. He didn't much care about the legal niceties—he was used to fixing them up later. He was still bitter about how much his father had lost in the War, and he aimed to get it back any way he could. If you crossed him, he was the kind of man who would pull a pistol and shoot you between the eyes in front of a hundred witnesses, then go take his supper.

George Rountree was the smartest of the bunch. Waddell liked him the least. In some ways, they thought alike—Rountree was always scouting out the board three moves ahead of everybody else. And they both served the law. But Rountree was a fanatic on the subject—he wouldn't cross the street without the proper paperwork. He knew precedents and counter-precedents, ordinances and codes, right down to their subsections and footnotes.

For Waddell, the law was a drama, the courtroom a theater— exactly like the courthouse meeting. The broad sweep of justice ranged from tragedy to farce. Each trial had its own set of players, protagonist and antagonist, and a rising curve of suspense as they struggled toward the climax—that moment of decision after which nothing would ever be the same.

At the center of each trial was the nut: one actor wanted something, and the other would stop at nothing to keep him from having it. A stage-managed combat by proxy. The consequences might be staggering—fines, hard labor, life imprisonment, even death.

But for George Rountree, the drama was a nuisance. Human passions interfered with the law. The law lived in books. The law was the fiction everyone in the community had agreed upon so that their collective life might proceed with a semblance of order and decorum. The law was a kind of story told over and over again. From time to time, one needed to revise it—as he was already revising the role of Negroes and the ballot, Waddell knew.

In the courtroom, Rountree was formidable. He could not match Waddell for fiery eloquence, for inflaming hearts and winning over an audience of nervous jurors. Instead, Rountree relied on the inexorable momentum of logic—fact following fact, figure proving figure, nothing overlooked, crushing his opponent by sheer weight of proof. Rountree won his cases in the law library.

Rountree thrived on information, on knowing more than anybody else. The way to keep him off-balance, then, was to keep him in the dark. Already, at Waddell's urging, Hugh MacRae had cut him out of some key meetings. It was time to cut him out of a few more.

Waddell pulled out his gold watch—already after seven. Before he finished his plate, the men began to arrive. Within a few minutes, they filled up his parlor, dining room, and library, milling about, pouring coffee down their throats, all dressed up and talking in low tones, like a board of directors.

Aunt Bessie disappeared. She did not even remove the breakfast dishes. Miz Gabby had not come down yet. What ailed her lately? No matter—women had no part in this morning's business. And where was Samuel Jenks? He had sent word for Jenks to meet him here bright and early. For what they were about to do, he wanted his biographer close at hand.

J. Allan Taylor stood in the entryway, thumbs hooked in the waistband of his trousers. He was nearly as tall as his brother but lacked Walker's bulk. He was a man with no room for extras. Every few minutes, he yanked his watch out of his vest, snapped it open like he was knifing open an oyster, then dropped it back into the flannel pocket.

Hugh MacRae said, "Expecting somebody?"

Taylor said, "You don't think the niggers will send word?"

MacRae barely smiled. "As if that matters."

"But if they give in to everything—"

MacRae clapped a hand on his shoulder. "Now listen, John. They can all sign over the deeds to their houses, it wouldn't change what we have to do."

Taylor took his thumbs out of his waistband. "I'm just thinking of George. He'll hold us to the paper. Like some goddamn contract or something."

MacRae had sent word to Rountree after yesterday's meeting that the thing was settled: no call for drastic measures. "You let me handle George," he said.

MacRae's eyes were flinty and bright, his face ruddy and smooth from good health and exercise. This morning, he moved in a kind of aura. His tweeds were crisp. His riding boots—which he rarely wore on a business day—were spit-shined to a rich chocolate brown. His thinning blond hair was slicked in a side part, and his ears were as pink as if he'd been standing in the cold for an hour. He fairly glowed.

Beside him, Waddell seemed spectral, a black-and-white figure cut from the fabric of an earlier century: pale gray eyes sunk in deep, dark circles, silver hair and spiked goatee sheeny with oil, moustaches waxed to stiff points, high celluloid collar yellow against the white of his throat, black clawhammer coat both ridiculous and somber at this hour of the morning.

With great ceremony, Waddell consulted his watch. Where was Jenks? No matter—he couldn't wait any longer. "Gentlemen," he said in a soft, deep voice, then snapped his watchcase shut as if it were loaded to fire. "Time."

MacRae donned his brown slouch hat, precisely blocked into a campaign crown, and led the Committee of Twenty-five across the porch and down the middle of Fifth Street to Market, where his saddled horse stood waiting at the armory. To J. Allan Taylor, he said, "Never doubt me, John."

Striding hard on his sore legs, Colonel Waddell passed the line of men and took his place at the head, beside MacRae and Taylor. In a few minutes, he would ride. He was walking so fast the breeze pushed at the broad front brim of his plumed chapeau, the same one he'd worn at Richmond and the Petersburg Pike. His hand reached reflexively to his left hip to pat the hilt of his cavalry saber—but in the rush, he had forgotten to buckle it on.

Sam Jenks met them coming the other way. He greeted Waddell and his cousin and fell into step with them. He could tell by the look on MacRae's face that these men were out to do serious business this morning. He could almost smell their nervous adrenaline, rank as sweat.

The Light Infantry had been mustering at the armory since before dawn. Everything had been arranged. All the right people had been told. Every man had his assignment. When Waddell's party arrived, Donald MacRae and Captain James were waiting. Several hundred men armed with Winchesters and Colt pistols were milling about in the yard by the steps. Some of them had spent the night guarding First Baptist Church or patrolling the neighborhoods, reporting at intervals to Colonel Roger Moore, grand marshal of the vigilantes. Moore had set up command a few blocks from Waddell's house in the other direction, at Fifth and Chestnut.

Moore had stopped by Waddell's house as a courtesy the previous evening. During the War Between the States, he had served with Waddell in the Forty-first Regiment of the Third North Carolina Cavalry. Moore had been commissioned a major on the same day Waddell had received his colonelcy. When Waddell had become ill, Moore had taken over command of the regiment.

Waddell figured a command post was a good place for Colonel Moore this morning—one less chief to contend with. Let him wait there until they sent him his orders.

When the assembled mob caught sight of Waddell, MacRae, and the other committee men, they cheered and pressed closer toward the armory, waiting for the word. The mob parted to let the leaders ascend the marble steps and enter the armory.

Standing just inside the thick double doors, the MacRae brothers conferred briefly. Donald was still technically in command of the Light Infantry men who had volunteered for the Cuban campaign but never gotten there.

"Form up your men," Hugh MacRae said without any inflection. His voice resounded in the high space. Waddell and J. Allan Taylor stood to either side.

Sam Jenks, loitering a step behind, said, "I don't get it. You're going to use force? But—"

"Keep quiet," MacRae said. "It's time to make a point."

Donald MacRae hesitated and rubbed his sharp chin. "I still hold my commission in the U.S. Army, Hugh," he said. "There may be ramifications."

J. Allan Taylor said, "He's right, Hugh—they could court-martial him for this. It would give them a pretext to send the federals down."

"Goddamnit!" Hugh MacRae said. "Why didn't you say something yesterday?"

"It didn't occur to me yesterday."

"Get Colonel Moore on the telephone."

The telephone hung on the wall in the meeting parlor just off the corridor. They clustered around it while MacRae rang Moore's house. He wasn't there. Of course he wasn't there, Waddell reflected: MacRae must not know about the command post.

Next, they rang Moore's office, but of course he wasn't there, either. Waddell knew that Colonel Moore was barely two blocks away, waiting by a telephone for this very call, but he didn't say anything. MacRae hung up, looking baffled. His hair was mussed, and there was soot on the sleeve of his tweed coat where he'd rubbed against the fireplace mantel.

"Get Walker on the telephone," J. Allan Taylor suggested. "Christ, why isn't he here already?"

MacRae rang him at home. "Walk? We've got a situation here. Come on over and straighten us out. We need a good officer out front." Then he listened, pressing the earpiece hard against his pink ear.

"What's he giving you?" J. Allan Taylor said. "Let's get on with this."

"Goddamnit, haul your fat ass over here!" MacRae shouted into the trumpet. The composure was gone from his voice. As he cursed, his tenor went shrill and broke. His face went scarlet. He listened some more. "We need some leadership on this thing," he said.

"Let me talk to him," J. Allan Taylor said. He reached for the earpiece, but MacRae held onto it with a white fist.

Sam said, "I still don't see why—"

Waddell grabbed him, hard.

"No, the city is not threatened, Walk, not directly," Hugh MacRae said. "Christ Jesus—we've gone over all that! This thing is necessary. The long-term threat is there. We've got to do this thing. We talked about that."

Walker Taylor was shouting into the other end—they all could hear the shrill buzz of his voice rattling the earpiece.

"We may not need you later!" Hugh MacRae said. "Later may be too late."

"Let me go get him," Donald MacRae offered. "He's only a block away."

Hugh ignored him and stared at the wall, still shouting. "We can't stop it now—it's too late, man!" He listened again, stamping his foot. "The Pinkertons' report? We talked to the Pinkertons!" He listened. "I don't give a good hoot in hell if you've changed your mind!"

Donald MacRae shook his head and stared at the Italian marble floor.

J. Allan Taylor stood by, wringing his hands, imagining what his grandfather would do at this moment if he were standing beside them here, in the family house he had built. They were all letting Hugh down. It was all a matter of technicalities. Rountree must have been talking to Walker—it had his stamp all over it. Legalities, that's all it was. Paper laws.

Hugh MacRae clapped the earpiece into the cradle so hard he nearly tore the wooden telephone box off the wall. He didn't have to explain—they'd all caught the gist.

Sam had never seen Hugh so worked up—almost too angry to speak.

"Do it yourself," J. Allan said.

MacRae shook his head violently. "That's not my place. It's a military operation, that's how we planned the goddamn thing." He chopped the air with his hands. "We want action taken by the proper authorities." He swore again. "I thought I had some goddamn soldiers I could count on."

His brother Donald said, "Tom James can do it. He's out on the steps."

MacRae flung open the big doors and marched out, boots clicking, onto the marble steps. The mob cheered. At the fringes, Red Shirts collected in knots and pumped their rifles over their heads. "Let's go get the niggers!" one of them cried, and the rest broke out in a chorus of cheering and hurrahs. They pressed closer.

Sam was scared in his stomach. This mob had an air of premeditation—it was no spontaneous lynching party. These men had waited all night for this moment. Some had been waiting weeks. The inflammatory articles in the newspapers, the rousing hate speeches, the bogus election—everything had been moving toward this. And Sam's job was to write the story.

The infantrymen and several squads of Naval Reserves stood in loose formation in the side yard, checking their weapons.

Hugh MacRae said, "Captain James, if you please."

Captain James turned on his heel, looking puzzled.

"Captain MacRae requests you take command of this operation."

Captain James backed up a step, glanced sidelong at the mob, looked to Donald MacRae for some explanation. Donald MacRae stood with his brother and said nothing. "What, me lead that mob?" Captain James said.

The MacRaes nodded. The blood rose in Captain James's face. Automatically, he braced himself at attention. "I am a soldier," he said. "I won't lead a mob."

Sam scribbled James's reply in his notebook—he wanted to get it right. He understood it immediately to be a defining moment, a vivid declaration of character. He wished he himself were capable of such a moment.

Donald MacRae said, "Somebody has to do it."

Captain James said, "Not me—never. I won't."

Hugh MacRae swore.

Donald MacRae turned up his palms. "Be reasonable, Tom."

Waddell stood beside them, beaming, then took one calculated step toward the crowd. "Waddell!" Solomon Fishblate shouted from the front of the crowd, and others took up the chant: "Waddell! Waddell! Waddell!" He stood at the top step and let them cheer. He waved. He bowed deeply from the waist, sweeping his plumed hat across his body in a graceful flourish.

Two of the Red Shirts grabbed him bodily and hauled him through the parting crowd, then hoisted him onto a horse. The stirrups were too long, but never mind that, he thought. He took the reins in one hand and, in a gesture he had not used in thirty-five years, lifted the other easily, naturally, palm open. He waited till the men had turned their attention from the armory steps to him. He sat above the crowd, feeding on their upturned faces, hand still raised. "We tried to reason with the niggers," he said, "but they have defied us. Alex Manly is still at large, free to slander the good name of our women. I say this nonsense has gone on long enough!"

The men hurrahed.

"Today, we march on the nigger newspaper and seize Manly— are you with me?"

The din rattled the windows of the armory. With all eyes fastened on him, Waddell casually let his arm drop forward, as if he were tossing a baseball, and their cheers started his horse forward up Market Street.

Hugh MacRae stood momentarily paralyzed. It was too late to stop Waddell. He had picked his moment with perfection, had outflanked him again. Colonel Moore, Walker Taylor, Tom James, even his own brother Donald—all had failed him at the crucial moment. He swore a string of oaths.

J. Allan Taylor grabbed MacRae's arm and led him around back to their stabled horses. "Come on, Hugh—we can catch ahold of this thing yet."

Sam Jenks sprinted down the steps and followed the mob.

On the bone-white marble steps of the armory, Captain James watched them go. When the infantrymen formed up in ranks and started marching out of the yard, he leaped off the steps to stop them. "If you follow that mob, leave your tunics here!" he shouted. The men milled about uncertainly.

Lieutenant White, the drillmaster, who wore wire-rimmed spectacles and styled himself after Colonel Roosevelt, said to Donald MacRae, "Captain, are we not to do our part?"

"I'm in command here," Captain James said. "If the city is threatened, we will move to keep the peace."

Donald MacRae swore, threw up a helpless hand, and retired inside the building.

The men remained standing in ranks, muttering. The tail of the mob was almost out of sight now, and a group of men and boys who had arrived late were sprinting through the pall of lime dust to catch up to it.

"At ease," Captain James said. "Stack your weapons. Go on about your business. But don't leave the compound."

The men shifted from foot to foot, talked briefly among themselves, swatted their gray, white-plumed hats against their thighs, and, with an exaggerated air of disappointment, began falling out. There were coffee and biscuits inside—they could smell the wood smoke from the old iron cookstove in the basement club rooms.

Colonel Alfred Moore Waddell walked his horse so that the men behind him could keep up. Mounted Red Shirts took up positions as outriders, Winchesters cocked on thighs. By the time Waddell reached the turn onto Seventh, the mob stretched two blocks behind him, all the way back to the Wilmington Light Infantry Armory.

Waddell made the turn onto Seventh Street with five hundred men trailing him. MacRae rode somewhere behind him—he didn't look back to see. An army could have only one leader. Mike Dowling jogged along the flank on his skittish sorrel, his red shirt freshly laundered for the occasion. Among the marchers on foot were Solomon Fishblate and the Reverend Peyton Hoge, both carrying Winchesters.

From out of nowhere appeared Father Dennen, waving his arms

to stop them. "For the love of Jesus, boys, you can't do this!" he shouted. "You can't do this!"

Waddell's horse shouldered past him, and the priest went sprawling onto the oyster shells. He picked himself up and brushed himself off in a cloud of lime dust, grabbing men by the elbow, pleading for tolerance. But the sheer momentum of the mob carried him along and spit him out into the gutter, where he lay, stunned, watching hundreds of wild-eyed men stream past.

Seventh was a quiet residential street. The mob flowed noisily along the narrow, tree-shaded corridor between modest frame houses, moving fast. They trampled flower beds, scattered stray dogs, sent whole flocks of blackbirds exploding out of the twisted live oaks in black, frenzied bursts.

A Red Shirt fired his rifle into the air. Pretty soon, a dozen ragged shots cracked into the overhanging branches. A shotgun boomed twice, bringing down a rain of twigs and shredded leaves. Men hooted and yelled. A frightened horse kicked down a picket fence at the corner of Dock. At Orange Street, a team of matched grays pulling a landau reared up at the sudden appearance of the mob, and the carriage fetched up against a porch, its front wheel busted. Dr. Silas Wright, the mayor, peered out of the landau, clutching the useless reins in his white gloves, praying to go unrecognized.

The mob rushed through the neighborhood like a flash flood, carrying away everything in its path. White women stared out from behind curtains. Occasionally, men ran outside to join the mob, buttoning their flies as they ran, pulling on coats, their pockets bulging with shotgun shells.

Past Orange Street, the faces turned darker. Negro workingmen, sleeping after the late shift at the mills, were roused abruptly. They fled out their back doors barefoot, wearing only flannel union suits. Many of the women were already at work in the better homes across town. Children dived under beds, stared through the broken boards of slat fences.

By the time it roared past Williston School on Ann Street, the

mob had swelled to almost a thousand men. Now, Waddell could
see a church and a white building just in front of it that must be
Free Love Hall. The sign proclaiming *The Record Publishing
Company* still hung from the second floor. A face appeared in the
upstairs window, then disappeared. Waddell reined up at a distance from the front door, men milling so close around him that he
could not move his feet in the stirrups. All at once, he realized he
was unarmed. The upraised barrel of a Winchester was bobbing
out of the crowd on his right. He gripped the barrel, hauled the
weapon out of the owner's hands, and planted the butt on his
thigh.

As the mob fetched up and surrounded the building, it went
deathly silent all at once, as if its angry roar had been caused by
the constant movement. Waddell looked behind him onto a sea of
hats. Rifle barrels poked up among the hats, here and there a
brickbat.

Waddell held up his hand—an old cavalry habit. He drew himself up in the saddle and addressed the closed door. "Open up, in
the name of the white citizens of Wilmington!"

On cue, a dismounted Red Shirt hammered at the door with a
brickbat.

"We want Manly!" Waddell proclaimed.

Nobody answered.

He gave a casual signal with his left hand. The mob spit out two
men in overalls, each hefting a fire ax. Taking turns, they whacked
at the door until it splintered off its hinges. Inside stood a lone
Negro, transfixed, wide-open mouth bubbling with saliva. A voice
shouted, "Manly!" A little pistol cracked, and the Negro grabbed
his neck, reeling as if he'd been punched. Then he vanished.

The mob rushed into Free Love Hall after him, but he was gone
out the back. They slipped on his blood.

They smashed chairs and tables with nine-pound railroad mauls,
gouged the walls with axes, shattered the windows with rifle butts
and brickbats. They swarmed upstairs to the printing room and
found the Hoe press. Four men heaved against it, but they could

not budge it. So they overturned the drawers full of type, scattering the heavy letters across the floor. They smashed more windows, busted every piece of furniture in sight, swept carefully filed stacks of back numbers of the *Record* off the shelves, then pulled down the shelves. Swinging axes and mauls, they pulverized two typewriters, a beer mug filled with sharpened pencils, an old desk, and a glass paperweight.

Mike Dowling was so caught up in the melee that, by the time he finished smashing things, the Winchester in his hand had a broken stock and a bent barrel. He flung it away, gave a blood-curdling rebel yell, and crawled out the window toward *The Record Publishing Company* sign. Hands gripped him by the belt as, swimming in thin air, he tore it loose from its chains and flung it down into the street. The mob axed it into kindling.

Downstairs, two Red Shirts discovered a storage closet. They smashed the padlock with a maul and raked cans of kerosene and turpentine off the shelves. Other men shouldered them aside, grabbed the kerosene and turpentine, and doused the broken furniture. Somebody struck a match. The men upstairs barely got out as the flames flared into the rafters.

Outside Free Love Hall, Waddell was furious. The mob was out of control. They had come to get Manly, and Manly had fled. Somebody had already been shot—what had become of him? Was he Alex Manly? Other men were firing freely into the flames. "Call the fire brigade!" he yelled to one of Dowling's men, who merely grinned at him and popped off another round.

Solly Fishblate found Waddell. "I've put in a call to the Negro fire brigade!" he shouted.

"Can't you do something about these Red Shirts?"

"Should have thought of that before."

The flames were leaping out of the roof now, and the northerly breeze threatened to spread the fire to the church next door. That would never do—you could not burn down a church and expect the world to bless your cause. Hundreds of rifles were firing now. Men and boys were cheering. Horses reared and plunged, neighing in fear. To Waddell, the clamor had an old, familiar taste.

Sam Jenks, who had finally worked his way to Waddell's side, said, "I thought there wasn't supposed to be any violence." He hadn't been this scared since Cuba.

Waddell bent from his horse. "Welcome to the chaos of battle, son."

"Manly doesn't even seem to be here."

"It's gone beyond that now. Men are going to die today."

A block north, at the intersection of Ann Street, a horde of Red Shirts surrounded the horse-drawn fire engine of Phoenix Hose Reel Company No. 1 as it turned onto Seventh. The Negro crew clutched the brass handrails, as if they could not be harmed unless they let go. A dozen men grabbed the horses and held them. The others trained their rifles on the firemen and shouted obscenities. The firemen didn't reply—they hugged their machine.

Free Love Hall blazed so hot that the crowd fell back. The cool air rushed past their ears toward the suction of the fire, and the heat gusted back into their faces. Flames shot fifty feet above the roof. The pine clapboards, saturated with natural resin, burned blue and orange. Boards crackled and spit. Rafters buckled with claps like pistol shots. The flames sucked at the cool air with a sound like heavy surf. The shake roof erupted in half a dozen places, the shingles fluttering onto the heads of the mob. Some of the clapboards literally exploded, rocketing embers into the crowd. The embers arced out from the building and bloomed like fireworks. The crowd cheered each one and danced out of the way.

The fire spit out flaming splinters. Little white boys scrapped over them, ran in gleeful circles trailing plumes of smoke.

All at once, a great tearing sound split the air—the joists were buckling. Waddell's horse heard it and reared, almost tossing him off. He got the horse under control and listened: the upstairs floor was giving way.

A thousand men and boys stopped their spree. Then they heard a great boom as the Jonah Hoe press crashed through.

At the intersection of Seventh and Ann, the Red Shirts backed away from the fire brigade and let them through unmolested. For two hours, they fought the blaze, but they didn't have a chance—

Free Love Hall was already a ruin by the time they arrived. They worked under the guns of the mob, concentrating on their apparatus.

Hugh MacRae watched the firemen work. "Such discipline," he observed.

One of the Red Shirts said, "You dress those monkeys up, they are crackerjack."

Sam could not turn away—his eyes were captured by the spectacle. When at last the heat made him look away, he spied the woman in the crimson Eaton jacket grinning toward the flames, scrawling onto her notebook pages with a blind hand.

Back at Colonel Waddell's house, Bessie King fretted. Her hands needed to be doing something. Those high-and-mighty men who had followed the Colonel out the door had murder in their eyes. She didn't want to know where they were going, or why. "Lord, bring my boy back to this house before the reckoning," she prayed out loud as she cleaned up the kitchen and rinsed the breakfast dishes at the sink. The cold water sloshed out of the pump and splashed her apron, but she didn't notice.

The parlor carpet was soiled from boots and men's heavy shoes. She fetched the vacuum sweeper, the newest gadget the Colonel had procured for the household. She could get the carpet much cleaner by hauling it out to the back porch, folding it over the banister, and whacking it with her broom, but her back was too tired today. She rolled the mechanical sweeper back and forth over the carpet, listening to the roller brush spin and the dirt rattle up into the metal canister. When she stopped, the house was silent. She rolled the gadget back into the kitchen closet and closed the door on it.

It was a powerful lonely morning. Her boy was out on the streets somewhere. Her little girl, too—slipped out during breakfast.

She sighed and held back tears. Humming softly to quiet her nerves, she climbed the stairs to see about Miz Gabrielle. Surely, she must crave some company, too.

*A man's life, his whole integrity, comes down to
little moments when he could have done the right
thing, but didn't—because he wasn't paying attention.*

> Samuel Jenks,
> Pulitzer Prize winner for
> journalism, addressing the
> University of Delaware
> class of 1922

CHAPTER SEVENTEEN

Thursday, November 10

THE VIGILANTES MARCHED back to the Wilmington Light Infantry
Armory in a boisterous, ragged column, men falling out here and
there along the way to take a drink or do mischief to the Negroes'
homes. As the last elements accumulated in the armory yard,
Waddell faced them from the marble steps, hands clasped behind
his back, plumed hat cocked over his right brow.

Sam stood off to the side watching the mob, taking notes. He
picked out the crimson Eaton jacket of the lady reporter.

"Gentlemen!" Waddell announced sternly. "We have done what
we set out to do! The Negro newspaper is finished. From this
moment on, the editor Manly is declared by this community to be
an outlaw, to be shot on sight—"

Their cheering interrupted him. He rocked back on his heels, and Sam could tell he was not savoring the cheers. He had lost control this morning, and he knew it. For a few minutes, Sam reflected, it had been like Cuba—the confusion of violence, the stomach-clenching fear, and afterward the guilt. It must not happen again. It might already be too late. Waddell, impatient, started talking again before the crowd had quieted.

"I assure you, whoever bags that black rascal shall not be prosecuted under law!"

This time, the cheering went on for some time, the Red Shirts chanting, "Kill Manly! Kill Manly!"

Waddell held up his hands for silence. "You called upon me to lead you. You have performed your duty. Now, go quietly about your business. Obey the law—unless we are forced to defend ourselves."

Here, he paused for a predictable round of hurrahs. Waddell desperately wanted to keep his audience assembled within the sound of his voice, yet part of him feared what he had inspired them to do, what they still might do. This morning, the clamor of battle had revisited him, and he had loved it. The kerosene smoke still burned his nostrils. Following his lead, the mob had displayed a power like a natural force. A man could get drunk on that power—and he must keep his head. There was intricate work to be done yet.

At first, the crowd knotted together, talking excitedly about what they had just accomplished. Captain James held the infantry inside the building.

His mouth suddenly cotton-dry, Waddell turned on his heels and went inside to fetch a glass of water. Sam followed. The mob began to disperse, men in small bands heading for their jobs, their neighborhoods. A good many of them lived in Brooklyn among the Negro workmen.

Waddell stomped the length of the marble hall into the back kitchen and drank from a tin ladle he filled at the pump. He slurped the water carelessly, splashing his shirt and lapels. His collar was already slippery with perspiration, and he smelled of horse sweat. His thighs were sore from the ride, and his knees ached. He was breathing hard.

Sam stood behind him, hands clasped in front, saying nothing. When Waddell turned, he said, "Thirsty work, eh, Colonel?"

Colonel Waddell rehung the ladle and dabbed his lips with a dishtowel. "You don't approve?"

"Didn't figure you for a vigilante."

Waddell heard the disappointment in his voice. He snapped the towel into the sink. "This is not what I had in mind. But men are men. You can lead them so far, but in the end they will do what they will do."

"You're resigned to it." Sam felt lightheaded from adrenaline.

Waddell stepped close to him, and Sam saw the power building again in his eyes, the light being turned up brighter. "I'm resigned to nothing," Waddell said. "Nothing is changed. Somebody got carried away. A building has been burned."

"A pretty big nothing."

"What exactly are you saying? Are you with me, or not?" He cocked his head and squinted one eye, as if he were sighting over a rifle. "I don't like your tone."

"A man was shot," Sam said. And Alex Manly soon would be, he thought—if he were stupid enough to still be in town.

"We don't know that."

"The blood."

"He rabbited right out the back window, though, didn't he? Pretty damned spry for a dead darky."

Sam hadn't meant to bully Waddell with his own guilty conscience. "You're right—what's done is done. But what happens now?"

Hugh MacRae shouldered his way into the kitchen next to Sam. "My question exactly," he said.

Waddell smiled, taking control again. MacRae wondered how he'd ever managed to get control in the first place. Now, he owned the mob.

Waddell said quietly, "I think we're about due for a meeting of the aldermen—say, this afternoon? Meantime, I'm going home to wash up properly."

Sam gathered his notes and went to the *Messenger* office, where he typed up the story of what he'd seen. What, exactly, was the story? There were lots of stories. It depended on your point of view.

White men calling a halt to Negro domination. A judgment of fire to satisfy the honor of white women all over the Old North State. That was one story. Waddell's heroic version.

That's how he wrote it. It would have been easier to do it with a drink.

Tired but in high spirits, Waddell retired to his home, where Bessie had just brought in the mail. Among the bills and correspondence was a broad envelope addressed to him and bearing the carefully penned notation, "Please deliver at House." He knifed it open and read it quickly, smiled, and folded it into the outside pocket of his clawhammer coat. It changed nothing.

Meta Rountree clambered up the stairs and banged open the bedroom door. "George! George, get up!"

George Rountree opened his eyes and jerked his head off the pillow. He felt the cold thrill of calamity in his heart. "What?" he stammered. "What is it?"

"I don't know for sure," she said, already laying his suit and a clean, boiled shirt across the arm of a chair. "Something's happening downtown. Gunshots. The whole north side is burning. The Negroes are in a riot!"

He regarded her stupidly, trying to clear the sand out of his burning eyes. "How—?"

"Chadbourn called on the telephone." The postmaster. "Come on, get up—get up!"

Rountree struggled into his clothes, then went into the indoor privy to urinate and splash water on his face. There was no time to shave. He burst out the door onto Front Street and jogged the three blocks to the post office, arriving out of breath. His old friend W. H. Chadbourn met him on the steps.

Chadbourn had dallied briefly with the Republicans and then backed off when the party fused with the Populists and the Negroes. He had no use for white supremacy, but he believed in civil order. It was Chadbourn who, leaving the Board of Audit and Finance to become postmaster, had turned over his vacant seat to a Democrat, setting up the current stalemate between the two boards.

"All hell's breaking loose, George," he said. "They burned out Manly. They say there's fires all over the north side. They say the Negroes are marching on city hall."

"Those goddamn cowboys! This puts everything in jeopardy."

"Too late for the fine points, George. Go home. Protect your family."

Rountree was thinking fast. "We've got to stop this foolishness. Can you get Mayor Wright to resign?"

"I can try."

"Can you get the board to go along?"

"I told you, I'll try."

Rountree grabbed his friend's arm. "If they don't, this city won't be here by nightfall."

Rountree hurried back home and searched the front hall closet for one of the Winchesters he had bought wholesale for the Businessmen's Committee back in August. He'd never fired it. He hadn't fired a gun in years. He couldn't remember whether he'd loaded it or not. He pumped the lever, and a bullet sprang up from the magazine into the open receiver. But it was already loaded, ready to be cocked and fired. The round in the chamber didn't eject, and the gun jammed. He swore. For five minutes, breathing hard and fighting panic, he worked at the jam with a silver pocketknife. At last, the jammed bullet popped free, and he carefully closed the lever. Then he let down the hammer, so he wouldn't accidentally shoot his foot off.

He banged out the front door and walked to the corner of Red Cross and Nutt streets—across from the offices of Sprunts' Champion Compress—with the gun on his shoulder, feeling like a damned fool. He loitered on the corner, watching in every direction for some sign of a mob, a riot. Nothing. He fished out his watch and checked it: ten o'clock exactly.

What was going on? Where was everybody? He thought he heard the report of a rifle, but it might have been a hammer. Down Nutt Street, the yard of the compress seemed quiet enough. Empty freight wagons were parked in a neat row, tailgates to the iron fence, tongues raised like a line of stubby, raked masts. The machinery in the long shed clattered and droned—business as usual. At the end of Red Cross, on the river, steam tugs charged back and forth, hauling fat barges up and down the river.

He listened. He squinted in every direction as far as he could see. He looked at his watch six times in ten minutes. He scratched his beard. He calmed down. He smoothed a hand over his bald head. He drew out a handkerchief and scrubbed a finger smudge off the oiled black receiver. He wondered how many shots he had—eight? No, seven: he had not replaced the jammed bullet. It was in his coat pocket.

He wondered if he could shoot a man. Would it be easier to shoot a Negro than a white? The whole idea made his stomach go queer. He thought it would be damned hard to shoot anybody. This was his home. Whatever violence happened here, he'd have to live with it.

He was a man of the law. He sighed and swore again softly, then carried the gun home and put it back in the closet. He would have unloaded it, but he didn't want to fool with that damned pocket-knife again. Instead, he rummaged in a kitchen drawer until he found a key that had never been used. With it, he locked the closet. He put the key in the top drawer of the desk in his study, then he locked that and slipped the desk key into his watch pocket.

When he turned to go back out, Meta was watching him. Her arms were crossed in a hug, as if she were cold, though the house was quite warm from the coal grates. Her eyes were full of fear, and the fear was in her soft voice. "What's happening, George?"

"Don't fret," he said gently. "I put up the gun. Don't know why I ever bought the thing."

She touched his arm. "Are we safe here?"

"For right now. Just keep the doors bolted. I need to find some-body who can tell me what's going on."

"Why can't you just leave it be?"

"Because I live here, Mrs. Rountree," he said quietly. "I have a responsibility for what happens."

She nodded and lowered her head, not watching him as he went out again.

Rountree went back to the same corner, intending to inquire at the Sprunt offices. Even as he walked, he realized he wasn't thinking clearly. He should have just gotten on the telephone and tried to reach MacRae or Walker Taylor. He would use the telephone at Sprunts'. Or perhaps somebody there had already received word. He must collect himself and keep a clear head. He must not let this thing get away from him.

Almost as soon as he reached the corner, he heard the crowd of Negroes advancing up Nutt Street through the gates of the Champion Compress—a hundred or more. Workers, unarmed but noisy. Rountree stopped walking. Seeing him, the crowd stopped, too. Out of the Sprunt offices spilled a collection of clerks and purchasing agents. Two pointed rifles. One of them, a young, slender man wearing shirtsleeves and a tie, took a step forward. "Where you think you're going?" he called out.

Several Negroes spoke at once.

"Going home."

"They're burning us down."

"Got to see our families."

The slender man said, "Get back to work."

Resolutely, the Negroes marched forward.

"Just hold it right there," the slender man said, backing up a step and glancing nervously at Rountree.

Rountree said, "Go get your boss." Here it is, he thought—this town's going to go off like a Fourth of July rocket.

The man disappeared into the office to use the telephone. By and by, as the men lingered, staring across the narrow street at the other race, the slender man returned from the office, and James Sprunt came striding up from the compress yard right through the ranks of the Negroes. "What goes on here?" he asked in a level voice. He was a tall, graying man with a handsome face, a mild manner, and a head for figures. He'd done his best to stay out of politics: he had work to do, a business to run.

"We just want to go see about our families, Mr. Sprunt," one of the Negroes said.

"What about this?" he asked the clerk in the shirtsleeves.

The clerk shifted his rifle from hand to hand. "I told these niggers to go back to work," he said.

Sprunt glared at him. "Don't ever use that word again on my time."

The clerk ducked his head.

Other white men materialized from nowhere and lined up behind the clerk and Rountree. Most of them carried Winchesters. Some wore red shirts. Rountree felt the atmosphere heating up like water in a kettle. Any minute now, it would cross a critical threshold and burst into steam. He ducked into the Sprunt offices and rang up the armory. He spoke to Captain James. "We've got a riot brewing," he said. "Get that machine gun down here right now." By the time he hung up the earpiece, he regretted making the call. He decided he had better stop making things worse.

Outside, Grand Marshal Roger Moore had arrived with a squad of vigilantes. Moore had a compact, military bearing. Stuck in his belt was a double-action army Colt. From a crimson sash across his gray shirt hung an artillery officer's short sword, blunt and sturdy. He deployed his men in a single line across Nutt Street and ordered them not to fire. The Negroes were getting restless and angry.

Moore said, "What's the situation, George?"

"We've got to break this up," Rountree said.

Moore rocked on his heels, arms crossed, and nodded. "Let me read them the riot act. Then we'll clear the street."

Sprunt joined them. "They're just scared," he observed. "Lots of bad rumors flying around. Let's see if we can't reassure them."

Moore touched the butt of his pistol. "We can reassure them, all right."

Rountree said, "Mr. Sprunt's right, Roger. They're not going anywhere, long as your men hold their position."

"I got damned few men."

At that moment, in a clatter of hoofs and shouted orders, Kenan's Gatling gun detail reined up their wagon behind the vigilantes. Only minutes behind them, a company of Wilmington Light Infantry jogged up double-time and deployed in skirmish formation. The vigilantes moved out of the way as Kenan's hostlers backed their wagon into position, tailgate to the crowd, so they would not be shooting over the horses.

Kenan stood behind the gun, sighting in on the crowd of Negroes. As an officer, he ought to delegate the actual firing to an enlisted man, but he was the only one with real experience on the gun. Besides, it was too much responsibility for a younger man. His crew hunkered beside him over a case of magazines, ready to reload on cue. The hostlers stood by the team, hands on the bridles, bowing the horses' heads so they would not plunge and bolt when the firing commenced. The last two men in the detail stood on either side of the wagon, guarding its flanks against snipers. They were well-drilled, deploying expertly in less than a minute.

The Negroes fell back a couple of steps, pointing at the gun, the ones in front glancing back nervously over their shoulders, where their escape was blocked by the press of their companions.

For a second, Rountree could not get his breath. Then he drew himself up and strolled as casually as he could toward the Negroes. Sprunt walked alongside. Moore held back, glancing at the gun, the vigilantes, the crowd, Rountree. Finally, he, too, moved toward the Negroes.

"What have we done to you?" a Negro in front asked. He was looking right at Rountree and pointing over Rountree's shoulder at the Gatling gun, Kenan's infantrymen, the vigilantes and their Winchesters. "Tell me, what have we done?"

"Nothing," Rountree said, trying to control his voice. He was angry at everybody, including himself, and more afraid than he'd ever been in his life. "You haven't done anything. Let's keep it that way."

"We want to go home, that's all."

"Why don't you just go back to work?" Rountree said. "Wouldn't that be the best thing?"

Another of the Negroes said, "They're burning us down. I got to see about my family."

Sprunt turned to Rountree. "What does he mean, George?"

"There's been talk that Brooklyn's burning. Probably nothing to it."

"Something to it, all right," said the Negro. He was a tall, skinny fellow in denim overalls. Against the powder blue of his clothes, his face was dark as coffee. "Burned down Manly at the *Record*, that's what we heard."

Sprunt muttered, "MacRae."

Grand Marshal Moore drew out a sheet of paper bearing small type. "I don't care what's happening in Brooklyn. These men are inciting to riot."

"I know the law," Rountree said. Did this little colonel want a massacre?

"Then read it to these rioters," Moore said.

"There's no riot," Sprunt said. "Let's work this thing out."

Behind the gun, Kenan watched the delegation of white men dickering with the crowd of Negroes. As long as they stand in the way, he reflected, I can't shoot. Let them keep standing there. There was not a single gun among the Negroes. He had no idea whether he would be capable of shooting them down. Let it be clear-cut, he prayed. Make them act decisively one way or the other. If the Negroes attacked Rountree and the others, he could shoot. It would not do to shoot over their heads, since the downhill trajectory would cause his fire to rake the Sprunt compress, probably killing innocent workers—white and black.

He would have to shoot into their mass. They were all pressed together. At this close range, he could not miss.

In the chilly November breeze off the river, Kenan sweated through his uniform. His fist closed on the crank. The gun swiveled noiselessly under his touch. The horses were standing still. His men were behaving like soldiers, not talking or moving.

James Sprunt was fast losing his temper—and he almost never lost his temper. He took pride in being a fair man. If his workers were shot down at the gates of his compress, the act would show up as a debit on every balance sheet for the next twenty years.

A man's life was a balancing act. Every small action contributed to the balance, or else tipped the scales out of level. The balance was always between personal ambition and obligation to your community, the place where you lived. The place and the people were the same thing.

He peered into the crowd of black faces, looking for one who would trust him. "Mr. Telfair," he called to a man in the thick of the crowd. Jim Telfair was one of his top managers. They'd always gotten along well.

The man shoved his way forward and faced Sprunt.

"Why don't you pick a friend and go up to Brooklyn to see what's what?" Sprunt said. "Don't take too long—nobody's going anywhere till you get back." He scribbled his signature on an envelope. "In case there's any trouble," he explained.

Telfair grabbed a man out of the front row, and the two strode quickly toward Kenan's infantrymen. "It's all right," Rountree called out. "Let them through."

For half an hour, both sides relaxed and tensed, relaxed and tensed. Kenan took his hand off the crank and sat on the sideboard of the wagon, feeling chilly now. Rountree and Sprunt continued to palaver with the Negroes.

Telfair and his companion returned with a third man, the Reverend J. T. Lee of St. Stephen's A.M.E. Church. Lee had been the lone minister at the meeting where the white ultimatum was given. Telfair introduced him, then reported, "They burned the *Record*, all right."

"You sure?" Rountree demanded.

"Seen it with my own eyes."

Sprunt said, "If he says it's so, it's so."

"But that's all," Telfair continued. "Nobody's burning our houses. Nobody's shooting anybody—not that we saw."

The Negroes talked among themselves. The Reverend Lee moved among them, urging restraint and calm.

A rider galloped up Red Cross and handed a note to Grand Marshal Moore. Moore came over to Sprunt and Rountree. "Tell them we'll give them all safe conduct passes home," he said. "Let them leave by twos and threes."

So by twos and threes, the Negroes hurried toward their homes. While Sprunt was signing passes, Rountree conferred with Moore and Captain Kenan, who had lit a cigar. Kenan's heart was singing at the way this thing had turned out so far, but the day wasn't over yet.

"What's the story?" Kenan asked Moore.

"Some Negroes killed in Brooklyn," Moore said. "Looks like the shooting has started. Got to move these men out before they get the news. Disperse them."

"Right," Kenan said.

A male secretary leaned out the doorway of Sprunts' offices. "A call for you, Captain Kenan."

Kenan bit down on his cigar and clomped up two board steps into the hot office. On the telephone was Colonel Walker Taylor.

"The State Guard is taking charge of all military units in the city," Taylor told him. "You're under my command now. We need you at Fourth and Bladen on the double. It's starting."

Kenan walked slowly back to the wagon—there were still a few dozen Negroes hanging around, and there was no sense in stirring them up again. He issued quiet commands, limbered the gun, and started his company back up Red Cross. An image crossed his mind for an instant: Lincoln on the parapet of Fort Stevens, that ridiculous stovepipe hat sticking up like a clay target at the county fair. He reflected that his boy was deep in the heart of Mexico, and he thought that was a good thing. He wasn't sure he wanted him to see what his father was about to do. He shrugged off dreams and memories, flung away his cigar, and focused on the lurching wagon, the heavy gun, the job at hand.

They were three blocks from Bladen Street now, moving fast.

———————

Waddell's mob moved in several directions at once. Dowling led his lieutenants off to find a drink at Jurgen Haar's Saloon down on Front. Most of the businessmen walked downtown to their offices, some with assignments—men to call, meetings to set up, information to be passed along. A skeleton guard was posted at First Baptist, with a courier dispatched to Grand Marshal Moore to tell him to stand down, for the moment. They had no idea he was already at Sprunts' Champion Compress talking down a riot. The streets around the armory were clear of Negroes. It was as if they had been erased from the city.

A gang of white laborers headed north up Fourth Street toward their homes. The men were elated and full of brag. At last, action. At last, a white man could walk the streets of his own town swinging a rifle and saying what he damn pleased. Following the streetcar tracks, they straggled across the railroad culvert on a narrow bridge between Campbell and Hanover streets, straight into the heart of black Wilmington.

Their own homes were mostly beyond this neighborhood, at the far end of Brooklyn. They hated living there.

The men were tired—they'd been up all night, then had marched on the *Record* this morning. Now, they trudged along the sandy street with their heads down, double-barreled shotguns broken for safety and cocked over the crooks of their arms.

"Darktown," Bert Chadwick remarked conversationally, waggling his sixteen-shot Remington rifle toward the row of shotgun shacks on his right, which looked deserted but which they all knew were full of scared Negroes. "Pretty soon, we'll clear out this breeding nest."

"They get back in those filthy shacks and hump like rabbits," Teddy Curtis said. "No notion of right or wrong, no work ethic, no love of family."

Chadwick said, "They got animal sacrifice in their churches, the African Zionist ones. Take a poor child's lost cat, carve it up for their heathen gods. Make a decent Christian man ashamed."

Hill Terry said, "You work them niggers hard from sunup to sundown, let 'em sing awhile after supper, keep the women separate from the men, and they live and die happy."

"That's the God's honest truth," Chadwick agreed. "And we sure as hell don't need any Republican carpetbaggers coming down here from Yankeeland to stir 'em up."

Up ahead, on the near side of the intersection with Harnett Street, a small crowd of Negro men was assembling. When the first of the white men saw the Negroes on the corner, the whole band halted in the middle of the street.

"Here they come," Tom Miller said, watching the whites advance up Fourth. He had a fine, new Colt .44 pistol, taken in pawn months ago and stowed away in a cupboard until he might need it. Today, he planned to need it.

Most of the men with him were unarmed. A few of them had old rabbit .22s or shotguns they had not fired in years. They had started as a dozen or so men drinking coffee and wondering out loud what was happening downtown, where there seemed to be some kind of demonstration. They'd heard the sporadic crack of rifles and the long-distance murmur of the crowd of white men.

Then David King had showed up gory as a butchered shoat,

blood splashed across his Sears-Roebuck mail-order shirt. He wore a hole in his neck you could stick your finger into.

"They burned it down!" he blurted out, spraying his listeners with spittle and blood. He fainted into their arms.

It was a few minutes before the sense of it dawned on them: the *Record* had been burned to the ground.

"They gonna murderize Mr. Manly!" David King shouted again as soon as he came to.

"Somebody shot this boy," an authoritative voice said. Heads turned toward its source: Ivanhoe Grant, splendid in his tailored dove-gray suit.

Norman Lindsay, a foreman at Wilmington Cotton Mills, pulled a red neckerchief out of the back pocket of his overalls and wrapped it around David King's neck to stanch the bleeding. "Boy's only nicked," he said. "Be hunky-dory in no time."

David King wandered away, searching for a quiet corner.

Grant kept his hand in the pocket of his coat, fingers wrapped around a two-shot nickel Bulldog derringer. "Going to be hell to pay," he said.

Now, the white men moved closer, cautiously. Bert Chadwick took his Remington in both hands.

"Get you boys on home now," one of the Negroes said. "Don't be making trouble out here."

The Negroes held their ground. More arrived, swelling their number, but most were unarmed. Several pried loose slats from a nearby fence and hefted them as clubs. All the whites were armed.

Tom Miller shouted, "What you doing with those guns?"

"Going hunting for blackbirds," Chadwick answered.

Some of the whites laughed nervously. They shuffled around, unsure what to do. Hill Terry and Teddy Curtis thumbed two shells apiece into the breeches of their shotguns and snapped them shut with a motion like breaking a chicken's neck.

"Round these parts," Miller shouted back, "the blackbirds shoot back!"

"Shut your mouth, boy!"

"I'll shut it when you carry those guns out of my homeplace!"

"Goddamn you, boy, I'll ram this Winchester up your—"

Chadwick was drowned out by taunts. The whites answered with threats and obscenities. The whites advanced slowly, and the Negroes retreated across the intersection to the far corner, their backs to Walker's Grocery. Old Mr. Walker, hair and beard gray as ash, rocked on a cane chair in the open doorway gnawing an unlit Missouri meerschaum, waiting to see what would happen.

The taunting continued. More Negroes arrived. A streetcar barreled up Fourth Street and through the intersection without stopping, and the crowd dodged out of its way. Several armed white men swung off the moving car and hit the street running to get their balance. One of them was Sam Matthews, a teamster, who carried a .44 Colt navy rifle. Another was Sergeant Alton Lockamy.

"Get off the street! Go home!" Matthews shouted, the big-game rifle cocked on his hip.

"Never!" one of the Negroes said. "This is our homeplace! Get you bullies gone!"

Lockamy, open hands raised in a gesture of conciliation, sidled over to the blacks. "Gentlemen, there's no sense to borrow trouble."

"Tell that to them that burned out Manly!" Tom Miller said.

"I know, I heard about that. But what's done is done."

"You're the police. I'm a citizen. Protect me from that mob, officer." Some of the men behind Miller laughed nervously.

"Listen to the sergeant," Norman Lindsay said, growing agitated. "For heaven's sake, listen!"

Lockamy shrugged. "Boys, they'll shoot me quick as you," he said. "Use your nut. Get you on out of here."

"No," Miller said. "They can't be coming around here toting shotguns—"

"Look, I'll try to make them clear out of here."

Lockamy sighed and crossed the street to the white side, where he conferred with more stubborn men.

Chadwick said, "About time a white man walks where he pleases in this town." Matthews, Curtis, and Terry loudly agreed.

Everybody was chawing tobacco, spitting nervously. Time was running out. Sergeant Lockamy knew he must find a telephone and get some help up here, fast. He went inside Brunjes Grocery & Saloon.

On the other side of the street, Ivanhoe Grant said, "Now's the chance we've been waiting for. This is the place, and now is the time."

Norman Lindsay, at the front of the black crowd, saw at once what was about to happen. He turned to his friends and neighbors. "In the name of God, go home."

"The Lord despises a coward!" Grant shouted, pointing his finger in accusation at Lindsay.

"For the sake of your lives, your children, your families—"

The crowd shouted Lindsay down. He was still imploring them to disperse, his back to the whites, when Grant slipped the Bulldog derringer out of his coat pocket, straight-armed it past Lindsay's ear, and snapped off a wild shot in the direction of the whites.

Their reaction was so immediate it might have been simultaneous. Chadwick's Remington went off. A dozen Winchesters fired at once, as if in volley. Two shotguns thumped—Curtis and Terry. The shotguns thumped again. Pistols cracked. Sam Matthews's big-game rifle boomed, the walnut stock punching him in the shoulder.

Norman Lindsay felt a fist in his back and was dead before he hit the dirt. Beside him, a brick mason named John Townsend screamed, twisted, and fell dead. William Mouson, an unarmed clerk, crumpled without a sound, astonished, shot clean through his open mouth.

Negro men fell wounded on either side of Tom Miller. He pumped six shots toward the whites and hit Bert Chadwick in the muscle of his left arm. Chadwick's Remington jumped out of his hands, and he fell on top of it.

A couple of men behind Miller got off shots, deafening him. He ducked into Walker's Grocery to reload and sent Mr. Walker sprawling into a pyramid of canned peaches. The crowd of Negroes scattered, dropping fence slats, trying to outrun the bullets. The whites kept shooting. George Henry Davis, himself shot in the thigh, shepherded a wounded friend around the corner and into a house, where the friend bled to death in his arms. Some of the wounded lay in the street, afraid to get up. Miller fled out the back of the store into the alley.

Ivanhoe Grant evaporated.

A white dentist named George Piner took a slug in the left side. Bill Mayo, who had proudly signed the White Man's Declaration of Independence, climbed onto his own porch on Fourth Street to be able to see above the crowd. From behind a board fence across Fourth Street came a single report. Mayo collapsed, shot through the chest.

Lockamy now had his hands full. He tried to stop any further shooting, but bands of white men rushed after the retreating Negroes in all directions. Still, no police arrived to help him. He feared it was deliberate.

A streetcar sparked to a wrenching stop. Father Dennen jumped off. A gang of white men lifted bloody Bill Mayo into the car, and Dennen was torn: should he stay here and try to do some good, or remain with a dying man who needed last rites?

He stayed on the streetcar with Mayo. A safe distance from the shooting, he helped carry the wounded man into Bernice Moore's drugstore. Dr. T. J. Schonwald happened to be there ordering medicine, and he tended Mayo while someone telephoned for an ambulance.

"Get out of the way, if you please, Father," Schonwald ordered curtly. "I'll tell you when you can have his soul."

Caught once again in the duty of his office, Father Dennen rode in the ambulance with Mayo to City-County Hospital at Tenth and Red Cross. Mayo's chest was a pulp of blood and bandages, and he was unconscious. In the ambulance, his ears rushing with the momentum of what was happening all around him, Dennen reached into the pocket of his cassock for a vial of holy ointment no larger than a fountain pen, dabbed his thumb, and murmured the Latin blessing of extreme unction.

He might have saved himself the trouble: Bill Mayo lived.

By the time Kenan's Gatling gun detail arrived at Fourth and Bladen, the violence was well under way. Grand Marshal Roger Moore arrived on horseback with two dozen riders and a hundred others on foot scattered behind him. Colonel Walker Taylor, also on horseback, arrived alone. A few minutes later, Hugh MacRae and J. Allan Taylor showed up at the head of the Wilmington Light Infantry. Dowling and his Red Shirts were already on the scene.

Rountree was still back at the compress conferring with James Sprunt.

Waddell was at home.

In the melee of competing commands and scattered firing, Walker Taylor found his brother. "Where's Captain James?" he asked. "He's supposed to be in command of the infantry."

J. Allan swore. "The son of a bitch refuses to come out of barracks. Hugh and I are in charge."

"You have no authority—this is a State Guard action now."

"We have all the authority we need. Just stay out of our way."

Kenan set up his gun in the intersection. The main activity seemed to be down Bladen Street, where the Negroes were regrouping in small bands. A rifle fired out of a window a block away and nicked the sideboard. Kenan steadied himself. Behind a nearby fence, he spied the heads of half a dozen black boys, curious about the excitement.

J. Allan Taylor pointed his pistol toward the fence. "Knock down that damned fence, Bill. Give 'em a little pepper."

Kenan was dumbfounded. J. Allan Taylor had no military authority. Kenan didn't move. His men waited for his orders. "There's no threat," he said.

"Goddamnit, I'll show you threat."

Taylor ordered the infantry to form a hollow square. The front ranks knelt, and the second ranks aimed over their heads—toward the fence on the left, the shacks on the right, and straight down the center of the street where the Negroes milled. He gave the orders. They cleared Bladen Street with volley fire. The sniping stopped.

Shots tore through the thin front planking of homes and right out the back walls, shattering everything in between. Gun smoke warmed the air and clouded the vision. At the far end of the street, black men went down in surprise. Inside the houses, women screamed. The board fence splintered from the high-powered rounds. The boys behind the fence ducked, but one didn't go down in time, and a Krag round tore his head off above the ears.

Kenan watched. His men waited. He gave no order to fire. His mouth went dry. His whole body was clenched. He had not signed on for this. Who was in charge here? Where was Captain James, or Colonel Walker Taylor?

The Light Infantry advanced up Bladen Street, bayonets fixed, firing as they went. When J. Allan Taylor spotted two Negro women attempting to remove the corpse of their brother, he ordered, "Make them leave the bodies in the street—as a lesson." Soldiers hustled the women away at bayonet point.

All along Bladen Street—on the stoop of Walker's Grocery, in the streets and alleys of Brooklyn—lay the bodies of black men and boys, cooling in the sun, stiffening into unnatural shapes.

Walker Taylor was busy rounding up his State Guard volunteers by telephone from Brunjes Grocery & Saloon. Within fifteen minutes, he assembled a sizable contingent. He stationed them on street corners with orders to detain and search all Negroes. He was nominally in command of the military district of Wilmington, but he couldn't control Dowling's Red Shirts or Roger Moore's vigilantes, which answered to Hugh MacRae. And he couldn't control the Naval Reserves or the Light Infantry, because his orders were being flouted by his own brother.

It was a hell of a mess. He would have to rein it in, street corner by street corner. He would do what he could to keep order. Without order, there was just a mob of scared people—the most dangerous kind.

Hugh MacRae was breathless with excitement, yet at the same time, he had never felt so cool-headed and alive. He stayed with J. Allan Taylor and the Light Infantry as they cleared the neighborhood. He fired and reloaded his own pistol so many times he lost count.

Somewhere along the line of march, Sam Jenks caught up with his cousin. He kept himself in the middle of the square, scribbling notes as he walked. "Keep your head down," MacRae said. "I don't want to be explaining to your pretty wife."

"Can't write it if I don't see it."

"Then take a good look. This is what history looks like."

A vigilante joined them. "Word is, they know who shot Bill Mayo," he said to J. Allan Taylor.

"They got him?" Taylor said.

"No, sir. But I know where the boy lives. Laborer, name of Dan Wright. Missing the thumb on his right hand." He splayed his right hand and crooked the thumb to illustrate.

MacRae said, "Take a flying squad over there. I'll stay with the boys."

J. Allan Taylor took a sergeant and fifteen men to Wright's home, two blocks over. Sam tagged along. Using rifle butts, they burst through the door and pointed their guns at Wright and his wife. Then they ransacked the house and found a Winchester .44 leaning in a bedroom corner. Taylor sniffed the muzzle—it had been fired recently. He worked the lever, and a spent shell ejected onto the pine floor. Taylor picked up the shell.

"I shot into the air," Wright explained. "Then I got scared."

"Didn't even have sense enough to get rid of the casing," Taylor said. "Bring him along, boys."

Taylor formed the men up in a gauntlet in the sandy street outside the house. Dan Wright stood uncertainly at the foot of his stoop, rubbing his maimed hand. His wife looked on from the stoop, weeping.

Taylor said, "Run to daylight, boy."

Wright hesitated. "Cap'n?"

"You heard me. We're letting you get away."

The men cocked their rifles.

"Have mercy, cap'n! I told you, I shot into the air."

Sam said, "You're not actually going to—"

"You'll get the same mercy you showed Bill Mayo," Taylor said. Wright stood fast. Taylor put his pistol to Wright's forehead. "Or I can give you a third eye right now."

Wright squinted his eyes closed and held his breath.

"Go on, run, boy. It's the only chance you'll get today."

Sam wanted to grab the black man and wrestle him to the ground, save him. He wanted to shout, protest, put a stop to what was about to happen. But he just stood there, mouth open.

Dan Wright put his head down and ran hard, grunting, through the gauntlet. He passed one man, another, gray and red blurs out of the corner of his eye. He kept his head down. His feet sank into the deep sand. He struggled for footing, running in slow motion. He would make it, he had to. He could see daylight at the end of the street.

And then a rifle butt punched him in the side, and he went down. His mouth tasted sand. A bullet shattered his knee. Another took part of his maimed hand clean off. He lay in the sand as nine more bullets kicked his body.

Sam fell to his knees and threw up. The infantrymen stood around and watched, curious about what they had just done. One of them poked Wright with a rifle barrel, and he moved. He was still alive.

After he collected his wits, Sam said, "You can't just let him lie there! For Christ's sake!"

J. Allan Taylor said, "Boy, don't crowd me."

They let Dan Wright lie in the street for half an hour. When it was clear he wasn't going to die anytime soon, Taylor had him taken to City-County Hospital, so his men could get on with their business. In a ward three hundred feet away from where Bill Mayo lay wounded, Dan Wright lingered till sundown the next day. He never lost consciousness. He never admitted shooting anybody. He uttered no last words.

———

When it became clearly a matter of keeping civil order, Captain Thomas James left barracks. He joined the main body of the Wilmington Light Infantry as they were preparing to advance on the Manhattan Dance Hall, a two-story frame building surrounded by a high wooden fence. A lone sniper was firing from a second-floor window. James's men took cover across the street in an alley.

"Get some sappers out there and knock down that fence," he commanded.

Three men disappeared and came back fifteen minutes later with axes looted from a hardware store. While their comrades covered them with volley fire, they hunkered low to give a scarce target and dodged across the street. The sniper fired once over their heads, kicking up sand in the street. Then, as volleys raked the second story, he quit firing. Windows burst. Clapboards sprang loose.

In half a minute, the sappers hacked down the rickety fence, and the infantry charged into the building. They arrested three unarmed men and caught a fourth, Josh Halsey, clambering over the back fence. They found a rifle upstairs.

James said to the prisoner, "As you were caught fleeing the scene, I can only assume you are the culprit." He ordered Halsey to stand against the back fence and formed his men into a firing squad.

One of infantrymen, Bill Robbins, said, "This ain't right."

The man beside him said, "You shoot him, Bill, or I'll shoot you."

On James's order, they fired. The high-powered rounds flung Halsey into the fence, and one of them tore the top of his head off. Robbins shut his eyes and fired into the fence.

David Jacobs, the coroner, later reported that he removed a pint of bullets from Halsey's body.

Sam Jenks couldn't believe the scene he had just witnessed outside Dan Wright's house. Not even Cuba had been like that. He had seen it coming. He had done nothing to stop it. His ears rang from the incredible noise of the guns. He could hardly catch his breath.

He could hear firing all over the city now. And another sound: the constant pealing of fire bells. The town was coming apart. He must find Gray Ellen and get her out of here. Was she at school? He couldn't remember. He was lost in a strange neighborhood. All around him moved armed men.

He would go to the house first. If she wasn't there, he'd search

for her. This was no town for a woman alone. Or a man. He broke
off from the infantry and ran back the other way, passing vigilantes and Red Shirts and men wearing half a dozen different uniforms. Half of them seemed to be giving orders. The other half
seemed to be running in all directions regardless of the orders.

Still a dozen blocks from home, he encountered a squad of
infantry detaining a young black woman—Saffron King James.

"What's that in your hand, missy?" one of them asked.

She held up her rock of virtue in her fist and threatened him.

"Strip off that dress and search this little gal," the squad leader
said.

Two men grabbed her arms, and the leader began to unbutton
her dress.

Without thinking, Sam stepped into the middle of things. "Don't
touch her," he said with authority. "She hasn't done anything."

"Just who the hell are you?" the squad leader asked.

Fighting down panic, Sam said, "She's on an errand for my
cousin, Hugh MacRae."

"Mr. MacRae? Well, that's different. Boys, let her pass."

Saffron shrugged them off and stalked away without looking
back. The fire bells were still ringing, joined now by church bells.
The squad of infantry began to move on.

At last, Sam made it home. He climbed onto his porch and
doubled over, his hands on his knees, to keep from being sick.

———

At Front and Princess streets, David King was stopped by a
vigilante patrol—Dowling and a band of Red Shirts. They had
been refreshing themselves at Jurgen Haar's and were now headed
back to Brooklyn. David was all mixed up. When the shooting had
started at Walker's Grocery, he had lit out. He had to get to his
mother, who was at Colonel Waddell's house. He would be safe
there—she had told him so. But he had come too far.

"Hold up there, boy," Dowling said, shoving the muzzle of a
Winchester in his face.

"Got to get to my mam," he said.

"And where would she be?"

"Don't know, perzactly. Fifth Street, at the big house."

"You're off your road, boy," Dowling said. "What's that thing on your neck?"

David King rubbed his bloody bandage.

One of the Red Shirts said, "Ain't you the boy was at Manly's place?"

"Not me, cap'n," he said, backing away.

"Sure, it's the same boy," another said. "I seen him there. Rabbited out the back."

"You going to rabbit on us, boy?" Dowling asked.

David King was befuddled. What did these men want from him? All day long, he had run from one bad place to another. It was time to run again.

He pumped his legs and got three steps before they shot him down.

"Come on, boys," Dowling said. "Open season on blackbirds. I know where there's a whole flock."

Before the day was out, Dowling would boast that he had bagged thirty.

Look around—do you see any monuments
to Alex Manly? Is there a Carter Peamon
Library on your pretty campus?

Saffron King James,
1964

CHAPTER EIGHTEEN

Thursday, November 10

THE KILLING WENT ON all afternoon.

The State Guard under Walker Taylor established a semblance of military order, methodically marching through Brooklyn, closing shops, ordering people off the streets. Before them scattered hundreds of Negroes—men, women, and children—fleeing the city. They took only what they could carry. They didn't look back. With bundles of bedding on their heads or stuffed into cloth satchels, they headed for Oakdale Cemetery, for the swamps along Smith's Creek, for anyplace they could lie low and wait for the mayhem to pass.

Meanwhile, the eighty men of the Light Infantry—now under command of Captain James—and the sixty Naval Reserves under Lieutenant George Morton raided Negro churches, where guns were rumored to be stockpiled. Where Manly was rumored to be hiding. Where armed squads of black assassins were rumored to be holed up. Where black secret fraternities were rumored to be torturing white prisoners.

Kenan's crew hauled the Gatling gun to the door of each church and trained it there. Then flying squads rushed the building. They overturned benches, desecrated holy places, outraged ministers, terrified custodians—but they found nothing except one stockpile of campaign leaflets.

On Fifth Street a block from Colonel Waddell's home, a Negro mailman was attacked by a crowd of white hooligans. They beat him unconscious and dumped out his leather mailbag in the street. The breeze scattered letters under the wheels of passing traffic. Gabrielle deRosset Waddell heard the commotion and rushed out to investigate. Discovering the mailman lying face down, she swabbed his bloody face with her handkerchief. Then she arranged a carriage to take him home.

All up and down her street, black servants were hiding out with their white employers.

Three blocks east of Colonel Waddell's home, two members of the Wilmington Light Infantry, on detached patrol, cornered another Negro mailman. They held the muzzles of their Krag-Jorgensen rifles to his head and ordered him to kneel on the oyster shells. "Beg for your life," they commanded. He did. They didn't shoot him.

First Baptist Church, half a block south of the Waddell home, was receiving white women and children from all over the city. A cordon of fifty armed men surrounded the building. Food, water, and blankets were stockpiled inside. A doctor, a nurse, and a pharmacist stood by. In the basement, a squad of vigilantes guarded the entrance to the tunnel that gave safe access to the Light Infantry Armory, a block away. Couriers came and went through the tunnel.

At St. Thomas's on Dock Street, three and a half blocks away, Negro parishioners were accumulating in the pews, waiting for Father Dennen. They knelt and prayed quietly, row upon row.

In Brooklyn, Negro families were furtively retrieving the bodies of loved ones and burying them in cellars, woodsheds, and stables, so the surviving family members wouldn't be implicated and hunted down by vigilantes. Some, according to custom, buried their dead with heads pointed east, toward Africa. The Negro mortuary on North Second was stacked with bodies.

It was difficult to keep track of how many were killed, who they were, who precisely was responsible. Nobody was trying very hard.

The only sure thing was that all the dead were black.

George Rountree took the streetcar up to Brooklyn to see for himself. He'd heard reports of six Negroes shot down at the Cape Fear Lumber Company, their bodies buried in a shallow ditch. Somebody else told him that, for sassing a white man, a Negro stevedore had been knocked into the river and drowned within sight of the Market Street ferry landing.

On Fourth Street, a boy no older than thirteen was bragging to all who would listen that he had ambushed a black man from behind a board fence. "Nailed that nigger rabble-rouser right between the eyes," he claimed.

One of Dowling's boys was boasting that he'd picked off nine blackbirds, one by one, as they fled from a shanty by the railroad.

When Rountree arrived at the Hilton Bridge on Fourth, several bodies lay sprawled against the iron railings. Barbaric, he thought—why wasn't somebody removing these dead out of common decency? He would speak to MacRae. Soldiers were in position here. Rumor had it that a Negro mob was heading into the city from Rocky Point. This seemed unlikely to Rountree, but if it kept the soldiers out of mischief, so be it. Somehow, he had to slow this thing down.

He was hoping the worst was over. He'd had word from Chadbourn that the aldermen were meeting right now to talk about resigning. In a little while, he'd go back downtown and hurry the process along. Bring some sanity back to this thing.

On the far side of the bridge, he caught up with MacRae, who was arguing with Walker Taylor about where to deploy the Gatling gun. A courier brought word of a mob of five hundred Negroes massing at Ninth and Nixon streets, preparing to march on the downtown area.

Rountree was skeptical. All day long, every report had been muddied by exaggeration. Discount all the numbers by half, he thought, and you might get a true picture.

"If there's really five hundred of them, or even two hundred, they won't scare so easy," Rountree said, recalling the mob of workers at Sprunts' Champion Compress, who, even unarmed, had not backed down from a Gatling gun.

"We'd better get somebody over there, stall for time," MacRae said.

"You're not going?"

"You handle it, George. We'll back you up."

"Hugh, this really isn't my—"

"Get Carter Peamon. They'll listen to one of their own people."

MacRae ordered Kenan to haul the gun to Ninth and Nixon. Meanwhile, he rounded up a contingent of infantry and Naval Reserves and double-timed them over to Nixon Street to put them between the black mob and downtown. Rountree located Carter Peamon, a ward boss, and fetched him over to the trouble spot.

Kenan unlimbered the gun and stood, once more, facing a mob. His dream washed over him in vivid color—the crowding faces, the reaching hands, the astonished eyes of old comrades—and his stomach went queer. He was sure that this time he would have to fire. The day was going on too long. Everybody was pressing too hard. Too much damage had already been done. Men were dying, and others were resigned to dying. He wished somebody would quiet those damned bells.

He forced himself to take deep breaths. The air was full of sun, and the brass receiver was warm under his hand. His men were more nervous this time. Up the street, shotguns and rifles poked out of the mob. The Negroes had positioned riflemen in the second-floor windows of the corner houses to make a crossfire. He elevated the gun—he would rake the windows first.

Kenan watched the delegation of three whites and Carter Peamon approach the mob, trying to make peace.

"Mr. Peamon," Ivanhoe Grant said. He slipped out of the crowd, his dove-gray suit still creased and immaculate despite all he'd been through today.

"Reverend? This your party?"

"It's no party, brother. This is the future."

Men behind him muttered approval. A few of them raised their fists. In some of the fists were rifles.

One of the whites, a business associate of MacRae's named Heiskel Gouvenier, said, "Gentlemen, don't you think there's been enough trouble for one day?"

"Trouble? Trouble hasn't even started yet," Grant said innocently.

"I don't believe I know you," Gouvenier said, squinting at him. He'd been told to look out for a light-skinned preacher, thought to be Manly in disguise.

Ivanhoe Grant mugged like a minstrel. "Don't you recognize me, white man? Don't you know me at all?"

"I said I don't. Now, look—"

"I'm the fly in the ointment, white man. The bogeyman in your fairy tale."

"You tell him, preacher!"

Grant put his face up close to Gouvenier's. "I am the spy in the land of Pharaoh."

"Now, there's no reason to start—"

Grant stuck a finger in his face. "We're not *starting* anything. We aim to finish a few things, though." With that, Grant waved his arm, and several young men behind him grabbed the white men roughly and pinned their arms behind their backs. Tom Miller bound their hands with baling twine.

"What do we do with him?" Miller asked. They had Peamon by the elbows, but nobody dared tie him.

Grant looked Peamon in the eye. "You with us?"

Peamon glared back, straightened up, shrugged off the men who were holding his elbows. He brushed off his sleeves with his hand. The gesture was so dignified that they let him alone. "So you're going to give them a reason?" Peamon said.

Tom Miller said, "It's time to decide, Carter. Declare yourself."

"They'll burn you down," Peamon said softly. "They'll burn you all down. Brooklyn will be a smoking hole in the ground. Don't you see it? Look yonder at that machine gun."

Miller and the others took a long look. A few of them had seen the gun in action on the river.

"They're shooting our people down in the street," Grant said in his sermonizing voice. "How long, O Lord?"

"*Our* people? Since when did you belong to us?"

" 'And lo the prophet came into their midst, and they knew him not.' "

To Miller and the others, Peamon said, "This man is putting you in danger." He pointed toward the Gatling gun. "He's putting your families in harm's way. For the love of God, get gone from here! Go to your homes! Stay with your families. If you provoke these people—"

"Why not fight back?" someone said. "We can't make it any worse."

Peamon swore. "It can always get worse."

A man behind Grant agreed: "Machine gun sure make it worse."

Ivanhoe Grant turned to the crowd of men and boys, now numbering in the hundreds. " 'Who will rise up for me against the evildoers? Who will stand up for me against the workers of iniquity?' "

Peamon answered him from the psalm: " 'He shall bring upon them their own iniquity, and shall cut them off in their own wickedness.' " He paused for effect, raised a hand, pointed directly at Grant. " 'Yea, the Lord our God shall cut them off.' Not you, Reverend—*the Lord our God!*"

The crowd of blacks began arguing among themselves. Down the street, they could see the infantry moving into position, flanking the Gatling gun. They knew what was bound to come next.

Tom Miller said, "If we let them go, maybe they'll fire on us anyway."

Grant widened his eyes triumphantly. "Are you willing to trust that they will not?"

Carter Peamon said, "I give you my word. Break this up, and I'll keep them off you. They don't want a war."

"Funny time to decide that," Grant said.

"More killing is not the answer."

Grant persisted. "I'm telling you, brothers—the white hostages protect us. They won't fire on their own."

"Just what do you plan to do with these men?" Peamon said. "Have you thought of that?"

Grant just smiled, then put a fist on his neck and crooked his head, as if he'd been hoisted up in a noose. Some of the men laughed nervously.

"That's brilliant! You lynch a white man, they will clear out this county of colored folk. We'll give up everything we've gained since the War."

"Damned little enough," Tom Miller said, resignation in his voice. It was becoming clear that they had not thought this thing through. They had a leader, but they didn't have a plan. Grant's only plan was mayhem.

"Let them go," Peamon insisted. "Untie their hands. Now. Do it."

Before Grant could reassert himself, Miller and the young men cut the twine with jackknives, and the white men stood there rubbing their wrists. One of them had pissed himself, and he stood with his hands clasped over his wet crotch.

Gouvenier said, "Well?"

Tom Miller turned him around bodily and pushed him away. "Go on, get out of here. All of you."

Peamon hesitated.

"You, too, Mr. Peamon—you've shown us your colors."

Head down, Peamon walked with Gouvenier and the other whites to the Light Infantry skirmish line, where Hugh MacRae waited.

MacRae clapped Gouvenier on the back. Immediately, infantry-men seized Carter Peamon and bound his hands with ropes. J. Allan Taylor supervised.

"Now, wait a minute, John," Gouvenier said. "This boy got us out of there."

Taylor said, "He stood by while they trussed you up like hogs." He tapped his field glasses.

"What are you going to do?" Peamon asked. He couldn't believe what was happening. He hoped to God they weren't going to turn the Gatling gun on his people. Get away, he thought—get far away and don't look back. "You can't just—"

"As we're under martial law," J. Allan Taylor said, "this colored boy will face a firing squad."

"What for?" Peamon was incredulous. He lived by the law—due process, presumption of innocence, a jury of peers. These were the forces of law.

"Inciting insurrection."

"Now, hold on," MacRae said. This was getting way out of hand. The boy had just done them a big favor. They had what they wanted—no sense pushing their luck. It was one thing to fire on a mob of laborers, another to lynch a prominent citizen—even a Negro. And a politician at that. There would be questions, interfer-ence from federal judges, grand juries. Besides, the boy had always cooperated. You wanted to give some incentive. "Nobody's declared martial law, John, not yet. You can't just shoot the boy."

"What, then?"

MacRae had a plan, a list, for later. He and J. Allan Taylor had worked it out weeks ago. Might as well start now. "Put him on a train," MacRae reminded him. "Banish him."

Peamon started to protest.

MacRae clapped him on the back. "Don't thank me, boy—you did us a good turn. Least I can do is see you safely out of here."

A detail of four infantrymen with fixed bayonets escorted Carter Peamon to the Atlantic Coastline depot on Red Cross Street. It was a rough escort—twice when Peamon tried to convince the men to reconsider, they clubbed him with rifle butts. When they arrived, his right eye was swollen shut, and he had lost a tooth.

The depot, like all the freight and passenger depots in the area, was patrolled by vigilantes. They had orders to let any Negro leave who could afford the fare, but they were also on the lookout for Alex Manly. There was no regular passenger train scheduled within the hour, so they flagged a Columbia & Augusta switcher engine that was heading across the river to Lake Waccamaw to pick up a string of boxcars. One of the soldiers cut Peamon's bindings with a bayonet, and he climbed up beside the engineer and fireman.

At Eagle Island, just across the river, the engine was shunted to a siding to let a freight pass. Peamon saw his chance. He was a man of property, with a family and interests, and he didn't intend to be hustled out of town like a bad character. He would not forfeit all he had worked for. He hopped down out of the cab onto the gravel roadbed and straightened his coat. He brushed his sleeves and hitched his trousers.

While Peamon was adjusting his tie, a vigilante down the track raised a deer rifle and shot him square between the shoulder blades. Then he ducked inside the crew shack and rang up Roger Moore's post. He shouted into the mouthpiece, "Tell the Colonel— I just shot Alex Manly!"

The Board of Aldermen assembled at the home of building contractor Charles D. Morrill, who was ill with pneumonia and could not make the short trip to city hall. They sat around the dining room table, hands clasped on the white linen tablecloth. It had the flavor of a religious service. Whenever they heard hoof-beats on the street outside, or the sound of men's voices, they glanced nervously over their shoulders at the unguarded windows.

Mayor Silas Wright, as usual wearing white gloves, called the meeting to order in a quiet voice. "You-all are aware of what is happening in our city," Wright began, speaking slowly and precisely, as if delivering an unpleasant diagnosis. As he spoke, his hands fluttered gracefully. It was impossible not to watch his hands. "We must take steps to restore order."

"That's putting it mildly," Benjamin Keith said. He stood and circled the table, punching one hand softly into the palm of the other. This was about utilities, he figured: private water, private electric, private gas, even a private ferry. And railroad rates, municipal bonds, dollars and cents. Monopolies, and how to keep them. This white versus black business was just a screen—heartfelt, but still just a screen. The real issue was business. "The greedy sons of bitches finally—"

"Sit down, Bennie. Keep a level head."

Abruptly, Keith parked himself in his chair, thudding his big fists onto the table. "Never thought I'd live to see this day," he said, then said it again. Across the table, John Norwood nodded solemnly.

Wright continued, "If we're lucky, we'll all live to see tomorrow."

"What do you propose?" Norwood asked.

"First, let's continue the ban on alcohol."

"Oh, that'll fix everything, all right," Keith said. "The town's full of vigilantes, and you're worried about beer. What we need is to wire Washington and ask for federal marshals! Federal troops!"

"Bennie," Wright chided.

"Go on, we're listening," Norwood said tiredly, as if he knew what was coming. Had he been such a fool to believe things were getting better?

"Extend the ban on liquor and beer," Wright said.

Alderman Daniel Gore, a bank vice president and insurance man, said, "Would that be all consumption, or just sale?"

Keith exploded. "Jesus Christ! The whole city is crumbling down around our ears, and all you can think to do is close down the saloons?"

Wright said, "Sometimes modest actions—"

"Modest actions? For Christ's sake!" Keith bolted from his chair and slammed it hard into the table. Morrill, who sat at the head of the table wrapped in a shawl, said nothing—he hardly looked conscious.

"Sit down, Bennie," Wright said again, but Keith remained standing. "The hooligans are fueled by liquor. If we can put an end to drunkenness—"

"Some of the hooligans are wearing uniforms," Norwood interrupted. He, too, was starting to lose his temper with Dr. Wright. They must act. Otherwise, they were going to lose their city for good.

"That's right," Elijah Green, the other black alderman, said. "We've got to do something, and now."

"There's a motion on the table," Wright said patiently.

"Second," Gore said.

"Discussion?"

Keith said, "Jesus Christ. Call the question."

Wright said, "All in favor of banning the sale of alcoholic beverages until further notice within a mile of the city limits, signify by saying 'Aye.' "

They voted in favor.

Keith sat down and clasped his hands eagerly. "Now, let's wire Washington."

"Let's not overreact," Wright said. "We don't want outsiders thinking we can't take care of our own house."

Keith gave him a look. Outsiders?

Norwood said, "The police seem to have disappeared from the streets. Where's Chief Melton?"

"I don't know."

"Who called in the State Guard? Has martial law been declared?"

Wright said, "Is the State Guard here?"

Keith said pointedly, "As long as it's still functioning, only this board can declare martial law. In a vacuum of civil authority, the governor."

Gore said, "Gentlemen, there is a solution." All eyes looked his way. None of them had forgotten that he'd caved in to the Redeemers under threat, then publicly announced support for the white supremacist platform. The rumor was that he'd actually contributed money to Rountree's campaign committee. "I have had certain conversations with leading individuals."

"Rountree," Keith said, and swore.

"Yes," Gore said. "And others. They assure me that order can be restored."

"I'll bet," Keith said. Who had broken the order in the first place? "Let me guess—they want a new board."

"That's it, yes."

"You resign if you want to—not me," Norwood said. Green agreed.

Gore said, "It won't work unless it's unanimous. That's the only way they can guarantee control."

"Never," Keith said. "This is still a democracy, and we're still the legally elected board."

Gore said, "It's beyond that now. No sense in arguing the finer points."

"The finer points! My God, if fair and legal election is a finer point, then what in the name of Christ are the broad principles?"

Gore got up, angry. "Suit yourselves. I only told them I'd try. It's going to come to that, sooner or later. You might as well resign yourselves to it. We're all lame ducks now—why not save what we can? I'll wait for your answer at city hall." He strode out and slammed the front door behind him.

Mayor Wright held his head in his white-gloved hands.

"So that's it?" Norwood said.

"Well, if you won't wire Washington," Keith said to the mayor, "I will."

Wright lifted his head. "Gentlemen, I'm afraid Dan has a point. We don't have a lot of options. We've got to end the bloodshed."

They talked for another hour, but nothing came of it. After they adjourned, Keith, Norwood, and Green went to Keith's home and called three federal judges before they found one who would intercede with Washington. An hour later, Keith received a telegram from the office of Attorney General John W. Griggs, who had conferred with President McKinley: *At this time no evidence to warrant action by Washington.*

Norwood said, "That's it, then."

Keith said, "Gentlemen, look out for yourselves from now on."

Norwood sat silently, tears streaming down his face. How had it all come to this?

Green lifted him gently by the elbow. "Come on, brother—we're on the wrong side of town."

———

George Rountree was determined to end the violence. It was already midafternoon. In just a few hours, when the sun went down, absolute terror would descend on the city. It wouldn't just be a few isolated confrontations, but wholesale shooting and burning.

When he arrived at his home to change into a fresh shirt and make some telephone calls, Chadbourn, the postmaster, was waiting in his parlor.

Chadbourn fanned a dozen telegrams toward Rountree and said without pleasantries, "Offers from all over the state to send down militia."

Rountree grunted. "Just what this fire needs—more kerosene."

"Colonel Waddell is calling the committee to meet."

"His idea?" Meta had fetched a clean shirt, and Rountree changed right there in the parlor in front of Chadbourn—unthinkable, for a man who called his wife "Mrs." even in private.

"Mine," Chadbourn said. "Dan Gore thinks he can persuade the board to resign."

Rountree buttoned his shirt, fixed the celluloid collar around his neck, knotted his tie. "I thought that was already settled."

"Take it easy. He has a couple of conditions."

Rountree swore. Meta ducked her head and pretended she hadn't heard. Couldn't everybody see it was way past that? They had to send a clear signal to MacRae and Moore and Dowling and all the other little generals roaming around loose that the government was back in firm control. That meant a new mayor and board.

Chadbourn said, "Police Chief Melton will disappear if we pay him the remainder of his year's salary. That's only two months."

"The job he's done, he ought to give back what we already paid him."

"Mayor Wright will resign if you let him pretend it's his idea."

"Great—let's all pretend. What else?"

"Gore has suggested a slate of candidates for a new board."

"I knew it!"

Chadbourn smiled. "It's okay, George. He's come over to our side. They're all our people."

All but three had signed the White Man's Declaration of Independence.

The meeting was already in progress in city hall in the room across from the board chamber. As Rountree entered, Waddell stopped in mid-sentence. "I see we have a stranger present," he said sharply. "George, this is a closed meeting."

"Stranger?" Rountree said. "What the hell?"

Hugh MacRae, who was seated up front with J. Allan Taylor, said, "It's all right, Colonel." MacRae had brushed his coat and changed his shirt, but his plantation boots were still spattered with mud, and his hair was disheveled. He looked wildly alive.

Waddell opened his arms in a mock-gracious gesture.

Rountree said, "I've got an offer from the board. Hear me out." He was still nonplussed by the hostile reception he had received. What new alliance was being formed?

"By all means," Waddell said.

Rountree gave the details.

"Splendid," Waddell said when Rountree finished. "Now, all we have to do is fill out the slate." He grabbed the lapels of his clawhammer coat and stared fiercely in the direction of MacRae and Taylor.

It was all happening so fast, Rountree still didn't quite have his bearings. The killing had spooked him, thrown him off. With Waddell presiding and Hugh MacRae offering in nomination some of the names Gore had suggested, they filled all but two of the seats.

Then, scarcely pausing for breath, Waddell said, "I move we add the illustrious names of Hugh MacRae and John Allan Taylor to our new board." He'd already worked it out with MacRae—part of their new relationship. They were approved by acclamation.

MacRae said immediately, "And I nominate for the office of mayor the man whose leadership has inspired us all—Colonel Alfred Moore Waddell." Taylor seconded, and Waddell, too, was approved by acclamation.

Rountree was stunned: so that was what Waddell had been after all along.

Waddell proclaimed, "We shall now adjourn to the chamber to be sworn in. Hugh, see if you can't round up the old board."

MacRae said, "Colonel, it's happening as we speak."

In a body, they marched out of the room. Solomon Fishblate was waiting in the hall. "Figured you'd be here," he whispered to Waddell. "When you didn't call. Where are we in the process?"

J. Allan Taylor bumped him out of the way, "Solly, allow me to present our new mayor."

Fishblate glared at Waddell. "You? You?"

Waddell patted him on the shoulder and smiled confidentially. "Solomon, events are proceeding very rapidly. One cannot always predict."

Then, in a rush of coats and guards, he swept into the chamber. Silas Wright and the old board, except for Benjamin Keith and Morrill, were waiting. Wright had already secured a letter of resignation from Morrill. They'd pick up Keith any minute.

One by one, in strict observance of the law, the aldermen resigned. After each stepped down, a name from Waddell's list was placed in nomination, and the board—gradually changing from Fusionist to Democratic—voted him in. Even the police chief resigned.

Finally, Dr. Wright resigned, and Colonel Alfred Moore Waddell, C.S.A., retired, became mayor of Wilmington.

Waddell smacked his hands together—it had all worked out perfectly. Once again, he was in command. "All that's left is the swearing in," he said. "Let's get a judge in here." Somebody went to fetch one.

"Just a minute, Colonel," MacRae said. He put an arm on J. Allan Taylor's shoulder. "John and I are going to forgo the ceremony for the present. We'll take up our offices first thing Monday morning."

Waddell was momentarily flummoxed. "But why?" Something was cooking—he'd thought they'd let him in on all of it. But he should have known. With MacRae, there was always one more item on the agenda.

"Unfinished business," Taylor said. "Nothing that concerns the board."

"Right," Waddell said. "Well. If there are no objections?" What were they up to? Whatever it was, they clearly didn't want to be encumbered with the legalities of office.

While he was pondering, a justice of the peace arrived with a

Bible, and, as they all raised their right hands, MacRae and Taylor slipped out.

After swearing in Waddell's government, the justice swore in 250 special constables. By God, Waddell meant to have order. It was four o'clock. As the courthouse clock next door was tolling the hour, the board unanimously voted to declare the city under martial law.

Meanwhile, MacRae and Taylor ducked from the corridor of city hall into the portal to the Thalian Hall mezzanine. Flanked by autographed portraits of Tom Thumb, Helena Modjeska, John Phillip Sousa, and Frederick Douglass, all of whom had played there, they pored over two sheets of paper. One was a railroad timetable. The other was a list of names—all the men who must be banished from the city, for good. Even now, Roger Moore's citizen-troops were rounding them up.

Alex Manly's name was still at the top of the list, though he had already been reported shot five different times in five separate locations.

"When we finally get that dandy nigger, we'll prop him up in a pine coffin outside city hall," Taylor said. "The way they did with Jesse James."

Manly's brothers, Frank, Lewin, and Henry, were also on the list.

Ivanhoe Grant was on the list, as were Tom Miller, the pawnbroker, and the former Negro aldermen, Norwood and Green, who would be taken just as soon as they left city hall. Ben Keith was also on the list, along with Silas Wright and the former police chief, Melton. Lawyer Armond Scott had made the list. So had the customs collector, John Dancy, the Reverend Jim Telfair, the Reverend J. T. Lee of St. Stephen's A.M.E., the Reverend J. Allen Kirk of Central Baptist, and Carter Peamon. Peamon's name was crossed off.

It was a long list. There were nearly a hundred names in all: preachers, lawyers, merchants, restaurateurs, barbers, politicians, policemen, magistrates. All men with a lot to lose. The leaders of the Negro professional class.

Sam Jenks sat on the steps of his porch, gathering his wits and vaguely listening to Callie Register prattle about her husband, Farley, who had returned only a couple of days ago, fired from the railroad gang. Now, he was prowling with the vigilantes.

"Got no use for a man such as that," she was saying. "Out chasing the colored folk. Him and his shotgun, both of 'em loaded."

"Do you know where she went?"

Callie shrugged, irked at being interrupted. "Gray Ellen? She didn't go nowheres. Never come home from school."

Sam tried to remember: had she gone to school today? This day had gone on so long that he couldn't remember when it had started, which things had happened today and which yesterday. He couldn't get the picture out of his mind—Dan Wright staggering into the sand while the infantrymen shot him again and again. Then they had just let him lie there for the longest time.

Norwood's office at the school must have a telephone. Sam walked down the street to the drugstore across from the courthouse and called the operator, who tried to connect him. But no one picked up on the other end. He would just have to go up there.

On Third Street, he spotted Harry Calabash crossing from city hall. "Harry!" he called. "For God's sake."

Harry had on a shabby gray duster over his frayed wool suit. A gray fedora was perched on his head as if someone else had carelessly put it there. "Where's your raincoat?" he said.

"Raincoat?" Sam looked at the sky and saw that it was clouding up with a low overcast. All at once, he shivered with the new chill. "Guess I wasn't paying attention."

"Come along with me," Harry said. "You've been missing all the news."

"Can't, Harry," Sam said, pulling away. "Got to get up to Williston and find Gray."

"Williston's closed. All the schools, hours ago. Where on earth have you been?"

"Brooklyn, mostly." If not Williston, where? He had no idea where to start looking. If she'd had any friends, he would have gone to their homes. But there was only Gabrielle, and Gray wouldn't go there.

"Then let's trade notes," Harry said.

Before Sam realized it, Harry had steered him past the guards and into the Cape Fear Club, which was full of businessmen and out-of-town reporters. Representatives of the Businessmen's Committee were meeting their trains and escorting them directly to the club, so they'd get the straight story from the men who knew it best. It wouldn't do to have them roaming around forming independent impressions. Only the woman in the crimson Eaton jacket was allowed to wander unmolested, and, Sam suspected, that was mainly because, as a woman, she was barred from the club.

They stood at the bar. Harry ordered a whiskey for himself and a Coca-Cola for Sam, but Sam was still shaken from what he had watched today. He was actually shivering.

"Give me a whiskey, water back," he said.

"Special occasion?" Harry asked. He wasn't smiling.

The Negro bartender delivered the drinks immediately and stood off in the corner. Sam could not tell whether he was in or out of earshot—he supposed people used to servants didn't worry about such things. Right now, he didn't care, either.

"You should have seen it, Harry. That poor son of a bitch," he said, and related the story of the capture and shooting of Dan Wright. He groped for the right word to describe what he had witnessed. "It was—"

"Obscene?" Harry said.

"That about covers it," Sam agreed.

As Sam reached for his glass, Harry covered it with his hand. "You sure about this?"

Sam nodded, then took a hot slug of whiskey on his tongue. He almost gagged. But he held the whiskey in his mouth, letting it burn. Already, he could hear his ears buzzing. He could feel his panic subside, replaced by a warm wash of reassurance.

Harry said, "I just came from city hall. We are now under martial law."

"Silas Wright did that?"

"We have a new mayor," Harry said.

"Who is it, Walker Taylor? Fishblate? Or Cousin Hugh?"

Harry Calabash smiled, recalling the look of utter bewilderment on Fishblate's face as Waddell's coterie had marched past him into the board chambers—somebody clearly had welshed on a deal. "Waddell," he said.

Sam took another slug of the whiskey and laughed. So Waddell had been wired in all along. Running a shadow government.

Harry clinked his glass against Sam's. "Congratulations, Samuel. You backed the right horse. Or the right horse backed you."

They drank together and ordered more. Sam was feeling a warm surge of euphoria. Maybe some good would come out of this after all. Maybe he and Gray Ellen would have the future here they deserved.

Harry drank hard and needed a new whiskey after two gulps. The bartender obliged. Looking away at the green-coated barman, he said to Sam, "You're fooling yourself if you think so."

"What? I didn't say anything."

Harry turned and drew closer to be heard above the growing noise of the newspapermen at the tables behind them. "No, but you're working out all the angles. Your ambition is trying to fool your conscience."

Sam finished his glass and demanded another.

Harry put a hand on his sleeve. Sam had never noticed before how crooked and bony Harry's fingers were. The sallow skin was stippled with liver spots. Suddenly, he didn't want Harry to touch him.

"You're a whisker away from the sweetest deal you've ever known," Harry said. "All it takes to clinch it is to say, 'Yes, sir,' next time they ask you something. Doesn't matter what they ask— might be murder, might be 'Pass the salt.' Just say, 'Yes, sir,' and you'll be sitting pretty. Young man on the rise. Way I was, once upon a time."

"Lay off, Harry."

Harry smiled. "You're about to find out if you have any character."

They had several more drinks, and the sun was already well down before Sam remembered he was looking for Gray Ellen. His stomach was boiling, and his cheeks were flushed. The conversations around him were just a buzzing racket. He stepped away from the bar and momentarily lost his balance. He wanted to pay for his drinks, but the barman stood in the corner and made no move to present a bill. Sam's thinking was fuzzy. He had no idea how bills were paid at the Cape Fear Club. Let Harry handle it— he could square with Harry tomorrow.

His head felt like a bag of water, sloshing back and forth behind his sore eyes. He could not focus properly—things kept going into and out of detail. He made it to the door. Outside, a cold drizzle matted his hair in minutes. The chill seeped into his body.

He stood in the drizzle, hands stuffed into his coat pockets. The pistol in his right pocket was warm against his hand. He tried to clear his head, recover his bearings. The river was behind him, his home off to the right. He started walking straight ahead. He had to find Gray Ellen.

Bessie King noticed somebody sneaking around the back of the house and stole out through the kitchen to investigate. "David?" she called softly into the darkness. "David boy?"

A light-skinned Negro in a pearl-gray overcoat and hat stepped out of the drizzle into the kitchen light. Drops of water beaded on the fine fabric of his coat and glistened along the brim of his fedora.

She said, "Mr. Manly?"

The man shook his head. "I am a preacher of the Lord, ma'am. Come to bring you sad news."

Bessie took a step back and braced herself against the doorjamb. The drizzle was on her face. "Oh, lordy, lordy. My David."

"I am sorry, ma'am."

She steadied herself. "Where is he?"

"At the mortuary down on Second, ma'am. You best wait until morning."

She nodded and put her face into her hands. When she lifted her head, the light-skinned man had melted away.

Bessie locked the back door and stood in the kitchen, looking stupidly at the pots and pans. Her mind was a rushing vacuum. Something deep inside her shuddered. She could feel herself falling, and she held onto the counter with both hands. Her soul was faltering. She tried to pray and could not. All she could utter was "Sweet Jesus."

She stood at the sink for several minutes to let the rushing go out of her head. She could feel her soul swirling around in her breast. She wished she had never set foot outside to see who the skulker was. If she didn't know, then it hadn't happened. Yet what he had told her must be true—it felt true. Felt truer than anything she had ever heard.

After a time, she heard sobbing and realized it was not her own. Almost automatically, she floated through the dining room and into the parlor, where Gabrielle sat folded into a sofa, sobbing into her hands. Her body convulsed with each sob. The tears ran out between her fingers.

Bessie laid a hand on her arm, and Gabrielle looked up. "Oh, Bessie," she whispered. "This is an awful day."

She must have overheard, Bessie thought. She sat down next to Gabrielle and put an arm around her shoulder. The two women hugged and cried together. Bessie prayed, "Father, do not forsake us in the hour of our trial."

Gabrielle said, "Do you know what today is?"

"A black day," Bessie said. "No blacker day has ever been."

"He's out there somewhere—who knows where? He should be here, with me."

What was she thinking of that old billy goat for at a time like this? "I know, honey, I know. Ain't right."

"You don't understand," Gabrielle said, sitting upright. "Today, this is the second anniversary of my wedding."

Bessie King looked away. So not even this one, she thought. "Honey, we all got troubles," she said, and went back to the kitchen to have her privacy.

*All the ones who left, they never came back. I
know—because I waited for them.*

Elizabeth "Bessie" King,
1918

CHAPTER NINETEEN

Thursday, November 10

ONCE AGAIN, Gray Ellen Jenks found herself in strange territory
with a man she did not trust. She wrapped her shawl around her
to keep off the drizzle as the driver steered the open buggy through
the arched wrought-iron gate of Oakdale Cemetery.

The driver was John Norwood, the only man in town who'd given
her a chance. To her left sat Ivanhoe Grant, the man who had
forced her to take a chance. Squeezed in the middle, she felt caught
between two radically different visions of the future.

Going home had seemed pointless—Sam would be out chasing
the action. Norwood had dismissed all the jittery children almost

as soon as the school day had begun, then had rushed off to attend some kind of meeting downtown. Nobody seemed to know what was going on, but everybody knew it was bad.

Later, Norwood had found her outside city hall, where she had gravitated hoping to find Sam. Never had she seen Norwood so angry and frightened.

"Can you get us a carriage?" he'd asked, hooding his face under the lowered brim of his hat. His tone had lost all confidence, all professional composure. He was just a black man asking a white woman to protect him. It made him ashamed.

She had not hesitated. She retrieved the buggy Cousin Hugh had made available to them. Norwood directed her down streets she had never traveled before, stopping only once to let a gray-coated shadow leap up onto the seat beside her—Ivanhoe Grant.

"What are we doing in the cemetery?" she asked now. She was already spooked enough without lurking around graveyards. She thought she caught a glimpse of a human shape, moving, out of the corner of her eye.

"I must minister to my flock," Grant said without smiling.

"What, here?"

The buggy moved softly in the drizzle along the narrow, rutted lanes, between hummocks planted with marble and granite monuments bearing the names of the finest families in Wilmington— invisible in the dark and rain. Grant lit a kerosene lantern and trimmed it low. They ducked under low-hanging dogwood branches, bare and heavily wet. Live oaks were splayed against the black sky, their twisted limbs casting grotesque shadows in the fickle play of light. Spanish moss draped the branches in gray shrouds.

"Dark as sin in this place," Norwood observed.

Grant signaled Norwood to stop the buggy. All at once, silent black shapes materialized out of the drizzle, human shapes gliding slowly toward them, as if the graves had opened and the dead were once again walking.

"Dear God."

"It's all right, schoolteacher," Grant said. He reached out and shook hands with one of the shadows, then another.

Now, Gray Ellen could hear murmuring, the fussing of infants, coughing, low voices singing. She recognized two of her students, the little sisters with the tightly braided hair, hanging onto a young woman in a green blanket coat.

"They've been coming out here all day," Norwood explained.

"Why here?"

Grant said, "These are the only white folks can't do 'em no harm."

"Are they all right?"

"All right as they're going to get," Grant said.

Norwood clucked the horse onward, and they rode slowly along the winding lanes. On either side of them under the trees, families huddled, tucked into the shadows, reclining against the berms, sheltering themselves as best they could from the drizzle and the fitful night wind. Saffron King James knelt over a wounded man, bandaging his leg and speaking softly.

"Why did you bring me here?" Gray Ellen asked after a while.

"Goddamnit, woman!" Grant said. "Does it always have to be about you?"

Norwood said, "I had to get out of town. I'm on some kind of a list."

"I'm sorry, Mr. Norwood."

"Running scared—no way for a man to do." Norwood's tone was soft, but it carried force.

"I didn't realize—"

"People had better start realizing. A shame has visited this city."

"Amen," said Grant, and all around them in the darkness, voices answered softly, "Amen."

They drove deep into the maze of burial plots until they came to the woods at the northern edge. "Looks like my stop," Norwood said. The horse stood with her head down. Norwood hopped out. He had no extra clothes, no blankets, just an overcoat.

"You'll catch your death out here," Gray Ellen whispered.

"Take care of yourself, hear?"

"Don't fret about me. It's you that—"

"Well, get gone from here. Don't tell a soul where you've been."

As if it were the most natural thing in the world, Norwood climbed a berm and disappeared into the tangled woods.

Grant took the reins. As they started up, he said, "He'll be all right—man's got a powerful anger to warm his heart tonight."

The way he said it, she knew he was the one with the most powerful anger of all, the kind that burned a man up. Anger was not enough, she thought, but she didn't say it. She was in no mood to argue, not here.

The buggy wound through the tree-tunneled lanes. Grant said softly, "And now I am going to take you somewhere."

He drove down a twisting, rutted track hemmed in on both sides by thick foliage, trees growing so close together a grown man could not slip between them. After a time, he whispered, "Put out that lantern," and she obeyed. It was raining harder—she could hear it pattering against the leaves, but the canopy was so overgrown that the rain reached them as a slow drip, then misted up into their bones from the wet forest floor.

The smell changed—an overwhelming odor of ferment and rot. The wheels of the buggy sank into the muddy road, and the horse had difficulty keeping her feet. The buggy slowed. Despite her coat, Gray Ellen was soaked through and shivering. Her face was coated with an oily, cold film—the rain, and whatever was in the air. The road turned into paste. The buggy wheels hissed along. The mare slopped one foot after the other, picking her way cautiously around ruts and holes. In the thick darkness, Gray Ellen could not see the horse anymore, but she could hear her plainly.

They were descending toward water, she could feel it. The air grew heavier. Over the steady patter of the rain, she heard bullfrogs and a shrieking night bird. An owl moaned in the trees. A rodent squealed.

"Please," she whispered. "Let me light the lantern again."

"Shh," he said. Then, "Whoa, now. Whoa." The buggy stopped.

"Where are we?"

He didn't say anything. It was as if he wanted to spook her. He knew the value of a pause.

"Tell me where we are."

"You always have to be talking?" His voice was so mean it frightened her.

"Take me back. Now."

He sighed theatrically. "Teacher, you are going to have to learn patience. And faith."

"I have plenty of faith."

"Shoot. You don't know the first thing about it."

"Take me back."

He reached over in the dark and grabbed her shoulders. "Shush. Now listen."

Too scared to do anything else, she listened hard. She heard the rain and the frogs. Then over the rain came another sound: voices. Human voices. Singing. She cocked her head to hear better. The incessant rain made it hard. The racket of frogs and insects disoriented her—she could not locate the direction of the singing.

But after a time, she could make out some of the words. "When the battle's over," a woman's voice sang, while deeper voices hummed along behind it, "we can wear a crown—in the new Je-ru-sa-lem."

"Over yonder, less than a mile," Grant said softly. "Smith's Creek Bridge."

He clasped his bare fingers gently around the back of her neck and swiveled her head. Twinkling like a low star, a faint light shone in the distance.

"A lantern?" she said.

"White soldiers up there. Sentries. They've sealed off the city."

"Then we'd better warn—"

"Shush, now. They won't come out here. Those white boys know better than to try and rout us out of the swamp."

She nodded in the dark. They must be huddled out there by the hundreds.

Grant said, "Runaways been hiding out in these swamps for a hundred and fifty years. It's a hole in the map." Alex Manly's father, mother, and two brothers were out there somewhere, he knew.

"Then they're safe? But it's so cold." She didn't think she could survive the night in the open.

He sighed. "Safe is an approximate thing, teacher. Nobody's going to shoot them out here. Nobody's going to get close enough."

She shivered in the rain. The mare snorted but stood patiently, waiting for the driver to take up slack on the reins. Gray Ellen said, "It's no night to be sleeping outdoors. My God."

"They dare not light fires," Grant said, his voice suddenly breaking.

She wished there were light enough to see his face. He had not hesitated to urge on the violence—was he now feeling remorse? Did he have any right? He had invented himself—a man who was not a man but a living cause, a flame burning toward a single purpose hallowed by a dead grandfather and two centuries of racial memory. But in this moment, in the dark, she glimpsed the man who lived inside the invention. He was close to breaking.

His voice recovered its matter-of-fact tone. "Some will catch pneumonia. Some will die. The old and infirm, the babies."

"The children," she said, suddenly realizing. The willowy, squirming bodies who lived behind the wooden desks in her classroom were tonight sleeping in the swamp, without even a fire.

Grant abruptly handed over the reins and started to climb out. She could only hear him. "What are you doing?" she said.

"It's all over now. They'll be hunting me down, too, by and by. Can't go back."

She thought quickly. She couldn't help all those invisible people out there in the darkness, but she could at least help this man. "Come back with me. Stay at the house until morning. Wait till things calm down."

"I ought to stay here. I belong with them."

"You can't do anything for them."

"Maybe not. But I am a preacher of the Lord—"

"Stop it. I'm giving you a chance—take it."

Without answering, Grant settled back into the seat and took the reins. He backed the mare and skillfully turned the buggy around. They headed back to town. Now that she knew the voices were out there, she heard the singing all the way back to the main road, long after it was too far away to hear. The eeriness of it thrilled her stomach—it was like riding among ghosts. She wept all the way home.

The Reverend J. Allen Kirk huddled under the Hilton Bridge in the railroad culvert. He heard the single horse and buggy clomp across the bridge—too slow to be vigilantes. He almost ventured a look, but at the last minute ducked back into the shadows. When the rain let up, he would follow the culvert farther out of town.

He ought to be braver, he knew. He wanted to stand at the head of his congregation in defiance of the white vigilantes. Once, he could have been a rock, a leader, a martyr—but then, in one sermon, Ivanhoe Grant had stolen his congregation away from him. Let Grant be their martyr.

The buggy was gone, and the rain came down harder than ever. A slow train rumbled past him. Through the windows in the lighted cars sat white men, their rifles poking up between the seats.

He prayed for courage. He bolted from under the shelter of the bridge and dodged from shadow to shadow along the deep culvert, running away.

By nightfall, companies of State Guards from the outlying towns of Clinton and Maxton and a detachment of Naval Reserves from Kinston arrived in town. The Kinston troops relieved the men of the Light Infantry at the jail. Half the Clinton men were assigned to patrol the perimeter of Brooklyn, and half were detailed to guard the hospital after a rumored attempt to finish off Bill Mayo. The Maxton men were billeted in reserve at the armory and in private homes nearby.

Colonel Walker Taylor now commanded some five hundred men in uniform. Mike Dowling still led eighty Red Shirts. Another fifty

Rough Riders prowled the streets. Colonel Roger Moore could count on three hundred vigilantes, many of whom were now deputized. Police Chief Parmele fielded about half his force of twenty-five patrolmen, three sergeants, and a captain. The rest had fled the city under threat.

Hugh MacRae and J. Allan Taylor had their own shadow force of men who reported directly to the Secret Nine. These men were scattered among the other organizations. Somewhere, four Pinkerton operatives—two white and two black, each team unaware of the other—were still rattling around, along with Special Constable John Taylor, a Negro, who patrolled Brooklyn trying to keep people indoors.

Three deputy sheriffs were also on duty, though the chief deputy, George Z. French, was in hiding in the rooms above his own at the Orton Hotel, the one place nobody thought to look for him. There had been open threats to hang him from an oak tree on Market Street. James Allen, a young man from Father Dennen's parish, was protecting him. Allen considered French a corrupt bully, but he wanted to be able to face Father Dennen at Sunday mass without shame for the life he could have saved but didn't.

Captain Walter G. MacRae, Hugh MacRae's uncle, was now acting sheriff.

All told, a thousand armed white men, taking often contradictory orders from a variety of military and dubiously constituted civil authorities, occupied the city.

Sam Jenks was dimly aware of the commotion. Reflexively, he turned right when he reached Third Street, heading for home. His route took him past the jail, where a mob of Red Shirts was holding some kind of torchlight vigil. The torches sputtered in the rain, sending up plumes of black smoke. He made his way shakily to the outskirts of the crowd.

"They got Tom Miller in there," a skinny man said. "And a bunch of other rabble-rousers." The man looked vaguely familiar. It was a minute or two before Sam could place him—he'd seen him at the house next door. Callie Register's itinerant husband, Farley.

"What you planning to do?" Sam was rocking back and forth,

trying to stay upright. His feet were soaked from walking through puddles and, standing still, he suddenly felt cold to the bone, and said so.

"Cold as a witch's tit," Farley agreed, standing close enough to smell the whiskey on Sam's breath. "Got any more of that save-the-baby?"

Sam shook his head. "Been at the club."

"Oh," Farley said, nodding but disappointed. "Drinking with the mucky-mucks. Don't I know you?"

"What's going on?" Sam asked again.

"Going to take them niggers out of here and decorate a few lampposts."

Sam was in no mood for another lynching.

The jail was a solid block of a building just behind the court-house. The mob was laying siege to the front door, the public entrance with its wide stairs and tall, barred windows. Sam made his way toward it through the crowd, shoving and getting shoved back.

He couldn't tell at first what was keeping the mob at bay. Why didn't they just rush the entrance and take the prisoners? What was stopping them? When he at last clawed his way through the crowd, he saw their obstacle: Father Christopher Dennen. The priest stood, back against the door, arguing in a loud voice with Mike Dowling. The skirts of his cassock were spattered with mud. His red hair was matted, and his fists were balled.

"Father," Dowling was saying, "I'm not going to ask you again. Now, if you'll kindly move aside—"

"There are soldiers behind me," Dennen warned.

Dowling laughed. "Kinston volunteers, Father. We know all about 'em. They won't fire on white men." The crowd behind him hurrahed. Sam saw worried faces at the windows inside.

"Mike, don't do this. There's been enough mayhem for one day."

"Father, you may as well try to stop the rain."

From deep in the pocket of his cassock, Father Dennen pulled out an ancient watch. "Mike, it's two minutes past midnight. This long, shameful day is over. Let the new one begin without blood."

Dowling grabbed the priest's arm and held it, unsure what to do next. A devout Catholic, he knew better than to strike a priest.

"Mike, if you care for your immortal soul—"

Made brave by the whiskey, Sam mounted the stairs. He grabbed for the priest to yank him out of Dowling's grip, but slipped on the wet stone and went sprawling on the steps. It took him two tries to get back up.

Father Dennen said, "Oh, for the love of God—another drunken hero of the white race."

"I came to help," Sam said.

"You've done enough already. I'm warning both of you, I'll have you excommunicated!"

"Father," Sam said, but he couldn't think of how to finish it.

From the back of the crowd came shouting. A column of men armed with Winchesters broke through and mounted the steps. At their head was Colonel Waddell, followed by the new sheriff, Walter MacRae. The men fanned out at the top of the steps on either side of Waddell, facing the crowd. Waddell was hatless, as if he'd been roused from sleep and had dressed in a hurry. His silver hair glistened in the rain. He said, "Mike, what do you think you're doing?"

"Colonel," Dowling said, smiling, "we're just carrying out your orders."

Sheriff MacRae brandished his pump shotgun. "You'll take those men over my dead body."

Waddell faced the crowd. "Listen to me, all of you. My position has radically changed. As your mayor, I am now a sworn officer of the law."

"Mayor?" Dowling said, incredulous. "When did all this happen?"

Many in the crowd were also hearing the news for the first time. There was scattered applause and a few rebel yells.

Waddell said, "This jail and these prisoners must have protection." A few in the crowd shouted objections. Waddell held up his hands, then spread his arms wide. "There are fifty rifles up here. Special deputies who answer to the law. They will shoot down any man who moves on the jail!" He paused to let that sink in. "We have carried the day and won the field. Now, we must govern impartially. We are civilized people—we cannot abide anarchy."

Father Dennen crossed his arms and cocked his head, mouth open, as if he could not believe his ears. Sam, too, was stunned at the hypocrisy.

"Now, go about your business. Leave justice to the proper authorities!"

In a few minutes, it was all over. Waddell left, the deputies relieved the Kinston men, and Sam stood in the rain. Mike Dowling shook a finger at him and said, "I'll remember your face." Then he left with his Red Shirts.

Father Dennen waited till he was alone on the jailhouse steps with Sam. Then he wound up and slammed a fist into Sam's cheek. Sam saw it coming and didn't even try to duck. Once again, he went down on the wet granite steps, too drunk to feel any pain. Father Dennen stood over him. "That's just the start of your penance. Shame on you."

———

Though they detoured down back streets to avoid the vigilance patrols, they were stopped twice on the way back to town. Gray Ellen explained that Grant was her servant. Grant played along—keeping his head down, shoulders slumped, eyes averted—and they let the buggy pass. They turned onto the alley behind the house on Third Street just before midnight. They were both soaked through and shivering—they'd been out since suppertime. The house was dark—where in the world was Sam? They left the rig in the alley, the mare still harnessed to the singletree, standing head down in the rain.

They entered the back door quietly. The last thing Gray Ellen wanted was for Callie to come around to share her troubles.

In the kitchen, she pulled the shades and warmed up a pot of stew. They sat across from each other at the plain wooden table and spooned the hot stew off their plates. Grant was finished with his helping almost before Gray Ellen had begun. "Been a hard day," he explained. "All this running around, a man can work up an appetite."

It was only then, when he leaned forward, winced, and steadied himself with both hands against the table, that she noticed the blood under his left arm.

"Take off your coat and vest," she commanded, rising.

"Leave me be."

"You're not going to die in my house."

"Nobody's dying, teacher."

She was already behind him, tugging at the sleeves of his coat. He groaned in pain. "Help me," she said.

He slipped off the coat and unbuttoned the vest, leaning forward so she could work it off his arms. The left side of his shirt was dark with old blood.

"When did this happen?" she said.

"Out in front of Walker's Grocery this morning."

"Are all men born fools, or do they learn it as they go?"

"There's no bullet," he said. "Just cut me a little."

"Lucky shot."

He laughed. "For who?"

"At least let me clean the wound. Take off your shirt."

She moved his jacket out of the way, noticing a heavy lump in the right pocket. Same place Sam keeps his, she thought. Fools.

Using a sponge, she swabbed away the blood. She scrubbed gingerly, as much afraid of opening up the old scars as the new wound. In the linen closet off the kitchen, she found a pillow slip and carefully scissored it down the sides, fashioning a long, wide bandage. She doubled it up and wrapped it around Grant. The wound wasn't bleeding much.

"Have you got a drink in the house?" he asked. "It would steady me down."

She shook her head. "We don't keep any. Sam doesn't use it."

"That a fact? Your man always leave you alone this late at night?"

"It's been sort of a special day. Lots of things happening that never happened before."

He sat at the table, still shirtless. He reached over to the chair on his right and felt in the pocket of his jacket.

"It's still there," she said. "You won't need it tonight."

"Never can tell," he said. "What's going to happen when your man comes home and finds a nigger in his kitchen?"

"Don't use that word," she said. "I abhor it." Without that word, she believed irrationally, what had happened today would have been impossible. "Why do you keep goading me? What is it you want?"

"What I want is to do it differently next time." There was no mistaking the cold rage in his voice.

"Next time?" She was amazed.

He stood and walked around the kitchen. He put his face up close to hers, and she drew back until she was trapped against the counter.

"Don't," she said.

"I wasn't." He reached behind her, picked out an apple from a bowl on the counter, and drew out a pocketknife, then backed off. He slit the apple expertly to its core and popped the two halves open in his hand. "Next time, I will not underestimate the white man." He sliced the apple into quarters and deftly scored the seeds from each wedge, then popped it into his mouth. In less than a minute, he devoured the whole apple. "We always underestimate the white man," he said wonderingly, as if talking out loud to himself. "We are always amazed at the lengths to which he will go. The things that do not make him ashamed."

"We're not all like that," she said. "You're not being fair."

He raised an accusing finger. "I have seen this city today. I am done being surprised. I am done being fair."

The rain let up a little as Sam wandered down Third Street, dimly aware that he was within a block of home. He walked closer. The rain and cold had sobered him up some, and now his cheekbone ached from Father Dennen's punch. His shoulder and back were sore from falling down on the jailhouse steps. He had trouble seeing out of his right eye unless he squinted.

There were lights on at the back of the house—Gray Ellen must still be awake. Probably, she had sat up for hours reading, fretting, wondering where he was. Guilt overcame him. He was drunk. He was a coward. Philadelphia, Chicago, Cuba—would he just keep on making the same mistakes over and over? He wasn't getting better, stronger, or braver. He was just getting older. He took a deep breath, trying to clear his head of the whiskey.

But the things he had seen today, the way he had felt—it was more than a man could bear with a clear head. Watching, he had been a part of it all. It was like the day on the tugboat, watching the Gatling gun tear apart pumpkins and trees. Just being there, a witness, had made him guilty. Now, he had another reason to feel guilty. He stumbled up the front porch stairs. When he grabbed the rotten railing for support, it broke off in his hand.

He took another deep breath, turned the key in the front door, and went inside.

Gray Ellen heard him clomping along the corridor to the kitchen and turned. "My God, what happened to you?" she said. "Your eye, your cheek."

"The wrath of God." Sam laughed shortly. "I'm all right." He was home.

She swept across the kitchen to the doorway and reached for him, then drew away. "I don't believe it—you're drunk!"

"Look, I can explain," Sam said, moving into the kitchen. Then he saw Ivanhoe Grant. "The hell's he doing here?"

"Calm down," Gray Ellen said. "You're a mess."

Sam's hand reached reflexively into his coat pocket and pulled out the little navy revolver. He wasn't sure what he meant to do with it.

"Oh, for God's sake," Gray Ellen said, reaching for the pistol.

He pushed her away with the other hand. "I want to know what he's doing in my house." Sam was bewildered. What was a black man doing half-undressed in his kitchen, after midnight, alone with his wife? What was any man doing there?

"Take it easy," Grant said, grinning. He strode forward casually, then picked up his coat off the back of the chair and folded it over his arm.

Sam stared at Grant. "What's all that?" he said, meaning the scars, the bandage. Where was the man's shirt?

Gray Ellen said, "Can't you see he's hurt?"

"I don't need a woman talking for me," Grant said. He turned on Sam. "You want to shoot me, you go right ahead." He puffed out his chest, crosshatched with livid scars.

Sam held the pistol at arm's length, watching it wobble as he took aim at Grant's torso. Father Dennen's penance came back to him: do no harm. Grant just stood there. What were all those scars? "Somebody whip you?"

"Are you going to shoot me or not?"

Sam didn't know what to do. He looked at Gray Ellen.

"Sam, Sam—trust me, Sam. It's all right. It was nothing improper."

He nodded. He did trust her. She never lied, not to him or anyone. He felt the whole day draining down into his shoes—the violence, the guilt, the whiskey, all of it. He lowered the revolver. "No, I'm not going to shoot you," he said. He wanted somebody to realize that he was trying to do the right thing—that he had been trying all day long.

Grant whipped out his two-shot Bulldog derringer. "Don't pity me, white man," he said softly. "So you don't have the stomach for it?" He straight-armed the derringer toward Sam's face. Sam just stood there, dumbstruck, drunk enough to wonder if it were really happening at all.

Gray Ellen's mouth fell open, but she had no words.

Grant cocked the hammer. "The fear of the Lord is the beginning of wisdom." He fired once. The kitchen exploded in Sam's ears. Something whizzed by his ear and slammed into the wall behind him. He dropped his revolver and staggered backward. Grant cocked the hammer and fired the second shot.

Sam was sitting on the hall floor, amazed to be alive. He moved his mouth until words came out. "You deliberately missed." Gray Ellen was a statue at the edge of his vision, smoke curling around her head. His ears rang—hard. His own voice sounded far away.

Grant said, "Did I?" He laughed heartily, an exaggerated laugh from deep in his belly. "Work it out for yourself. Write the story." Then he was gone out the back door. His bloody shirt still hung across the chair back. Sam heard a buggy clattering down the alley in the rain.

Only then did Gray Ellen move to his side. She knelt next to him and cradled his head to her breast. He sobbed into her damp bosom. She was done crying. She knew Ivanhoe Grant had missed on purpose. Against all his instincts, he had shown mercy. For her sake, she believed.

In a few minutes, she would make a pot of coffee. They would sit up all night at the kitchen table. It had been a long day. They had a lot to tell each other.

After a while, Gray Ellen said, "You have to be better than what goes on around you. We all must. Promise me."

He promised. Then he went to work.

It was a very complicated story. Sam would have to remember the details carefully, for somewhere along the way he had lost his notebook. He would write it from memory. He would tell the whole truth. Memory did not lie.

William Rand Kenan hunkered against the sideboard of the wagon, which was backed up onto Smith's Creek Bridge. As usual, they'd left the horses in harness. The tarp was draped over the gun against the rain—loosely, so it could be hauled off quickly in the event of action. The rain was slackening. There was reported to be a mob of Negroes headed this way, but Kenan didn't trust the report. They'd been hearing that same rumor all day long. He was tired of being alert.

Things were quieting down. After being in the thick of it all day, he liked being on the outskirts.

The cigar tasted good. He drew in the rich smoke and blew it out again, savoring the smell. It went right to his head, making it a little light. The air held the smoke low around his face and made him feel warmer somehow. He and his crew sat quietly in the dark. The boys weren't even talking. He hoped they were still awake. Across the bridge, they had hung a lantern to illuminate whoever might be coming up the road toward them.

A little while ago, he'd heard a horse and carriage moving along the old swamp road. When he was a kid, he used to gig bullfrogs down here. Nobody went down there much anymore—the road was all overgrown. Three years back, the creek and river had risen, flooding out most of the road and making more swamp. He wouldn't go back there now.

But he'd been hearing the Negroes out there all night. They were just voices, invisible as every other creature that lived in the swamp. Go home, he wanted to tell them. It's under control now. It wasn't before, but it is now. But would they ever trust any white man again?

Maybe Silas Wright and James Sprunt. Kenan had spied the two of them rushing between trouble spots in the doctor's black landau, imploring men on both sides to put up their guns and back off. He could still see Dr. Wright's white-gloved hands fluttering as he talked, and James Sprunt nodding and gathering men around him with the sweep of his long arms. Both men had endangered their lives for the sake of peace.

But after it got going good, they didn't have a chance. Kenan had lost track of them in the mayhem.

Jesus, he thought—volley-firing along Bladen Street. What in the hell were those boys thinking of? You could shoot a Krag through both walls of one of those flimsy shotgun shacks and kill a mule standing out back. The army had used the Krag in Cuba against dug-in professional troops and killed them through adobe walls.

He could hear them singing now. He'd heard them off and on all night, as the breeze shifted. Hymns, mostly. From time to time, when he recognized the tune, he hummed along quietly. Sometimes, the rain drowned out the voices, but now it was letting up. The government weather office predicted tomorrow would be crisp and clear. They'd freeze out there. Why had they taken their children? Fear, he supposed. A powerful fear, to drive a man and his whole family into a cold swamp on a November night.

He puffed on his cigar and thought fondly of his wife, Mary, asleep back at the house. Then he thought of his boy in Mexico, building a dam. Maybe he would take Mary down for a visit. But the boy might be gone before they could make it down there—he was always on the move, always building, soaring along as if he had a perfect map of the complicated future. Lord, how he missed that boy.

Kenan studied the sky—still black. When the stars came out, he would pull the tarp off the gun and wipe it down good with an oily rag.

There was still a good six hours till first light. If anything happened tonight, they would be ready. There was no need to inventory the ammunition—he'd worked hard all day to make sure they didn't fire a single shot.

*When the high-hat preacher, with his spike-tailed
coat and with gun on his shoulder, went out
hunting blackbirds, it was not much of a surprise
to see others not so prominent in church affairs
acting as he did.*

Benjamin F. Keith,
wholesale merchant

CHAPTER TWENTY

Sunday, November 13

BY FRIDAY MORNING, the killing was mostly done, and the banish-
ments began. Squads operating under the orders of Hugh MacRae,
J. Allan Taylor, and the others of the Secret Nine combed the city
for the men on their list. Many of them, including all the Manlys,
had already fled. Some, such as Silas Wright, they simply could
not find.

First, they emptied the jail. Former Police Chief Melton, United
States Commissioner Robert Bunting, and Bunting's mulatto wife,
Nancy, were placed on the three-fifteen northbound Zephyr, along
with four Negroes prominent in local politics: lawyer William
Henderson, a police sergeant, Charles Gilbert, and merchants

Isaac Loftin and Charles McAllister. McAllister was said to have sold guns to blacks.

Another caravan from the jail included Tom Miller, Magistrate R. B. Pickens, the Reverend Isaac Bell, James Loughlin, who was clerk of the Front Street City Market, and ward boss A. I. Bryant. All of them were herded aboard the southbound Limited. Miller was especially bitter—he left behind dozens of rental properties, a pawnshop inventory worth fifty thousand dollars, and a fat portfolio of debts owed to him by white clients, none of which would ever be paid.

His assets, like those of the Manlys and others, would enrich some of the leading white families in town. All the papers would be legal, notarized by the Democratic register of deeds.

They caught Chief Deputy George Z. French sneaking out the back door of the Orton Hotel and hauled him in a wagon to the Atlantic Coastline depot on Red Cross Street, escorted by a forest of Wilmington Light Infantry bayonets. Outside the depot, Red Shirts swarmed aboard the wagon and seized the reins. They stopped it under the twisted limbs of a grandfather live oak and tossed a rope over the stoutest one, then looped a noose around his neck. Before they could drive the wagon out from under him, he cried out in gibberish. His high voice carried the weird ring of incantation.

Harry Calabash was watching. "I'll be damned," he said out loud to the woman reporter in the crimson jacket.

"What? Has he lost his mind?"

Calabash laughed sweetly. "It's code—the secret Masonic cry for help. His brother Freemasons can't refuse."

And even as he spoke, men in suits came streaming out of the crowd. Two of them held the horses while Heiskel Gouvenier and others climbed aboard and took the noose off French's neck.

"What's so funny about that?"

Calabash laughed again. Sam ought to be here to see this, he thought. "Fellow's got the hangman's noose around his neck, and he still believes his club won't let him down."

Armond Scott, the young Negro lawyer who had failed to deliver the answer to Waddell's ultimatum, was put on the seven o'clock northbound train that evening—the same train that carried Deputy French. But Scott was escorted to the Negro car.

And so it went. The city was being systematically emptied of the opposition party—the party of carpetbaggers, Negroes, Populists, and Republicans. Order was being restored. The black middle class disappeared.

No Negroes were allowed to come into the city limits without first being searched. Men and women alike were frisked, and some suspicious characters were required to strip. Parcels and bags were ransacked for weapons. Wagons were unloaded onto the street. The posses confiscated several billy clubs, a razor, a broken pistol, and three old case knives.

But blacks were allowed to leave the city unmolested, and they fled in droves. The road over Smith's Creek Bridge was clogged with pedestrians. The mill workers and domestic servants who chose to remain were escorted to their jobs by squads of mounted vigilantes. White boys were pressed into escort duty. Safe conduct passes were issued. White men were quickly hired to fill the places of black men dismissed from the police and fire departments. The bureaucracy of order was taking hold.

By Saturday, it was becoming clear that the city could not function without Negro labor. Sprunts' Champion Compress, largely because of James Sprunt's reputation for fairness, had retained most of its men, but MacRae's Wilmington Cotton Mills and other large concerns were nearly deserted. It was impossible to train ordinary laborers to be skilled machinists overnight. Construction sites were abandoned, waiting for brick masons, carpenters, and glaziers.

Most of the forty-four restaurants in town had been owned and run by Negroes. Now, all but a handful were closed. On the waterfront, nothing was moving. Steamships and coastal packets lay idle at the wharf, accumulating wharfage fees, with no stevedores to unload their cargoes and no teamsters to haul them away if they did.

Blacks were no longer allowed to leave the city but were directed back to their homes. They left anyway: in boxcars, on trails through the swamp, along unguarded lanes, in small boats across the Cape Fear River.

Colonel Waddell sent delegation after delegation into the swamps to persuade the Negroes to come back into town and return to their jobs, but none met with much success. He even wrote an appeal for the *Messenger*, explaining away the violence as isolated, spontaneous acts: "Self-appointed vigilantes are responsible for much of this misery, because of the indiscriminate way they have gone about banishing objectionable persons; and, in some instances, unscrupulous whites have gratified their personal spite in dealing with the Negroes."

But nobody was reading the newspaper out in the swamps, along the lanes of Oakdale Cemetery, or under makeshift cover in the great railroad culvert that was the boundary between Brooklyn and white Wilmington.

As a last resort, Waddell sent black search parties into the swamps—men borrowed from Sprunts' Champion Compress. These brought back a few dozen workers, but not enough. Brooklyn was a ghost town.

The city was still technically under martial law. At the suggestion of George Rountree, Waddell's board took advantage of the situation and approved Rountree's draft of two temporary ordinances designed to consolidate power and ease the labor shortage: first, any person arrested within the city limits could be tried only before the mayor, not a magistrate, since there were still a handful of Republican magistrates legally in office; second, any vagrant was ordered to find employment within twenty-four hours or leave the city. If he refused, he could be summarily sentenced to work without wages on city property for up to thirty days.

Rountree planned to include these ordinances in the new city charter he would champion in Raleigh when he took his seat in the legislature in January.

On Sunday, Sam and Gray Ellen Jenks walked to St. Thomas's for the ten o'clock mass. But Father Dennen was not there. The place was empty. The Negro janitor watched them warily from the sacristy as they stood, bewildered, in the center aisle of the little frame church. When he was sure they meant him no harm, he emerged into the sanctuary. "Father's gone north," he said.

"There's no mass today?" Gray Ellen asked. This morning, it seemed very important to attend mass, to listen for reassurance in the old Latin prayers, to come away with at least a qualified blessing.

"All the whitefolks over at First Presbyterian. All the ministers, too."

"How do you know?" Sam asked.

The janitor shrugged. "Man keep his ear to the ground, hear all kind of news."

By the time they arrived at First Presbyterian Church, the meeting was already well under way. J. Allan Taylor was in the pulpit, addressing the crowd of ministers and white citizens. He was explaining the banishment policy. "And that," he concluded, "is how we deal with agitators—now and in the future. Colored or white."

All at once, Sam realized that was what had happened to Father Dennen.

"My God," Gray Ellen said under her breath, "who do these people think they are?"

A minister Sam did not recognize stood up in the front pew and protested. "That's illegal! What about a man's rights under law?"

"Of course it's not legal!" Taylor said. "Nothing is legal here just now. Where have you been? We've been fighting anarchy, and we're trying to establish orderly government." He went on to name all the leading citizens who had supported the actions to take back the government, beginning with Waddell, MacRae, and his brother Walker, all of whom were seated on choir chairs in the sanctuary. "Do you want to stand there and tell these men that they are not honorable men? Not the finest men in this city?"

There was a burst of applause, and the minister sat down.

Someone was missing, Sam realized: Captain Kenan.

The white pastor of Brooklyn Baptist Church, now an alderman, stood up and said, "In the riot on Thursday, the Negro was the aggressor."

"Hear, hear!"

Gray Ellen said loudly, "Riot? It was a massacre."

"I believe the whites were doing God's service," Taylor said. "Just consider all that has been done for the good of business, politics, and the church."

The Reverend Peyton Hoge, presiding in his own church, ascended the pulpit. "Let us pray and give thanks to God," he said, raising his eyes to the ceiling, hands upturned as though he were expecting rain. " 'He that ruleth his spirit is better than he that taketh a city.' " He lowered his eyes and swept a hand toward the men assembled behind him. "We have done both."

"Amen," said the congregation.

But Hoge wasn't finished. He held up an index finger. "That is much. But it is more—because it is our own city we have taken."

——————

Later that afternoon, Sam went by the *Messenger* office. Even on a Sunday, he knew he'd find Tom Clawson there. He would appeal to Clawson's sense of fair play. Clawson had never wanted things to go this far—he'd warned Alex Manly.

"Well, look who's here," Clawson said.

"I've got a story," Sam said. He'd been up all night writing it longhand. Gray Ellen had proofed it.

"I'll bet you have. Where the hell have you been for the past two days?"

He was right, Sam knew. He hadn't even bothered to check in during the worst of the violence. His thinking had been all cloudy. The whiskey hadn't helped.

"Out in the field," he said.

"Yeah, that's what Harry said. See anything?"

"I saw plenty."

"Did you? Did you really?" Clawson's voice had an edge to it. The tone was all wrong, as if there were something important and obvious that he wouldn't say out loud but expected Sam to hear anyway.

"Read all about it," Sam said, holding up the handwritten sheets.

"Never mind that. You're wanted at the mayor's house. They've been looking for you all day."

"They?"

"Waddell and your cousin."

"Look," Sam said, standing up. "I'm sorry I left you in the lurch. It was a mess out there. I got caught up in something. Lost my bearings, you know?" His eyes burned from lack of sleep. Again, he held out the pages of the true story of what he had witnessed.

Clawson just stood there.

Sam said, "Is there some kind of problem?"

"I'm sorry as hell it worked out this way."

"What do you mean?"

Clawson rubbed his own tired eyes. "From the start, it was all wrong. You've got no business here. You haven't got a clue."

Sam offered the pages a third time. "It's all true. Fact after fact."

"You think the facts make it true?" Clawson snapped the pages out of his hand. "Get out of here. You've kept them waiting long enough."

———————

Bessie King wordlessly ushered Sam into Waddell's library, where the mayor sat smoking a cheroot and going through a sheaf of carbons. In his shirtsleeves and garters, he looked skinny and frail, a harmless old gentleman of letters. His shirt was yellow and shiny.

"Samuel—glad you could make it. May I offer—?"

"No, thanks. I was working. Tom Clawson sent me over. Things have quieted down a good deal."

Waddell smiled and winked. "It's so peaceful right now, I could patrol this city with six nannies and a willow switch." He rose from his desk and peeked out the door into the hallway. "Miz Gabby, dear—would you please bring in the mail?"

"Mail on a Sunday?" Sam asked.

Waddell smiled and ambled back to his desk. He sat on the edge of it puffing his cheroot. He looked well rested but pale. Framed by his silver hair and goatee, his face seemed positively translucent. Now comes the pitch, Sam thought. That must be why Clawson was so upset—Sam was about to be included in the inner circle. J. Allan Taylor was Clawson's man, and now that the dust had settled, J. Allan Taylor wasn't mayor of anything. It had been like watching a chaotic game of billiards, in which a dozen men were all shooting at once on the same table. All the vectors had converged, intersected, and deflected, and now it was clear which balls were in whose pockets.

Whatever happened now, Sam had a clear conscience. He had, for once, done the right thing. And still come out ahead. Waddell wasn't perfect, but he had saved those men at the jail from lynching. Not like the soldiers running amok in Brooklyn. Sam could work for the man, honorably.

"As you can see," Waddell said to the windows, "events have borne out my predictions."

"They sure have."

"It's all turned out better than I dared hope."

Sam thought briefly of Dan Wright peddling for his life in deep sand, the crack of the rifle shots. Then he put the image out of his mind. What was done was done—it couldn't be fixed now. Best get on with the future.

The library door clicked open and in glided Gabrielle deRosset Waddell, lovely in a gray woolen dress that looked almost military. From collar to waist, a line of red buttons ran between stripes of black velvet. Her dark hair floated in black combs, swept up from her neck and ears, which were rose-pale. She nodded a greeting and held out a handful of envelopes, all of which had already been knifed open.

Waddell set his cheroot on the ashtray and clapped his hands like a happy child. "This place has turned into a branch office of Western Union and the United States Postal Service. Miz Gabby, read some of them."

Without enthusiasm, Gabrielle slipped a letter out of the envelope on top. " 'My dear Colonel—Just a few lines to congratulate you on your courage, and the people of Wilmington on their nerve.' "

"When a public man acts," Waddell said, rubbing his hands and then taking up his cheroot again, "other men take notice. Keep reading, Miz Gabby."

Gabrielle glanced at Sam and chose another letter. He suddenly understood that she had read all these letters out loud before, perhaps many times. " 'I beg to congratulate you on the struggle in dear old North Carolina—' "

"You see, Sam," Waddell said, as Gabrielle kept reading in a monotone, "we have made history here. We have seized the moment."

" '. . . have dragged the dear old state out of the slough of black mud and degradation into which she was fast sinking.' "

"The whole country is paying attention to what has happened down here."

"A revolution," Sam said quietly.

Gabrielle read, " 'Should you want any more help in redeeming this state from Negro rule and tyranny, there are many sons of North Carolina here in Georgia who will cheerfully go to your aid.' "

Waddell nodded vigorously. "Revolution—good word for it. Washington and Jefferson would approve. The Anglo-Saxon tradition— when a government becomes intolerable, openly and manfully overthrow it."

Sam started to argue with him, but Gabrielle distracted him with her reading. " 'Brooklyn Wharf and Warehouse Company, New York: We congratulate you on the result, in whose solution your own courage, eloquence, and self-control in the moment of success have been such potent elements.' "

"We're in every newspaper from New York to San Francisco! *Collier's* wants me to write them a memoir."

Gabrielle mechanically opened another letter. " 'Astronomers, open your telescopes!' "

"Frank Wagnells has wired me for a photograph to accompany an article in the *Literary Digest*."

" '—Tell me what bright star I see rising which not only shines on but warms the sons of North Carolina!' " This time, Sam heard the merest hint of irony in her voice. Still, her eyes were hard and steady.

She picked out another letter. " 'As you know,' " Gabrielle read, " 'I have always admired you, and now I am almost a hero worshipper—' "

Waddell smiled, stood from the desk, and turned to the window. Sam watched his narrow back, the crisp yellow-white shirt creased by his sharp little shoulder blades.

The Colonel said, "Thing is, I have some hard news for you, Samuel."

" 'For your deliverance of your good people, you will be loved by them all their lives—' "

"Bad news?" Sam said. "What do you mean?" He sat forward in his chair. Had Clawson called about the story already?

" '—and a remote posterity will call you blessed.' " Tears were forming in her eyes.

Waddell spun around abruptly. "Read the one from Congressman Thompson."

Gabrielle did not react immediately. She stood stiffly at attention, aware that Sam was watching her. He wanted to speak to her—clearly, something awful had happened in this house—but he had no idea what question to ask. She made no attempt to wipe the tears from her cheeks. Sam's attention was riveted on her face, which seemed hotly alive, yet rigid.

She read, " 'While I am an uncompromising Republican, I—like you—would stand up for and defend the honor and good name of the white women of North Carolina, the South, the North, of America—' "

"That's the nub of it, Samuel."

"I don't understand."

"Women. Honor. Discretion. A sense of propriety and, well, manners. Knowing one's place."

" '—Americans should be proud of their mothers, sisters, daughters, and wives.' "

"Yes, wives, Sam. *Your* wife."

"What about her?" His face flushed. He glanced at Gabrielle, but she gave nothing away. Gabrielle stood just inside the door holding the packet of letters, saying nothing, staring at the floor.

"A man must be able to control his woman, Sam. A woman depends on her man to set limits." He was still not facing Sam. He stood, hands clasped behind his back, staring out the window, a thin spiral of smoke rising from his cigar. "I have certain reports," Waddell stated calmly. "We understand she has been, well, *sympathetic* to the Negro cause."

"She makes up her own mind, if that's what you mean." Sam had a vivid image of Gray Ellen swinging around the lamppost after Waddell's speech, screaming, "You lost the War!" then tumbling under him in the lime dust.

Waddell shook his head like a patient schoolmaster. He still wouldn't face Sam. "Your mistake, then. It's one thing to hold a few sentimental opinions."

Gabrielle opened her mouth and then closed it on the back of her hand.

"It's quite another to interfere with the business of men—*public* men."

Sam stood up. "Why don't you just come out and say what's on your mind?"

Behind Gabrielle, a man entered brusquely: Hugh MacRae.

Waddell at last turned. "You want to tell him, Hugh?" He opened a drawer and fished something out.

MacRae said, "It cost me something to bring you down here."

"I paid my way," Sam said.

"I'm not talking about money. Money's easy. Reputation, that's what I'm talking about. Foreign correspondent. War hero."

"I never claimed—"

"You didn't have to."

So somebody had wired Chicago—he'd almost managed to forget Cuba. He felt his cheeks go hot.

MacRae said, "You came here on the strength of my name. My poor relation from up north. You asked for a job, and I obliged you."

"And I'm grateful."

"Don't be," Waddell said mildly. "You don't have it anymore." He held a rag in his hand.

MacRae said, "I didn't expect much. Didn't ask for anything but a little gratitude. Is that so much to ask? Instead, look how you repay me."

Sam started for the door. "I don't have to stand here and take this."

MacRae blocked his way. "Yes, cousin—I'm afraid you do."

Gabrielle moved off to the side. He thought he heard her say, "I'm sorry," but it might have been only a sharp intake of breath.

"Look, it must be some kind of mistake." Sam's insides were churning. Everything was going wrong again. He had been so close.

"Mrs. Waddell, please leave us," MacRae said. She didn't move. "Very well, then. I don't mean to be indelicate. But since Cousin Sam here has no ear for subtlety, let me ask him straight out." He stood on the balls of his feet, fists at his side. "Sam, did you know your wife was sleeping with a nigger?"

Sam swung his fist at MacRae's face, but MacRae adroitly dodged it, then boxed Sam neatly on the ear. Sam dropped to the floor and banged his head. Gabrielle looked away. Bessie King, hearing the ruckus, stuck her head in the door to see what was wrong and just as quickly ducked out again.

Sam sat up. MacRae drew an envelope from his coat and flicked it into Sam's lap—tickets. "The Yankee Clipper leaves at quarter past seven."

Shakily, Sam got to his feet, but MacRae was already gone. He had trouble with his equilibrium and grabbed a chair for balance. He couldn't believe it—he was being run out of town. What was their word? *Banished.* A word right out of the Bible.

Waddell said in a kindly voice, "I had such great hopes for you, Samuel. You had such a promising future." Now, he'd have to write his own story—you just couldn't count on a man anymore, not like in the old days.

Sam rubbed his ear and tried to focus his eyes on Gabrielle. It mattered a great deal to him at that moment what she thought of him. Why wouldn't she speak?

"The worst thing, of course," Waddell went on, as if he were reporting a postmortem, "is the Manly business."

"What Manly business?"

Waddell smiled. "You're out, Samuel. No need to dissemble. We know perfectly well that your *wife*"—he said it like it was a dirty word—"helped Alex Manly to escape."

The absurd logic was coming clear to Sam: Ivanhoe Grant naked to the waist in his kitchen. The buggy Cousin Hugh had loaned them.

Waddell held up the rag—Ivanhoe Grant's bloody shirt. "The buggy was recovered at Castle Hayne, near the depot," Waddell said. "There was an eyewitness, a neighbor."

Sam cocked his head. "Man or woman?"

"Neither—a little boy. Two little boys, in fact."

Sam nodded. The two little gangsters next door. It was almost funny. He waited a moment until he got his equilibrium back, then slowly walked to the door. As he opened it, he turned and said, "I wrote it all down, you know. The whole story. Gave it to Tom Clawson."

Waddell chuckled. "You don't actually think he'll print it?"

"Then I'll write it again, someplace else. I will."

"You do that. You scribble away to your heart's content. I can't use that kind of scribbler."

"My God," Sam said. "To think I admired you."

"Of course, you did, Samuel." Waddell smiled, stepped closer, and patted him on the shoulder. "You still do."

Sam staggered into the foyer, still dizzy from MacRae's blow. Gabrielle appeared at his elbow. "So you're going along with all this?" he said.

She looked him right in the eye. "A woman doesn't have as many lucky choices as a man."

Sam nodded. He almost understood. "Did he hurt you?"

She shook her head. "He's my husband."

"That's it?"

"I have to live here."

Sam turned and reached for the doorknob. "Gray will miss you."

"Please tell her goodbye for me."

"Tell her yourself."

"No. She'll understand."

Of course she would. Sam nodded and left.

———

From the window of the train, Sam and Gray Ellen watched the flickering lights of the city reel by. They sat side by side, not talking. Gray Ellen was nearer the window.

Crowded around them in the dimly lighted car were other silent passengers, all white—the Negro coaches were up ahead, just behind the engine, where the noise and soot were worst. Every seat was filled. People crouched in the aisle. The passengers rocked gently with the motion of the train, heads bobbing. Many of them had their eyes closed, though Sam was sure they were not sleeping.

Shame, he thought—that's what they were all feeling. Humiliation. Anger. Disbelief. He was feeling it acutely. Next to him, Gray Ellen had her eyes glued to the passing lights, but he had no idea what she was feeling.

They were headed back to Philadelphia, but what they would do there, whether they would even remain there, was an open question.

Sam hadn't told Harry Calabash that he was leaving, but somehow Harry had known. He'd been waiting back at the house when Sam returned home from Waddell's. He shook Sam's hand solemnly. "Good luck in Yankeeland," he said.

"How can you stay?" Sam asked.

Harry looked old and used up. He was sober now, but Sam knew he'd be deep in the whiskey by train time. Harry shrugged, as if the answer were too obvious to bother saying out loud. "This is where I live."

"After everything that's happened?"

"You've got to forgive a city, same as a person."

Sam thought, how can you forgive anybody who won't admit they've done wrong? "It's as simple as that?" he said.

"I didn't say it was simple. It's just the way it is."

They were losing the city now. The lights were going out behind them. There were no stars to light the overcast sky. Somewhere off to the left, Sam knew, lay the river—brown, swollen with the rains, clogged with anchored ships waiting to be unloaded.

Beyond the city, he knew, lay beautiful, unspoiled country. Lowland forests full of deer and stubble fields thick with Canada geese, clear creeks swimming with trout and tidal basins brimming with oysters and clams. Wide-open beaches he had walked with Gray Ellen, dunes where plovers and giant turtles nested. But tonight, the country was invisible under the black sky. He might never see it again. Already, he missed it.

The train rattled over the trestle at Smith's Creek and through the swamps—were the people still out there, huddling in the cold rain? Then they were moving away from the river for good.

Harry Calabash had told him rumors of bodies—wagonloads of Negro bodies—being dumped into the river in the dead of Thursday night. Sam had no idea if it were true. He knew for sure that dozens of Negroes had been killed. He had carefully tallied all the reports and corrected for redundancy, rumor, and exaggeration. He guessed that 120 to 150 Negroes had been massacred. That was the only accurate word—*massacred*. They never had a chance.

He had no idea if any of those had been dumped into the river. But he imagined them now, bloated and stiff—a fleet of faceless, nameless black corpses drifting out on the tide, floating down the Cape Fear to the sea.

EPILOGUE

New Year's Eve 1 8 9 9

GRAY ELLEN STARES out the window of her bedroom while Sam fusses with the bottle of champagne. Two stories below, Chestnut Street is thronged with holiday revelers heading to Independence Mall to cheer in the new year, as church bells toll all over the city. Snow has been falling for hours, drifting soft against doorways and curbs.

He twists off the wire and turns the bottle while holding the cork till it pops out softly. He can smell the sweet bouquet. Gray Ellen looks radiant tonight in a midnight-blue satin evening gown—a gift from Gabrielle deRosset Waddell. It arrived last week without a note. Perhaps Gabrielle had waited a suitable period, as if in mourning. Still, a whole year. Sam could not fathom why she sent it, why she even bothered to finish making it. Yet Gray Ellen was not surprised, acted almost as if she expected it.

Its arrival unsettled Sam, but now, fitted onto Gray Ellen's slim figure, it gives him a kind of hope. Her black hair shines.

Gray Ellen is newly pregnant. She will not show for weeks. It is the best secret they have ever shared.

Sam pours the champagne into two crystal flutes, wedding presents, and watches the bubbles. He has not had a drink since his last whiskey with Harry Calabash. Tonight, they are allowing themselves one bottle of French vintage, a gift from her family, to celebrate.

This time, it has been easier for Sam to stop drinking. What he needed all along was not the drink but the foggy sense of well-being that came with the drink. The escape from himself. But he doesn't feel the urgent desire to escape from himself anymore. He isn't a hero, just a newspaperman who is sometimes ambitious, often afraid, full of venial sins, and dodging mortal ones. *Be better than what goes on around you.* He promised her.

Sometimes at night, though, he dreams of escaping. He is underwater, his feet planted to his boot tops in thick river mud, holding his breath. The current is tugging him downriver, toward the ocean.

In the murky water, large, lumpish objects drift by. Some of them have faces—eyes wide open in astonishment, mouths agape. Their fingers are splayed, reaching, trying to grab the brown water and hold on. Trying to grab hold of Sam.

Always, he pushes them away, his lungs burning from lack of breath. Far overhead, something moves on the surface, casting its fat shadow all the way down to the bottom of the river. What is casting the shadow? It is never clear. Something big, looming out of the dark future. He cannot hold his breath any longer. His feet are stuck, as in cement. One of the floating corpses latches onto him. He gulps cold water that tastes of tea. He tries to cry out, but his voice is lost in water.

The black corpse has him and won't let go. He feels his feet lifting free of the mud, his body caught in the current, flying to the sea.

Then he wakes to Gray Ellen, peacefully asleep beside him.

"Look at the lights," Sam says now, stepping beside her and offering her a flute of champagne. Through the mist of blowing snow, the lights of the city glimmer yellow and blue and orange against the drifts in the street.

"Every light in the world is on tonight," she says. She is not happy, but she is content. She feels safe, here on home ground. Sam covers the city desk for the *Bulletin*. She teaches at Friends School. There are no mobs in the street, except for the revelers.

"It will be a good year for us," Sam says. "I can feel it."

"You say that every year."

He always expects too much, and then the disappointment overwhelms him. Better to expect nothing, to be grateful for small blessings. But she doesn't really believe that—who can live without hopes? It is only the future, bright as a field of new snow, that makes it possible to survive the present.

Still, she doesn't want to know what the new year will hold. She will trust herself to bear it.

Outside, the world seems frozen. It is two minutes till midnight.

She watches the hands on the clock across the street, and they don't move. It's as if time is going to grind to a halt at midnight and then, with a great gnashing of celestial gears, begin to move backward.

"Did I tell you that I ran into Alex Manly on the street this morning?"

She has heard he moved to Philadelphia. So have many other Wilmington Negroes—they've formed a club they call the Sons of Liberty.

"Got a job as a painter—passing himself off as Irish."

She doesn't answer. She never wants to talk about that time again. She wants it to remain a hole in their life. To talk about it is to bring it all back, and all the bad luck with it. The dress is lovely. The woman who made it is a lovely memory. If Gray Ellen's life goes as she hopes it will, she will never see her again.

Sam realizes he shouldn't have said anything. She is at peace now—leave her be. He had a letter from Harry last week that he hasn't told her about, the first letter since they left. Mike Dowling is now a captain in the fire department. George Rountree is an important man in the legislature. Hugh MacRae keeps getting richer. Wilmington is a one-party town.

According to Harry, by the time it was all over, a thousand Negroes fled the county, most of them skilled workers and professionals. A thousand people, Sam reflects—one for every armed man who helped take the city. Where were the other seven thousand whites? Couldn't they stand up to the minority with guns?

In the year since the uprising, Wilmington has been struck by a blizzard and two hurricanes. Business is stagnant—nobody is investing. The bottom has dropped out of cotton. Wooden ships are rotting at their moorings, waiting for cargo.

But Sam can't help feeling it is not over. Harry said it—you have to forgive a city, if it is your city. Sam longs to go back there. He didn't realize until he left, but somehow it is his city now. Part of him remains there. It will always be there, urging him to do better, to live up to a wife who believes in grace.

He misses the racket of the wharf, the opal sky, even the oyster-shell dust. Someday, he must go back. It will be different. A year from now, ten years, twenty. He will return and claim it.

Meanwhile, you've got to be where you live.

John Norwood went back, Harry wrote. Sam wishes he knew Norwood better. It's always the quiet ones who make the lasting difference. You can charge around, make speeches, shoot guns, but in the end, it's the quiet ones.

Gray Ellen sips her champagne. The bubbles tickle her nose. The revelers have passed. She cannot see them beyond the roofs of the houses, but they cast their dancing lights into the snowy sky, a modest aurora borealis. She sets her glass on the window sill.

There descends a great silence, like the silence of held breath. She trembles, feels her spine tingle. She imagines him out there in the silence, and his image sticks in her eye like a ghost: Ivanhoe Grant. She hears his strident voice, thinned by distance. He is a kind of devil made by men. A thing created out of suffering. There will be no easy rest for anybody while he is loose on the land. She does not approve of him, but she believes in him.

Somehow, knowing he is still out there—believing it—reassures her. "Can you hear it?" she says.

But Sam hears nothing beyond the silence.

"Listen," she says. Ivanhoe Grant—he's still out there somewhere, chasing away sin, gathering his anger, seething with the white man's poison. He will call them back. He is a sinner, too wicked for this world, but he will call them all back. He will outlast them all.

She stares into the snowy night and wills his image into focus: a hobo jungle at the edge of a swamp. A black man in a pearl-gray suit headed south. In his hand, he carries a Bible he knows by heart. He walks alone beside the tracks, head up, back straight, a man burning at the core. Behind him, a train is approaching around a long curve, whistle moaning. He turns. In the beam of the locomotive, his skin is the color of wheat dust, and his eyes shine with ferocious anger.

Yet, in the thundering darkness, he smiles.

Sam says, "But I don't hear—"

"Shh." She takes his face firmly in her hands, touches his ears with her fingertips. "Shh," she whispers again. "Don't talk. Don't answer. Don't say anything. Listen—just listen."

Any second now, the gong will strike the hour.

Gray Ellen stares across the street at the black hands of the clock, frozen against the luminescent, pearly face at one minute until midnight. One minute until the twentieth century.

———

Armond Scott, the young lawyer who failed to deliver the Committee of Colored Citizens' reply to the white ultimatum, became a judge of the Twelfth Municipal Court in Washington, D.C. George Rountree and Walker Taylor engineered the appointment, leading to speculation that Scott had been bought off by the white supremacy movement.

Father Christopher Dennen disappeared from Wilmington in 1898, leaving behind a tradition of social activism among the Catholic parishes of Wilmington.

Dr. Silas Wright, the mayor ousted by Waddell, showed uncharacteristic bravery in his futile effort to restore calm during the events of Thursday, November 10, 1898. He remained in the city until November 14, then fled. He was rumored to be in Knoxville, Tennessee, leading a quiet life as a general practitioner.

Hugh MacRae realized his lifelong dream of colonizing the Cape Fear region with "utopian" agrarian communities of Germans, Hungarians, Poles, Dutchmen, and Italians. In 1900, he became head of the Wilmington Gas Light Company, consolidating that utility with the Wrightsville Street Railway and Seacoast Railway.

He was largely responsible for developing Wrightsville Beach as a resort destination for tourists from all over the country. Because of his expertise with real estate and agriculture, he was considered for a position in the administration of Herbert Hoover.

Colonel Walker Taylor never achieved his ambition of becoming mayor of Wilmington, but he was appointed collector of customs by President Woodrow Wilson in 1913. He was lauded on several public occasions for his performance during the coup of 1898. His Boys Brigade was reorganized under the auspices of the Kiwanis in 1921 as the Brigade Boys Club and remains active today as a model for training young men to be good citizens.

Widely traveled, Taylor visited Rome in 1928. There, he was granted an interview with Mussolini, whom he characterized with admiration as a combination Caesar and Napoleon.

Sam Jenks worked for various Eastern newspapers and later for newsreel syndicates. Trying his hand again as a war correspondent, he accompanied Blackjack Pershing's expedition into Mexico in vain pursuit of Pancho Villa. For his coverage of the repression of striking copper miners in Bisbee, Arizona, in 1917—during which he was run out of town in a boxcar and left to die in the New Mexico desert along with the strikers—he was awarded the Pulitzer Prize for journalism. He never returned to Wilmington.

Gray Ellen Jenks taught reading and history at Friends School for thirty-one years. Her memoir, *Through a Woman's Eyes*, won her international celebrity, including an invitation to the inauguration of Franklin D. Roosevelt. She corresponded with Eleanor Roosevelt and frequently lectured at universities and clubs.

Gray Ellen and Sam's first daughter, Christine, became an aviatrix and for a time held the women's solo speed record from San Francisco to New York. Two other daughters, Margaret and Kathleen, became champions of women's rights.

Their only son, Harry, became an archaeologist and disappeared in the Yucatan in 1955.

George Rountree distinguished himself as a judge on the North Carolina Superior Court. As chairman of the Committee on Constitutional Amendments of the North Carolina General Assembly, he authored the so-called grandfather clause, requiring voters to qualify as literate and to pay a poll tax before voting. For generations, it effectively barred blacks from casting votes.

Elizabeth "Bessie" King never left Wilmington. She continued her employment as a domestic servant to various leading families until forced to retire because of arthritis in 1926 at the age of sixty-six. She finished her days in a private retirement home, where she lived for forty more years, supported by an anonymous benefactor.

Saffron King James went to Baltimore in 1902. There, she attended the Baltimore College of Nursing and Medical Arts. After stints in various hospitals, she returned to Wilmington's James Walker Hospital in 1917 and was cited for her service during the influenza epidemic the following year. She outlived three husbands, the last a minister, and was struck and killed by an automobile in 1966 while going to the bedside of her dying mother.

John G. Norwood left Wilmington briefly during the coup but returned six months later. He continued to work behind the political scenes to improve the treatment of Afro-Americans.

Harry Calabash continued to reside in Wilmington. He was found dead of a heart attack on the night that the armistice was signed ending the Great War. On the floor next to his chair was an empty fifth of bourbon.

Captain William Rand Kenan, in the peak of health and

vigor, died suddenly of unexplained causes in 1903 on the thirty-eighth anniversary of the assassination of Abraham Lincoln.

Colonel Alfred Moore Waddell served three terms as mayor of Wilmington, becoming one of the city's wealthiest and most distinguished citizens. He died in his bed at the age of seventy-six on St. Patrick's Day 1911, after an eight-hour illness. His funeral at St. James Episcopal Church was attended by hundreds of mourners, including representatives of many of the best clubs in Wilmington. The *Raleigh News & Observer* eulogized him as a model for Southern manhood: "When Waddell died, the South lost one of the cleanest and purest types of the chivalrous gentleman." He was interred at Oakdale Cemetery.

Gabrielle deRosset Waddell survived her husband by many years. She became conspicuous for her public and private philanthropy, and she traveled widely. She never remarried.

Ivanhoe Grant disappeared from history in 1898. But an elderly man rumored to be Grant appears in an Associated Press wire photo, standing on the steps of the Lincoln Memorial behind the Reverend Dr. Martin Luther King, Jr., as King delivered his famous "I Have a Dream" oratory. Grant would have been a hundred years old. The man in the photograph has never been positively identified.

Alex Manly returned to Wilmington only once, in 1925, with his wife, Carrie. He visited the courthouse, where he attempted to regain title to his properties confiscated in 1898. But there was no record that he had ever owned any real estate or other assets in New Hanover County.

In the aftermath of the coup, reporters from numerous papers in New York, Boston, and Philadelphia requested interviews, but he refused them all, claiming that he would someday write the definitive account of his experiences during the uprising. No such account was ever published.

MAP OF
WILMINGTON
NORTH CAROLINA